Triumph or Trap?

Katherine stood trembling in the great hall of Clandara, awaiting the arrival of her lover. She had persuaded her father and her brother that she would not renounce her love for James Macdonald, hate him though they did, slander him as they tried, raking up the women and the killings in his notorious past. She had persuaded James to rein his fearful temper, and to remain mild and meek before the insults he was sure to face when he demanded her hand in marriage.

But now as she watched James enter through the great stone archway, and saw the sudden hard gleam in her father's eyes, the vicious tightening of her brother's mouth, she was filled with sudden fear.

Had she led her lover to his heart's desire—or to his certain death . . . ?

CLANDARA

A sweeping epic of violent wills and unleashed passion.

SIGNET Titles by Evelyn Anthony

CLANDARA

by

Evelyn Anthony

A SIGNET BOOK

NEW AMERICAN LIBRARY

TIMES MIRROR

Library of Congress Catalog Card Number: 63-8765

This is an authorized reprint of a hardcover edition published by
Doubleday and Company, Inc.

SIGNET TRADEMARK REG. U.S. PAT. OFF. AND FOREIGN COUNTRIES
REGISTERED TRADEMARK—MARCA REGISTRADA
HECHO EN CHICAGO, U.S.A.

SIGNET, SIGNET CLASSICS, MENTOR, PLUME AND MERIDIAN BOOKS
are published by The New American Library, Inc.,
1301 Avenue of the Americas, New York, New York 10019

First Printing, March, 1976

5 6 7 8 9

PRINTED IN THE UNITED STATES OF AMERICA

Prologue

The twelfth century was just beginning when the first of the Frasers built his great fortress at Clandara at the top of the sweeping hillside that overlooked Loch Ness. The great grey castle walls were weathered by hundreds of years of biting Highland winds and mellowing suns. It stood like a sentinel above the clear blue waters of the Loch, magnificent yet dwarfed by the majestic purple mountains that rose up behind it, their peaks shrouded in eternal mists. Little had changed in the wild and lovely land of Scotland itself since the great Highland chieftain began his fortress; the castle itself had seen the passage of time and dynasties. The Stuarts had ruled from Edinburgh and the tragic Mary, Queen of Scots, had stayed a night at Clandara, and her great-grandson James II had been driven from the throne of England, and his son the Old Pretender, James Stuart, was a homeless exile in Rome. Many wars had raged about Clandara, but none fiercer than the bitter siege of two hundred years before when the Red Fraser seized the child of his neighbours, the Macdonalds, and held her for ransom in the castle.

The Macdonalds had invested Clandara with two hundred clansmen and brought up crude battering rams to break down the massive oak doors, but at the end of two months the dead lay thick around the unbreeched walls and the siege was raised.

The unhappy daughter of the Macdonald chief was never seen again, but tradition in both families held that the Red Fraser had starved his prisoner to death and then buried her somewhere within the eight-foot-thick walls. So began the feud which ravaged the surrounding countryside and brought *generations of Macdonalds out on raids against the crofts and cattle of the Frasers, burning and laying waste what they could not carry off.*

The Macdonalds revenged the kidnapping and murder of their ancestress by some of the cruellest warfare ever conducted in the Highlands, and both families came at last to the end of their resources when mutual ruin threatened them as a result of the feud. It was then that Andrew, Earl of Clandara and chief of the Frasers, signed a peace treaty with his enemies and married as his second wife Margaret Macdonald, cousin and ward of Sir Alexander Macdonald of Dundrenan. At the time of that marriage his children Robert and Katherine were almost grown up, and for the next five years there was an uneasy peace between the warring families. By the summer of 1744 the truce was still unbroken; war seemed far indeed from the Houses of Fraser and Macdonald and further still from all the clans of Scotland. Across the English Channel the rightful heir to Scotland's throne, Prince Charles Edward Stuart, dreamed and planned his return, and at the end of a stay in France with her mother's relatives, Katherine Fraser came back once more to Clandara.

Chapter 1

"BEFORE I LET you marry that scoundrel, I'd sooner see you dead!"

It was the first time in her life that Katherine had seen her father really angry with her. He stood in the Green Salon at Clandara with a table between them like a barrier between enemies, and ended the argument by shouting at her in a voice so altered by shock and outrage that she hardly recognised it.

"Father," Katherine's tone was calm. "You made peace with the Macdonalds. You married a Macdonald! How can you forbid me?"

The Earl swung round towards a figure sitting so still and silent in a chair that she might have been a statue; a pale, plain woman forever sewing in some corner. She was the cousin of his old enemy, Sir Alexander Macdonald of Dundrenan, and she had been bartered to him like so many head of cattle when the two families made their peace. He had married her, but he loathed her as he loathed all her kin. His face flushed angrily. He turned to his daughter again, his beautiful, spoilt, wilful child with her high courage and her blue eyes blazing angrily at him. The sun was on her and it changed her red hair to fire. She was his child but he could see the grace and beauty and spirit which had brought so many suitors to Clandara in the past while she was scarcely of an age to marry.

"How dare you tell me I married a Macdonald as if that were an excuse for what you've done! I made a marriage of convenience with that woman to put an end to a clan war! Nothing gives you the right to even *look* at a ruffian like

1

James Macdonald. . . . I sent you to France to your cousin Marie to befit yourself for a proper marriage to someone like Henry Ogilvie and you come back here and tell me you want to marry the most notorious scoundrel in the Highlands!"

"He is not a scoundrel," Katherine retorted. She was desperately trying to keep calm, to avoid losing her temper or bursting into tears, and already the tears were threatening to come. She and James had discussed this so often and both had agreed that she must be quiet and reasonable.

"A murderer," the Earl countered, "a lecher . . . a man of such infamous reputation that no respectable woman would speak to him. And you dare to ask me if I will receive him as your suitor? My poor child, I think you must be mad!"

"I don't believe you," Katherine said. "I don't believe anything you say about him, and even if it's true, I love him and I don't care! I loved him from the moment I met him at cousin Marie's house. If only you knew, Father, if only I could make you understand how gentle he is, how generous and loving. . . ."

"Ach!" The Earl turned away from her in disgust. Privately he cursed his kinswoman, the Marquise de Betrand, to hell and back again for allowing his precious Katherine, committed to her charge after all, he thought furiously, to meet a man like James Macdonald. Mischievous, frivolous little wretch . . . he could hardly wait to compose a letter to her expressing his opinion of the way she had abused her position as Katherine's chaperone. James Macdonald. It was inconceivable, horrifying. He turned back to his daughter and tried again.

"This noble gentleman of whom you speak," he said, "bolted three of our families into their crofts and set fire to them. That was when you were still a child. This same man killed Andrew Crawford's son because he spilled a glass of wine over his sleeve at dinner. He's known up and down the Highlands for picking quarrels with anyone just for the love of killing them. As for his morals . . . no woman of good reputation can afford to be seen in his company. Ask anything in the world of me and I'll give it to you," he entreated. "But no father would permit his child to marry such a man. I'd sooner see you dead first."

Katherine had been brought up with hatred of the Macdonalds as part of the accepted pattern of life, like rising in the morning and eating and drinking. As a child her old nurse had whispered dreadful tales of the evil deeds of the Black Macdonald, as the Highlanders called the heir to Dundrenan. More cruel than his father, more quarrelsome, more violent and pitiless than all his fearful kindred put together. His name was a bogey with which the Fraser mothers frightened their children. Katherine too had been afraid; afraid because she was not permitted to ride out alone or far beyond the confines of Clandara without an escort of a half dozen armed clansmen to protect her. The Macdonalds lurked like birds of prey, waiting for the unwary Fraser, irrespective of age or sex, in order to fall upon them. When her own people had returned after a savage foray into the land of the Macdonalds, their exploits were praised as if, in killing the women and children of their enemies, they were merely hunting down the devil. And then with all this heritage of hate and prejudice behind her, Katherine had met her family's enemy himself, but far away from the pervasive Scottish atmosphere, brought face to face with him in the supper room of a French château.

What use were her father's warnings, what use her own impassioned denials of what she knew very well to be the truth? "I love him." Her own avowal came back to her and it was at once her only weapon and the only one she needed.

"Father," Katherine said slowly, "Father, I don't expect you to believe me when I say that, whatever James was or has done, loving me has changed him. I know that if I tell you that he was the most gentle, tender man that I have ever met, you will laugh and say that he was only making mock of me. I cannot persuade you. And yet," she said, "it's true."

"He has bewitched you," the Earl answered her. "Nothing could change that scoundrel. Nothing could erase the infamy of his life for the last twenty years. If you must have it plain, Katherine, he was frequenting the stews of Edinburgh at fifteen!"

Again she pleaded with him, and as she did so she was unaware of her stepmother's eyes watching her, their expression so guarded that they might have been the eyes of a blind woman.

"And if he did," Katherine countered passionately, "have we Frasers never done the same or worse? Are we so perfect, Father, that you condemn James as if our whole family and all who went before were saints in virtue? Oh, I beg of you to consider a little. Please, please, forget all the old hates and wrongs that lie in the past. Receive James and give him your blessing . . ."

"My blessing!" The Earl swung round upon her. "My curse, and the curse of your ancestors for generations! Enough now, Katherine. I've heard enough. I shall write to Marie de Betrand and inform her of the harm her stupidity has done us all, and I advise you to put all thought of this ruffian out of your head. If you cannot forget him I shall devise another journey for you. There is an excellent convent in Bavaria where you would have time to consider your folly and your disobedience. Now go to your room!" Unlike his favourite child, he had not inherited the flaming Fraser colouring. He was gray now, and he wore a powdered periwig in the French style, but in his youth the Earl had been as fair as his only son Robert. Even Robert would not have supported his sister on this issue. Since their mother's death the two had been inseparable, bound by common loss and loneliness, and when the first Countess of Clandara died, he himself had been too grieved and selfish to admit his children into his life until they were grown up and the bonds of love between them transcended the duty they owed their father. He adored Katherine; he loved her spirit and her recklessness, so terribly evident in this tragic passion for a man so unfit to approach her that his name alone was never spoken in the castle. He loved her and he meant what he said when he told her death was preferable to the marriage she proposed. But if his love for Robert was less, his pride in him was greater. Robert was sound and kind and sensible, yet his character was strong, stronger perhaps than his father's own, more reminiscent of the firm and gentle woman who had won Clandara's heart twenty-five years ago and retained it even after she was long years in her grave.

Robert. Robert must see that what that foolish, headstrong child was asking was impossible. The Earl did not look at Katherine as she passed him. He opened the door for her and she went out without a word. He slammed the door on her and suddenly, intensely irritable, he turned angrily upon the silent witness sitting in her chair.

"If I had known, madam," he snapped, "that our convenient alliance would result in Katherine thinking of a Macdonald as a husband, I would sooner have fought your family for the rest of my life. How dare that ruffianly cousin of yours aspire to my daughter!" He had never liked his second wife; as a young woman in her early thirties Margaret Macdonald had been silent and unattractive. As the despised wife and ignored stepmother she was a source of constant irritation to him. It infuriated the Earl to see her sitting in the late Countess' chair at the dining table, or sewing by the west window in the Green Salon as Katherine's mother used to do. Her presence was an affront to him; he despised her and he resented the necessity which had forced him into a miserable travesty of a marriage.

"He is a ruffian and a scoundrel, do you hear?" he repeated, suddenly wishing that his wife would give him the satisfaction of a quarrel.

The Countess got up; she folded her needlework and put it away. "James Macdonald is my cousin," she said quietly. "I cannot listen while you insult him to my face."

"Are you suggesting," the Earl demanded, "that he is a fit husband for my daughter?"

The Countess was very pale; the Earl seldom attacked her on the subject of her family, or indeed discussed anything with her even in anger, if he could help it, but on the few occasions when he was angry, she inevitably burst into tears. It was a weakness which made her hate him all the more.

"James is the bravest man I've ever known," she said. "He has never had a serious thought for a woman in his head until now. If he courts Katherine, you can be sure it is because he loves her. And if they marry"—her voice broke and the humiliating tears began to gather—"if they do marry, she will be very lucky!" And before he could answer her she ran out of the room.

Katherine had not dared to disobey her father, but she sent one of the house servants to find her brother. Robert Fraser was the elder by five years; he was a tall fair man with a gentle face and regular features, enhanced by eyes as piercing and blue as his sister's. He was liked and respected as a man whose word was his bond, a serious, just, and responsible landlord, better-tempered than the old Earl. He loved only two things in his life and that love was typical of his whole nature. He loved his home and he adored his sister Katherine.

She ran into his arms and he held her, comforting and soothing as if she were a little girl again and he the older brother who had so often picked her up after a fall.

"Kate, Kate, dry your tears. . . . What is it, my sweet one?"

"It's Father! I told him I want to get married and he has refused . . . refused finally and absolutely!"

"Married?" Robert held her away from him in surprise. "I knew nothing of it! Why didn't you say something to me . . . we've never had secrets before."

"Oh, Robert, Robert, I didn't tell you because you'd have said just the same as Father. Only I knew you'd make me feel ashamed as Father never could. Anyway, I'm telling you now, because you've got to help me!"

"Who is it?" her brother asked.

Katherine turned away from him and went to the window overlooking the moors beyond the castle walls. "James Macdonald."

"What!" Robert was upon her and he caught her arm and swung her round facing him. "The Macdonald of Dundrenan! Kate, are you out of your wits? Marry him? Good God above, I didn't know you had even *seen* him!"

"We met in France," she said. "He knew cousin Marie well and she introduced us. Robert, please listen to me first before you condemn him. I saw him every day for months, nearly six months we were together, and he's the most wonderful man, Robert, the most gentle, tender man . . . I love him so," she said and her voice trembled. "I love him more than I believed it possible to love anyone. If I am kept apart from him I'll never have another happy moment. Please, my sweet and darling brother, help me now. I have not one friend in the world in this if you turn against me too."

. "Oh, Kate," he whispered, "Kate, what have you done? What are you asking of me? Do you know what this man is? Not just as a Macdonald whom we've hated for centuries, but in his own right, he's got the worst name in the Highlands. How could you have loved him ... how could you have let yourself be duped ..."

"I am not duped," she said fiercely. "He loves me as much as I love him. And he's not a man on whom that love sits lightly, I can tell you. He has no friends in this business either. But he's willing to defy his family for my sake. He's willing to do anything if only you and Father will receive him."

"Father will never do that," Robert said slowly. "A match between you is unthinkable."

"He threatened to send me away to Bavaria to a convent," Katherine said. "I didn't argue with him any more. I knew it was no use. But I swear to you, Robert, that I won't give up James. If we're not allowed to marry, I shall run away with him."

She saw her brother's eyes turn hard, and the set of his mouth was very like the Earl's as she had seen it less than an hour before.

"You will do nothing of the kind," he said coldly. "If you ever speak of such a thing again I will personally have you confined to your rooms until a safe place can be found for you." And then a thought came to him which changed his colour from white to red. "Has he seduced you?" he said. "Katherine, tell me the truth ... don't be afraid to tell me ..."

"Afraid!" She laughed angrily. "God's life, I wouldn't dare confess it if he had! But you can rest easy. James has never touched me. And I can promise you he's had the opportunity!"

"Thank God for that." Robert put his arm around her

shoulders. "I was only so afraid for you that something had happened. I would have killed him, you know that."

"I know," she said. "I know you love me. That's why you've got to help me in spite of yourself. I'll accept that you hate James. I'll even accept that you may have some cause. But I love him, Robert. If I don't have him, my heart will break. And so will his. Please help us. Speak to Father. Agree with him, say anything, but at least let James come here and plead his own case."

"And do you really think that that will make a difference?" he asked her slowly.

She looked at him and smiled. "I know the man I love," she answered. "Nothing in heaven or hell will stop him getting what he wants. He will win you and Father over."

"Very well then. I shall speak to him, but I promise nothing. You'll have to be patient, Kate."

"Dear Robert." Katherine put her arms around his neck and kissed him. "Go and see Father now and ask if I may go out riding tomorrow."

"Why tomorrow?" he asked her.

She smiled as she answered him. "Because James is expecting to meet me at Loch Ness. We have been meeting there for the past month. I want to be able to tell him he can come to Clandara!"

The following morning the Countess was at her usual place in the Green Salon, sewing one of the dozens of samplers with which she occupied her time. She knew every sound of the castle; its routine never varied, and when she heard the noise of horses in the courtyard she left her chair and went to the window to watch.

Below her she saw Katherine, accompanied by her old servant Angus, mounting up on a fine chestnut. Katherine rode well; she handled the fresh horse as if it were a placid old cob. She did everything well; sometimes Margaret Clandara reflected that life was unjust in the distribution of gifts, giving so much to some and so little to others. Beauty, grace, character . . . her stepdaughter had them all.

She must have needed them and more, she thought dryly,

to have captured James Macdonald. She had not seen him for five years, not since he stood behind her in the chapel at Clandara on the day she married the Earl, and almost the last thing she could remember as she went to the altar to take her vows was the expression of anger in his eyes. Such dark eyes, as black as pitch, but with that curious red light in them which made them seem almost brown when he was angry. His grandmother had been a Spaniard, and she had given her colouring to all the Macdonalds, except Margaret, who was only a cousin.

James had not wanted her to marry the head of the Frasers. James had not wanted to make peace with them or set foot in their house. And he had never known that he was the object of his insignificant cousin's undying love. Margaret had not blamed him. He was the kind of man she was content to worship silently, allowing herself a daydream in which she was the partner in all the shameful deeds of which he was accused. But it was only a fantasy and she was a practical girl who did not expect the secret longings of a plain and elder cousin to become reality. And then at last, when she was resigned to spinsterhood, the offer came for her from the Earl of Clandara.

There was a time after she was first married when she had tried hard to make herself agreeable to him. He was a man she could have cared for, indeed her empty heart and untouched body were only too eager to respond to love if the opportunity were offered her. But that opportunity never came. She had been exchanged in a treaty and married with pomp to a man who walked out of her bedroom on their wedding night with the remark that he was sure she would prefer to be alone. And nothing had changed between them since. Her efforts to please him and her one timid overture at affection had all been repulsed with coldness and scorn and now she hated him as she had never believed it possible to hate another human being. Not just for his harshness and indifference, but for the virginity which made her a mockery in his eyes and her own. She would never forgive him until the day she died.

Leaning forward, she saw Katherine move out towards the

castle gate, followed by the old servant on a sturdy grey mare, and she knew suddenly that she was going to meet James Macdonald. The Earl had lost. Margaret began to laugh, holding her hands to her mouth to muffle the sound; she laughed until she shook and then the laughter changed to the most bitter weeping.

Katherine had been riding for nearly an hour, with her personal servant, Angus Fraser, trotting a few paces behind. He was an old man who had been her guardian on riding and walking trips since childhood and she could hear him muttering and cursing under his breath as he followed. For the last month he had escorted her on this journey to Loch Ness and been the unwilling witness of her meetings with James Macdonald. She had made him swear an oath to keep it secret and after the first few mornings when the old man stood with his pistol cocked, watching his mistress and her lover from behind a hillock, he had come to the astonishing conclusion that the Macdonald meant the Lady Katherine no harm. She half turned in the saddle and called out to him, laughing.

"Stop cursing, Angus, you'll have some beastie putting the horse's foot in a hole if they hear you muttering on so!"

"It's no' my cursing that offends the beasties, milady," he called back. "It's the sight o' that murderin' Macdonald holding speech with ye and putting his black hands upon ye!"

His love for his mistress and his abhorrence of her actions had so upset the worthy Angus that he had been caught stealing the Earl's whisky and severely reprimanded. As he had been stealing it undetected for over thirty years, his carelessness showed how deep was his distress of mind.

"You're a peeping old woman!" Katherine retorted. "If you don't like what you see, cease your spying, you old rascal. This time you can stay here by the Loch road. And don't let me find you one inch nearer."

She touched her horse's sides and broke into a canter down the rough path that ran by the Loch waters. The Loch itself was smooth and blue, its surface shadowed by the majestic mountains that rose up from its farther shore. The sun was shining and the sharp clear air stung her face, and as the horse responded to the wind it broke into a gallop; as they turned the bend in the rough road she saw another horseman coming fast towards her, his pace wilder than her own. She called out to him and her cry was caught by the wind and torn away, and then they met and the man riding a big black horse pulled it up onto its haunches and threw himself down almost before the animal was back on its feet. He came and lifted her from the saddle and she abandoned herself into his arms.

"James, oh, James beloved . . ."

He was exceptionally tall for a Highlander; his shoulders were very broad and his strength was a legend. When he gathered Katherine close to him he lifted her off the ground. His dark face came down and his hard mouth pressed on her lips; she felt the muscles in his arms contract and marvelled at the power in them, and then perversely rejoiced because he was always so careful not to hurt her.

"Katherine! My bonny, beautiful Katherine . . . I rode like the devil to get here in time."

"So I see," she said gently. His splendid horse was lathered and sweating, its flanks heaved. "You ride too hard, my love. The poor beast is worn out."

"I'm an impatient man," the Macdonald answered. "And that's the least of my faults."

She reached up and touched the swarthy cheek and immediately he turned her hand to his lips and kissed it. "You have no faults in my eyes, James. Come, darling, tether the horses and let us sit down. I have some news for you and it won't wait a moment longer!"

They walked upwards through the short grass and he found a place where the heather grew thick and spread his cloak for her.

He tried to take her in his arms again but she held him back and whispered, "Wait, James, wait for a moment, let me speak first. Don't you want to hear my news?"

"Only if it's good," he answered. He found it more and more difficult to control his furious desire to hold her and kiss the lovely soft lips until they ached, and yet he would never have outraged the virtue which was so rare and so precious to him.

"I spoke to my father yesterday," Katherine told him.

"And he refused to hear of me and threatened to send you out of Scotland," James finished for her. "I expected as much. Is this your good news, my beloved?"

"No," she laughed, "no, my wild, impatient one. That's only the beginning. He was furious and he said exactly that—about my being sent abroad. And he banished me to my rooms. He was very, very angry, James. I could do nothing with him, nothing at all. It was my brother Robert who persuaded him."

"Your brother! By God, I didn't expect him to be our ally."

"You don't know him," she answered. "Robert is the sweetest of men, and next to you he is the dearest person in the world to me. He would do anything to make me happy, James. I told him how much I loved you and it was he who saw Father and made him agree to receive you. You are to come to Clandara tomorrow! Now, is that good news or not?"

"The best in the world, Katherine my love. If I can see your father I will convince him. If I was the devil I'd win over St. Peter in order to get you!"

"From what they both said of you, you might indeed *be* the devil," she said. "James, tell me something. Are you as wicked as they say? Not that I care, beloved ... I don't care what you are or what you've done. But I should like to know from you."

For a moment James did not answer her. Twenty years of violence and debauchery rose up and mocked him. So many fights that he had lost count; nights when he roamed the streets of Edinburgh when he and his brothers were students at the university, looking for women and accosting the passers-by, fights and drunken forays into the brothels, and raids upon the lands of the Frasers, stealing their cattle and chasing their people out into the moors to die.

He had never been aware of evil until he met Katherine;

he had lived like a wild animal, without pity or remorse. She sensed his shame and regret for the past.

"James, my darling," said Katherine, "forgive me. I had no right to ask. The past is your affair. Forget I ever asked you. Please."

"You have every right, if you're to marry me," he said at last. "And whatever I've been, Katherine, I never lied in my life. It's a poor virtue but the only one I can boast. I shan't lie now. If your father said I was a murderer, he told the truth; a cattle thief and a whoremonger ... all these things and more.

"But since I met you," he said, "I've changed myself. I've not laid a hand on a woman or drawn my sword on any man. I have tried to be worthy of you, Katherine. If you marry me, I will spend my life trying."

She put her arms around him and drew down his head and kissed him, long and passionately as he had taught her, and then his arms came round her and she was pressed so tightly against him that she could hardly breathe. They went backwards down upon the ground, and her desire rose to meet his until she trembled. Their world grew dark; the bright sun, the wind receded, and her senses clamoured and begged and a cry of surrender was torn from her shaking lips. As he held her he felt as if he were on fire; for a moment he hesitated, fighting himself and her, and then he thrust her away from him. She lay looking up at him, her blazing hair loose over her shoulders, and there were tears in her eyes.

"James, James, what did I do wrong?"

"Nothing, my love. Nothing. The danger is past, and it was all my fault."

"You could have taken me," she whispered. "I wished it."

"I know," he said. "But this is one time I know what it is to love as well as want. And I am not going to anticipate our wedding. Sit up, my darling heart, and braid up your hair. I must look your father in the eye tomorrow."

He smiled and helped her upright, and touched the shining red hair as she bound it up again. "What colouring will our children be?" he wondered. "If our son has your hair he will be the first Red Macdonald for generations."

"My son will be like you," she answered. "Black as the night crow. And brave and splendid above all other men. Promise me one thing."

"Anything. Anything in the world."

"Promise me that, whatever my father says to you tomorrow, you won't be goaded into a quarrel. I know Father. He may have agreed to Robert but only because he thinks he'll win. And if you lose your temper with him, then all is lost. I know he'll try to make you."

"I will be as meek as milk," he promised her. "I have too much to lose to mind a few insults. But I've a feeling I'll get a bonny reception all the same!" He laughed and held her close to him. "Don't be afraid of me; I shan't fall into any trap. I'll go to him, bonnet in hand."

"What of your own father?" Katherine asked him. "Does he know you intend to marry me?"

"He does," James answered grimly.

"And what did *he* say?"

James did not answer immediately. Sir Alexander's reply had been shouted from the head of the dinner table in the Great Hall at Dundrenan, and it bellowed still in his son's ears.

"Katherine Fraser! I'd sooner ye brought back a common hoor as a bride. If it isn't one and the same thing."

Only the intervention of his younger brother Hugh had stopped father and son leaping at each other. They had stood glaring and spitting with fury, and for the first time in his life the evil old man had retreated before the greater rage of his elder son. "Marry her then, but I warn ye, if you bring her here, the servants'll poison her inside a week!"

James shrugged and said lightly: "He was not pleased. But you've no need to worry on his account. I have no mind to live at Dundrenan under his shadow when we're married. I have a fine house at Kincarrig which is empty. It will make a bonny home for us until I inherit Dundrenan. Father is an old devil, but he won't trouble us. As for my brothers, they'll like you well enough."

"When they see that we are happy, both families will be

reconciled," Katherine said. "But we may have to wait, James. Father won't agree to any hurried marriage."

"All I pray is that he'll agree to a marriage at all. The time of it will come about of its own accord. And when I come to Clandara tomorrow, I shan't come empty-handed."

"What will you bring?" She teased him. "Some of our cattle that you drove off in the night?"

"They've been slaughtered," he reminded her. "I haven't raided your people since our cousin married your father. I must say I've been tempted once or twice. There's little enough to do on the long evenings. . . . How is Margaret? I'd half forgotten her existence."

"Well enough," Katherine said. "I think she must find it dull."

"She's a dull woman, but a kind one. Sweetheart, shall we go back to France after we're married? Why not visit the Marquise—she'd be delighted. I used to watch her watching us. I swear she hasn't enjoyed herself so much for years as she did while you and I were there."

"She was very sweet to me," Katherine laughed. "She used to come into my room at night—do you know, James, she wore rouge and rice powder even in her nightgown—she looked so ridiculous, like a little painted doll—and ask me what we had done and what you had said and whether you had kissed me! I think she enjoyed imagining how furious Father would be. She was my grandmother's cousin and she never liked Father."

"I'll never forget the first time I saw you," he said. "I was bored to death with my visit to the Château Charanton, but I knew I had to stay abroad for a while—there was that duel with Angus Mackecknie and the scandal got too much even for us . . . and then I went to the Marquise's supper party and saw you. You were wearing a white dress and there was a little crowd of Frenchmen standing by you, all ogling as if their eyes were about to fall out of their heads. I remember how angry it made me."

She was the most beautiful girl he had ever seen. She stood out in the crowd of overpainted, twittering Frenchwomen like a magnificent rose in her simple white satin gown, with lace at her breasts and elbows, and her glorious hair unpowdered. He had wanted her from the first moment, and then when he had arranged an introduction, the sound of her name only inflamed him more. A Fraser. Clandara's daughter. And a virgin; he had an unerring instinct for the uninitiated. What a triumph, he had thought, what a godsent means of dissipating the idle days. The vileness of his intentions made him shudder when he remembered them. But they had not lasted long.

"I remember you," she said. "And when I met you and knew who you were—oh, James, it doesn't seem possible! When you think, if we'd met here in Scotland we'd have hated each other and turned away."

"We would," he agreed. "The only difference is, I'd have taken some men and lain in wait for you one night. I could never have forgotten you, Katherine, or let you go to someone else."

"And if it had begun like that," she murmured, "instead of going out together, hunting and dancing at the Marquise's parties, I would have ended by loving you just as I do now."

"And always will, I pray to God," he said.

"I must go back." She stood up, and they embraced again, tenderly this time and a little afraid of themselves.

"Where's that old servant of yours?" he asked her.

"Over there by the bend in the Loch road. It's a miracle that he's held his tongue about our meetings. Do you know he nearly shot you once when he saw you take me in your arms! He told me afterwards that he was just about to fire when he saw me reach up and kiss you and realised it was not taking place against my will! Poor old Angus. He's very good and devoted and he's so angry with me that he can hardly speak. Can I take him with me to Kincarrig?"

"You can take what servants you wish, my love. The household will be composed and run according to your pleasure. Come, we must walk back, the sun is nearly over the edge of the mountain there. It will be dark in half an hour."

They walked back holding hands, James helping her down the steeper part of the hillside until they came to the two horses which were placidly cropping at the stubbly grass.

"My darling." He held both her hands and suddenly went down upon his knee before her. She stroked the black head which was bent over her hand.

"Pray that all will go well with us tomorrow. Pray that God will help us to gain our happiness."

"I will pray," he promised her. "I haven't spoken the name of God except to swear by it since I was a child at my mother's knee. But I'll pray tonight as never before. Now mount up, Katherine my love. And farewell until tomorrow!"

"Go to the courtyard and see if that's the Macdonald returned!"

The old man sitting in his chair by the open fireplace in the Great Hall of Dundrenan had been listening for the sound of a horse for the past hour. His grey head was thrust round the tall back of the oak chair and he scowled at the servant who ran to obey him.

Sir Alexander Macdonald was nearly seventy; he was short and thickset, with powerful arms and a trunk like a wrestler. Even at his age, he could break a man's back if once he managed to lock him. As a young man he had been feared and hated by his enemies and loved by his own clansmen, for there was no one like him in a fight. When James Stuart, the rightful King of Scotland, returned from exile in France and tried to wrest his throne back from the English in the rising of 1715, Alexander of Dundrenan had dragged his men away from their fields and their cattle and ridden out to do battle. He was fortunate in suffering no more than a heavy fine for his part in the rebellion, for along with his courage he possessed a high degree of cunning, and he had made useful friends among the Scots who governed on behalf of England. While other men lost their heads and their estates, Dundrenan remained safe and its chief confined his activities to harassing the Frasers. But he had never forgiven or forgotten the money he had been forced to pay to bribe his way out of a charge of treason. If he hated anything as much as he hated the Clan Fraser and its chief, he hated King George II of England and the English.

" 'Tis the Macdonald himself, lord."

"Tell him to come straight to me," the old man snapped and settled back in his chair. His eyes were not black like his son's; they were a peculiar colour, almost the same yellow as the agates he wore in his dagger hilt, and they had earned him the nickname of "The Lion." There was an ugly light in them as he waited for his son. Sir Alexander knew where he had gone.

When he heard James's step on the stone floor he did not look up or move. He stayed motionless until his son's shadow fell upon him and then he raised his eyes and glared at him and said slowly: "Come back, are ye? Fresh from courting, I suppose."

"You may suppose what you please," James snapped back at him. "If you've a mind to repeat your insults of last night, I have no mind to listen to you." And he turned as if he were going to walk away.

"Wait!" The old man sprang up. "Don't dare to turn your back on me, you renegade! Snuffling round the skirts of our enemy . . . Ach, James, you smell of where you've been!"

"I've been to see my intended wife," James answered. "I told you last night that I had made up my mind and Katherine has spoken to her father. He was as displeased as you. But that makes no difference to either of us. And since you betray so much curiosity, the Earl has agreed to receive me tomorrow!"

"It's a trick," Sir Alexander shouted. "A trick to get you inside their damned castle and then cut your throat. . . . Son, son, are you bewitched? Go there—alone, I suppose. God's wounds, if you go, you'll go with a company of men and your brothers at your back!"

"I'll go alone," James answered coldly. "And all I hope is that I return with his permission to marry Katherine. The feud is over, Father. It ended when we all stood in the chapel at Clandara and watched our cousin Margaret marry, do you remember? And it was you who insisted that peace must be made . . ."

"We were poor," his father retorted. "Poorer by ten thousand golden guineas after the '15. We couldn't stand the loss of cattle and the burning down of our crofts. But then is then and now is now. . . . We've prospered; I dare swear we're richer than that old swine Clandara could ever hope to be. There's no reason for this," he shouted, and there was a genuine note of pain in his voice. "No reason in the world why you couldn't have chosen a wife from any one of half a dozen Highland families if you've an itch to settle down. But this woman . . . No, James, I can't believe it of you!"

His son looked down at him and shrugged. The indifference on his face stung his father like a blow. There had always been love between him and his sons; love and loyalty and a bond of common taste. No other woman had set foot in Dundrenan since the old chief's wife died giving birth to his last son, David, and her influence had vanished with her into the grave. There was no sign in the great grim house that it had ever had a mistress. The walls were bare stone, hung here and there with fading tapestries which stirred in a perpetual draught; the open fires smoked, and there were hunting dogs sprawled in front of them; in some rooms the floors were still carpeted with straw as they had been a hundred years before. The only incongruous note was the Macdonald plate spread out upon a huge oak sideboard, the gold and silver dishes, cups and ewers gleaming in the dull light.

It was a fortress, garrisoned by fighters; the chief employed only half a dozen women in the house and these were usually pregnant by some member of the family. It was a common means of increasing the household staff, and the prized blood of the chief and his sons bred them devoted servants. Now their precious unity was gone, spoilt by this madman's passion for the daughter of their enemy.

"You're not intending to bring her here?" he demanded. "I told you what would happen if you did."

"This is no place for her," James answered shortly. "I'll not take her anywhere where she's not loved as she deserves. I have my mother's house at Kincarrig. We will live there."

The old man stared at him in absolute disbelief. "You'd leave your home—your heritage—your own father and family, just for the sake of bedding a *woman?* Son, I'll not quarrel with you, for it's obvious you're out of your mind.

You stand there, telling me you'll go off to Kincarrig and leave me in my old age . . . James, have you no love left for any of us?"

"I have love for all my kin," James answered. "I love you all," he repeated. "But I love Katherine more. You do not know her, Father, you have no idea of her graces and virtues . . ."

"Her *virtues!* God in heaven, I can't believe my ears. You, who were laying with scullery maids at fourteen, prating to me of virtue . . . Enough, James, enough. Go to Clandara tomorrow; there's no stopping a fool from his doom. Out of my sight now, and tell that old laggard Ian to bring me some whisky. Maybe your brothers can talk to you, it's certain that I can't any longer."

"If my brothers try to interfere with me," James told him quietly, "I'll break their necks. I will send the whisky to you, Father. It may have put you in a better mood by the time we dine."

The night came and the moon that rose over the sweeping hills and touched the mountaintops with silver made the wild and lovely countryside appear as cold and unreal as if it were part of some undiscovered planet. The lights in Clandara were extinguished, so too were those at Dundrenan, where the old chief lay drunk in his bed, and his son slept on and dreamed of the woman he loved, and turned impatiently in his empty bed as if in his dream he might find her there. And the sleep that came to Katherine far away at Clandara was as sweet and full of tender fantasies as those of James. Everywhere else in both great houses there was hatred and disquiet.

Katherine had awoken very early; lying in the slow drowsy state between sleep and wakefulness, she had closed her eyes and thought of James, and with the thought of him came the memory of those moments in the hollow, and it drove her out of bed, restless and longing and exhilarated because this was the day when he was coming to claim her. In spite of everything she was not afraid. Her maid, Annie, granddaughter of old Angus, helped her ladyship into her fine copper bath and poured in more hot water with a great deal of jasmine essence in it, and scrubbed her ladyship's white shoulders, bursting with such curiosity that she could contain herself no longer. The gossip was all over the castle.

"Is it true there's a suitor comin' for Your Ladyship today? Is it true it's a Macdonald? I didna believe my grandfather, he's an auld fool as Your Ladyship knows, but he was blatherin' and talkin' all night long . . ."

"Annie." Katherine drew the soft towel round her and stepped onto the floor, leaving patches of scented water as she walked. "Annie, your grandfather is not such an old fool as you make him out. There is a suitor coming here today, and he is not just a Macdonald, but *the* Macdonald himself. How will you like serving me in Kincarrig after we're married?"

"God protect me!" Annie stared at her mistress, her mouth opening in horror. "I'd as soon serve the devil in hell!"

"Then I'll take someone else," Katherine said firmly. "See if you can find a likely girl, Annie, and teach her my ways so that she can dress me and care for the clothes closets as well as you. I shall miss you though," she added gently.

Annie did not answer at once. She had a thin, ugly, humourous little face; she was only ten years older than Katherine but she treated her mistress with a mixture of protectiveness and awe as if there were thirty years between them. No one had ever wanted to marry Annie. She was too plain and too sharp-tongued. The whole of her affections had been channelled into devotion for the beautiful girl she had waited on since they were both children. She held out Katherine's shift and, seeing the perfect young body, thought of the loathsome Macdonald, and shut her eyes with a grimace of disgust.

There had been a cousin of the Earl's a year ago, a kind, soft-spoken gentleman—Henry Ogilvie—she remembered the name immediately. There had been talk of him and the Lady Katherine and everyone from the Earl down to Angus and the house servants had approved. Then her ladyship had gone to France and met this ruffian and Henry Ogilvie ceased his visits. Annie had gone with her, hating every moment of her exile. She had not learnt one word of the new language or eaten a mouthful of the food without complaining and comparing everything indignantly with the glories of Scotland. And not even she had known that the reason for her mistress' high spirits was the black and surly man she had seen dancing with her once or twice.

"Milady," she said at last. "Stand still, if ye please, or I can't tie these laces.... Milady, there's not one lassie within miles could care for ye as well as I can. If they weren't pickin' and stealin', they'd be asleep or sneaking off with some footman when your back was turned."

"In that case," Katherine said, understanding the game and enjoying it, "I shall have to employ a Macdonald as my maid."

It was too much for Annie. "No Macdonald shall put her dirty hands on you!" she snapped. "If you're going to this place to live with this villain, ye'll have need of me to take care of ye. But I don't believe your father will permit it, not for one moment. Employ a Macdonald, indeed!" She pulled in the corset laces so sharply that Katherine winced.

"If he refuses," she said, "I'll go with James Macdonald without the benefit of clergy. Will you come with me then, Annie?"

Annie stood back and held out a petticoat of white lawn, trimmed with a profusion of Carrickmacross lace. "I will not come with ye," she retorted, "and what's more, milady, I'll tell your father what you've said so he can keep the key turned on you."

"Annie! Have you never been in love?"

"With this muckle lot of ne'er-do-wells? I have not, thanks be to God. And don't think I believe that talk about running off. That's all well enough for the common folk, but wellborn ladies like yourself don't throw themselves away on wicked scoundrels like the Macdonald who'd as soon cut their throats as marry them afterwards!"

"The Macdonald is not a wicked scoundrel." Katherine's voice had lost its teasing tone. It was cold and sharp and Annie kept her head down. She knew when she had gone too far. "You will speak of him with respect in future, or not at all. Now open the clothes press; I wish to choose my dress for today."

"I put out the yellow velvet," Annie ventured.

"It is not good enough," Katherine said. She was still angry with Annie. There was not one person, she thought bitterly, not one to whom she could turn for encouragement. Hatred and prejudice blinded them all. She missed her dead mother at that moment as she had not done since she was a little girl.

The first Countess of Clandara was a gentle, calm woman, renowned for her kind heart and generosity. The portrait of her which hung in the Green Salon showed a slight, pretty girl with soft brown hair and hazel eyes. It was painted when she was still a bride. All the Fraser wives had been painted after marriage; the pictures went back in a long line in the Green Salon and round the walls of the enormous main staircase, even including the three women unlucky enough to marry the Red Fraser. Their pale, undistinguished faces looked down the centuries, framed by the ugly sixteenth-century caps and veils. He had married them and buried them and taken their substantial dowries. Katherine used to wander up and down the salon and the gallery, listening to her nurse explaining the history of each portrait, and she had often wondered whether one of the Red Fraser's wives had been alive at the time of the Macdonald siege and whether she had tried to help his unfortunate prisoner. But of the long line of Frasers and their wives and daughters, only one was not represented. The present Countess had not been painted according to tradition. The space beside the Earl's portrait was occupied by a magnificent picture of Katherine in hunting dress, painted just before she went to France.

Katherine went to the big mahogany clothes press that ran the length of one wall in her room, and pulled out the dresses one after the other.

"This," she said suddenly, "I will wear this. And the green slippers."

The dress had been made for her in France. It was taffeta, its colour a lovely, elusive sea green shot with blue, the bodice cut low and straight across her breast. Tiny flowers of turquoise and crystal were sewn on the bodice and scattered cleverly in the folds of the very full skirt. It was a beautiful dress, and she chose a long velvet scarf of brilliant turquoise blue to cover her shoulders. Annie laid out the dress on her bed and put the slippers and scarf beside it, and then, still in silence, Katherine sat down to have her hair dressed.

Annie was as proud of that thick, burnished hair as if it were her own. She brushed it with two of her mistress' silver brushes until it gleamed like fire.

Katherine had never needed to direct her; she had an unerring instinct for what was beautiful and in good taste where her mistress was concerned. She combed her hair back off her forehead, slipping two dark tortoise-shell combs into place, and caught it up behind with a double knot of blue silk ribbons, twisting the ends of hair so that they fell in ringlets over Katherine's shoulder.

"Thank you, Annie. That looks very well."

"I've done it a hundred times before. There's nothing special in it. For someone as bonny as you, it'd take a great fool to make you look other than the beauty ye are. Stand up now, milady, and I'll lace ye into your dress."

Katherine paused and turned slowly round in front of her long mirror, and saw Annie's expression confirming what she saw. She had never looked more beautiful.

"If your father says no," Annie said suddenly, "yon Macdonald will murder him to get his hands on you."

"There'll be no murder, Annie," she said quietly. "There'll be no violence and no argument. I have James Macdonald's word and I know he will not break it. We are all tired of fighting; after all, we've had a Macdonald living in this house for the last five years."

"We have that," her maid agreed. "And much good it's done her or us." She looked at the watch hanging from her waist. It was a present from her mistress and she was immensely proud of it. She was the only servant in the castle who possessed a watch, and she had taught herself to tell the time. "It's past ten. Ye've been so long dressing, milady, ye'll keep your family waiting for their morning chocolate."

The chocolate was a ritual which never varied. At eleven, the Earl and his son and daughter and his wife drank chocolate in the long library and discussed the business of the day. It was a leisurely habit which had originated with the Earl's French mother. She had been an heiress and a gay and lively woman, though not particularly pretty, and she had begun to improve and civilise her new home and seduce her fierce husband from his uncouth tastes in food and drink and a day beginning with porridge and meat at sunrise and the same diet, followed by bed, as soon as the sun had set. She had panelled the Green Salon and covered the walls in soft green silk, and filled it with beautiful furniture made by some of the best craftsmen in her native France. The tulipwood table and the elegant walnut chairs with their fine embroidery were hers. Over the years she had transformed other of the state rooms in the bleak, forbidding castle, filling them with colour and elegance, and catching the Scottish sun by the reflection of many mirrors. The Great Hall was untouched. It was said that her husband had looked on with an indulgent, even an approving eye, while his wife brought comfort and grace into his home. But his indulgence did not permit the dispersal of his family's collection of arms and armour or the hundred heads of stag which decorated the Great Hall.

It was never known what the Countess planned to do with it, because the Frasers took part in the rebellion of 1715 in favour of the Catholic claimant to the thrones of Scotland and England. James Stuart, the Old Pretender, as his English Protestant enemies described him, was no more fortunate than the other members of his race. He fled Scotland in defeat, and the Frasers of Clandara were among those ruined on his account. The little French Countess was widowed by the executioner in the public square at Edinburgh, where her husband prepared himself for the block by sending her a gallant message and a greeting to His Majesty King George I of England that was so obscenely insulting that he was hurriedly beheaded in the middle of it. Katherine's father had bought back his lands and his title by the payment of a huge fine, and kept both by living for some years in exile on his estates.

The Earl and his Countess were long dead, but the morning chocolate survived in their memory. But when Katherine went down, only the Countess was there, waiting.

"Where is my father, and Robert?" she asked Margaret.

"I don't know," she answered. "I have been here for some ten minutes or more." The Countess looked quickly at her stepdaughter. She knew the significance of the beautiful dress; she even admitted, for her nature was not a grudging one, that if her cousin won her he would have the loveliest woman in Scotland as his wife. After a moment she coughed. "Katherine, I don't wish to pry into your affairs, but—is my cousin James coming today?"

"Oh yes, he is!" Katherine turned to her. "He's coming at noon to ask Father for me. Oh, God, how I pray he succeeds. . . . What do you think Father will do, madam?"

"I have no way of knowing what your father thinks," the Countess said quietly. "He does not confide in me. But I am afraid it is unlikely; his feelings for my family have not changed."

"I know," Katherine said. Remembering her father's remarks about his own wedding, she felt suddenly sorry for her stepmother. "I hope you were not too hurt, madam, yesterday morning. I am sure my father values you; he is not a demonstrative man."

"He fondles his dogs," the Countess answered, her tone very calm. "He has never once even offered his hand to me."

"But you did not expect love," Katherine reminded her. She was embarrassed and uncomfortable at discussing her father with this woman to whom she hardly spoke at all.

"No, perhaps not." The Countess looked up at her. "I don't know quite what I did expect. I had long ceased to think of marriage when your father's offer came. I was brought up to think it could be a sweet thing. As it will be for you, if you have really won my cousin James's heart. It is a brave one, but from his childhood it was always empty. No woman filled it, and believe me, many tried. I congratulate you. You will have love and children . . . your marriage will not be like mine. God go with you today."

As she finished speaking, Robert Fraser came into the room. The Countess curtsied and then hid herself in a chair in a corner by the fireplace.

"He won't come down," Robert said, speaking to Katherine. "He won't see you or speak to you, and I've had the devil's own trouble making him keep his promise to receive the Macdonald today. He's in a bad mood, Katherine. I don't know what the result may be."

"He's preparing himself to meet James with insults, that's what he's doing. I know Father! He couldn't move me, and then you supported me, and now he thinks he'll rile James into a quarrel. But he won't, Robert!" She came to her brother and he put his arm round her. "Can't you do anything with him? Try once more, I beg of you. Tell him at least that James is of our faith and we can be married here in the chapel ... think, if it was Andrew Cameron, or the Macgregor—they were both suitors once, and neither of them Catholics. Please, Robert, think of something to make him more reasonable before he sees James!"

"I'll try," her brother said gently. "Ring for Davie, and after you've finished here, go to your room and wait."

The hour was endless. She finished her chocolate without speaking to her stepmother, who sat back in the shadow of the tall chair, and then ran back to her own rooms where Annie waited, and there she spent the time pacing up and down by the windows, looking out and asking her maid the time every few minutes. At five minutes to noon she heard horses and the thud and rattle of the gates being opened, and ran to the window to open it. But Annie got there first.

"Away with ye," she said fiercely. "Hanging out the window like any wee crofter's lass looking for her lover! Remember yourself, and who you are, and don't let the man see you. God forgive ye, where's your pride and your sense of what's proper?"

"Is it him, Annie?" Katherine demanded. "Can you see him, tell me!"

"Aye, I can," the maid answered. "He's riding past through the outer courtyard and he has one of his clansmen with him. A mighty ruffian he is too. No," she amended as Katherine tried to push past her, "not the Macdonald, he's all dressed in velvets like a gentleman and riding a horse as black as himself. It's the servant I meant."

Katherine put out her arms to her suddenly, and instantly

Annie enfolded her. "Annie, pray for me. If I lose him I'll never have another happy day. And say that you'll come to Kincarrig with me."

"Ach," Annie said crossly, "do ye think I'd let you go anywhere without me to look after ye! Go down now, milady, or you'll keep your father and the Macdonald waiting."

Five years ago the Earl had met face to face with the man who now came to claim his daughter. Five years ago both families had met in the Great Hall to sign the marriage treaty and witness the wedding of their kinswoman to the Earl, and apart from the squat, dark figure of Sir Alexander Macdonald, Katherine's father had remembered his eldest son best, only because his arrogance had impressed itself upon him like the scar of some old wound.

He had changed very little. He was as tall as the Earl remembered, and even darker if that were possible. His dress, of deep green velvet doublet, lace cuffs and jabot, was immaculate, and a red and green plaid hung from his shoulder. The Earl noticed with surprise that James Macdonald was not wearing a sword.

"I cannot welcome you," the Earl said coldly, "because I know the reason for your visit, and I must tell you, sir, that whatever you have to say to me is a waste of time."

"My compliments, my lord." James came closer to where the Earl and his son Robert stood, and bowed low to both of them. The expression on his dark face was quite calm. "I accept your sentiments but may I ask you to be patient with me. Is the Lady Katherine coming down?" He glanced round the Great Hall and at that moment he saw her at the top of the sweeping stairs, one hand on the stone balustrade, and forgetting her father and brother, James turned his back on them and went to meet her. At the end of the stairs she gave him her hand and bending low, he kissed it. For a moment they gazed at each other, and she heard him whisper, "I promised you . . . as meek as milk . . ."

When they came face to face with the Earl, Katherine's hand was firmly held in his.

"Release my daughter." Her father's voice was icy. James pressed her fingers and then let them go.

"Lord Clandara," he began, "I wish to make formal suit for your daughter. I am well aware of my own unworthiness, but in spite of it I value the virtue and grace of Katherine above any treasure in the world. I will spend the rest of my life making her happy if you will agree to our marriage."

"Those are fine sentiments," the Earl retorted, "but they hardly sound convincing in the mouth of a man whose reputation is the scandal of the Highlands. Your estimate of women's virtue is well known, sir. Do you seriously suggest that I deliver my daughter to a man like yourself? Come," he said sarcastically, "don't let us descend to farce. I am prepared to overlook Katherine's folly and find a suitable husband for her as soon as possible. As for you, I advise you to seek a wife among your own kin. If you can find any father who will receive you!"

"My lord," James answered quietly, "if I don't marry your daughter I shall never marry. Your advice to me is therefore useless."

"And useless to me too." Katherine spoke up for the first time. She stepped closer to James and in defiance of the Earl's angry frown put her arm through his. "I will never marry either," she said slowly. "Nothing will change me. Father, we beg of you, at least give us a little time to prove our love for one another. At least give James a chance!"

"That's all I ask."

The Earl's expression did not soften. It angered him beyond endurance to see Katherine with her arm through the Macdonald's; it made him painfully aware of the physical consequences of what they asked and the thought of that swarthy, murderous son of his enemy bestriding his child made him turn sick with rage.

He stood up. "You have made your pleas," he said. "I see no point in continuing this discussion. You, sir, leave the house; there's no more to be said."

"One moment!" Robert's voice was very firm. Until then he had not spoken. Katherine's face was ashen and there was a stricken, desperate look in the Macdonald's eyes. Whatever he was—and his type was as odious to Robert as his reputation—he was passionately and helplessly in love with his sister.

"We have not treated this submission honourably, and I am sure that it was made in honour. Angus, wine for her ladyship and for us. Drink that, Kate, it will put some blood back into your cheeks. Let us be calm; and let there be no scoring of points"—he glanced quickly at his father—"for whoever wins, it will be poor Kate's heart that breaks. Now." He turned to James. "You have a very bad name. Is it deserved or not?"

"It is deserved," James answered without hesitating. "But in my own defence I've never wronged an innocent woman save once."

"We know," the Earl interposed sharply. "At Glengannock. You raided the mansion house there for some slight or other and ravished Gannock's daughter."

James did not excuse himself, but his dark face flushed and he did not look at Katherine. "I was drunk," he said.

After a moment Katherine put out her hand and laid it on his. "If I can forgive him," she said gently, "why can't both of you?"

"And your duelling, sir," the Earl interrupted quickly. "How many men have you killed, and how many times have you gone out raiding since you were a wee boy? ... Your hands are covered in blood; the blood of my people more than any other! Tell my daughter how you shut in the women and the children when you set my crofts on fire! Were you drunk then too?"

"No, my lord. But I was not on that raid; it was led by my father. It was he who did the burning, not I. And all this slaying and bad living that you bring against me—what can I say to it? We are not saints. We are not saints, but nor are you. If you have qualms about Katherine living at Dundrenan, she can fill my house at Kincarrig with her own servants, and we will live there. As for money, I am not a poor man, I assure you. She'll want for nothing. Donal! Bring the casket here!"

The Macdonald servant moved up quietly behind his master's chair. He put down a leather box on the table and handed James the key. There was a necklace inside the box on a bed of faded blue velvet; on each side of it there hung two pendant earrings. The stones were emeralds and diamonds of such a magnificent size and lustre that even the Earl was silenced.

"These were part of my mother's dowry," James explained. "They came from Spain originally with my grandmother. She left these and others to me when she died. I give them to you, Katherine. It was my mother's wish that they should be given to my wife. No other woman but you will ever wear them."

Robert put his hand on the Earl's shoulder before he had time to speak.

"Katherine, do you love the Macdonald? Are you ready to leave your home and family and go and live with him among his people?"

"I love James with all my heart," she answered. "I will follow him as the Queen of Scots said she'd follow Bothwell—to the world's end in a white petticoat! If I don't marry him, I will never marry anyone."

"So." Robert turned then to James. "Do you love my sister enough to abandon your old way of living and make her happy if she becomes your wife?"

"I love your sister enough to cut out my heart and give it to her," was the answer. "Before God, my old life is finished. If I fail to make her happy"—James spoke to both the Earl and Robert then—"you can call me to any accounting you please."

"In that case, Father," Robert said, "there is nothing to do but agree."

"Agree!" The Earl turned to stare at his son in astonishment. "Robert, you must be mad. . . . I listened to you in the first place, that's why I received him—but now you sit there and tell me I must agree to this marriage . . ."

"You must," Robert asserted quietly. "For I am ready to give permission, and as your heir I have a say in my sister's future. Please, Father. Agree to the betrothal."

"I implore you." Katherine spoke then. "We won't set a date for the wedding without your approval. But let me be betrothed to James. Please, Father . . ."

The Earl did not answer at once. He had expected Katherine to oppose him, but his son's defection was a complete surprise. He was alone in his refusal. And he knew his daughter. If she said she would never marry anyone but that ruffian sitting opposite to him, then she would keep her word. But betrothal was not marriage. She would have time to find the Macdonald out.

"As you wish, my child," he said at last. "We will announce it. But there will be no wedding for a year."

James stood up and bowed to him. "My lord, I'm afraid that expressing gratitude is hard to me; I am better at giving insults than compliments," and he smiled. "But I thank you with all my heart, and I repeat my promise." He turned to Katherine and she stood beside him, her hand in his. James raised it to his lips and kissed it. "I will make Katherine happy."

Katherine left them then. Robert seemed to have taken full control and had suggested that they discuss the question of a dowry and a settlement from James, and the men had withdrawn to the long library to drink whisky and draft out an arrangement from both sides. She ran up the stairs, holding the skirts of her dress in one hand and exposing her ankles to the horrified sight of Annie, who had been waiting and trying to listen from the top of the staircase.

Katherine flew to her and threw her arms around her. Firmly, Annie disengaged herself. "Ye needn't tell me," she said, "but you're very happy about something. His lordship didn't throw him out, I see."

"No." Katherine looked up at her; she was flushed and laughing. "No, he didn't. And you can go and get out your baggage for Kincarrig!"

"Oh, God protect us," Annie said. "There's no possible good can come of this!"

Chapter 2

NINE LONG months had passed since James Macdonald first came to the castle. The time had seemed an eternity to the lovers, and in the beginning it had not been made easy by the relentless hostility of the heads of their families. The Earl lost his old affectionate way with his daughter; in spite of his promise he was sullen and disapproving, and when James first began to present himself as her affianced husband, it was only the influence of Robert which prevented the old Earl from breaking his word and ordering him out of the castle. But try as he would, he could find no fault with James.

Clandara could only describe him as besotted. His harsh voice became gentle, his fierce eyes lit with tenderness whenever Katherine appeared; his hand was always out to steady her step, his arm supported her, his extraordinary passion would have been ridiculous in a lesser man. And Katherine adored him.

The old Earl saw his daughter's wilful character, with its slight element of spoiltness, flower and soften under the impetus of her radiant love for James Macdonald. When he was present they were very circumspect, making conversation and only waiting for the moment when he left them alone again. And then he would hear them laughing, or listen to Katherine playing on the virginals while he stood by her, and there was always the low murmur of their talk, broken by laughter, shutting everyone out of their lives. Her father was very angry, as angry as the father of James, who seldom saw his son or could begin a conversation without ending in a violent quarrel, but they were helpless against their children. Robert did not mind; he understood that Katherine's heart was full and he loved her enough to withdraw gracefully when he was satisfied that she had chosen a man who could be trusted with her happiness. On the day her father surrendered and set a date in August for their wedding, Katherine went to her brother, and with gratitude and love she thanked him for helping her and James.

"You made it possible," she told him. "Today is the happiest day in my entire life, and I owe it all to you." She came to him and put her arms around his neck as she had done when they were children. "My dear brother," she said gently, "I know how I've neglected you these last few months. You've had to go riding alone and walking alone, while I did all the things we used to do with James. But never believe that I've stopped loving you. The only thing that troubles me is the fear of your being lonely when I've gone."

"I shall be very lonely, Kate," Robert answered her. "I have been lonely already. But I didn't mind, because I saw how happy you were. I must admit, your James adores you. I can't see any harm befalling you with him."

"Nor can I," she said softly. "But, dearest Robert, when I'm married, why don't you think of a wife for yourself? This house is gloomy sometimes, when Father reads for hours on end and that poor dull woman sits there sewing her endless samplers. Find a gay and pretty girl and think about it. . . . Will you promise?"

Robert kissed her cheek. "I will promise to think about it," he said. "Much as I love Clandara, it will be insufferable without you. It was dull enough when you went to France. Oh, Kate, I'm glad you're happy! That's all that really matters."

"I am so happy," she said to him, "that I cannot believe I am not dreaming and will suddenly wake up to find that James has gone or never existed. . . . I want to marry him, Robert, I want to be his wife and bear his children and do all the things with him that I have never done. And now I know, in two short months, I shall. God bless you, brother. I am going to meet him this afternoon and I can hear Angus downstairs grumbling because he's got to be the chaperone again. We'll both see you this evening."

When she was gone, Robert waited alone in the room for a few moments. In spite of his reassurance to Katherine, he suddenly felt sad and abandoned and, for the first time, a little jealous. But his feeling was unworthy and he vanquished it, and went to the window when he heard her leaving and leaned out to wave good-bye. And after that there was little time for loneliness, for the wedding of the Earl's daughter claimed the time and attentions of everyone from the chief himself down to the humble crofters who began weaving and embroidering gifts for the bride. And a month before the wedding, on the twenty-sixth of July, the Earl gave a ball at Clandara for Katherine and her bridegroom, to which the chief of the Macdonalds and his family and all the families in the county were invited.

The Great Hall had been transformed; its walls were hung with tapestries, and hundreds of candles burnt in the bronze chandeliers that hung from the vaulted roof. There were more lights burning in tall sconces, and the Earl's piper played in the gallery above the guests. The huge library had been turned into a supper room, one wall lined by tables on which every variety of meat and game and great quantities of fish were arranged, while servants waited to serve food and wine.

It was the gayest and most brilliant assembly of the local noble families that had been gathered at Clandara for thirty years. The last time had been before the rising of 1715, when the Earl's mother had entertained her cousins from France and given a reception for them. Few who were present then had met again after the rebellion was crushed by the English forces and the King in exile had been once more driven from Scotland. Many had joined the ninth Earl of Clandara on the scaffold, and many had lost their fortunes and estates and fled the country. And now, thirty years after, when a new German King, George II, sat on the throne of England and the veterans of the '15 were either exiled in penury or in Rome where the unhappy James Stuart lived on the bounty of the Pope, the talk had begun again, and it was once again of rebellion and war.

James Stuart was the son of James II of England, the last

Catholic King of that obdurately Protestant country, whom they had driven out and replaced by members of his own family who were of the right persuasion. It was for this King's heir that old Clandara had lost his head, and though he himself had retired, unwilling that more blood should be shed for him, James Stuart had a young son, Prince Charles Edward, already a veteran of the European wars, a youth of twenty-four but a man in the coinage of valour and spirit. The old Jacobites drank to the King across the seas, giving the forbidden toast by passing the wine glass over a cup of water, but now the young men were talking of the Prince. They were tired of laws which were originated in England being promulgated in Edinburgh and enforced by Lowlanders or traitors who had purchased the lands of the loyalists in their absence. The Highland chiefs were bored and their young sons were restless, drawn by the idea of a man as young as themselves who spoke and wrote with passion of his native Scotland and of his wish to return there if it were only to die among his own in battle.

There was talk and there was uneasiness because something was going to happen soon, though no one among them all seemed to know where or when it would be. But there was no shadow over the happiness of Katherine and James that night; war was not in the heart of that indomitable fighter James, who hated the English and the Protestants and had been reared on his father's tales of blood and vengeance. War was far indeed from the mind of Katherine as she danced the reel with him, so flushed and radiant with happiness that her beauty surpassed itself and drew all eyes on them both. Among those who watched were the chief of the Macdonalds and his two younger sons.

Hugh Macdonald was thirty; like James, he was dark and his handsome face was as swarthy as a Spaniard's, but the eyes were a curious grey-green. They gave him an almost boyish look accentuated by his elegant, yet raffish manners. His rather thin lips were always curled up in a smile, and of all his dour family he was the only one who laughed continuously. He was once described with great pride by his father as the most heartless young scoundrel he had ever encountered, not excluding the terrible James himself. Hugh's wits were as quick and agile as his body; he resembled his younger brother David as a fine rapier did a claymore. David, at twenty-two, was the physical model of his father: thickset, powerful, dark as night, and with a spirit consumed by the desire to fight and kill. He had little conversation and little mental process. He was essentially a savage and out of his time even in that savage age.

"I've not seen your cousin Margaret," Sir Alexander remarked. They had dined earlier on with their host and his family, and the Countess had spoken so little that she might just as well not have been there. While the men remained at the table and before the other guests arrived, she had excused herself and vanished. Now, bored and enraged because he had been unable to find fault, the old chief searched for some other cause of grievance. "Clandara has not danced once with her," he snarled to Hugh, who was leaning up against the tapestried wall, watching the dancers through his narrow, light eyes.

"I can't say I blame him," he answered. "Cousin Margaret always looked a little like a horse. You're feeling quarrelsome, Father. Think of something else. You can't pick a quarrel with a man because he doesn't fancy *Margaret . . .*"

"I have no intention of picking a quarrel," his father snapped. "This is not the time or the place. I let it get too far; one month more and they'll be married. If you're talking about quarrels, that should have been arranged months ago!"

"I don't see why it's late." David spoke for the first time for half an hour. "Anything would be justified if it stopped our brother making a fool of himself."

"He's bewitched," his father said. "There's no other explanation for it. He's defied me—his father—cast off his own kind and given himself body and soul to that damned woman. Where's the whisky? . . . David, call that servant over there. My glass is empty, like their hospitality and my son James's head!"

"Oh, I wouldn't condemn him too hard," Hugh remarked. "Look at them dancing there. You must admit she's a fine beauty. One of the finest I've seen. It's a pity it's James, you know. He was always too rough and uncomprehending of women's pretty ways. Such a pity he's hiding her away at Kincarrig, I might have had some gay evenings with her if he were absent at all. . . ."

"I wouldn't touch her." David Macdonald spoke suddenly. "I wouldn't put a hand on any Fraser except to kill them."

"No wonder the women run away from you," his brother said. "You're so violent, Davie, you remind me of our dear James before love transfigured his black soul. Now, my soul is just as black as yours but I'm a sight more pleasant with it! I'd take that redheaded madam from under his nose in a week if he brought her to Dundrenan."

"That's a good reason why she's going to Kincarrig," Sir Alexander retorted. "I'd have you and James killing each other over a Fraser—that would be the last irony. Where the hell is the whisky?"

A servant came with a silver jug and some water and re-filled their glasses. Hugh took a long drink of his and then set the glass down.

"Since we're here, we may as well enjoy it. While you and Father get drunk, Davie, I'm going to pay court to some of these charming ladies I see here. That little child with the fair hair from Glendar . . ."

"Lord Glendar's niece," his father said. "Mind yourself, Hugh. They're a powerful family; you'll not get away with your tricks there."

"I have no tricks in mind," Hugh protested. "Seeing my brother James dancing there with a fair bride-to-be on his arm, I'm in a romantic mood, that's all. Glendar's niece, is she? Charming. In that gown you can see quite a lot of her little breasts. Farewell, Father. Brother." He bowed to them and began to make his way towards the seventeen-year-old Fiona Mackintosh of Glendar.

"Your brother's dancing," Katherine whispered. The reel had finished and new partnerships were forming for the next dance. James had not relinquished her to anyone except Robert. They stood very close together, her arm through his, and even those who disliked both families, and had grudges against one or other, admitted that they were a perfect complement to each other. She was graceful, yet voluptuous, with beautiful shoulders and arms, and the combination of her colouring was startlingly brilliant. Her dress was white, crossed by a silk tartan sash, and the magnificent emerald necklace shone round her neck. And James did credit to his ancient blood and the blood of the noble Spanish lady who had been his grandmother. His black hair was powdered and tied back in a queue with a velvet ribbon; his red velvet coat and dress kilt fitted his splendid muscular figure, and there was a large diamond pin in his lace cravat. They matched each other, and they knew it and were proud.

"I hoped your brothers would enjoy themselves," Katherine said. "Look, isn't that Hugh partnering the little Glendar child?"

"It is," James said, "and I rather wish it wasn't. I hope her uncle chases him off. You don't know my brother Hugh, sweetheart, or you wouldn't wish him on any innocent of seventeen. Not even for a reel."

"Are you all really so bad, then?" she teased him. "And are they worse than you were?"

"Little different," he answered gently. "Except Hugh perhaps. Hugh has what his old nurse described as the devil's grin. It's seldom off his face. Do you know, my darling, we were in a fight once outside some tavern in Edinburgh when we were all very young, and I heard someone laughing. It was Hugh, fighting like Lucifer and laughing like a madman."

"Your brother David is a little difficult," she said. "Hugh has spoken to me once or twice and been quite charming, but David—"

"David belongs to the past," James told her. "David should have been born two or three centuries back when we were all little better than pirates, preying off the Lowlanders and each other. He would have been perfectly happy then."

"Robert is fond of you," Katherine said suddenly. "I hope you like him a little, James, just for my sake."

"I have a great respect for him," he said, "and gratitude too. Without him, we'd never have won your father over.

Come, my love, let's walk a little in the air. It's hot in here and I have a mind to be alone with you."

"Four more weeks," she said to him. "We'll have so little time for meeting between now and our wedding. Come with me, James. I know a turret walk with the most beautiful view in the world."

They climbed the narrow stone steps that wound up the inside of the castle wall and came to a little door. It opened out to a parapet walk which ran halfway round the wall and ended at the entrance to a smaller turret.

"This is called the Ladies' Walk," Katherine said. "When my ancestors were away at the Crusades, their wives used to stand here and watch for them."

James drew her back against the shelter of a buttress and took her in his arms. "You'll have no need to watch for me," he said. "I'll never leave you for a day!"

Eagerly she met his lips and hers opened under the urgent pressure of his kiss. Desire blazed up between them; even the least contact ignited their senses and brought them trembling and breathless into each other's arms. Katherine had been inexperienced and shy at first; now, after long months of waiting, her woman's instincts clamoured for the ultimate release, the final leap into the precipice which opened out beneath her every time they touched. His hands and his mouth and the muscles in his magnificent body were all things she knew and loved and which affected her like a drug. And she had seen him struggle with his own desire, winning each time and yet losing a little, until he was as helpless in his way before her as she was before him. And then again the temptation swept over them both as it had done that day so long ago on the moorland by Loch Ness, and again it was James who drew back, begging her forgiveness, tenderly caressing the soft face which he held close to his heart, and as he held her, she felt him trembling with the crisis through which they had both passed.

"Darling heart ... such a madness possessed me ... I feel ashamed before you."

"There is no shame in love," she whispered. "I am your wanton, James. I have no shame at all."

"You're not to say that," he said fiercely. "I forbid you to speak that word. *I* know what wanton means. . . . Beautiful, sweet, foolish Katherine, mistress of my heart, come back to the ball before I lose my head again."

"Is there a turret walk at Kincarrig?" She looked over her shoulder at him as they turned to go back, and her eyes shone in competition with the great stones round her neck.

"There is no turret walk," he answered. "But we won't need one there. Wait till you see it tomorrow."

"I'm so excited," she said. "I don't even want to go to bed. Why don't we ride straight there, my love, after this ball is over?" He opened the door and helped her down the narrow winding steps.

"Because it's a five-hour ride, and I have arranged for our grieve to meet us. I shall have to go to Dundrenan tonight and then we will go together tomorrow morning; I'll bring my grieve with me and we'll meet at the Black River Bridge and ride on together. How I hope you like what I have done!"

"I'm sure I shall," she reassured him. "But you've made such a secret of it I've been tempted to slip over alone in the last month and see. . . . Supposing Father had not made a wedding date—didn't you even think of that when you began all these preparations of yours?"

"I knew you would be my wife," he said quietly. "And I have prepared Kincarrig accordingly. But if you don't like it, my love, then we will pull it down and build another house. Come, isn't this the door into the main corridor?"

In the corridor, halfway down to the head of the main staircase, they suddenly came upon the Countess Margaret. She had dressed for the ball in a gown of pale pink velvet and satin, more suitable for a girl of Katherine's age than her own. The soft youthful colour of her dress only accentuated the pale face and the tired eyes.

"Why, Margaret!" James stopped and, taking her hand, kissed it and bowed. "I've hardly seen you tonight. We looked for you below but I couldn't find you anywhere."

"I have been in the library," she answered. She looked at him and then very slowly at Katherine, and after a second's pause her stepdaughter began to blush. "You have been taking the air, I see," she said.

"Yes, Maggie." James's tone changed to the friendly, mocking voice she had known when they were both children and she had paid long visits to Dundrenan House. "Yes, Maggie, we've been taking the air, as you call it. And haven't you done the same yourself, an old married woman like you?"

To his surprise, Margaret's pale face flushed a deep painful red. She did not look at Katherine. "No," she said, and her voice in contrast to her strained, unhappy face, was flat and calm. "No, I haven't. Or anything like it. If you want to know why, you had best ask your future wife. I'm not surprised she hasn't told you. Now I'm going to bed. I'm not used to festivities," and she gave her cousin a terrible smile. "Good night."

"Well I'll be damned." James stood looking after his cousin as she walked quickly back down the corridor and disappeared into one of the rooms. "What the devil did she mean by all that?"

"I don't think she's very happy," Katherine said; suddenly she felt almost guilty about the Countess. "She told me the other day that a marriage of convenience was not what she expected when she married Father."

When James looked down at her, it was the first time she had seen him frown. "Forgive me," he said quietly. "What is meant here by a marriage of convenience? Explain it to me, I feel a little confused. . . ."

"It is not consummated." Katherine was so nervous that she spoke quite curtly. "I think she thought Father might care for her and have children by her . . . it's a pity the situation was not explained to her before. It would have saved the poor thing a lot of disappointment."

"It was not explained to us either," he said. Now they were standing facing each other in the empty corridor, and Katherine thought suddenly, "We're going to quarrel, and over Margaret Clandara, of all people in the world. It's too ridiculous. . . ."

"Are you telling me that your father has offered my cousin

that insult for all these years? Good God, Katherine, I'd rather he'd treated her as I did Gannock's daughter ... it's less cruel!"

"James, don't be angry, I beg of you," she said. "I am not responsible for what happened between Father and Margaret. Don't look so angry with me, as if it were my fault ..."

"Of course it's not your fault," he said, and he put his arm around her again. But his face was set and his eyes were angry. "I was not aware of the calculated insult to the honour of my family. No wonder your father is against our marriage; what a fine irony of fate on him, that now he'll have Macdonald grandchildren instead of the children he's denied poor Margaret!"

"James," Katherine interrupted, "James, he didn't love her. He never pretended that, surely. Why must you start all this talk of insults and honour now? Do you want to lose me even at the last moment? Don't you know that your father and mine would seize any excuse to start a clan war with each other and stop our marriage?"

"Of course I know," he said. "I know very well that there's nothing I can do for Margaret without risking our happiness. But I'm not used to swallowing my honour and the taste is bitter, I assure you."

"When we're married," she said suddenly, "perhaps Margaret could go back to her own people. Darling James, please don't think about it. Don't nurse a new grudge against my father or we will never be happy. If Margaret went back to Dundrenan, she would be happy then. I will ask her, if you like."

"Margaret may not have your wit and beauty, my Katherine, but she has the Macdonald's sense of what is fitting. She will never be returned to her own people as the repudiated wife of a Fraser. She will stay here and suffer for as long as your father lives. But you can be kind to her, my love; for my sake, ease her hurt a little if you can. We were brought up together and she was all of a sister that I ever knew."

"I will," she promised eagerly. "I will do my best. I will do anything if only you will look at me and smile again."

He did as she asked and, when he saw how pale she

looked, he gathered her quickly into his arms and kissed her, begging her forgiveness.

"I was a boor," he apologised. "My darling, I didn't mean to hurt you and accuse you when you are wholly innocent. I was upset for my cousin. Did you see the look on her face when she left us? We won't talk of it again, but I wonder if your father knows what an enemy he's made. . . . Come now, kiss me and we'll go back to the ball. I love you so, my Katherine. To hell with Margaret and Clandara. Come."

In the Great Hall once more, Robert advanced to meet them. He smiled at his sister and took James by the arm. "Come into the supper room; some of our guests have still to meet you."

In the supper room they were surrounded; Katherine found herself in the centre of a group of women, some of whom were married, and soon the talk was of dresses and the mysterious Kincarrig, which she was going to see for the first time tomorrow. With the men, among them James's cousin, the Macdonald of Keppoch, and the younger son of Lovat, head of all the Clan Fraser and a distant cousin of Clandara himself, the talk was more serious.

"There are rumours that there'll be a landing soon from France," Macdonald of Keppoch said. "One of my sons has just come back from Paris and he said the Prince, God bless him, was ready to muster an army and set sail weeks ago. He hoped for support from the King of France, but so far the King has not received him. But he'll come one day, he'll come whether the French help him or not."

"I hope not," Robert said. "I hope nobody tempts the Prince into doing anything rash like his father in '15 and thereby ruining us and the Stuart cause forever. If he comes, then he must bring an army with him and a proper plan of action. We wouldn't be dealing with each other in a new rebellion. The English are a people to be taken seriously when it comes to war."

"I'd match one of my men against ten of their damned redcoats any day," James snapped. "They've run from the Highland charge again and again. Personally, I'd rather put our King back on his throne without the help of France or any other foreigners. Scotsmen alone should do it, and Scotsmen can."

The son of Lord Lovat lifted his wineglass and immediately Robert and James and Keppoch raised theirs. There was a large pitcher of water standing on the table near them, and James moved it into the centre and then slowly passed his glass above it.

"To the King, gentlemen!"

"To the King over the water! God save King James!"

"And now, if we do have to fight for the Prince," the young Lovat said, "I hope we'll all meet together on the field. But it's only a hope for the future, I'm afraid. If he comes without French aid, my father won't support him. And he must know that others won't. In the meantime, we'll drink to him! Gentlemen, I give you the Prince!"

As they moved away, Macdonald of Keppoch turned to James. He was an old man of nearly seventy, chief of a powerful branch of the great clan which spread through glen and island, bound by many chieftains under the supreme lordship of the Macdonald of the Isles. He loved to tell how he discomfited a guest who boasted in his fortress home of the fine silver candelabra that graced the tables of the English nobility. That evening when he came to dine with Keppoch, the table was ringed with his tallest clansmen, each holding aloft a resin torch to light the meal. And Keppoch remarked to the astonished guest that he doubted if in England there were candelabra to match his. He had not seen James for nearly five years and he was surprised and intrigued to learn of the betrothal of Dundrenan's heir with the daughter of the Fraser of Clandara; he had not shared in the feud himself, but he knew about it, and in early times some of his men had joined their cousins on a raid or two against the Fraser cattle herds.

"Soft words from the Frasers," he said under his breath. "They're not overburdened with fighting spirit. Did ye hear that young whelp of Lovat's saying his father wouldn't come out without a French army? And your brother-in-law-to-be wasn't much bolder. My sons will go with the Prince and I'll ride out myself if I have to be held up on my horse. If the day comes, James, if the day comes."

"Who knows?" James answered. "Rumours come and go on the wind and the time goes with them and nothing happens. It's the wish being father to the thought, Keppoch. As for me, I'm a month off my wedding and the last thing I have thought about is a rising."

"You've a fine bride," the old man said. "And it's always wise to marry the enemy, for you never know when you might need to have them at your back. My greetings to your father, James. I saw him a while past in the Great Hall but he was drunk and in none too good a humour. But my greetings just the same. I'll see you on your wedding day no doubt."

James bowed to him. "No doubt. God go with you, till then." He moved over to take Katherine back to the Great Hall where they joined in one of the lively Fraser reels. His father and David Macdonald were standing where he had last seen them, both too drunk to speak to each other but still firmly on their legs. He made a mocking bow to his brother Hugh, who was talking to the gentle Fiona Mackintosh. He was leaning as close to her as he dared, and she was staring up at him, her large hazel eyes wide open as if she were being hynotised by a snake. Hugh glanced at his brother and winked.

"If he seduces her tonight," James said under his breath, "we'll have the biggest clan war for a hundred years."

Katherine looked quickly over at them both and then away. For a moment she had found Hugh's eyes fixed on her and there was something in them that made her shudder.

There was a new light coming into the room, competing with the hundreds of candles, and it was the soft grey light of the coming dawn. As it turned from grey to palest pink, the first of Clandara's guests began to leave, among them the chief of Dundrenan and his three sons. They travelled fast over the rough tracks and moors, and reached their own fortress home within three hours, tired and eager for a few hours' sleep. But there was a strange horse tethered in Sir Alexander's stables and a stranger waiting for them in the Great Hall, dozing in a chair by the open fire. There was no sleep for any of the Macdonalds that July day.

Katherine was awoken early by the vigilant Annie. She stretched and turned over, settling deeper into her pillows, until the maid leant over the bed and shook her.

"Wake up, milady. It's past six."

"Oh, Annie! I'm still half asleep. Go away!"

"Ye told me yesterday to wake you, for we're going to see this house at Kincarrig today. Wake up, milady!"

"Of course!" Katherine sat up quickly. "I promised to take you with me. Dear Annie, I'm sure you'll like it. James says it's beautiful and he's spent a fortune having it made comfortable for me. Give me my robe and prepare some hot water."

"Your robe's here," said Annie, holding out the brocade dressing gown, "and the hot water's in your bath."

Katherine sang to herself as she washed and let Annie dry her and help her into her chemise and corselet. She dressed in a riding habit of blue cloth with a Scots bonnet in dark blue velvet, and held out her hand for her gloves.

"There's a picnic to come with us," Annie said. "I took the liberty of ordering some chicken and pasties and two bottles of wine. Angus says it'll take us the best part of the day to ride there and back."

"The Macdonald is meeting us halfway," Katherine reminded her. "Did you take him into consideration when you ordered the food?"

"I did, milady. Mrs. Duncan showed me the parcels before she packed them. There's more than enough for everyone."

"Thank you," Katherine said. "You are very good, Annie, when you're not scolding and grumbling, and I really don't know what I'd do without you."

Annie tied her cloak under her chin and pulled the plain bonnet over her sandy hair. "No more do I," she said. "Angus was told to bring the horses round at half past eight. I think I hear them now."

The Earl was not yet awake; Katherine sent a message to his steward telling him that she had gone without disturbing him and would be back that evening. There was no sign of Robert either. She walked very quickly past the Countess' door and then suddenly, remembering her promise to James, she astounded Annie by turning back and knocking on it.

"Who is there?" Margaret was up. No one even knew what time she rose. She had her own maid to wait on her; she was a dark sullen girl who had come from Dundrenan and made friends with nobody in the six years she had been among the Frasers.

"It's Katherine. May I come in?" She paused a little awkwardly by the door until her stepmother came out of the inner room where she slept. She looked very tired and her eyes were red, though whether from sleeplessness or weeping it was hard to say.

"What can I do for you?" she asked.

Katherine shook her head. "Nothing, madam. I only came to wish you a good morning and to say I am going to see Kincarrig today. I wondered if you knew it."

"I have been there," Margaret answered dully. "But it was empty then. My family preferred Dundrenan; it was easier to fortify. Kincarrig is a very fine, large house. I am sure you will like it."

"I'm sure I will." Katherine hesitated. She had nothing to say to the other woman; her effort had been made and she was embarrassed and anxious to escape. For James's sake she made one more.

"After we are married, madam, I hope you come and visit us from time to time."

"If your father gives permission, I would like that very much. James will be going to Kincarrig with you, of course."

"He's meeting us," Katherine answered.

"Then give him my greetings. I wish you a good journey." And the Countess opened the door for her and closed it firmly on her.

Her maid, Jean Macdonald, came out of the Countess' powder closet where she had been listening.

"We are invited to Kincarrig," Margaret announced. "After the wedding."

"Will ye go, milady?"

"I would rather die than see a Fraser mistress of Kincarrig

or any other house belonging to our people. If he had taken
her to Dundrenan it would have broken my heart."

"Och, milady, maybe it'll be easier for you when they're
married."

Jean, whom everyone despised as stupid and taciturn, was
the possessor of a particularly warm heart as well as an im-
mutably unforgiving nature regarding her enemies. She loved
her mistress as much as Annie Fraser loved hers, but it was
the devotion of the servant, awkward and ill expressed in
words.

"Nothing will be easier for me," Margaret said, "until the
day his lordship dies and I can go back to my own people.
And take you with me, you poor child. There's no man for
you here among these people."

"I don't want one," Jean said quickly. "I'm content as I
am. Come, milady, your toilette is ready for the day."

Margaret still used her trousseau. She had not bought a
new gown or a fresh set of underclothes for six years. She
would wear the silks and velvets and the flowing robes of lace
and lawn until they were patched and darned and fell to
pieces. She would not spend one penny on herself nor ask a
penny from her husband. It was a curious and dangerous idi-
osyncrasy which no one had noticed because they so seldom
noticed her. She dressed and prepared herself for another day
spent in organising the household in opposition to the Earl's
steward, who hated her, and the servants, who disobeyed her
if they could. A day spent in boredom; riding alone except
for a Fraser trotting behind her as custom decreed; drinking
chocolate in the library with her husband and Robert while
they talked over her head as if she were not there, dining and
supping with them in the draughty Great Hall at the end of a
long table, and then retiring early to sit and sew in her own
rooms until she chose to go to bed. And there was no release
that she could see but Clandara's death or her own.

It was a lovely morning. The month of July had been
warm with little rain, and the countryside had blossomed into
heather and patches of bright yellow gorse. The mountains
rose high in the distance, their sides a dark purple wreathed

in drifting clouds; the little cavalcade rode down the rough and sometimes precipitous track towards Kincarrig and before noon they were well into Macdonald country. James had arranged to meet them at a small wooden bridge crossing one of the wider streams which found their way down from the mountains. When they arrived there, a Macdonald was waiting for them with a message. Katherine read it and exclaimed in disappointment. James could not meet them; the Macdonalds had found a most important guest waiting for them when they returned from Clandara last night, and it was impossible for James to leave Dundrenan that day. The man he had sent in his place was his new grieve and would be in charge of the household at Kincarrig. He could show Katherine the house and carry out any orders she might have for him.

Led by the grieve, who presented himself as Ian Macdonald, the horses rode onwards towards Kincarrig and at last they came within sight of the lodge gates leading to the house.

The gates were opened by an old servant who saluted them, bowing and taking off his bonnet, and behind him Katherine saw a woman bustling several half-grown children out of sight.

James's descriptions had not prepared her for Kincarrig. It was built of grey Scots stone, the remains of some ancient castle long fallen into ruins, and the architect had been influenced by the elegant and decorative styles of the great French country houses. It was a beautiful mellowed house, large but not forbidding like Clandara, with a multitude of windows and a splendid entrance up a long flight of wide stone steps. He had told her the gardens were a wilderness, but they had been transformed into a gracious landscape, reminiscent of the rolling parklands of a French château, with shrubs and trees and shaded walks. A stone fountain played in the centre of the long drive up to the house; the waters cascaded from a centre group of nymphs, attending the dominant, triumphant figure of Pan, the pagan god of love.

At the steps, when she dismounted, servants appeared from

inside to take the horses; Ian Macdonald introduced them all by name and, according to Highland custom, Katherine shook their hands and thanked them for their greeting. The house had a Great Hall, smaller than the enormous room where she had danced the night before, but panelled in oak with a huge ancient fireplace, surmounted by the arms of the Macdonalds. The stairs were oak, with a magnificent carved balustrade, the work of the same craftsmen who had made the panelling. The smell of paint and cedar polish was over-powering, though every window was open to admit the sun, making patterns of dappled light upon the shining floors.

Preceded by the grieve, Katherine went into the main rooms of her new home.

"This is the Grey Salon, milady," Ian Macdonald said. "The Macdonald chose everything in it himself. Some of the best furniture from Dundrenan is in this room."

It was a lovely room; she stood in the doorway, looking at the walls which were pannelled in grey silk and hung with portraits. Macdonalds, every one of them. The same dark faces, arrogant and inscrutable with their curious likeness to the man she loved, stared down at her from the past, and over a magnificent silver-gilt table she saw the picture of a beautiful woman, dark-eyed and black-haired, with a wide white ruff outlining her pale face, and knew even before she asked the grieve that this was James's grandmother who had been a cousin of the Duke of Alba and married Sir Donald Macdonald in Spain in 1671.

"I hope Your Ladyship is pleased," the grieve said. "I know how much the Macdonald wanted to show this room to you himself."

"I think it is beautiful," she said at last. "The most beautiful room in Scotland." And she turned triumphantly to Annie.

"There's not a room in Clandara to match it! Where are the private apartments?"

"This way, if you will follow me." He led them through the Grey Salon and on past two smaller antechambers, all furnished and decorated in exquisite taste, and then at last she saw the bedchamber which she and James would share in a few weeks.

She had never imagined him to be artistic or to possess such an imaginative sense of colour and proportion, and yet the bedroom was the result of an artist's inspiration. It was golden from the tapestries which covered the walls to the enormous tester bed which stood in the center of the floor, its brilliant embroidered hangings sweeping the ground. Her dressing table and closets were made of the faded golden walnut which so closely matched the scheme of the whole room. It was luxurious beyond belief, and yet it seemed to be full of sun. Even on the greyest Scottish day, with the fine Highland rain streaming past the windows, it would always seem as if it were full of morning sunshine.

Impulsively, she turned to the grieve, and his rather solemn face softened and he smiled. She was a Fraser, and though he had thought her beautiful and gracious, he had been polite but unenthusiastic. But her appreciation touched him; he could not help thinking how well her golden beauty would enrich the lovely room.

"How I wish your master were here," she said. "He never told me what a wonderful place Kincarrig was. It is a palace, not a house."

"Six months ago it was a shell, milady. The walls were peeling, half the windows without glass, and not more than a few sticks of mildewed furniture in the whole place. The Macdonald has spent a lot of money to make it fit for you."

"And the furnishings," she asked him, "those wonderful tapestries and bed ... surely he did not buy them? ... Such things are not for sale in Scotland."

"The hangings and furniture were in the attics at Dundrenan," the grieve replied. "Sir Alexander has no mind for fancy things, and they had been put away since my father's time. He was the old laird's steward, and his father before him. ... I know the Macdonald ordered the bed from France four months ago. It came by ship and we assembled it the week before. If you have finished here, I'll show you the kitchens. My brother will be steward to the lord and yourself. He will be here next time to greet you."

"Nothing would please me more," Katherine answered. "But now we'll dine; it's been a long ride, and I'd be honoured if you'll join me. We brought some provisions with us."

"They won't be needed," he assured her. "The Macdonald gave orders and everything is prepared. It is ready in the library. I thought you would wish to dine quietly today."

As they sat down in the narrow library, panelled in oak and filled with books from the floor to the ceiling, Katherine whispered to Annie, who stood behind her chair. "Now, can you find one word of complaint? Come, woman, tell the truth without spleen . . . isn't this a house you will be proud to live in with me?"

"I'm proud to live anywhere with you," Annie retorted. "Whether you end in a croft or a palace like this, masquerading as a simple Scottish dower house. And I've no spleen, milady. It's a fine house and so long as you're happy in it, so shall I be. But I don't like yon dour Macdonald . . . he's overfull of himself if you ask me. But have no fear—I'll bring him down to his right size when the time comes." And Annie contented herself with seeing that her mistress had all she needed and waving the Macdonald serving maids aside with an air of authority.

It was a long day, for Katherine wanted to see everything. She inspected the kitchens and walked through the fine gardens, talking earnestly to Ian Macdonald, until Annie's legs ached and the sun was sinking behind the purple mountains.

When they remounted and the grieve parted from them at the bridge where they had met, old Angus muttered disagreeably under his breath that he had never seen a place less like a Scottish house nor met people meaner with the whisky to an old man who had been ridden off his legs.

"Ach," Annie snapped at him, "hold your tongue, Grandfather. . . . It's no matter if ye don't like it. I dare say there'll be servants enough for her ladyship there and ye won't be coming!"

It was dark when they reached Clandara, and Katherine went up to her rooms and changed out of the creased and dusty riding dress into a warm cloth gown trimmed with miniver.

"What a beautiful house," she said again as Annie brushed and combed her hair and dressed it simply round her head. "I never imagined that I would live anywhere so beautiful! I do wish James could have been with us—I can't wait to tell him how I love it. I wonder who the visitor was that kept him?"

"Ach," Annie shrugged, "who knows, milady? There's always business of one kind or another for the chiefs. Your own brother is out tonight; I heard the steward ordering some supper to be sent to your father's room."

"Then you can bring mine there too. I'll go and see him now."

The Earl was sitting by a blazing fire, for the nights were cold even in July, and Katherine was surprised to see that he had left his meal half finished. She came over to him and, bending down, kissed his cheek. He looked up at her and in spite of his smile he looked suddenly very old and tired.

"You're late, my child. Did you have a good journey?"

"Very good, Father. And worth every mile to see Kincarrig!"

"I hope it's a fitting home for you," he said. "Sit down a moment, I want to talk to you."

"Won't you let me tell you about the house?" she asked gently.

"Later, Katherine. I know you're pleased with it and that's enough for the moment. Did the Macdonald meet you there?"

"No," she said, "no, he sent a message. He was detained at Dundrenan. Where's Robert? The steward said he was out."

"Robert is at Dundrenan too," her father answered. "A messenger came not half an hour after you left this morning, summoning both of us to the Macdonald's house. I felt too tired to go; besides, Robert deals better with them than I do."

For a moment there was silence between them. The Earl was staring at the fire; he seemed hardly aware of her.

"Father, what is wrong? I know something has happened. . . . Why has Robert gone to Dundrenan?"

"The Macdonald's messenger brought this," he said, and he

opened his hand and held out a crumpled piece of white silk sewn into the shape of a cockade.

"The Stuarts!" Katherine exclaimed. "Oh, Father, no!"

"That is their emblem," he answered. "Thirty years ago one of these was brought here to my father in the dead of the night and he rode out as Robert has done. When he returned, he had sworn himself to the cause of the King. Before he gathered our people and went out to war, he sent me by ship to France. I was his only son, Katherine, and he knew if he fell that I might be spared if I had taken no part in the rising."

"Father, what is going to happen? Has the King returned?" She was as pale as the silk she twisted in her fingers.

"I don't know," he said slowly. "But it's certainly not the King who's coming. He's old and retired from the struggle. I believe it's his son, Prince Charles, who's making the claim for him this time. And it's a claim we will not answer. That's why I sent your brother. If the Stuarts are coming back to bring war and ruin to Scotland, the Frasers of Clandara are not going to join them. We lost all in the '15. Our lands and people could not survive another failure. And, by God, I know it will fail, whatever the enterprise!"

"But he cannot come back," she said. "We've been at peace for all these years . . . nobody wants to fight now!"

"You speak for yourself and for us, my child," he said. "But that's not the thinking of men like Alexander Macdonald and others. There have been rumours that the Prince would land with a French army for the past six months. I thought it would come to nothing, but now I fear it has. And there will be men mad enough to join him and destroy themselves and beguile others to destruction with them."

"But what was the message, besides this? Did the man say nothing?"

"He brought a summons from the Macdonald of Dundrenan which he said was one of many going out to families all over the glens. And he gave me that cockade."

"Has the Prince landed? If not, surely there is still time to dissuade him. Oh, Father, I cannot bear it! When will Robert be back?"

"By dawn tomorrow," the Earl said. "As we are not joining, there is naught to keep him there."

She looked down at the piece of silk which was now pulled and torn loose from its design. Her voice was very low. "Do you think James will fight?"

"Ha, you know him better than I," he said shortly. "Do you think that his love for you and his wedding and the fine house will keep him or any of his kin out of a battle? He'll fight, my child, don't doubt it. They'll come out and call their clansmen with them if there's any prospect of a war. Nothing could stop them. And I'll not let you marry into a family that will soon enough be ruined and hunted down for vengeance by the English. My name would not protect you then. If he wants you, let him remain neutral."

"James does not know the meaning of that word," she said slowly. "You know that, Father. And what he elects to do, I shall do also. I shall be his wife, and if he fights for the Prince I shall fight with him." She stood up and held out the white ribbons to him. "What shall I do with this?"

"Throw it on the fire! I want nothing connected with this business in my house!"

"When Robert returns tomorrow we will know more," Katherine said. "It may not be as bad as we fear. But whatever befalls, nothing will stop my marriage to James. I want you to know that. Good night, Father."

She slept little that night, not even confiding her fears to Annie, who slept on her straw palliasse outside her mistress' door. If James joined with the Stuarts, then she would follow James. She had no doubt of that. Her love and allegiance were given to him and she would travel to the battlefield with him in common with the other ladies and the poor wives and children of the clansmen, to succour their men or to mourn them when the fighting was over. She rose before dawn, and Annie found her watching by the window as the sky grew light, and then at last she told her in whispers that her brother was returning with news of a new war which would alter all their lives. But the dawn became day and the castle was full of the sounds of ordinary activities; it was midafternoon and Robert had not returned to Clandara.

The Great Hall at Dundrenan was full of men. Robert arrived early and stood drinking whisky and talking to James as, one after another, the heads of the local families and their sons came to Dundrenan.

Macdonald of Keppoch was already there, with his brother Donald and the two brothers of the Lord of Kinlochmoidart, Ranald and Clanranald Macdonald. The Macgregor of Macgregor, a small redheaded man with a notoriously fiery temper, sat speaking to David and Hugh Macdonald and from time to time they laughed among themselves. The Glengarry chieftain came, and Robert greeted him; they were cousins by blood and old friends. The last was Cameron of Lochiel, a tall and splendid figure in coat and trews of tartan, head and shoulders above all but James, with the piercing light eye of the Highlander and hair tied back in a stiff queue with an ominous white ribbon.

"Now, gentlemen!" Sir Alexander stood and addressed them all. "We are all assembled, I think? James, is anyone else expected?"

"All are here, Father."

Robert turned to Glengarry. "Who are we brought here to see? What more do you know of all this?"

"Nothing, save the summons and the badge that came with it. As for the reason, I'd not be surprised to see Prince Charles himself come through the door!"

"Hugh, bring in our guest!"

The man who walked in and shook hands with their host was not the twenty-four-year-old heir to the throne of Scotland, but a lean, tall man of sixty years, with a pale aristocratic face and light green eyes that travelled swiftly over them all without a flicker.

"May I present to you Sir John O'Reilly, emissary from His Royal Highness Prince Charles Edward!"

The stranger was introduced to them one by one and when he came to Robert he shook hands with him and said quietly: "Fraser of Clandara. It is a noble name. Your grandfather did great service to the King."

Robert bowed without answering. There were always men like O'Reilly in the courts of exiled kings; mercenaries without home or fortune, driven from their native Ireland by English strictures and persecution and ready to serve anyone who might unseat their enemy in London and restore them to their lands and titles. There were many Irish in the entourage of the King in Rome; tutors to the young Princes, military advisers, adventurers of every kind. This pale fanatical aristocrat was one of these, sent on to rouse the Prince's countrymen to war on his behalf.

"You have all received a summons," Sir John O'Reilly said. "And you must know from whom. But first, before I make my mission clear, I ask that all of you will take an oath of secrecy."

Each man drew his dirk according to the custom and kissed it as he gave his oath.

"Swear that you will keep every word spoken in this room a secret until such time as it is publicly proclaimed!"

"On pain of dishonour and eternal damnation, we swear! May we be stabbed by this same dirk if we dishonour our oath!"

"And now," the Irishman said, "I will deliver my message. I come to bring you this!"

It was no ordinary crucifix he held up before them, but a cross made of two sticks bound with white cloth, and when they saw it there was a murmur and a stir among the men assembled there.

It was the cross of war; the cross which each chief lit and then extinguished, the fiery cross which was carried from man to man across the glens, summoning the clansmen to arms.

"The moment of delivery has come. The hour for which you and all loyal subjects of the rightful King have waited for thirty years has struck again for Scotland. Gentlemen, the Prince landed at Eriska four days ago! I have come from there myself."

"In Scotland! Good God, man . . ."

"The Prince himself . . . Glengarry, did you hear that, the Prince is here among his own!" That was old Keppoch, his face suffused, his eyes alight and filling with tears.

"Aye, here among us," Alexander Macdonald shouted. "Speak up, Sir John, tell us his message."

"Quiet, quiet if you please. First let me tell you that the Prince came here by ship from France. That ship is now anchored in Loch nan Uamh, where His Royal Highness is receiving other chieftains."

The Macgregor spoke up then. "What troops has he brought with him?"

The pale eyes glittered at him and there was a note of contempt as O'Reilly replied. "If you are hoping for a French army, sir, then I must disappoint you. There are no troops. France would not help him. The Prince has returned to Scotland with seven men. That's all."

There was a moment when no one spoke then, and at last Robert broke in upon the silence. "What arms and ammunition then?"

"Hardly enough to equip a hundred men," the answer came. "There is nothing aboard but the Prince and seven others. There is no money, no stores, no foreign troops. There is only the Prince. So great is his trust in all of you," he added.

"In that case," the Glengarry said, "the enterprise is madness. Without men and money, there is not a hope for the Prince or for anyone who joins him. For the love of God, sir, persuade him to go home!"

"The Macdonald of Sleat used those same words to him, and do you know the Prince's answer? 'Thank you, but I am *come* home!' "

"Well spoken!" James stood out in front of them all, ranging himself beside the Irishman. His eyes were blazing. "God's life and death, look at you all, standing there with your mouths open like a lot of shivering women, bleating about foreign troops and foreign money! Is he or is he not the Prince of Scotland? What man among all of you here can quibble about guns and silver and a lot of mercenaries when our own Prince is landed and waiting for our help!"

He swung round to O'Reilly and drew his sword. "Give back my answer to the Prince," he shouted. "If no other man in the Highlands will draw his sword for him, I will and I'm ready to die for him!"

"And I, by God, and all of mine to the last man!" That was Macdonald of Keppoch's cry, and at once every man in the room was shouting and swearing allegiance, including Glengarry, who had tried to withdraw a moment before.

"The Camerons are with him." That was Lochiel, committing himself to crippling wounds and exile and his people to extermination. Lord Nairne, one of the great landowners and reputed to be very cautious, came to the Prince's representative and held out his hand. It seemed to Robert, standing still and silent among the shouting throng, that there was a look of desperation in his face as if he could foresee his doom and was yet powerless to escape it.

"My possessions and my men are at his service," Nairne said.

"Where will the royal army assemble?" demanded Sir Alexander Macdonald.

"At Glenfinnan, on August 15. The Prince will raise his standard there and then set out for Perth."

"Two hundred Macdonalds of Dundrenan will march with him," James's father promised, "with myself and my three sons at their head!"

"One hundred and fifty of us," called out Glengarry.

"Seven hundred Camerons, brought by myself!" Lochiel's voice rang out.

"And you, sir." Sir John O'Reilly swung round to the one man who had not pledged a sword or a clansman. "What will the Frasers of Clandara bring to Glenfinnan?"

Robert could see that one by one the other chiefs were watching him; the eyes of James, his sister's future husband, seemed to burn into his back as he turned to face his questioner. When he answered, his voice was quite steady.

"The Frasers of Clandara will not be at Glenfinnan," he said. "We are not joining the Prince. That is my father's decision and so he instructed me to say if such a thing were asked of me. We supported the Prince's father in '15, as you pointed out," he added. "My grandfather was beheaded and a fine was levied against us that has made us poor for generations to come. In my opinion, now more than ever, the whole enterprise is utter madness and I see nothing but death and disaster for the Prince and for Scotland. I make no heroic gesture, gentlemen, in which I do not believe," and he looked coldly at Glengarry. "We will not support the Prince, but you have our word that what I have heard will be kept secret, and that not one cup of meal or a drop of water will we give to the Prince's enemies."

"You will not fight!" James pushed forward, thrusting aside O'Reilly, and stood glaring at Robert, one hand upon his dagger. "You stand there and talk about your grandfather and a miserable sum of money! Mother of God, were the Frasers at Clandara the only ones who shed their blood and emptied their purses for the Stuarts? I say you are a coward and a dog, to stand there and refuse to aid your Prince!"

Robert flushed. "You may say what you please," he said. "You are my sister's affianced husband and for that reason I will not call you to account. You are at liberty to rush to your ruin and carry as many others with you out of folly and moral cowardice as you can. But your insults do not move me. I wish the Prince well, sir." He turned to Sir John O'Reilly. "If he wins, and I hope indeed that he does, he may exact what vengeance he pleases for our neutrality. And now, my lords and gentlemen, I bid you good day. I have no further business here."

No one spoke or moved as he left them; they could hear his voice in the courtyard outside calling for his servants and horses, and then very quietly Sir John O'Reilly turned to the Macdonalds.

"I hope you know what you have done," he said. "Inviting that traitor here has betrayed the whole enterprise. The Prince's life and the life of every man in this room is forfeit because of your misjudgment!"

"That is a lie." James swung on him angrily. "The Fraser gave his word. He will not break it. He may be a coward but he's not a traitor!"

"There's a short step between the one and the other," was the answer. "For my part, I believe there will be a message sent to the English garrison at Inverness as soon as that renegade sets foot in his own house. And if they hear of it and intercept the Prince, it will be your doing, sir." He pointed to

Alexander Macdonald. "Yours and yours alone. There will be no meeting at Glenfinnan, because most of you will be arrested before the fifteenth!"

"If this is true"—Lord Nairne's ruddy face had grown pale—"all our lives are lost before we fight. . . ."

"You brought him," O'Reilly said to James's father. "And you must see that, whatever happens, the Prince and the cause are not betrayed."

"It shall be done! James, David, Hugh, ride after him. Take three men with you."

"Father!" James faced him desperately. His own fierce anger against Robert had vanished and in its place there was a sense of horror. "Father, Robert Fraser will never break this oath! I swear it. They may not be joining us but didn't you hear him swear to give no succour to our enemies? Whatever he is, and I'm not defending him, neither he nor his father will speak one word to injure the Prince or any of us here! What are you asking, sir," he demanded savagely of the Irishman, "safety or vengeance, because the Frasers have not joined you?"

"In the name of your honour," O'Reilly addressed the old chief, "I ask for that traitor's life."

"It shall be granted you. My sons, mount up! Hurry, he's had a good start already! And when you find them, leave no witnesses alive."

As they mounted up some minutes later, accompanied by two clansmen armed with broadswords and dirks, Hugh moved over to his brother. "You'll have to kill him. . . . Ach, Jamie, what will the bride say?"

"Hold your damned tongue or I'll cut it out for you!" James snarled, and he raised his fist to strike the handsome grinning face that mocked him. But Hugh only kicked his horse and bounded forwards towards the gate. James could hear him laughing as he galloped through it.

"Is it the Fraser we're after?" Red Murdoch, his milk brother and therefore closest friend among the clansmen and one of the ugliest fighters he had ever known, came close up beside him, both horses stretching into a gallop.

"It is," James shouted. "He has two men with him. None

must escape alive. But they've a start on us, Murdoch. We'll have to ride like the devil to catch up with them before dark."

"I know a short cut," Murdoch said. "There's a wee path up Ben Mohire which comes down to the main track before it disappears into the moor altogether. We can take the horses up there and we'll be down at the foot of Ben Mohire before the Frasers have ridden around it."

James shouted to his brothers and they slowed up and took the rough, steep track in the wake of the big red-haired Highlander who urged his sturdy horse along, talking and arguing with it as it stumbled among rocks and potholes. He had killed a dozen men in everything from a brawl over the whisky pots to an ambush in the dark, but he cared for his horse with the tenderness of a woman for her favourite child.

"Och, come on now; you're a wee clever lassie and you'll get to the top before the Macdonald's horse now, and shame the devil out of them all. . . . Come on now, my wee one . . . ye'll see a fine fight before the day is out, just step lightly and be patient now . . ."

The others followed him in single file, James staring straight ahead, his mind a terrible blank, refusing to think further than the murderous task which lay ahead of him, refusing to imagine that within an hour he was likely to kill the brother of the woman he loved. But the thought and all its implications forced itself upon him and for a moment he weakened and pulled up his horse so violently that it reared and slipped on the treacherous path.

"Gently," Red Murdoch admonished. "It's a horrible pebbly place this, and even my wee mare goes easy. Another fifteen minutes and we'll be at the top; the descent is no' so step as this."

"What are you stopping for?" David Macdonald demanded suddenly. "You heard our father. We're in honour bound to do it. Ride on, James." In honour bound. Men had died for their honour and killed for it because it distinguished the gentlemen from the lowly born. It was possible for a man of ignoble birth to be a liar and a coward or to think of himself and his own happiness in a situation such as this, but it was impossible for one who was a gentleman. Whatever it cost him in terms of Robert Fraser's life or his own happiness, or Katherine's grief, James knew what had to be done.

"Be of good cheer," Hugh called out to him. "Do it properly and she'll never know it was you. . . . No one can prove it, brother, and if she does find out later, she'll be married and there'll be little enough she can do about it then. Come, Murdoch's a hundred yards ahead of us!"

"She will never forgive me," James said. "But that can't stop me now."

"If you can't make her fond enough to forget a mere brother, then you're not the man I thought you," Hugh mocked. "Besides, he's a fair fighter, our canny Fraser. Who knows, he might kill you!"

The Red Murdoch glanced back at the sound of Hugh Macdonald's laughter. He was a superstitious man and it disturbed him; at Dundrenan it was whispered that the devil himself had got into the bed with Lady Jean and sired that terrible, evil, laughing boy. . . .

The light was just beginning to fade when they reached the bottom of Ben Mohire and here James took command, disposing his brothers and Murdoch and the second clansman among the bushes in a bend in the narrow mountain track. Their horses were hidden farther up. Nearly an hour later they heard the sound of horses round the bend of the mountain. James drew his sword and, drawing the long thick end of his plaid round his left arm, sprang out into the middle of the path.

It was Annie's suggestion that Katherine should try on her wedding dress to pass the time while they waited for Robert. The seamstress and her two little assistants at Clandara had been working on it for nearly two months, and now it was finally ready. They slipped into her ladyship's bedroom under the austere eye of Annie, and watched while the dress was tried on. It was made of pure white satin, and Jeannie the seamstress had embroidered the whole bodice with a delicate design of flowers in silver thread and hundreds of split pearls. Magnificent lace hung in ruffles round the low neck and covered Katherine's arms from the elbow to the upper wrist. The under petticoat was cloth of silver and the same shining, silver tracery of flowers crept down the sides of the satin overskirt and vanished round the hem where the dress fell into a short train. Her veil was a priceless piece of Brussels lace, as fine as cobweb and worked with such intricacy that it seemed impossible that the human eye and hand could have fashioned it more than three centuries before. The veil had been an altar covering once, until the Reformation when one of the Earls of Clandara had gone over to the Reformed religion and given the exquisite veiling to his wife as a present. His descendants had returned to the old faith of Rome, but the veil passed on from mother to daughter, and it hung down from the narrow pearl and diamond diadem which was all that remained of the once famous Clandara jewels. Her father had given the diadem to Katherine, remarking ungraciously that it was not as fine as the great vulgar necklace given her by James, but it was one of the few family pieces saved from the depredations of the English after the rising in 1715. She stood before the long pier glass, watched by Annie and the women who had made the dress, and slowly turned to see herself from every side.

"I am very well pleased," she said at last. "My thanks to you, Jeannie, and to you, Mary and Morag. The dress is perfect."

"May God send Your Ladyship every happiness," they said quickly.

"Don't be too proud of yourselves now," Annie said sharply. "It's not the dress that's taking all our breaths away, but her ladyship's beauty. She'd be the fairest bride in Scotland if she were dressed in rags." In four weeks her mistress would be married, standing before the altar in the thirteenth-century chapel with James Macdonald beside her, and a new life in a new home would take her, and Annie with her, away from the place where both had been born. At the thought of children, Annie's eyes brightened. There would be a wet nurse of course; it was unthinkable that ladies of high birth should breast-feed their children, but Annie would have the care of them, wet nurse or not.... Life held great compensations through others whom one loved. Annie often said that and firmly believed it. All her happiness had been centred, unselfishly, on the interests of her mistress.

They were still standing there, grouped round the glass, when the door of Katherine's room opened suddenly and she turned round to find her father standing there. He was dressed in his riding coat and boots and was wearing the plaid wound round his shoulders. She could see the shadows of men behind him.

"I know your mind is occupied with dressing up for this damned wedding," he snapped. "But I thought I'd inform you that Robert has still not returned and there's no sight of him. I sent Angus out to meet him at midday and he came back at two o'clock and said there was not a sign of Robert or his men. I'm going to look for him, if I have to go to Dundrenan itself!"

"Father, I'm sure there's no need. Perhaps he decided to stay on?"

"Robert told me he would be back at dawn. He's nearly ten hours late and that's not like Robert. And *I* know he's not stayed on at Dundrenan unless it's against his will. I'm going out now. You'd better pray to God I find him!"

"Wait!" Katherine ran to him. "Wait for me ... I'll be changed and mounted in ten minutes. ... Please, Father, don't leave me behind. I didn't mean to be unthinking but Jeannie brought my dress and I was trying it. Here, help me out of it and hurry.... Annie, my riding dress and boots." And then, suddenly tormented by fear, a fear which held Robert in its cold centre, she tore the delicate fastenings in her hurry to take off the glittering dress and trampled it impatiently on the floor.

Twenty minutes later Katherine and her father rode out of Clandara at the head of twenty men.

"Father, we'll find him," she said. "I know we will; we'll probably meet him on the way."

"Some harm has come to him," the Earl said. "I know it. I've known since last night when he did not return. For your sake, my child, I hope the Macdonalds have not had a part in it...."

"Nothing has happened to him," she insisted, but even as she spoke her heart began to race, and the fear which was growing with every yard they rode rose up and shrieked at her, "He's dead, he's dead ... and you will find ... you know what you will find. ..."

"And if it has," she cried out, "why should you think James would hurt him? James would never touch a hair of Robert's head!"

But before he could answer her she whipped her horse into a gallop. And at the end of two hours' gruelling ride along the route to Dundrenan they found Robert and his two clansmen lying in the heather by the foot of Ben Mohire.

It was Hugh Macdonald who killed Robert and he ran him through the back because he had watched James duelling with him for ten minutes and seen him lose a dozen opportunities of finishing the fight. So Hugh came up to Robert as the two men circled each other and drove his sword through him so hard that the point protruded through his chest.

"Good Christ, you killed him from behind!" James stared at him in horror. Hugh put his foot on Robert's back and, using both hands, pulled out the bloody sword and wiped it on the dead man's plaid.

"Well, I realised you were never going to kill him from the front," he said. "You damned fool!" Suddenly his mood had changed and his face was dark and furiously angry. "He might have killed you while you danced around him like an old woman! What's become of you, can't you kill a man any more? Is that what that redheaded bitch has done to you? David! Murdoch! Haven't you finished that dog yet? Cut his throat and let's be off!"

David turned over the two Fraser clansmen. Blood was oozing out of the mouth of the last who had fought both him and Murdoch. Murdoch's dirk was sticking in his chest. David pulled it out and threw it to it owner.

"Leave nothing behind," he said. "These two are dead! Make sure of the Fraser himself."

James bent over Robert's body and turned him face upwards. The eyes were still open and the mouth twisted in the pain and surprise which was the last thing he felt as Hugh's blade pierced his heart.

"He's dead," he called out. He did not look at his brother Hugh. "Mount up and let's get back. It'll be completely dark in half an hour."

Murdoch walked slowly over to the body of the young fair man lying face upwards and kicked aside the sword which had fallen from his hand. He bent over him and quickly searched his pockets, slipping a purse with a few guineas in it and a golden fob watch into his sporran.

"Och," he said, looking down, "ye're prettier in death than any Fraser is alive. . . . Refuse to join the Prince, would ye. . . . Ye've got off a might too easy for a dirty traitor," and dropping on one knee, the Red Murdoch made his own contribution to the cause by quickly cutting the dead man's throat.

And that was how Katherine and his father found him.

The night had come and gone and the sun was high in the skies, turning the distant peaks of the purple mountain to a glorious golden colour, but still Katherine sat on in her chair by the window, looking out with eyes that saw nothing, refusing the food that Annie placed beside her, refusing to undress or go to bed. She still wore the crumpled riding dress and there was a great stain of blood across the skirt where her brother's head had lain in her lap until her father dragged her forcibly away.

She had come upon the dreadful sight quite suddenly and the valley round Ben Mohire echoed and re-echoed with her screams of horror. And then hysteria gave way to silence; the terrible silence of shock which nothing had been able to break since she returned to Clandara.

Robert and his men had been laid out in the chapel where she was to have married James Macdonald. The tenants were coming in to mourn and prepare for the funeral, and her father spent his time kneeling by his son's coffin, his head bowed upon his hands and his heart empty of everything except a consuming grief and an equally consuming hatred.

David Macdonald had made a mistake when he said that all the Frasers were dead.

One of Robert's servants had been alive when they were found, and he forced out four words as the Earl and Katherine bent over him.

"The Macdonald did it. . . ." That was all. Though they called to him and shook him, the man only lolled back and rolled up his eyes and died. But he had condemned James and doomed Katherine, and his words ran round her brain as she sat by her window.

"The Macdonald did it. . . ." The Macdonald; the son and heir, James, the eldest . . . there could be no doubt. She could not deny it or excuse it or pretend that the words of a dying man were a lie. James had killed Robert. The man she loved had murdered the brother she loved and then let his men cut his throat. . . . The nightmare memory came back to her and she groaned and hid her face in her hands to try and shut it out. Her father's terrible accusing cry shouted through her mind, as it had done for all the long hours of the night. "You brought that murderer into our home . . . and this is his doing!" If she closed her eyes she could see Robert as clearly as if he were in the room. The voice which would never speak again whispered over and over in her imagination. "My sweet Kate, all I want is your happiness. . . . I bear no hatred for any man. . . . Let the feud die. . . . Your James adores you. . . ."

The dance they had had on the night of the ball, when he told her gallantly how beautiful she looked, and for a moment she had thought how sadly she would miss him when she was married and living at Kincarrig They had been inseparable as children, and the bond of love between them was stronger than anything in her life until she met James. And now Robert was dead. The man who had taken her out onto the Ladies' Walk and kissed her until her lips were bruised, and put his hands upon her, had not scrupled to murder the human being she loved so much and who had actually befriended them. It was so dreadful that she could hardly force herself to believe it. She could not banish the sight of that mutilated body, but neither could she avoid the image of

James which besieged her thoughts and tore at her heart with its taunting memories of their passion and their hopes all now blighted and betrayed.

"I wish he had killed me."

They were the first words she had spoken, and they brought Annie rushing to her side, where she was just in time to take her mistress in her arms as she slid off the chair to the ground, rocking backwards and forwards, the tears pouring down her face.

"Oh, milady, my love, don't cry ... don't break your heart like that! Ach now, for the love of God, ye'll be ill if ye greet so ... the Lord Robert wouldn't wish it—ye know how he hated ye to cry!"

"I loved him so," Katherine wept, "but I loved that other more than anything in the world ... and he said he loved me. ... Oh, Mother of God, Annie, how often he said it and swore it and how I believed him! And then he kills Robert, my sweet Robert, who never harmed anyone in his life and was the only friend we had in the beginning, I wish he had killed me! I wish he had driven his sword into me . . ."

Annie said no more. She held the distracted girl in her arms, soothing her and wiping the tears away, and after a little while she persuaded her to go over to the bed, where she undressed her and helped her between the covers. Exhausted at last, Katherine lay back upon the pillows.

"Now rest there a moment," Annie said. "I'm going down to the kitchen and make you a wee draught to help you sleep."

"Where is my father?"

"He's in the chapel with the Lord Robert and the other two poor laddies," Annie answered.

"What has he done about this?" Katherine asked, and her voice shook.

"He's sent a message to Dundrenan," Annie admitted. "Dugal the steward said he's accused them of the murder and he sent another letter to the Courts of Justice at Inverness impeaching the Macdonalds. That's all, child, and it'll do ye no good to think about it. It's out of your hands now."

"I wonder what Father will do to *her?*" Katherine said suddenly. No one had thought of the Countess. She had run to her rooms and locked herself in when the cavalcade returned with the bodies of the three men, and no one had seen her since.

"Ach, I don't know," Annie said slowly. "But I wouldn't be her for all the wealth of the world."

"Nor would I," Katherine muttered. "He should have thought of his cousin before he murdered Robert. . . . He was quite concerned for her happiness the last time he was here," and to Annie's horror she gave a wild laugh. "Ah, and to think that I so nearly yielded to him that very night . . . and do you know what he did, the liar and hypocrite? He stood away from me and made a fine speech about abusing the trust I had placed in him, and took me back to the ball. Oh, my God, my God, if only I could kill him! If only You'd let me revenge Robert and redeem myself for ever having touched him . . ."

Ten minutes later Annie was back with a cup of hot herb tea into which she had put a strong measure of whisky, and she sat by the bed until at last Katherine fell asleep.

Silence descended upon Clandara. It was the silence of death and grief, muffling the movements of servants and muting the sounds of the human voice. But the night before the funeral of the Lord Robert the corridors filled with maids and servingmen who came creeping up to listen to the screams coming from the Countess Margaret's room.

The Earl's steward came out in his night robe and ordered them back to their quarters. He had seen the Earl go in to his wife with a hunting whip, and he thought it quite likely that, since the Earl was a little drunk and quite unbalanced with grief for his son, he would beat the luckless creature to death. In any case it was no concern of the household. There was no one in it with the slightest inclination to interfere.

Only Annie came to her mistress and suggested that she might intervene; it would not look well for the Earl if his wife died of injuries. Katherine looked at her and her eyes were as hard and cold as ice.

"If it were James Macdonald in that room, I'd go and watch my father kill him," she said coldly. "But as it's only that miserable woman, I'm not interested what he does. Now go to bed and shut that door, Annie. I don't want to be disturbed."

Robert had been dead and in his grave for nearly two weeks when the gatekeeper came running into the library with the news that he had seen a Macdonald approaching on horseback. One of the ordinary clansmen, he reported in answer to the Earl's question. And then, to his amazement, Clandara ordered him to admit the enemy. As he went back to his post the old man saw the Lady Katherine hurrying down the stairs to join her father.

She stood side by side with him when the man was brought in. He was young and dark, with bright blue eyes that watched them with a mixture of wariness and pride as if to tell them that he was not afraid to come alone and unarmed into their house. She remembered then that he had come with James that first morning nearly a year ago. He pulled off his bonnet and bowed.

"I am Donal Macdonald, servant to the Macdonald of Dundrenan," he announced. "I have a message for the Lady Katherine from my master."

"Have you?" the Earl said quietly. "May I ask why the Macdonald did not deliver it in person instead of sending you? Was he afraid to face the father and sister of the man he murdered?"

The young man looked at him stonily. "The Macdonald is afraid of nothing," he answered shortly. "But you must know, my lord, though the talk is that you're not joining him, that the Prince has landed here and the clans are rising with him. The Macdonald is preparing for war. All he asks is a fair hearing from you before he leaves for the campaign."

"Is that his message?" Clandara asked.

"His message is for you, milady; I have it here." He held out a letter towards her.

For a moment Katherine hesitated. She saw the familiar writing and the seal and remembered the impassioned letters which were still locked in her desk drawer in her room. Then she took it between the tips of her fingers and looked at it, turning it over.

"The Macdonald has explained what happened there," his servant said. "I will take back your answer, milady. My master is waiting for one word from you before he leaves." He was still speaking when she began to tear the letter across the middle. She tore it in four pieces and then slowly dropped them on the floor at the messenger's feet.

"Your master wants an answer to take with him to the war," she said quietly. "Then he shall have one. Wait." She rang the bell rope by the fire and, when Annie came in answer to it, Katherine went and whispered to her. Then she went back to her father and, taking him by the arm, she led him down to the far end of the room. The Macdonald could hear them talking together and shifted a little. There was something very dangerous in this cool reception. Something in the face of the old man and his daughter as they looked at him that told him to turn and leap through the window and escape while he could. But that would be showing fear, and these were Frasers and people on whom a self-respecting Macdonald would not spit. He stayed where he was.

"Here is my answer for the Macdonald." Katherine came and held out to him the great emerald necklace and earrings which James had given her. "Take them," she commanded. "Tell him to sell them and give the money to the Prince."

The Macdonald could hear noises behind him. He glanced quickly behind his back and saw that the door was open and half a dozen men were standing inside the library waiting for him. He looked into the face of the woman standing in front of him, her hands full of the splendid jewels, and saw that he was going to die. Before the Earl gave a single command, Donal Macdonald spat on the floor at Katherine's feet.

They sent him back to Dundrenan over the back of his horse, with the Macdonald emeralds round his neck, where they became entangled by the cord with which he had been strangled. Five of the Frasers escorted the horse and its burden to within three hundred yards of Dundrenan itself and then with yells of encouragement they whipped it up so that it came to the house at the gallop. By the time the gates were opened and the horse and the dead man were taken inside, the Frasers were riding hard back to Clandara. And that same night the Earl and his men rode out to Kincarrig, and when they left, the blaze from the burning house lit the night sky for miles around.

At Clandara, Katherine resumed her old life with its former duties of attending to the household and the servants and helping her father with the estate, and as the days passed and the rumours of the rising reached them, it seemed as if the walls of Clandara grew taller and the light in the great castle less as hope died in her heart and hatred turned everything to bitterness. Katherine lived and talked and worked until she was so tired at night that she sometimes fell asleep in her chair sitting opposite her father. One night when he tried to comfort her for the ruin of all her hopes, she had told him gently that there was nothing to regret.

"My life," she said to him, "is over. I shall never marry, Father, and I only want to live to try and make up to you for Robert. I am as happy now as I will ever be. When he killed Robert, he also killed me." And that was true, as the Earl knew. And when the knowledge of his son's loss and his daughter's terrible corroding grief became too much for him to bear, he bethought him of the woman who was imprisoned in her room upstairs, and then he would empty his whisky glass and go and take down the key of her room and go into it and relieve his pain by beating Margaret Macdonald until his arm ached.

But for Katherine there was no relief. She had destroyed James's letters and systematically ripped her wedding dress to pieces and ordered Annie to burn it. There was no sign of him anywhere in her room, no gifts or notes or even the dress in which they had become betrothed, for that too she had destroyed. And now the hated name was never mentioned between her father and herself and Annie was forbidden to speak of what had happened.

As Annie said to her grandfather, it would have been better for her ladyship to die, than live without love or hope or joy in life.

Chapter 3

AUGUST CAME and the days were warm, with the fleeting brilliance of the Scottish summer; the days were so lovely and so full of the radiance of sun and fulfilment that Katherine preferred the coolness and gloom of the castle. With the emptiness and tragedy of what had become her daily life, it was impossible to control the traitorous imaginings which pictured Kincarrig and the idyllic days which might have been. She had tried not to think of James; his name was forbidden, even Robert was no longer mentioned, though his tomb in the vault was covered in fresh flowers, the gift of the servants who had known and loved him, and she often searched in vain for her father, only to find him kneeling in the cold beside the new stone sarcophagus in the vault.

Nothing could bring her brother back, and all she could do was to try and bury the memory of her love and the man who had betrayed it until it was as dead as the companion of her childhood. News came to them through friends who passed to offer their sympathy, but they were on their way to join the Prince at Glenfinnan, for the banner of the Stuarts was flying once again in the Highlands and the clans were rallying to it and to the romantic, dashing symbol of their vanished independence, Prince Charles himself. It was the middle of the month and their last visitor, the young laird Grant of Glenmoriston, had left them after a stay of two nights to join the royal army. The castle was silent and empty. The Earl had gone to his rooms; he retired early, and often now Angus and his steward helped him to bed and took the empty whisky bottle out of his hand. The night was warm, and as Katherine sat on alone in the Green Salon, unable to sleep and unwilling to retire to her room, the heat became oppressive to her. She threw her needlework aside and, opening the long windows out onto the terrace, she stepped through into the moonlit garden. There was no sound but the movement of a gentle wind that stirred the trees. Beyond the terrace there was an arbour, shaded by creepers and flowering shrubs. The smell of them was sweet and strong and she began to walk towards it. In the days of her engagement, James had often walked with her there and sat beside her on the stone seat, hidden from view of the house; there he had kissed her and held her and talked of their future. . . .

She was in the shadow of the trees when someone sprang on her, and a hand covered her mouth, stifling her cry of fear, and then the arms which held her were familiar and the voice that whispered turned her to stone. Her body recognised him and her senses leapt in agony at the warmth and the touch which had been denied them for so long.

He turned her round and held her, still covering her lips with his hand, and then the hand was gone and his mouth met hers and took possession of it, demanding, desperate, and in that second she was lost and her lips opened. For a long moment they stayed still, the man and the woman, fused by his physical strength so that she was incapable of struggling free. His hold was so powerful that he hurt her, but the pain in her pinioned arms only added to the torturing delight of that wild savage kiss which denied her speech and breath until, at last, he raised his head and they were face to face.

"My love," he said. "My love, my darling . . . I had to see you." She pulled away from him, appalled at herself, her body trembling, her skin burning where he touched her.

"You devil," she spat at him. "You murdering devil . . ."

"Abuse me all you wish," he told her, and she heard his voice break. "I knew if I could only find you it would be all right again. . . . Oh, Katherine, Katherine, whatever you say I know what happened when I held you in my arms . . . beloved, listen to me for one moment!"

"Listen to you!" Katherine backed away from him, but he had caught her hands and held them. "Listen to the man who took my love and my trust and then betrayed me. . . . You must be mad, Macdonald of Dundrenan, to come here and think that I would stand and listen to you! Are you so eager for death? Have you forgotten your servant who came here to give your lying message?"

"They said it was your doing but I did not believe them," James whispered. "Even when I took the necklace from his neck, I didn't believe that you had taken any part in it. . . ."

"Then you were wrong," Katherine answered, and now her voice was cold and level, and the moment of abandonment was gone. He stood in front of her, holding her hands in his until she dug her nails into him and he released her.

"I watched my father's men kill your messenger," she said. "And all I regretted was that it was him and not you. . . . Do you suppose I have forgotten my brother? Robert, who loved me and whom I loved better than anyone in the world . . . he helped us, do you remember? He persuaded my father to receive you and agree to our betrothal. And then you killed him, foully and vilely in an ambush!"

"I had no choice," James said. "He wouldn't join the Prince; the Prince's emissary demanded his life of us as a point of honour. My father sent us after him, but I swear to God, Katherine, that it was not I who killed him. I fought him fairly and he might as well have killed me. My brother Hugh ran him through the back. And that's the truth!"

"You're lying," she said. "There was a witness. One of our men was still alive and I heard his dying words as I held my brother's body in my arms. . . . 'The Macdonald did it.' You, James, not your brother, but you!"

"It was dark," he countered. "The man must have been wounded to death. He didn't see what really happened. Katherine, why should I lie to you now? I didn't kill Robert—whether I meant to is not the point between us now. I didn't kill him."

He came close to her and fell on his knees. "I've never knelt to God or man for as long as I can remember," he said hoarsely. "But I'm at your feet now, and all I ask is that you will believe me and forgive me. Call for your father, let him revenge himself as he will. I'll die contented if you will only say you love me still!"

His face was in shadow and she could not be sure but from the sound of his voice she thought that he was weeping.

"I never loved you," she said slowly. "As you never loved me. There was nothing between us but lust. And lust is all you've ever known. I am defiled from ever touching you."

"I don't believe you," he said; he stood up and they remained still, close enough to touch but without moving. "If I took you now, you'd submit. And I know it, and you know it. There may be blood between us, but if you truly loved me you'd forgive and come to me of your own will. I'm going to Perth to join the Prince tomorrow, but I couldn't go without one word from you, one sight of you ... and your forgiveness. Katherine, my only love, I beg of you. Forgive me."

There was a moment when madness came upon her, a temptation so strong that she felt herself move and knew that in one more moment she would throw herself into his arms and swear that nothing mattered, neither Robert nor her father nor anything in the world but the overwhelming passion which had woken again when she believed it killed by hatred. Her only defence against herself was to attack him, and the hand which had reached out towards him now swung round and struck him a violent blow across his face.

"That is my forgiveness! And I pray to God you find an early grave. Now go!"

He touched his cheek very slowly. The moonlight was on her now and all he could see was the beautiful face he loved contorted by loathing, and the hatred in her eyes was like a second blow.

"I was prepared for death," he said at last. "I was prepared for you to call out and deliver me to your people. I offered it, if you remember. If you had loved me, I would have been content if my death was what you wanted. But now, I see I was a fool to come. Your love was given lightly, as lightly as you gave your kiss only a few moments ago. Whatever you had done, Katherine, I would have followed you to the end of the earth and defended you against God and all the hosts of heaven. I imagined that you had that kind of love for me. Good Christ," he said savagely, "the poor harlots in Edinburgh have better hearts than you! What a fool, what a besotted fool, to think that a Fraser could be generous and give back love for love. Now listen well to me, for it's the last time you and I will ever speak.... I didn't kill your brother. I thought he was a coward and a traitor to refuse to fight for his Prince and I might well have killed him, but I didn't. And now it doesn't matter to me. Give this message to your father. When the war is over and we are victorious, he'll know where to find Macdonald of Dundrenan! And now you can scream for help without any hindrance from me. I wouldn't put a hand on you even to save my life!"

"James!" She cried out his name before she could stop herself but he had gone, and there was nothing but the shadowed arbour and the sound of the rising wind. He did not look back; he ran through the garden and out through the little side gate whose lock he had forced to get in and see her. He did not look back and he did not see her slowly sink down on her knees or hear the sound of desperate weeping.

It was nearly midnight when Annie came down to the Green Salon and out through the open window and found her mistress kneeling on the damp path, crying as if her heart would break. Gently she gathered Katherine into her arms. And then her sharp instincts told her what had happened.

"He's been here!" she whispered. "I know it.... What happened, milady? Dry your poor eyes and tell me."

"Oh, God! I was out walking in the garden alone when suddenly someone sprang out on me ... it was him, Annie. He said he'd come to ask me to forgive him. He swore he didn't kill Robert."

"And what did ye do?" the maid asked her quietly.

"I struck him," Katherine said slowly. "I told him I hated him and wished him dead."

"It's as well you did," Annie said. "He might well have abducted ye otherwise. . . . Ach, thank God no harm came to ye. It makes my heart stop to think what might have happened. . . ."

"He wouldn't hurt me," she said. "I knew that. And at the end he scorned to put a hand on me. I could have called out and betrayed him to his death and all he did was turn his back on me and walk away."

"But you didn't call," Annie muttered, helping her mistress to her feet again. "He'd have been run down in a few minutes and killed if anyone here had known. . . ."

"I didn't call," Katherine admitted. "Because I couldn't. Until this moment I thought I truly hated him; I thought of my brother and all I imagined was how happy I would be if only James were dead. But now I know the truth. Whatever he did, it makes no difference. I sent him away, Annie, and I know I shall never see him again. . . . Let's go in now. And swear to me that you will never speak a word of this to anyone."

"I swear," the maid said. "God help you, milady. Whatever he is, he must have loved you too to seek you here. Thank God," she said suddenly, "that I don't know what love is. Come now."

A column of men were marching through the hills, and they marched to the music of the Macdonalds' piper. There were nearly three hundred of them, and the majority were the tenants and their sons who farmed the bleak Macdonald lands, and they were dressed for the campaign in kilts and skin jackets lined with fleece, their chests and arms bare, the heavy broadsword swinging from a belt at their sides and the short dirk on the hip. Their plaids were wrapped around them, and in these they slept, rolled into them as if they were blankets, and some carried their crude cooking pots and packs of oatmeal for kneading into cakes and baking in hot ashes. The men were the same as their ancestors of centuries past. Primitive, hardy, bound only by the intense loyalty of the clan for its chief, they followed that chief and his sons who rode at the head of the column as it made its way slowly across country towards Perth and the army of Prince Charles.

Sir Alexander Macdonald was humming the piper's rant under his breath. He felt young and vigourous at the prospect of the war. Peace did not agree with him; he had been bored for a number of years and now his inertia was gone and a jovial enthusiasm had taken its place. His men smiled and murmured among themselves that the old lion scented a fight. It was a great pity, they said in the calm discursive manner of the Highlander, that the chief's son James was in such a black and bloody mood. James Macdonald rode beside his father but hours passed without a word being spoken between them, and after a few attempts even the mischievous and intrepid Hugh decided it was best to leave him alone. No one had dared to ask him where he had been the night before they set out, but his father and his brothers guessed.

He had come back to Dundrenan and thrust past them without waiting to answer their questions and the door of his room shut with a crash that rattled the windows. And all that night Hugh heard him walking up and down in his room behind the door which no one dared to open, cursing and muttering to himself. And when he came down in the morning the devil was back in him again; the old fierce light gleamed in his eye and the ugly, quarrelsome sneer was on his mouth again. As Hugh remarked, brother James was back to his old self, and life would be a deal less tranquil.

"James," his father said at last, "we'll halt at the Black Rock tonight. There's some crofts which can give us shelter and the men can camp and provide for themselves in the glen."

"As you wish," he answered. "I see no reason why we can't march through the night. We're not a lot of women that we can't lose a few hours' sleep!"

"We need food, and while you're on horseback, the rest of our people have been walking the last twenty miles. We stop at the Black Rock," his father snapped. He was suddenly so irritated with his son that he could have struck him. That damned woman, that redheaded bitch . . . She had ruined his son, his favourite son if he were honest, for he found David too stupid and brutish and Hugh too sinister. Sir Alexander was not deceived by James's silence nor by the aggressive and scathing way in which he answered even the simplest question. He knew his son. He had been amused by his dissipations and his quarrels when he was a boy and proud of his ferocity and his courage when he became a man. But what he saw now was a man fighting the world and himself with it. And all on account of a woman. His patience suddenly came to an end.

"James, where did you go off to the night before last?"

He turned in his saddle to look at his father, and his black eyes were red-rimmed and burning. "I went to Clandara, as you know very well," he said. "There was something that had to be done before I could come with you."

"I hope you did it," the old man said dryly. "But from the misery in your heart, I doubt you had the sense. If you went to see *her,* as I know you did, I only hope you took advantage of the situation to rid yourself of the taste for her once and for all!"

"Father," James answered him, "rape is not the cure for everything. I'm surprised you haven't learnt that."

"It's the best cure I know for an obsession like yours," his father retorted. "There's only one way to find out that one woman is much like another and that's to try her. More fool you if you risked your neck for nothing. I've no patience with you!"

"I've asked for none," his son replied. "I feel for her as she feels for me. And that's an end to it."

"Tenderly, I trust?" Hugh had ridden close up behind them and he grinned.

"You may be my brother," James said very quietly, "but watch your tongue. You're a bonny swordsman, especially when it's from behind, but you're no match for me!"

"Keep your fighting for the English," the old chief snapped.

Hugh shrugged and dropped his horse back to a level with his father. "You know, he'd draw on me," he said. "He's never forgiven me for killing the Fraser. Now there's ingratitude for you, Father! If I hadn't done it, he might just as well have been killed. You never saw anything like him, dancing and dawdling about as if he were holding a needle instead of a sword."

"He's out of his head," the old man said. "From the moment he saw that cursed girl, he's been possessed. No women, no trips into Inverness any more with you and David. Good Christ, he lived like a monk for a whole year, and then he strips Dundrenan of its treasures to furnish Kincarrig for her. And what is the end of it all? Eh? What is the end? Her brother turns out to be a traitor and a coward and we have to put an end to him. . . . Not that it came very hard on *you*," he added, and Hugh made him a little bow from the saddle. "Then Clandara lodges a complaint against us and the wedding is off. That's one good thing at least. What do you think happened when he went there?"

"I think she spat in his face," Hugh said. "That's my judgment of her. I also think she's less bitter than he thinks or she'd have found some way to have him taken. They served poor Donal a bonny turn when he went there. James was lucky to return at all."

"He'll recover," the old man said. "All this is just the heat of the moment. He'll cool. He'll cool when he joins with the Prince and has a few women and gets the taste of battle. That's all James needs. He'll forget her then and be himself again."

"Maybe," Hugh said softly. "Maybe. I hope you're right, Father, but I'm not so confident. He loves her still, whatever he says to the contrary. I doubt if he'll forget her as long as he lives."

Prince Charles Edward entered the city of Perth with one golden guinea in his pocket at the head of an army of Camerons, and the Macdonalds of Keppoch, Tirnadris, and Glengarry; and to the joy of his men the Prince wore the kilt and kept them company on foot. He was anxious to prove himself as hardy as they were, and he outmarched many of the strongest who had lived all their lives in the mountains.

His reception at Perth was a triumph. The people came out dancing and singing in the streets and the clan pipers played their ancient rants, extolling the glorious battles of the past, and everywhere the Prince looked, the windows were full of women waving and throwing flowers down on the army as it marched below. For thirty long years Scotland had been subdued, and the memory of the executions and deprivations inflicted upon those who rebelled for his royal father were still painfully fresh. History was not written in the Highlands so much as spoken and preserved in the songs of the clans, and children were brought up on the tales of the valour of their distant forefathers in the endless wars which ravaged the glens. The Prince spent the evening of September 4 in a house in the city and held what passed for a court reception for the leading citizens of the town. By the end of that meeting his funds were increased by a promised five hundred pounds and every hour he received reports of men coming in from all over the Highlands to join him. On the following day Sir John O'Reilly brought the news that the Macdonald of Dundrenan and his clansmen were marching into the city.

James and his brothers walked behind their father as they entered the large room which the Prince used as an audience chamber. It was lit by many candles and a big carved oak chair had been set up at one end, with an improvised canopy of velvet hung above it. It was full of people, all crowded round the young man who sat in the chair under the canopy, and to the astonishment and delight of Alexander Macdonald, Prince Charles got up and came down the room to greet them. He was tall and slightly built, with a rather round face, regular features, and a clear, ruddy complexion; like so many of his ancestors, he was a "red" Stuart, with the deep brown eyes that sometimes accompany the colouring.

Father and three sons went down on their knees and Alexander kissed the hand the Prince held out to him and then presented his sons.

"Welcome." Charles spoke with an accent so slight that it seemed like a lisp. It was already said of him that he was learning Gaelic and studying the ancient lore of his country. Generations of royal Stuarts had given him his dignity and grace, but his mother, the Polish Princess, had added a touch of fiery temperament and extravagant gesture which escaped him when he was excited.

"My eldest son James, Your Royal Highness." James met the younger man's eyes for a moment and was surprised to see that in spite of the gracious smile he was being shrewdly examined.

"I have heard much of you," Charles said. "There are already so many Macdonalds at my side that I have trouble in distinguishing them. But none so dark as you, sir, and your family."

"And none so brave." O'Reilly came up to them and bowed. "The Macdonalds of Dundrenan are rightly famous for their warlike spirit, Highness, and for their hospitality, as I well know," and his thin lips smiled at Sir Alexander.

"My heart is touched," the Prince said gravely. "Believe me, gentlemen. I came home with nothing but my faith in Scottish loyalty, and within a month I have an army which grows greater every day. I hope to keep you close about my person. I am your Prince, but on the day we shall all stand together as soldiers, and we shall confer as soldiers, all men having a voice."

The Macdonalds joined the crowd of people, while Charles went among them, speaking pleasantly to as many as he knew and asking for introductions to the rest.

"He's a fine Prince," Sir Alexander said; "fine manners and a real way with him. Look yonder: he's got the fat merchants and their wives simpering and blushing with contentment!"

"More than the merchants," James remarked. "Lord George Murray is here; that means all the Atholls will be with us, and there's the Duke of Perth standing over there. He's got the charm of the devil. I only hope he's got the devil's luck as well!"

"He's the Prince," David Macdonald snapped. "That is enough for me and all loyal Scotsmen. How long must we stay here, Father? The Prince has done with us now . . ."

"You stay while the Prince stays," O'Reilly answered smoothly. "It is the custom to remain until royalty leaves. This may not be Holyrood Palace yet, gentlemen, but this is the court of the Regent of Scotland."

"It's as well the Prince came," Alexander Macdonald said. "The King would have less sway than this bonny Prince with all the promise of youth to his advantage. If he stays on as Regent, that will be acceptable to all of us."

"There are quite a few women here, I see." Hugh had not spoken before. Of them all he was the least impressed. His natural cynicism accepted the gracious manners and flattering words of royalty with reservations; all men are pleasing when they seek favours, and in his view the Prince was seeking the greatest of favours from them all. He wanted their lives, their fortunes, and the future of their estates in order to secure a throne. He could well afford to come a few steps to meet them, and speak a few soft words. He nudged James.

"Look over there, that's a bonny female! The fair one in the green dress . . ."

As if she knew that he were watching her, the pretty young wife of one of the city's most prominent lawyers glanced away from her husband and, seeing the handsome, impudent young man staring at her, blushed and looked away.

"If you're looking for lechery, this isn't the place for it," James said. "These are respectable women. What of Fiona Mackintosh? I thought you were quite taken by her; you've been over there visiting often enough in the past few weeks."

"There's nothing like choosing a rich wife when the time comes to marry, and nothing better than finding a pretty one as well." Hugh grinned at him. "We're not all fools like you, James, to lose your soul over one woman and then have her spit in your eye! As for lechery—what else are we to do before the fighting? Excuse me. I'm going to introduce myself." He was gone before James could answer him, and within a few minutes James heard the sound of his brother's mocking laugh as he talked to the rather apprehensive lawyer, watching the lawyer's wife with the intensity of an animal stalking its prey.

James turned away and began a short conversation with O'Reilly about the number of their men and the arms they had brought with them. He was not really listening; he heard the Irishman's enthusiastic account of the strength of the Camerons and the petition which was still being pressed on the powerful chief of the Macleods to join them. He answered mechanically, while the pain and anger grew in his heart at the mention of Katherine and the jeer with which Hugh had left him. To lose his soul over a woman. All through the long march to Perth, through nights spent sleeping in wretched crofts where the only light was from a smoking fire of peat, or lying wrapped in a plaid on the heather, Katherine's image had tortured him, driving away sleep, or filling what rest he got with savage dreams of sensuality and nightmare caricatures of that last meeting.

He believed that he had killed his love for her. He believed that he hated her, and for that at least he was grateful, but he could not rid himself of his desire, and that desire grew worse now that all love for her was gone. His father had mocked him for not taking her, but not nearly as bitterly as he had mocked himself. His faith in her love, his belief that if he could once see and speak to her all would be well; had brought him very close to death. Her answer was the blow she struck him. And yet the memory of her lips and the response which she had been unable to control in the garden at Clandara tore at him until he felt as if he would go mad. Lechery. The word stung him and brought him round so abruptly that he left O'Reilly in the middle of a sentence. What else was there to do before the fighting? Hugh was right. Hugh would seduce that simpering woman and climb into bed with her under her pompous husband's nose, while he remained alone with nothing but his memories and his terrible regrets to warm him. He had not touched a woman except his perfidious love for more than a year. His taunt returned to him, as bitter an insult as he could offer her. "The poor harlots in Edinburgh have better hearts than you!"

He walked over to Hugh and bowed curtly to the two startled members of respectable Perth society. He did not even trouble to address them. It was unlikely the woman would have heard him if he did; she was gazing at his brother with large, excited blue eyes. In vulgar soldiers' parlance, she was ready to lie down if he took off his hat.

"Brother," James said. "I don't know your plans for this evening, but when we are dismissed from the Prince, I have a mind to see something of the city."

Hugh looked at him and a slow smile spread from his lips to his green eyes. "I'm glad to hear it," he said softly. "I thought you would be bored after a while, but not so quickly. . . . Mistress Macpherson has very kindly invited me to dine. With Mr. Macpherson, of course. I'm sure, madam," he said, turning to the young woman, "you will excuse me, if I decline so as to keep my brother company?"

"Oh, but your brother's more than welcome too." Margaret Macpherson spoke so quickly that her husband, who did not

wish to entertain one and certainly not two of these aggressive aristocrats, had no time to accept Hugh's excuse. She
knew perfectly well that dull, stuffy Donald with his law-
books and his tedious attitude to everything resented their in-
trusion; but there was something very flattering and fascinat-
ing about this young Highland gentleman and the way in
which he looked at her without caring whether Donald noticed it or not. She was determined not to lose him, even if it
meant entertaining his ferocious looking brother. There was
nothing to attract her about James. She felt quite nervous
when those black eyes were turned on her; they seemed to
burn as if there were a light behind them. She saw in them
an astonishing mixture of contempt and rage, as if the man
were casting about for someone with whom he could pick a
quarrel.

"We would be delighted," Hugh said gaily. "How charming
of you both to entertain us. Have you perhaps a sister,
madam, who could make conversation with my brother? He's
a man of genial taste and he delights in the company of
charming ladies . . ."

"A sister-in-law," Margaret Macpherson murmured. "She's
there, wearing a red gown, talking to Colonel O'Sullivan, the
Prince's quartermaster general."

"Enchanting," murmured Hugh, and the remark was accompanied by a look which assured Mistress Macpherson
that the honours were still hers. James glanced across at the
woman with whom he was to dine that evening, and what he
saw made no impression on him. He had never liked women
of his own colouring, and this woman in her bright scarlet
silk dress was very dark. She was tall and handsome in a
curiously patrician way. She resembled her brother the lawyer
a little; both had rather pronounced features, but as she came
towards them he could see that her eyes, unlike Macpherson's, were brilliantly blue.

"James Macdonald of Dundrenan, his brother Hugh, my
sister-in-law Mrs. Douglas. These gentlemen are dining with
us tonight."

Janet Douglas gave James her hand to kiss and smiled
slightly without speaking. It was a very cool hand and steady.

She did not appeal to him at all, but at least she possessed some air of distinction, however accidental, and he far preferred her to the soft and fluffy creature Hugh had marked out for himself.

"If you will excuse us," James said, "we must speak to our father for a moment. We will rejoin you here."

As soon as they had moved away he turned angrily to Hugh. "What the devil have you done, inviting me to these damned people's house for dinner? Go and lay that stupid wife of his if you want to, but don't ruin my few hours this evening!"

"My dear brother, keep your temper. I know exactly what I'm doing."

"And how do you propose to do it, with her husband looking on?" James demanded.

"Leave that to me," Hugh said pleasantly. "But we shall have an excellent dinner for which we shan't pay a penny, and then I shall have her and you shall have the sister-in-law if you have a mind to."

"And if I haven't a mind to, or she hasn't?" James exploded. "What then?"

"Then we will go down to the stews and you can take your pick of the whores," his brother answered. "But it will cost you and you will probably catch the pox from one of them; this place has been full of men for the past two days. Try my little plan first. Mistress Douglas looks likely enough; I'm not sure I wouldn't sooner have her than my little eager chicken. . . . But we will see. Perhaps we'll try it turn and turn about." And he laughed.

James did not join him, but before his inner eye he saw himself with Katherine in his arms, so tender and eager and completely within his grasp. In the heather by the Loch, and again on the night of the ball on the Ladies' Walk at Clandara. And himself, so wild with chivalrous love that he had put her from him. Turn and turn about. First that tall, self-possessed bitch with her shrewd blue eyes, and then the other, all fluttering and full-bosomed. Why not? He had done as much before, and sat down laughing with his brothers to compare notes. Anything, anything to drive the thought of Katherine from his mind.

"Why not indeed?" he said. "But we may have to kill the husband and that would hardly endear us to the Prince."

"We'll kill nobody," Hugh said. "We'll take two clansmen with us and they can keep Macpherson company while we dine. He won't protest, I promise you."

"Some more wine," James said. "Hugh, pass it here, damn you!" The meal was already finished, and the four of them, the Macdonalds and the two women, were sitting at the table still, propping their elbows on it, finishing off another bottle of the absent Macpherson's best claret. As Hugh had promised, the dinner was excellent, and under a firm pressure on each arm from the two Macdonald clansmen who had escorted them through the streets, their host had been removed to an upper room where James informed him curtly that his men had orders to cut his throat if he called out. And once the position was established, their hostess had abandoned herself to the enjoyment of a situation for which she could not possibly be blamed, and her sister-in-law, Janet Douglas, had made no comment whatever but began serving James with meat and wine. He ate less than he drank, and he drank with furious intent, not savouring the good claret but pouring it down his throat as if it were whisky, while his brother sat with his arm around Margaret Macpherson and grew bolder as he received encouragement. She leant back against him, a little tipsy herself, her dress slipping from her shoulders.

"Poor Donald," she sighed. "He must be so terribly frightened for me. I hope your men won't hurt him?"

"Of course they won't," Hugh said. "They're just like lambs. I told you he wouldn't make a to-do about it."

James looked across at the woman, her eyes heavy, pressing herself against his grinning brother, and suddenly irritated, he said coldly, "Would you like us to look, madam, in case our lambs have cut his throat as I directed? Maybe that's why he's silent."

"Knowing Donald," Janet Douglas said suddenly, "I'm sure

he gave them no cause. What a remarkably clever plan; which one of you gentlemen thought of it?"

"I did." Hugh grinned. "We were so enamoured by the sight of you that we couldn't allow a mere husband to stand in our way. Come, come, sweetheart, you're yawning. . . ." He whispered in her ear, and Margaret giggled. "Excuse us." Hugh got up and made a bow to the two left at the table. "Take care of my brother, my dear lady. He's in need of comfort."

When they were alone James upended the last bottle and cursed to find it empty.

Janet looked at him. "How much do you need?" she asked him.

He raised his head and looked at her. His eyes were bloodshot, but though he had drunk twice as much as Hugh, he was still sober. "What the devil do you mean?" he said.

Janet went to the cabinet and came back to the table. She carried a decanter of whisky. "You know very well what I mean," she said. "Here, try this. Why did you come here, when you've no stomach for any of it?"

"I was invited," he said sarcastically. "What's the matter, madam, can't you wait? If I don't oblige you, have a little patience and my brother will when he's finished with your sister-in-law."

"I don't care for your brother," she said quietly. "I think he and that worthless woman are well matched. But don't underestimate her; he won't be back as soon as you think. Be kind enough to pass me a glass; I'll have a little whisky myself."

She poured out a measure and began to sip it slowly. James watched her without speaking. In the candlelight she seemed very handsome; her pale, chiselled face was strangely composed. She might have been sitting at any dinner table in Perth with a sober company instead of drinking with a man she had never met before whose followers were holding her brother prisoner, while his wife was being seduced in his own bed.

"What manner of woman are you?" he said suddenly. "You can't be related to that poltroon upstairs?"

"As it happens I am," she said. "But brothers and sisters don't have to be alike. Witness yourself and your own brother. You look alike and so do Donald and I, but you're quite different from each other. What ails you, Macdonald of Dundrenan? Do you find me ugly?"

"Not ugly, no. But unpleasingly bold. I don't care for it."

"Oh dear me." She smiled, and her eyes flashed at him with genuine amusement. "Don't tell me I've shocked you. I know all about you, sir. Your reputation has gone before you. Long before," she added. "Don't tell me you prefer women to be hypocrites?"

"What do you know of me?" he demanded. She disturbed him when she was silent; her personality was strong and disturbing. He had never met anyone like her before. When she talked, she made him extremely angry, but angry as if he were dealing with a man.

"I know that you have a very bad name," she said gently. "Friends of mind had cause to curse it. A particular friend; Alice Gannoch, to be precise. Do you remember her at all?"

"I do." He looked at her, his eyes slowly and insultingly considering her, from her shining black hair to the line of her breasts above the neck of her red dress. "But I was drunk, and she was unwilling. Things are different this time. Are you still eager to find out if what she said was true, madam? There must be another bedroom in the house and I'm damned sure you'll know where to find it."

Janet rose. Her pale face had not altered. Instead she watched him with an expression that was full of curiosity and quite without fear. "Alice Gannoch never told me anything," she said slowly. "I heard of it from her mother. She is safely married now to a man who thought more of a large dowry than virginity. She is quite happy. Before we find that bedroom, Macdonald, let me tell you one thing. At seventeen I was married to a man who was so much in love with my money that he killed himself spending it. I have spent all my time since then searching for a man who *is* a man. I believe you are such a one. In any case, I would like to find out. Come then."

They went to a room up the first flight of stairs, and for a moment they stood facing each other, hesitating like two combatants before the final challenge is accepted. Then Janet came to him and stood against him, not moving, not putting her arms around him, just watching his face. James looked down at her and, putting both hands on her shoulders, he tore the red dress off her back. In the furious encounter which followed, he was astonished to hear her laughing.

He must have slept because he found that she had covered him, and when he opened his eyes she had lit a candle by the bedside and was sitting up beside him. She had a beautiful, voluptuous body, feminine and yet superbly strong. The sight of it left him so cold and so sickened with rage and disappointment that he turned away from her.

"Cover yourself," he said brutally. "You look like a whore."

"As you wish. I'm sorry, Macdonald. I should have gone and left you sleeping."

James did not answer her. He did not know how long he had slept but sleep had engulfed him as if he had stepped over a precipice.

Now his mind was clear, and with his memory came the most acute revulsion for himself and for the woman so close to him that he could hear her breathing. He had made love to scores of women, including some of the lowest drabs, who gave themselves to any drunken young gentleman for a few shillings; now he felt unclean and full of despair. He had escaped from nothing.

"I am sorry," Janet said again. "I found what I wanted, I only wish that you had too. Please look at me; I've done as you asked."

He pulled himself upright and jumped out of the bed. He began dressing, still without speaking or looking at her. It was incredible that he could have embraced and possessed one of the most passionate women he had ever encountered and yet remained horribly aloof and empty as if he were outside his body and critically watching the empty manifestations of his own lust. When he was ready she came up to him; she was wearing a long silk and velvet robe, and as if she could read his mind, she said quietly: "This is mine. This is my room; I live here with Donald and Margaret. I think I can hear her and your brother stirring. It will be daylight soon. You had better release my brother and be gone before anyone sees you. I will persuade him to accept the inevitable. He's a cautious man and inclined to be greedy. He won't want to lose his good standing with the Prince by complaining against his officers."

"It's of no consequence to me," he said roughly. "I'll stand any paltry lawyer's accusation and make him eat it!"

"I'm sure you would," she said gently. "But it's better not to have to do it. Before you go, tell me one thing."

He turned unwillingly and looked at her. "What is it?"

"Will you see me again? I have a house of my own here in Perth."

"I doubt it," he said. "There's been little profit in our meeting."

"Then I shall seek you," she said. "She must be very beautiful."

"Who? What do you mean?"

"I mean the woman whose name you called when you were making love to me. Good night, Macdonald of Dundrenan. We shall meet again."

The rest of the week was spent in assembling the Prince's army, checking and storing the ammunition, and holding councils of war with the chiefs. The day after their encounter with the family of Macpherson, the Macdonalds were present at one of these. The Prince was at the head of the table and on the right and left of him were Lord George Murray, brother of the Duke of Atholl, and the twenty-two-year-old Duke of Perth. Lord Nairne was there, and Lord Ogilvie, a new arrival. The news Colonel O'Sullivan gave them was encouraging.

The British garrison had left Edinburgh and was on its way to Stirling to give battle to the Prince's forces. Its commander, Sir John Cope, was not optimistic about his chances of success, and his force of English troops was already depleted by desertions. Rumours of the terrible barbarians from the north were terrifying his men, who numbered only twenty-five hundred and imagined themselves being cut to pieces by a force ten times that number. The size and ferocity of the Highland army gathering at Perth was joyfully exaggerated by those Scottish civilians who advised Cope gravely to escape them while he could. And not one man had answered the English call to volunteer while more and more small chiefs and their tacksmen tenants came in by horse and on foot to Perth, some armed only with scythes lashed to long poles, others equipped with basket-handled sword and the small buckler which was the standard equipment of the Highlander in war.

Compared with the regular soldiers in the Lowlands and across the border, very few carried muskets but this did not dismay the company present in Perth that day.

"My last accounting of our forces was about six thousand," Colonel Sullivan announced, "and more are coming every hour."

"But there is still no word from Macdonald of Sleat or Macleod of Macleod," Lord George Murray interposed.

James nudged his father and said quietly. "The new joint commander-in-chief of the army. The Prince has divided the appointment between him and the Duke of Perth. I don't like his looks."

"You like nothing and no one," his father snapped. "There's nothing wrong with the Murrays."

He was irritable and profoundly disappointed to find that James was unchanged by the encounter of the previous evening, of which he had received a full report from Hugh. He had found himself a woman, and a rich and handsome one according to his brother, and slammed out of the house without a word, as dour and quarrelsome as ever. He had already insulted one of the junior officers of Glengarry's men until their followers had to put between them to prevent a duel, and that was only an hour before they were summoned to the Prince. The itch to fight was on him; the old man could see it in his son's eye and the taut muscles in neck and jaw. James reminded him of some tethered beast of prey, straining at the chains which kept it from leaping off and flying at the world. Murray was still speaking.

"I hope you realise, Highness, how important these two chieftains are; they can call up hundreds of men and their money would be of equal use to us at this moment. I must advise you that their neutrality is a serious blow to us."

"There is no serious blow which can't be parried," the Prince remarked. "Personally, gentlemen, if the Macdonald of Sleat and the Macleod don't have the courage to join me, then I prefer to fight with a few brave men rather than any number of cowards. Let these two remain aloof, we shall not need them."

Lord George bowed and sat down. He was not impressed by the bravado of the young man sitting beside him, so full of belief in himself and his own power to charm that he could dismiss the defection of two of the most powerful men in the Highlands as if it were a trifle and beneath his notice. Lord George had joined Charles because his family had risen for the Prince's father in the '15, and the rightful Duke of Atholl was an old man who had come back with his young master after an exile of thirty years. Lord George had a brother sufficiently venal to accept the dukedom when it was withdrawn from the rebel holder, but this brother had fled before the Prince's advance. There were moments even after two days, when Lord George began to wish he had gone with him. It was all very well for Prince Charles Edward to set out on the conquest of Scotland, but it horrified the older man to hear him talk of marching into England.

He leant back in his chair with an expression of disapproval and listened to Aenas Macdonald, the sober-minded banker who had also come from France with Charles. Like most men with financial connections, he had contacts everywhere, and the information he gathered through dealings in London and Paris was the best source the Prince had on how his enemies were reacting to him.

Aenas was a pleasant man, with a streak of fierce fanaticism, a passionate attachment to his country and that country's rightful ruling family. He informed the Prince that his finances were good and would be better when a full accounting of the gifts of plate and jewels from sympathisers were converted into sterling. And then he put his hand up to his mouth and coughed; it was a gesture which James and all those men of war who sat around the Prince were to know very well in the long months to come.

"Your Royal Highness. I have one item of bad news. I have heard from an impeccable source that the Duke of Argyll and the Earl of Breadalbane and all the clan Campbell have declared for the Elector of Hanover." There was a moment of silence, broken only by the whisper of one of the young chiefs who enquired of his neighbour who the Elector of Hanover was, and was told angrily that this was the correct title for the German Prince illegally known as King of England. Old Macdonald of Keppoch was the first to speak.

"Well, sir, I say what of it! There's not one of us could sleep easily at night with the most treacherous ruffians in the Highlands among us. Let them fight for England! By God, there'll be enough Macdonalds ready to march in and punish them for it when Your Highness is victorious!"

"Let them march with the Hanoverians." James sprang up. "They've always been the scum of Scotland. There's no place for any Campbell here!"

"One moment, sir." That was a Fraser, younger son of one of Lord Lovat's cousins. "It's all very well for you and Keppoch to dismiss the Campbells. I, for one, would rather have them with us than ready to fall on our backs on the march. We're not all Macdonalds, remember."

In the long, cruel history of the clan wars, no deed of savage treachery surpassed the murder of the Macdonalds at Glencoe by John Campbell and his men. They had broken the sacred laws of hospitality by falling on the Macdonalds who gave them shelter and putting men, women, and children to the sword while they slept.

James glared at him; he seemed unaware of his surroundings or of the presence of the Prince as he faced a distant kinsman of the Frasers of Clandara, and all his hate and bitterness boiled up in him.

"It may seem a trifle to you, sir, that our kinsmen at Glencoe were murdered by those swine of Campbells, who ate their bread and then fell upon them in the night," he said very slowly. "No doubt the Frasers would do the same if there was any clan fool enough to turn their backs upon them!"

"Repeat that plainly, sir!" The young Fraser shouted, and now he was on his feet, his hand on his sword. "Repeat it and be ready to give satisfaction for it!"

"Gentlemen!"

Lord George Murray cut across them with a roar of anger. He pointed to James.

"Apologise! You're here to fight for the Prince, not for any private grievance. Apologise, sir, or leave the Prince's presence."

James faced him and he began to smile. His voice was very soft and almost mocking when he answered. "I'm damned if I'll do anything of the kind."

Charles had been silent while the quarrel developed, but he had been watching James carefully. He possessed a violent temper himself and he was on the point of losing it. Murray had already irritated him with his gloomy expression and gloomier remarks. Now he stared round the table at the men he had summoned to help him, two of whom were about to fight in his presence, and the rest arguing and standing up as if they were at a cockfight instead of a council.

"One moment! Sir Alexander Macdonald of Dundrenan, remove yourself and your sons since you cannot control them. And you, sir." He glared at the Fraser. "Leave us, and do not return until you know how to behave in my presence. If you want to fight so badly, make ready to engage Sir John Cope and the English. The first man here who risks his own life or takes another's will be imprisoned at Perth until after the war. Now, my lords, perhaps we can resume our business!"

Without a word the Fraser bowed and walked out of the room.

"Come!" The old Macdonald rose and saluted the Prince. "My apologies, Highness. My son will earn your pardon for this by leading his men in the first rank of the first battle. We will retire as you command."

As they left the house he turned furiously to James, who walked in silence beside him. "I ought to break your skull," he snarled. "You damned fool! You've brought disgrace upon us! What's the matter with you; can't you see a Fraser without venting your spleen about that cursed woman at the expense of your Prince and your family's honour? Don't argue with me," he roared as James started to reply. "Hold your tongue, sir, and listen to me. You may be my eldest son, but by the living God, if you can't behave like it, I'll send you back to Dundrenan to wait with the women and children!"

"I will see you and the Prince himself damned to hell before I stand and apologise to any man for speaking my mind," James snapped at him. "And if I go back to Dundrenan, half our clan will go with me. If you think they follow you alone, Father, try them and see!" And then he turned and walked away from them.

"He's mad," his father said savagely. "God knows what's to be done with him. . . . Hugh, go after him. In this mood he's likely to begin a brawl in the street and you heard what the Prince said. David, come with me!"

James walked on through the narrow streets and those who were in his path stepped hurriedly aside. He walked without seeing where he went and when Hugh caught up with him he turned on him with an oath. "To hell with you! Stop following me!"

"I want a drink," Hugh said. "There's a tavern at the end of the street there. Come on."

It was a small place, badly lit by guttering torches, and roughly furnished with benches round the walls and stale straw on the uneven floor. It smelt of sweat and liquor, and there were a few men in it already drinking and talking in little groups. Most of these were members of the Prince's army and a few called out to the Macdonalds as they entered, but James did not answer and Hugh only gestured, indicating that they wished to be alone.

James drank a cup of whisky down in one long draught and then looked round contemptuously. "We're in good company, I see," he said. "This place stinks like a cesspit. You've had your drink now, brother. Get out and leave me alone!"

"Before I go," Hugh said quietly, "let me tell you one thing. This is a war we've undertaken, not a gentleman's game or a foray after someone else's cattle. If you can't take it seriously, and I mean this, James, you'd better to do as Father threatened and go back to Dundrenan. Or to Clandara, if you like, and finish your business there. Here, give me your cup."

"I want no advice from you," James said slowly. "Unless it's how to kill a man by running him through from behind!"

Hugh grinned at him and filled his own cup with whisky. "I told Father you had never forgiven me for that," he said. "What a fool that woman made of you. How did she do it, James? How did she kill your love for your own family and still send you away like an outcast cur when you went to her that night at Clandara?"

"If you speak of her," James told him, "I'll kill you here and now."

"As you wish." Hugh shrugged. "But tell me one thing, brother, and then we'll talk of something else. Did you tell her it was I who killed her precious brother?"

"I did," James muttered. He did not want to talk to anyone of that last meeting with Katherine, least of all to the mocking, cynical younger brother sitting opposite and watching him with his pale eyes like a mountain cat. But the words came, torn from him by loneliness and a desperate need to confide in someone.

"I did, but she did not believe me. You left one of his men alive and they said I was the one. I made no pretence about it; I told her I would have done it if you had not, but that in fact I wasn't guilty. But she would not listen." He raised his head and looked at his brother. "You want to know what happened, don't you, so that you can mock and jeer? . . . Well, so you shall. I went on my knees to her and begged forgiveness . . . yes, Hugh, I knelt, and I'd have died happy if she had forgiven me. But do you know what she did? She struck me in the face and wished me dead. And then I left her. Does that satisfy you, or must I tell you more? Tell you how I sprang on her and held her and how she weakened for a moment and responded to me . . ."

"You love her still," Hugh said slowly. "You were weak, James. You should have seized her that night and kept her at

Dundrenan. She would have submitted in the end. Now there will never be peace between us or happiness for you as long as she lives."

"Submitted!" James laughed bitterly. "It's you who are the fool, my clever brother, with all your talk of women and your knowledge of their ways. I didn't want her lust! I loved her; I valued her virtue because I loved her. I thought she loved me as much in return. But that woman yesterday, that woman who lay in my arms and gave me everything of herself in exchange for nothing but insults, she was more true than Katherine Fraser ever was. . . ."

"Then why not seek her out?" his brother suggested. "We've another day or two here before the army marches out to catch up with Cope and the English. You could do worse, James. You need company and not the company of men this time. I'm meeting my little Macpherson this evening; her husband has taken fright and gone off on a visit to his uncle. I'm afraid our men were none too gentle with him and he doesn't care to complain or to stay here while we remain in Perth. I'll give a message to Mrs. Douglas. She'll expect you this evening. Come on now, we'll go and find David and Father. As I said, we've got to fight a war."

Chapter 4

"MILADY!"

Katherine was alone in the library, sewing. The whisper was so close to her chair that she started; she had heard no one enter the room.

Jean Macdonald, maid to her stepmother, stood by her, her eyes blinking nervously in her pale face.

"What do you mean by creeping up on me like that, girl? What do you want?"

"Milady, if you please, come with me. It's my mistress sends for ye. I daren't make a noise for fear the Earl would hear and send me back."

Katherine folded her sewing, threading the needle carefully into the work. The Countess had not been allowed to leave her rooms since Robert Fraser's body had been brought back from Ben Mohire.

"What does your mistress want with me?" she asked coldly.

"She's sick, milady, fearfu' sick, and she needs help. I beg of ye, show a little pity to the poor lady and come with me!"

"Very well. But if my father hears that you came down here and approached me behind his back, it will go hard with you. Come then."

Jean stood back and curtsied as Katherine rose and went ahead. She did not see the servile expression on the girl's face vanish as she passed and a look of intense hatred take its place as she followed her out of the room. The Countess had not sent for Katherine. She was hardly able to walk, and there were moments when she wandered in her speech and woke crying out with terrible dreams, so that her maid suspected that her mind was going. And still there were nights

102

when the Earl came in to her and threw Jean outside the door, and she crouched there, listening to his voice raised, cursing and threatening, and the helpless weeping of her mistress. Jean had taken the initiative in asking Katherine's help. Unless the Countess was reprieved from her husband's sentence of confinement and ill treatment she would die within the next few weeks. Jean was sure of this. She was ready to beg and whine to the hated Fraser's hated daughter, if she could trick her into helping the Countess.

When Katherine entered her stepmother's room and saw the figure lying in the big four-poster bed, she did not recognise her for a moment. And then as she came closer her colour went and she was as pale as the woman who turned her head and started with a cry of fear, clutching the sheets to her for protection.

She had not seen Margaret Clandara for nearly two months. And now her face was hollow-cheeked and sallow and a half-healed cut surrounded by a livid bruise showed on the side of her mouth. Her eyes were wild as they stared up at her stepdaughter, and suddenly overcome with shame and horror, Katherine ran to the bed and caught one of the shaking hands in hers.

"Oh, madam, madam, forgive me, I had no idea ... Jean, this mark is terrible; it needs attention."

"There are other marks, milady," Jean said slowly. "Your father did that with his fist. He used a whip on her more than once."

"What are you doing here? Jean, did you bring her? Oh, you wicked creature, you fool, don't you know she'll tell him and he'll come up here tonight and punish me!" Margaret sat upright and began to cry, the tears pouring uncontrolled down her face.

"I had to, madam, or you would have died here, after one of his lordship's visits. There's naught *I* could do to protect ye, God knows."

"You did well, Jean," Katherine said. "God in heaven, you look so thin, Margaret. ... Margaret, why didn't you send word to me before? I could have stopped him ... I had no idea!"

"I thought you knew," her stepmother said slowly. "I thought everyone knew that he was starving me and beating me to death because of what happened to his son."

"I knew at first," Katherine admitted; she was so ashamed and horrified that she could hardly speak. "But I too was mad with grief.... I didn't interfere. May God forgive me. Margaret, what can I do to help you?"

"Get me away," the Countess whispered. "Get me back to my own people. ..."

"There's no one there to take you in," Katherine said slowly. "All your clan have joined the war with Prince Charles Edward. My father would send men to take you back again."

"Oh, Mother of God." The Countess began to weep, her hurt mouth twisting with pain. "Then there's no hope for me. Give me a knife to kill myself! That's all I ask of you. God will reward you, it wouldn't be sinful. Don't leave me to suffer like this for something I know nothing of.... You loved my cousin once, you did, didn't you?"

"I did," Katherine answered her, and the watchful Jean saw her colour change and her hands clench until her rings made marks upon her fingers. "But if you want help from me, don't mention him. Don't speak his name!"

"I won't, I won't," the Countess promised. "But only let me die! It will be kinder ... kinder than this vengeance of your father's!"

Katherine got up from her knees. She turned to the maid. "Go down to the kitchens and get some broth and some meat for the Countess," she said. "Say those are my orders. I will send for a doctor from Inverness; he should be here by nightfall and he can treat the Countess. But you must say you had a fall." She turned to her stepmother. "No, I will not give you a knife or connive at anything like that. I will speak to my father. You have my word of honour that he will not illtreat you again. Rest easy now, madam. I shall do my best for you and you won't have anything more to fear."

She walked out through the door which Jean held open for her. "God bless you, milady," the girl said and curtsied to the ground. She closed the door after her and then she opened her lips and spat. "And may Christ curse you and all yours," she added.

She came to the Countess and helped her up on the pillows. For a moment the two women held onto each other without speaking. Jean said at last, "I did the right thing madam. Misbegotten though she is, she'll speak to her father and get the physician for ye. That's all that matters."

"You're a brave child, Jean," the Countess murmured. "What do you think that fiend would have done to you if she'd reported you to him?"

"Little worse than he's done to you," she answered. "May God blight him—it was as much as I could do to look her in the face when I was pleading . . ."

"Shush, Jean," her mistress said. "She's going to help me, didn't you hear?" Her pale eyes glittered into the girl's face above her. "We'll take her help, Jean my child. I asked for a knife to kill myself, and she refused. If God gives me strength I'll see the day when she'll regret not having done it."

Jean's round face softened in a smile and she squeezed her mistress' thin hand. "Thank God to hear ye say that," she whispered. "For a moment then I thought you'd been taken in by all those gentle words of hers. I thought ye'd lost your mind and forgiven her for being what she is."

"She is his daughter," the older woman muttered, and her red-rimmed eyes flickered and half closed. "Nothing can redeem that to me. I have as much forgiven her as I've forgiven *him*. Rest easy, Jean. I'm a Macdonald yet, in spite of what's been done to me."

"I know," the girl whispered. "And so am I, madam. Rest easy you too, for we'll have our vengeance when the time comes. As it will," she added. "I know it. Just be patient."

The light was fading and Katherine had ordered the candles in the library to be lit. The long, deep autumn dusk was the part of the day which depressed her most; she spent many mornings riding, galloping until her horse was exhausted and the unwilling Angus caught up with her, complaining of her carelessness of the poor beast. But she no longer went to the Loch or rode through the purple moorland where she and James had met so often, and when she returned to the castle it was only to occupy herself with details of its management which were the steward's concern and did not really need her. She sewed and she read and she went every day to Robert's grave, but as evening came she was alone, and the hour before her father returned was only one degree less wretched than the nights when she lay without sleeping.

The Earl spent as much time as possible out visiting his tenants and talking to his grieve; there was some escape for him in the management of his estate now that Robert was dead. In the evenings he and Katherine dined together and talked, and soon he would excuse himself and shut himself up in the writing room with his whisky, sometimes sending for the grieve, who remained with him late into the night.

When he came in that evening Katherie did not come forward and kiss him. She was still haunted by the results of his cruelty and his vengeance; Margaret Clandara's frightened, injured face had never left her mind, nor had the hysterical cry for a knife with which to end her suffering. It was incredible to Katherine that the father she had respected and loved could be capable of such brutality.

"You are very quiet, my child," he said. "Why do you sew at this hour? Candlelight is very trying for the eyes. I used to tell your mother so. Well, haven't you a word to say to me?"

"Yes." Katherine put down the cloth and looked at him. "Yes, Father, I have something to say to you. I saw Margaret today."

His eyes narrowed. "Who gave you permission to go in there?"

"No one, I just went to see her. And I've sent for a doctor from Inverness; he should be here sometime tonight." She faced him very calmly and her voice was steady. "We will tell him that she had a fall."

"We will tell him nothing," the Earl said, "because I'll have him turned back at the door. How dare you take it on yourself to interfere! How dare you go to that woman and defy my orders. No one but her maid is allowed near her."

"What do you want to do, Father?" she asked him. "Torture her to death? ... Ill-treat her until one night she falls dead at your feet?"

"Yes," he shouted, "yes, that's why I didn't make an end of her the day I brought Robert's body home! I want her to live as long as possible and suffer as much as I can make her. ... They should have remembered her before they murdered my son. ... I can't make them pay until this war is over, but I can punish her for being one of them."

"If I were to beg you, would you stop ill-using her? I *am* begging you, Father. Killing her by inches won't bring Robert back; if he could see what you are doing it would only shame him. She had no part in it. You can't blame Margaret. And if she dies there'll be a charge of murder laid against you."

He leant back in his chair and laughed. "Oh, will there? And by whom?"

"By Jean Macdonald," she said quietly. "Don't you see that any hope of accusing the Macdonalds will be lost if you are known to have killed their kinswoman, your own wife? I know you want vengeance on those who murdered Robert— don't you think I want it too? But this is not the way to get it. Which would you rather see: that poor helpless woman hounded to death and used in evidence against your claim, or the Macdonalds standing trial for murder?"

"*I* may want vengeance," the Earl said, "but are you sure you do? I've watched you, Katherine, and I've doubted. You brought Robert to his death by your betrothal to the man who killed him. I've never reproached you with it save once, when I held my son's body in my arms. But it hardly befits you to plead for anyone who bears that name."

"But I do plead," she said. "And not just for her but for you. I love you, Father, you are all I have left in the world now. Do not destroy that love by proving yourself as cruel as any Macdonald of Dundrenan. Nothing excuses what I saw today, neither Robert's death nor my betrayal nor your own grief. She begged me to give her a knife so she might kill herself. Please, my dear Father, don't do this terrible thing."

She got up and knelt beside his chair, and in spite of his

anger he put his arm around her. He looked suddenly very old.

"I always hated her," he muttered. "I put her in your mother's place and gave her our name to save my people from starvation and ruin. But I hated her even then. How can you ask me to relent and keep my hatred in my heart until it poisons what's left of my life? . . . Now that Robert is gone I have only you to live for; that creature doesn't matter to me, I feel only loathing and contempt for her. If she had defended herself even once I might have stopped. But she just cringes, looking at me like an animal, trembling with fear."

"Leave her alone," Katherine begged. "She's suffered enough. Let her stay in her rooms, but don't hurt her again. Send her away if you like, but don't degrade yourself and Robert's memory."

"I'll not send her away," he said. "You were right when you said she'd be good evidence for the Macdonalds. She'll stay here, where no one can listen to her tales."

"But you won't harm her," Katherine whispered. "Promise me that whatever happens you won't go up to that room again."

"Ah, God, what does it matter?" he said wearily. "You kneel there begging for her after what her kin did to your brother . . . even my own child turns against me. So be it. I'll give that maid of hers a key and she can lock the door. But no doctor will come into this house. One of the crofters' wives can tend her; there's a woman over at Glen Urquhart who knows about healing. She can't read or write and she'll know better than to spread any tales if she wents to keep the roof over her head. But the doctor returns to Inverness. That's my last word on the subject, and I won't have you mention it again. Besides, I've some news for you. I received a letter from Henry Ogilvie today. He's on his way to Inverness and he wants to spend a few nights with us."

Henry Ogilvie. The friend of her childhood who had come back as a young man and fallen in love with her. Gentle, kindly Henry Ogilvie whom she had refused and sent away on her return from France because she had lost her heart and soul to James.

"I wonder he comes," she said slowly, "after what happened."

"I think he comes because of it," her father said. "He comes to comfort both of us, my child. You should have married him long ago. It was always my wish."

"I know," Katherine answered. "But I didn't love him, Father. If I had never known love I would have been content with him, but it was not to be. God didn't mean me to be happy. But I'll be glad to see him for your sake."

"It will be good for both of us," the Earl said. "He was always close to Robert too."

They dined and Clandara excused himself, leaving Katherine alone in the silent room, her sewing in her lap, staring into the big log fire until Annie looked round the door and asked if she were ready to retire or did she wish for anything.

"No, thank you, Annie. I'm tired, I'll come up now. I thought I heard voices in the Hall outside a few moments ago——"

"You did, milady," Annie said. " 'Twas a doctor come all the way from Inverness and he was turned away by your father's orders. He was mightily aggrieved too, I can tell ye, after coming all that way for an urgent call. Who sent for him?"

"I did," Katherine said. "I wanted him to attend the Countess, but my father wouldn't allow it."

"That's a pity," Annie murmured. "I've heard much talk in the house that she's no' likely to last long. They've been giving food to that maid of hers today, and it's the first time she's been sent up anything decent to eat for weeks. What's going to become of her? Can't you speak to your father?"

"I have spoken to him." Katherine got up and Annie gathered her sewing bag and frame and put them away for her. "There'll be no more visits at night; he promised me."

"Thank God for that." Annie opened the door for her and then went out across the Great Hall, their steps echoing on the stone floor, and up the staircase to her rooms. "I've been afraid to sleep at night sometimes for fear that she'd be found dead and word would get out of what was happening.

Not that I care," she added hastily, "but I was thinking of you and the lord himself. He might send her away, maybe?"

"He daren't," Katherine said. "She'll have to stay where she can't speak. Who knows what will have happened by the time this war is over or where any one of us will be? . . . Mr. Ogilvie is coming to stay with us at the end of the next week."

"Mr. Ogilvie!" Annie's thin face grew bright. "Ach, but that's great news! He hasn't been to this house for more than a year. . . . Ye'll be happy to see him, I dare say. He was always a favourite with the lord and Lord Robert. . . . Everyone at Clandara liked him."

"I know." Katherine stood before her mirror, while Annie unfastened her dress and helped her out of it. Her cambric nightgown was laid out to warm before the fire. "He's on his way to Inverness; he'll only be here a few nights."

Annie pulled the nightgown over her mistress' head and straightened it, coming round to fasten the strings at her neck and wrists.

"Sit down, milady, and I'll brush out your hair for ye. The end of next week, you said?" She began to hum, and it was the first time she had dared to do so since Robert's death. She remembered Henry Ogilvie well; a fine gentleman, handsome and quiet-spoken and so much in love with the Lady Katherine that he used to follow her about the house like a dog. If she hadn't been sent on that trip to France and met that scoundrel, she'd have been married and living at the Ogilvie's fine mansion house by the Spey. She brushed hard at the long shining hair. If he were coming again there was still hope.

There was always hope in Annie's heart; hope that the Macdonalds would be killed to a man in the first battle, hope that this time Katherine would find in Ogilvie what she had never found before, but hope for her happiness most of all.

When Katherine was in bed, she tucked in the covers, settled her dressing robe and slippers by the end of the bed, and then began to examine the dresses hanging in the cupboards.

"What are you doing?" Katherine called out.

"Ach, just looking through your wardrobe," Annie said cheerfully. "It wouldn't do if he were to see you in the same dress you wore when he was last here."

"It will make no difference what he sees." Katherine lay back and closed her eyes. "Put out the candles, Annie, and go to bed. I know what you're thinking and if you dressed me in gold and silver it would make no difference. I sent Mr. Ogilvie away. Nothing has changed since that day. He's coming as an old friend, and it is of no consequence to me whether I see him or not. Now go to bed."

Annie curtsied and closed the door. She had taken no notice of her mistress, and she went to sleep listing the different gowns she would put out for each day and evening of the visit. She had a very shrewd instinct developed by long and fond observation of the woman she served. That instinct had recognised love, when it came in the shape of the Macdonald of Dundrenan, it had recognised passion such as she herself had never known and had no desire to know, and it divined and pitied the agony of mind and desolation of heart which brought her mistress weeping to the ground that night in the gardens a few weeks before, when the marks of her lover's hands were still imprinted on her arms. There was no fighting the Macdonald on his own terms. No swaggering chieftain in the length and breadth of the Highlands could compete with him, but the comforting arms and gentle understanding of someone like Mr. Ogilvie might prove a serious temptation. And, incurably optimistic as always, Annie felt that with the rebellion spreading everywhere and English troops marching out to stop it, it would soon be only the ghost of James that Henry Ogilvie would have to lay.

"If your late husband spent all your money, how is it you've such a fine house?"

Janet Douglas laughed. "I didn't say he spent all," she corrected. "Besides, I've taken good care of what was left. I'm a thrifty woman, James."

He looked up at her over his wineglass. Like everything in the house, her table silver and vessels were of magnificent quality. So was her wine and the food they had just eaten which was served by two footmen.

"Thrift is a great virtue," he said. "You're an admirable woman. Your late husband must have been a fool to leave you all alone so early."

"On the contrary, I'm very grateful to him. I couldn't have deceived him with you if he had been alive. He would have squeezed a fortune out of me to cover his blind eye."

She was so cynical at times that it irritated him. He did not like women to express their distrust of the world. He did not like women to do anything at all except accommodate him when and where he felt like it, to ask no questions and make no demands. And Janet certainly accommodated him, but she did it without any suggestion that she was bestowing favours. In that situation and in that only in their developing relationship, she gave the impression that she was receiving one. James finished his wine and she signalled for more to be served him. She did everything quietly and efficiently and with great self-confidence. It made him long to raise his arm and sweep everything off the table. And yet he came. He came most nights during his stay in Perth, and every time he went to bed with her and rose up empty and angry with himself. She had moved out of her brother's house and reopened her own to receive him. It was less embarrassing than meeting in her sister-in-law's home, for Hugh's interest was waning, and already there were nights when Margaret Macpherson had waited until dawn for the lover who did not come. She was suffering so bitterly from wounded pride that she was packing up to follow her indignant husband, hoping to be forgiven.

"I saw the Prince again today," Janet said. "He was out riding in the main street and he was surrounded by women, all clamouring to kiss his hand or touch him—his horse could hardly move!"

"If he could lay them all he'd be King of Scotland sooner than he thinks," James said. "By popular acclaim."

"What a pity he can't," she said. "It would save a great deal of bloodshed and give everyone what they want. Will

Edinburgh, he has no hope of winning. Is that sensible, Katherine, or do you think it cowardly?"

She smiled at him for the first time. "I think it very like you, Henry. You always thought well before making a decision, but when you made it, nothing could move you."

"Or you," he retorted gently. "Only you never thought at all, my dear. You were always wild; I used to have the very devil stopping you from taking every jump when you were a child, just because Robert and I did."

There was silence then, and the Earl snapped his fingers for more wine. The two Fraser servants who waited on them filled his glass and Henry's, and removed the dishes from the table. Then suddenly Katherine spoke.

"Robert's name is never mentioned now," she said. "And that's wrong. Father, it's wrong to grieve for him like this. Henry, I'm so glad you came to see us." She leant across and touched his hand and he flushed. "I feel as if you have brought Robert back."

"I feel it too," her father said. "You were always like a second son to me, my dear boy. And the child is right; my son is dead, but I can almost imagine him here with us, seeing you sitting down with us as you used to do in the old days. Stay longer than a week! Wait till we hear how the Prince has done on his march. . . . What's the use of going to Inverness when he may have run straight into the English army?"

"I hoped you'd ask me," Henry said. "I last heard that a force was marching out under the commander of the garrison, Sir John Cope, hoping to intercept the Prince. I met Cope once at a reception—a fearfully dull fellow like all the English, not a word to say for himself, and his officers were little better. I think," and his eyes gleamed, "that our people will run them into the ground the first time they meet them!"

"Maybe, maybe," the Earl said. "But it's the last battle that decides, not the first. I hope the Prince and his advisers remember that. Nobody did in the '15."

"I always wanted to know what your father said on the

scaffold," Henry asked, "that they had to execute him so hurriedly in the middle of it."

The Earl smiled a little. "My father was a blunt man," he said, "with a good turn of phrase. He said: 'God save King James,' and he was wishing a physical calamity upon the Elector of Hanover and one of his ugly German women, a most embarrassing calamity"—he was chuckling as he spoke—"which doesn't bear translation in front of you, Katherine, when the executioner swung at him with the axe! My mother used to repeat it with tears of pride in her eyes. Come, we've sat here long enough. Take Katherine into the Green Salon and I'll join you before bed. I've some business to see to with my grieve Dugal. Now that Robert's gone, I've little time to do anything but watch these tenants of mine and listen to their complaints."

They went into the Green Salon, and Katherine turned to him and asked if he would like to hear her play. "You used to like the spinet," she reminded him. "But I haven't touched it for so long I doubt if it's in tune."

"Then leave it for another time," he told her. "Come and walk in the gardens, it's a perfect night."

He opened the long windows for her and they stepped out into the cool grounds, and after a few steps he gently took her arm. The moon was high, casting a pale soft light over the waving trees, outlining the splendid moutains that towered over them like sentinels against the sky. He began leading her to the arbour where the stone seat was, and suddenly she stopped him and drew back.

"Not that way," she said. "Please, take the other path, Henry; it leads to the lower lawn."

"As you wish; I thought we might sit down."

"It's too cold," she said quickly. "Much too cold. I want to walk a little longer, then we can go in."

For some moments they said nothing. He held her arm against him, but the pressure was not returned. She walked with him but her thoughts were of that other night when in her desperation and grief she had wandered alone into the garden, taking the path to which Henry had tried to lead her, and found James waiting for her.

The memory was so intense and painful that she closed her eyes to drive it out, but the longing for him came upon her so violently that she shivered. It was as if her body belonged to someone else, and all the wrongs she had suffered and all the hatred she had encouraged were in vain, helpless to still the cry of desire for the arms which had captured her that night. Henry had felt that shiver, and immediately he turned back.

"You *are* cold," he said gently. "Come, Katherine, we'll go back. It was selfish of me, but I wanted to be alone with you for a little while."

"Selfish!" She turned and faced him with a cry. "Oh, Henry, how foolish you are . . . you don't know the meaning of the word! You're the gentlest and kindest man I've ever known—saving only Robert! I know what selfishness is, and cruelty, and lust. . . . I shock you, don't I? You never expected me to speak like this."

"I want you to," he urged her. He put his arms around her, and though she was stiff and cold, he held her close to him. "I want you to tell me what happened. Go on, Katherine, tell me. Everything!"

"You know what happened," she said fiercely. "You know how I sent you away for him, for the Macdonald of Dundrenan, the son of our enemy!"

"I know all that," he said slowly. "I know what he was; I couldn't believe that you could love him . . ."

"Nor could anyone," she said bitterly. "They all warned me—Father, Robert, everyone—but I didn't listen. I wanted him and I was blind. I loved him, Henry. There, I haven't said that even to myself since Robert died, but I've known it in my heart. I loved him in spite of everything and, God forgive me, I love him still!"

In the pale light his face was grey but he still held her, and one hand stroked her hair. "That doesn't matter. These things take time to die."

"He came back," she whispered. "He came here after Robert's death and hid in the garden and sprang on me in the arbour—that's why I won't go there with you tonight. He came to beg me to forgive him."

"And did you?" he asked her.

"No!" She pulled away from him, her eyes blazing. "No, thank God, I had that much honour left. I cursed him and struck him! That was my forgiveness for killing my Robert, my brother, who was *his* friend as well as mine. . . ."

"And he escaped," Henry said. "How did he escape?"

"I let him go," she said, and her voice was a whisper. "Can you understand that, Henry? I let him get away, I never raised the alarm or made a sound. If my father knew it, I think he'd kill me."

"He will never know," he said gently. "My poor Katherine, my beloved Katherine . . . Let me comfort you. Forget the past. Come, I'm going to take you in."

She was crying as they walked, still with his arm around her, and all his old love was alive in him, stronger than ever and deeper because of the pain and disappointment he had suffered. If the Macdonald had seduced her, Henry would not have cared. He would have gone out to find him and kill him, but he would not have loved her any less. But he knew too that then was not the moment to tell her or to offer more than comfort. He longed to take her in his arms and kiss her and wipe away the tears and the memory of the other, but he was sensible enough to know that it could not be done. Not then; not yet. He was a cautious man and, in spite of his gentleness, a determined one. He knew how to wait for what he wanted, and he wanted Katherine, weeping and desolate for the man who had betrayed her trust, as he had never wanted anything in his whole life. And he felt suddenly quite sure that this time he was going to get her.

"Wipe your eyes," he said. "Your father may be in the salon; what will he think if he sees you crying?" He gave her his handkerchief and she used it quickly, turning her face up for his inspection. The soft mouth was so close to him; it was still quivering.

"How is it now? Would he see anything?"

"Nothing . . . nothing now." His eyes were on her mouth and he made an involuntary movement towards her and then quickly stopped.

"Thank you for that, Henry," she said slowly. "Thank you

for not doing that. I couldn't have borne it yet, even from you."

"I understand," he told her. "I will be patient, Katherine. Before I go to Inverness I will ask you if I may. Just for the sake of my old love and your old fondness."

As they walked into the salon, she saw to her relief that it was empty. As he shut the windows, she went to a sofa and sat down, closing her eyes. She felt terribly weak and tired and very much afraid that she would give way to still more tears.

She heard him moving round the room and opened her eyes and watched him. He had changed very little. He was still as slim and elegant as ever; he always affected tartan coats and breeches of a different colour; she and Robert used to tease him for being a dandy. His dark brown hair was unpowdered and there was a little grey in it, just enough to accentuate the ten years' difference in their ages. They had been two wild youths, he and her brother Robert, and she a wilful, boisterous child who tried so hard to match them and keep up. Once, when she was fourteen, she had fallen in love with him for a month or two and flirted innocently to his great delight. But that was past, buried in Robert's grave with all the rest of her youth and its innocence. James had destroyed that as he had destroyed everything she loved. She was a woman now, marked by a furious and thwarted passion, embittered by hatred and sorrow and tortured by her own weakness. The soft-spoken, gentle companion of her youth had nothing to offer her now; there would be no peace in his arms from the devil with the face and voice of James Macdonald.

The door opened and one of the servants came in and curtsied. "You rang, sir?"

"Bring a decanter of brandy and two glasses for her ladyship and myself," he said. The girl curtsied again and withdrew.

"It will do you good." Henry came over and sat beside her. "Ah, that's excellent. I'll pour it. You may go."

She took the glass and he poured some for himself and sat down again beside her.

"Drink that," he said. "And then go up to bed; it's been a

long and distressing day for you, I know that. I've brought the past back, Katherine. Just give me a little time and see if I can show you something of the future."

Katherine shook her head. She felt better after the brandy. "What a fool I was," she said slowly. "What a fool to lose you, Henry. Can you really forgive me? I was so young and so thoughtless. I know I hurt you."

"That's not important now." He smiled down at her. "You were not in love with me, my dearest. I was still something of a brother; I realise that now; only a fool would have proposed to you when I did."

"If I'd accepted you, all would have been well. Instead . . ." She shrugged in despair. "My life is ruined, my brother gone, my father—I don't dare tell you what grief for his son and hate and whisky have driven him to doing. I saved my stepmother's life by a hair. He was starving and beating her. . . . It was indescribable. And for a time I knew it and did nothing. You have no idea what has become of us!"

"I'm beginning to," he said slowly. He was shocked in spite of himself, but even more determined that Clandara was no place for her to stay alone. "I'm going to speak to your father in the morning. I'm going to tell him that he should open his house again for your sake, receive people, try and forget Robert until he can bring the Macdonalds to a legal accounting."

"He may listen to you," she said wearily. "But it's no use. If you're trying to marry me off, my dear Henry, I can save you the trouble. I have done with marriage." She looked up at him and her eyes were full of tears. "Thanks to James Macdonald, I have done with life. I can truly say that, for I know I shall never be happy again."

"You think that now," Henry Ogilvie answered her steadily. "But I am going to warn you, Katherine. I shan't press you or make one advance against your wishes. But I lost you once and I don't intend to let you go again. All I ask is that you will allow me to remain a little while. Your father will end his mourning and you will begin to see people and live a normal life again. But I am going to stay here and live it with you."

"What of the Prince? I thought you were going to join him." She felt too weak and tired to argue. It all seemed quite unreal and she felt as if she would wake tomorrow and discover the whole evening had taken place in her imagination.

"The Prince can wait." He said it very firmly. "He's got to conquer the rest of Scotland yet. There'll be plenty of time for the Prince. And now I'm going to ring for your woman and get you to bed."

By the middle of September the royal army had left Perth, followed by a crowd of wives and loyalist ladies of indifferent reputation. Accompanied by pack horses and three servants, Janet Douglas rode out of the city behind the army, and James Macdonald left with his brothers in command of a regiment of his clansmen to seek the English forces.

The night of the sixteenth of September was very quiet and, considering that the army of Prince Charles was encamped outside the city's walls, Edinburgh itself was comparatively calm. They had sent out a civic deputation to plead with the Prince for time before they answered his call for unconditional surrender. The worthy gentlemen explained that though the main English army had marched out and left them unprotected, there was still a loyal garrison in Edinburgh Castle, and they dared not admit the Prince and his men without some thought for the consequences to themselves. Charles was reasonable and polite but firm in his demand. He hoped to make a good impression on the deputies, but at the same time he sent a message to his favourite, Cameron of Lochiel, with orders to take nine hundred men and see if they could storm one of the city gates by a trick. But he forbade violence. It would not do to harden the capital's resistance to him. The time passed and nothing was agreed by either side.

One of the coaches belonging to the deputation returned empty to its stable inside the Netherbow Port, and as soon as the gate was opened for it the gatekeeper was taken quickly by the throat by a certain Captain Ewan Macgregor, who then walked quietly through with the Camerons. The city was occupied without a shot being fired, and by noon the following day the heralds proclaimed King James III and his son Charles as Regent to the wild enthusiasm of the crowd. Contrary to their expectations, the Highlanders behaved with admirable courtesy and restraint, and since the people had nothing to fear immediately and nothing whatever to gain by being sour, they threw their hats in the air and shouted for the Prince, while the English garrison in the castle looked down on the crowded streets and celebrating crowds and told the Prince's emissaries to take their terms of surrender and go to hell. If any attempt were made to attack the castle, its English commander made it clear that he would turn his guns upon the city.

Within the day, it was reported that Sir John Cope and his men had landed at Dunbar, too late to rescue Edinburgh, but effectively barring the royal army's path to the south.

When he was summoned to join the main force marching to the attack, James Macdonald sent the Prince a note reminding him of his father's promise. "The forefront of the battle is my place. Otherwise I cannot come into your presence and I would consider myself better dead in battle than alive and in your continued disfavour." When the note was given to him, Charles read it and smiled. He looked up at Lord George Murray, his constant companion and the one man in the world whose pessimistic temperament suited him the least.

"The Macdonald of Dundrenan wants to make amends for that quarrel," he said. "I like the man's spirit; I wish we had more like him."

"I'm afraid I disagree." The older man prefaced so many of his remarks with those words that the Prince often felt tempted to say them for him. "The Macdonald is a man of notoriously bad temper and aggressive spirit; he is not particular about the cause, Highness, only about the chance to fight his fellow men. What does he ask in that letter then?"

"The right to go in the front of the attack on Cope," the Prince answered. His voice was a little curt. He was not used to being lectured and his opinions questioned. Lord George was more like a pedantic tutor than the commander of an army.

"In that case I should grant his wish," Lord George said.

"I have every intention," Charles remarked, "of doing so, and welcoming him back into my councils when he returns alive. Which he will, I know. Men like that bear charmed lives. I think I'll sleep now. In a day or so we must face our first battle with the English. I can hardly wait for it!"

Lord George bowed without answering and backed out. He was old and he had been in arms against the English often enough to have a hearty respect for them. He might hate them, but there were men among his own compatriots who were equally odious to him. The young Duke of Perth and the Prince's secretary, Murray of Broughton, were two who offended him constantly by their rashness and their lack of respect for his superior intelligence and past experience in fighting for the Prince's father.

All these young men were the same; he could see more in common between the Prince and that ruffianly Macdonald and his dreadful sons, more like pirates than gentlemen, than he could between the Prince and himself, one of the children of a duke, a man of sense and property and reputation. More and more he had to resist the conclusion that he had been mad to engage himself in the business at all. If they suffered a quick defeat at the hands of Cope, they might all be lucky to disband and escape.

Two nights later, on the evening of the twentieth, the two armies faced each other on Gladsmuir, midway between the villages of Prestonpans and Cockenzie. Sir John Cope had the advantage, for his front was protected by a treacherous bog. The position justified all Lord George's forebodings, and in despair at the enthusiasm of the Prince and his captains for the coming battle, the joint commander went to his tent to sleep. The Prince had insisted on lying down wrapped in his plaid like the Highlanders, in the middle of a field of cut pease, happy, as he said to the protests of Lord George and others, to share the discomforts with his men as he hoped to share the dangers.

But at a little after twelve Lord George was roused by his servant.

"Wake up, my lord. There's a man says he must see you urgently!"

The joint commander sat up irritably, rubbing his tired eyes.

"Send him away! Whatever it is, let him go to someone else with it or wait till morning."

"It had better not," the servant whispered. " 'Tis a Mr. Anderson; he says he's brother to the lassie that gave the Prince a drink on the road this afternoon."

"Ach, what of it? Go away, man, and tell him to do the same!"

Lord George remembered the little scene, so often duplicated all over the country wherever the Prince appeared. A blushing girl had offered him a glass of wine and been given a kiss on the cheek and a piece of cloth from his dirk scabbard as a souvenir. It was not a practice that recommended itself to Lord George's sense of how royalty should behave. It was too familiar and even—vulgar—he hesitated and then chose the word deliberately. Vulgar and foreign. Perhaps the Polish Princess who had borne him was to blame. . . .

"But, my lord, this Mr. Anderson says he knows a safe way over the bog!" Lord George was out of bed in a moment. He gave the man a push and told him to bring in the gentleman without another moment's delay. Five minutes later, Mr. Anderson was brought into the presence of the Prince's commander and was a little embarrassed to see him without wig or coat, sitting in his shirt and breeches, obviously just out of bed.

"I understand you have some information for us," Lord George said.

Mr. Anderson was a small man with sandy hair and a freckled complexion like a chicken. "I heard from my sister about the Prince," he said. "She showed me the red piece from his own dirk sheath. She spoke of him so well I thought I'd best come and help you for the battle tomorrow. I shoot snipe in these parts, sir, and I've gone over that bog many a time without wetting my feet. If it'll be of use, I can show you the path."

"Mr. Anderson." Lord George held out his hand and shook the little man's so hard that he winced. "All I ask is that you wait here while I wake the Prince. Wait here, there's a good fellow. My servant will give you anything you need."

"A wee glass of whisky if that's not too much to ask," Mr. Anderson said modestly. "I'll be needing it if we're going over the bog; it's a devilish cold damp place at night."

At three o'clock in the morning the army began to move out over the quagmire, and Mr. Anderson found himself at the head with the Macdonald of Dundrenan. The path was only wide enough for three men to walk abreast and their progress was slow, for they travelled as silently as possible. James walked by the side of their guide, and after the first half hour when they were safely on the firm ground and within sight of the lights of Cope's camp, he said suddenly: "Why did you wait so long to give this information?"

"I wasn't sure whether or not to interfere," Mr. Anderson said. They were standing on the edge of the bog and a long file of men, carrying their weapons and their brogues, crept past them away from the sodden ground and began dispersing into groups. A thousand men had crossed already and there was another hour to go before the dawn.

"My sister decided me," he continued. "She's aye mad for the Prince, you see, talking of nothing else but how bonny he was and how he kissed her." The little man smiled up into the fierce dark face above his. "I thought to myself, 'If he's as bonny as that to a poor, silly lassie like my sister, he'd make a bonny King of Scotland instead of the German King in London.' That's why I came, sir."

"Ah, the good guide, sent providentially to lead us!" Hugh Macdonald loomed up at them out of the darkness; he carried his sword wrapped in his plaid to prevent it clanking against his legs as he picked his way through the mud. He paused beside his brother to salute the small man. "Thank God for you, sir. We could no more have crossed through that than flown over it. One of our men strayed off the path a foot or two and it took three of us to pull him out again. All our men are through now." He turned to James. "We'd better begin re-forming before the light grows and they see us."

"If you'll excuse us, sir." James bowed to Mr. Anderson, who was to pay a terrible price for that night's work before a year had passed. "Call up your men, Hugh, but do it from mouth to mouth, passing the word on. No one is to make a sound. Good night, sir." He shook Mr. Anderson's hand and disappeared into the darkness.

By six o'clock the English pickets on duty were sure that something had gone wrong; they could hear the rattle and thud of men moving very close to them, but they could see nothing, for a thick white mist rose up from the bog as the sun began to warm it, obscuring everything in a phantom fog. It was most unnerving for the British troops who had been sick from the sea journey after their forced march to Aberdeen, and were tired and hungry as well. Scotland held no attractions for any of them. Most were veterans of the French campaign and they said among themselves that they preferred to stand in the field at Dettingen or Fontenoy and face a force of civilised troops like themselves than garrison a country like Scotland and come to blows with a people who were half mad with superstition and wholly mad in their language, customs, and means of making war. And behind the fortuitous haar of white, Prince Charles's army assembled in line of battle, with the regiment of Macdonalds in the forefront of the attack, James and Hugh standing before their men, their broadswords in their right hands, their round brass-studded bucklers fastened securely to their left arms, the deadly dirk in their hands.

When the haar lifted, they were going to charge straight into the enemy.

"It's thinning," James said. "Look, I can see the outline of that hummock over there and it's fifteen paces or more distant."

"In less than half an hour we'll be looking down their throats," Hugh answered. "I saw the Prince a moment ago. He sent a message to you. 'Tell him a brave man is never in my disfavour; I shall expect him to wait on me after the victory.' "

"Father will be satisfied," James said. "I'll bring him some little token of the battle as a peace offering."

"An Englishman's head would be appropriate," Hugh laughed softly. "Choose something above the rank of major if you can find one that hasn't run away. Do you know the definition of an English officer? One who remains at the rear so as to beat back his men as they retreat!"

"Keep your judgment until after we've fought them," James said. "I doubt their cowardice. You wouldn't get our people to stand in little lines firing and reloading like so many clockwork toys while their enemies rushed on them. Wait till later. And don't make a fool of yourself and be killed."

Hugh looked sideways at him and his grin faded. "That's what I was going to say to you. Kill, my dear brother, and do it until you're red to the elbows, but don't throw yourself on death. Remember Janet, waiting patiently for you in Edinburgh. She's worth coming back to; I only wish I had found myself some little consolation," and he sighed mockingly.

"Think of Fiona Mackintosh," James snapped back at him.

"Ah, that I will. She's promised to come to Edinburgh to see me if we go back before moving down on England. Alas, if I were killed today, she'd lose me, and I'd lose her fortune!"

"A true calamity," James agreed. He glanced over his shoulder. The Red Murdoch had taken his dead servant Donal's place; now he followed James into battle and rode after him when he went out, and he was just behind him on his right.

"Pass the word," James said. "The haar is lifting fast. Those men who have muskets, prime and load them and be ready to fire. After the volley, strip off and charge!"

The mist was vanishing like smoke, thinning so quickly before their eyes that the forward ranks of the enemy were visible and the sound of their shouts of alarm and the officers barking commands carried back through the mist to the Prince and his escort of picked cavalry, the Fitzjames Life Guards.

The battle opened with a round of shot from the English

artillery which fell on the right wing among Lochiel's Camerons, killing and injuring so few that his men greeted it with a derisive cheer. The first Highland line began to run forward, and at a distance of twenty paces James turned and halted, yelling to his men to fire. There was a loud discharge of muskets and many of the English soldiers in their distinctive red coats fell backwards, bowled over like rabbits, and the second and most terrible sound of battle was heard for the first time: the dreadful howling of the wounded. It was followed by a sound unknown to the veterans of many foreign wars, the terrifying war cry of the clans that rose and echoed over the moor from more than two thousand throats. And then the Macdonalds were upon them. The clansmen had stripped off their plaids and they ran down on them almost naked, the buckler held out in defence on the left arm, the heavy broadsword whirling over their heads and that unearthly yell of fighting spirit in their throats.

James leaped over the body of an English soldier who had fallen with his head opened by that first fusillade of musket fire, and he slashed at faces and redcoats everywhere, thrusting the spike of his buckler against their bodies as they pressed upon him, cutting and slashing and shouting encouragement to his men. He saw Murdoch for a moment, wielding a Lochaber axe, yelling with joy as he cleaved a head or an arm at a single stroke. The noise of firing and men screaming in fury, exultation, or pain was like the sound of a great storm. James lived an eternity within those first few minutes. His arm had a life of its own; his strength seemed to grow in him and the redness before his eyes was sometimes the bodies of the enemy, sometimes the fighting madness which possessed him. He came suddenly upon a young Englishman, wearing the crimson coat and blue facings and gold epaulettes of an officer. And he sprang upon him, his sword raised high to bring it down upon his shoulder at the point where arm and trunk were joined. In those few seconds he saw fear in that other human face and the mouth open in a soundless yell, and then it changed and the yell was a curse of defiance. He saw then that the arm was already hanging useless from another wound. As his sword came down, shearing through cloth and flesh and bone, the wounded man fired a pistol point-blank at his chest. For a moment he faltered; there was a searing pain in his side and then he drew back the sword and, aiming it at the man's body, threw his weight upon it. Murdoch found him, leaning on his weapon above a dead officer, armless and skewered into the ground for a depth of six inches. It was all over. Everywhere James looked through the remnants of mist, mutilated and dead men were lying over the moor; the axes and scythepoles had done terrible damage. Almost all the wounds were hacked-off limbs or heads, and the place was full of clansmen standing up, panting with excitement and exhaustion while the dead and wounded Englishmen lay at their feet. The rest had fled. Prince Charles had won his first battle at Prestonpans in exactly seven minutes.

"Ye're wounded!" Murdoch exclaimed. "Hold to me now, hold fast. . . ."

James's coat was soaked with blood and the weight of his buckler on his left arm hurt him intolerably. "That swine shot at me," he mumbled. "Pull out my sword, Murdoch. I'll lean on it."

"Ye'll lean on me," the clansman insisted. "Ye've no' been wounded badly, sir, there's nothing missing. . . . Ach, what a bonny morning this has been! I saw you going through them like a reaper! What a bonny morning!"

As he supported his chief's son back through the heaps of dead and injured men, he threw back his head and began to sing a wild triumphant lay of the glories of his clan and its great chiefs in the old battles of the past.

The victorious Scots pursued and captured what was left of the fleeing enemy, and the Prince showed yet another engaging side to his character by personally attending some of the wounded and sending to Edinburgh for surgeons to care for the casualties on both sides, for the English medical officers had followed hard on the retreating figure of Sir John Cope. James lay under an improvised tent, cared for by Murdoch and his brother David. Hugh had gone so far after the flying enemy that he had not returned to the field eight hours after the battle was over.

The wound did not seem to be a serious one; the dying man's hand had been aimed at James's heart but he had wavered and the shot went in high above the chest, almost in the shoulder. But he had lost a lot of blood and in the middle of a violent argument with his brother David, who would insist that he was injured, James fainted, and after that he was at Murdoch's mercy until one of the Prince's surgeons came to see him. There were a score of wounded lying under the canvas with him; most of them were English, many suffering terribly and without hope of recovery. James raised himself on one elbow as a Highlander passed him and began feeding drops of water to an English soldier.

"There are good Scotsmen thirsty here," James called out. "Don't waste your water on dogs who wouldn't give you a drop if you were in their place. Bring it here, man! Give it to your own!"

The man looked over his shoulder; his face was quite impassive, with nothing showing but his native courtesy, bland and impenetrable as steel. He recognised the wounded officer; everyone had heard of the Macdonald of Dundrenan and he had personally seen him in the battle. It was an awesome sight, but a pity he spoiled his bravery with cruelty to the beaten foe. The Prince had ordered mercy, and mercy the captives were going to get. Had he told his men to cut their throats, there would not have been one man left alive by midday. He supported the dying boy's head on his arm and tipped a little more water into his mouth.

"Did you hear me, damn you!"

"I did, sir, but I've orders from the Prince."

There was an ugly choking sound and the water came back red with blood; the boy's head fell sideways. He had received a dirk thrust down the belly which had laid him open. He was dead, and the Highlander put him back on the ground and came over to James with a bow. "Ye can have the rest of the water now. The laddie's dead."

James stared into the disapproving face above him; the man wore the seaweed badge of the MacNeils in his bonnet.

The Prince had ordered mercy. To hell with the Prince, to hell with playing at war and cutting men to pieces only to waste time caring for them afterwards.

"Next time there'll be no prisoners taken by the Macdonalds. Water for the dying! You damned fool. Take it to that poor devil over there!" He pointed to an injured man whose chest was roughly bandaged, his head pillowed on a bloody plaid, its pattern common to many of Lochiel's Camerons. The MacNeil went over as he was told without looking back at James. He left the tent to tell his fellow clansmen, and anyone else who would listen to him, that the Macdonalds of Dundrenan had sworn to take no prisoners in the future. The Macdonald was certainly a bonny fighter, but he was a man of blood. He, the speaker, did not envy the clansmen under his command. These men smelt of death and death travelled with them like a shadow. He made the sign of the cross and many others did the same. In the tent, David ran out anxiously to seek a surgeon, for James was unconscious again and neither he nor Murdoch could stanch a sudden flow of blood.

"There have been some casualties. That's all he said, Annie, some casualties."

Sir Andrew Maclean had called at Clandara that day, fresh from a stay at the capital; he described the rapturous reception given to the victorious Prince on his return and the amazing victory won over the English troops at Prestonpans. Seven minutes and they were flying for their lives. . . . And most of it done by the Maconalds and the Camerons. Katherine had felt the colour leaving her face; she had been listening politely, caring little whether or not fickle Edinburgh were making much of the occupying power, until their guest began his description of the battle, and she suddenly saw the lines of men advancing, and the men were Macdonalds and the tallest leading them was James . . . James going into battle with her curse of death upon him. She remained silent while her father and Henry talked with Maclean, and then excused herself and slipped out of the room. And then she shut and locked her door and fell on her knees and began to pray that,

much as she hated him, much as he deserved a slow and ago-
nising death, he had been spared this time. She was roused by
Annie's knocking.

"Milady, what was the matter with ye? Locking the door
like that!"

"I didn't want to be disturbed. Get me some water, Annie.
I feel faint."

Annie saw the pale and drawn face and the eyes wet with
tears and, tightening her lips, she went and brought a pitcher
of cold drinking water and filled a basin and scented it. Then
she made her mistress sit while she unlaced her bodice and
bathed her face, and gave her a cup of cool water to sip.

"There's been a battle," Katherine said at last. "Sir Andrew
Maclean brought us news."

Annie did not look at her. "Is he dead, or only wounded?"
she asked abruptly.

"I don't know," Katherine whispered. "Sir Andrew said the
Macdonalds and the Camerons did most of the fighting and
there were some casualties."

"But he didn't mention *him?*" Annie asked. "How do you
know it was those Macdonalds? It could have been any of the
clan."

"He spoke of Sir Alexander Macdonald," Katherine said.
"Then I knew it was them. Oh, my God, my God, I don't
even know what's happened to him!"

"Nothing at all, I should say," Annie retorted. "He's not
the kind that gets himself killed easily. He's making merry in
Edinburgh."

"I don't think so," Katherine whispered. "I feel in my heart
that something's happened to him. Oh, Annie, if I only knew,
it wouldn't be so bad! But every battle, every skirmish . . ."

"Ye'd have done better to go with him when he came here
that night," Annie said at last. "Ye loved him always and ye
do still . . . God pity you. He's a scoundrel and a murderer
and he's laid your whole life waste. Whatever you say to me,
I wish him dead a hundred times over! Perhaps then ye could
think of that good and gentle man who loves ye, and forget
this villain."

"Annie, I asked you once if you had ever been in love. Do you remember? You said no, and you were very scornful. . . . Now I'll ask you something else. Do you care for me at all?"

She gazed into the plain, anxious face and saw the answer in the painful blush that covered it from forehead to neck and the bright little brown eyes growing dim with emotion.

"I care for you more than anything in the world, milady. And I know what ye're going to ask me."

"Find out where he is, and if he's safe," Katherine begged her. "That's all I want—just tell me whether he's alive or not."

"How?" Annie asked her. "Why can't ye ask Sir Andrew Maclean?"

"I daren't," Katherine said. "He knows I was betrothed to him. I cannot possibly betray any interest in him. And if he gave me bad news, God knows how I'd betray myself! Oh, Annie, what can I do? Can't you talk to his servants, find out from them?"

"I can try," she said. "But if nobody knows anything . . . what then?"

"Then," Katherine said quietly, "you must go to Edinburgh and see what you can find out there."

"That's what I thought ye'd ask," Annie said sadly. "And I knew I'd be fool enough to agree to it, instead of telling your father what ye were about!"

"Try Maclean's men first," Katherine urged her. "Please, Annie, leave the water and let me fasten my own bodice; I'm quite all right now . . . all I want is news. I don't know how I can go down to dinner and face them all and see Mr. Ogilvie watching me. . . . I knew he was watching me this afternoon. Go down now and see what you can find out and then come back quickly and tell me!"

"When I've tidied ye," Annie said firmly. "and made you look as ye should with guests in the house. And not one minute sooner!"

And then when she was gone, Katherine began to pace up and down the room, listening for Annie's steps returning, listening also for the heavier tread of Henry, who she feared might come upstairs to seek her out. He had postponed his trip to Inverness; neither she nor her father was anxious that he should leave them. The Earl depended upon him, asked his advice, and talked to him about the affairs of Clandara as if he were his son, and slowly Katherine warmed towards him. She, too, depended and he gave all she asked, without demanding anything of her. And as the days had become weeks, some of her turbulent sorrow died and she grew calmer. Until this afternoon, when the cheerful old neighbour of theirs was describing the three weeks' old battle and there was James in her mind's eye again, and suddenly Henry became a ghost and everything unreal except the torture of not knowing whether or not James was safe.

"Annie!" She ran forward and caught the girl by the shoulders. "What did they say?"

"Nothing." Annie shook her head. "They knew nothing of the Macdonalds, father or sons, except that they were in the forefront of the battle. But our people lost little more than a hundred in all, so it's unlikely, most unlikely, that *he* was one of them. They said some of the worst wounded were taken back by litter to Edinburgh, but there's very few of them, mostly being cared for in private houses and enjoying themselves mightily."

"Then you had better go there and find out," Katherine said. "Annie, I'm going to send you on a shopping expedition. I need some new stuffs for gowns and some shoes and some patterns in the latest style. My father won't suspect anything. You can go tomorrow."

"Ach, God help me, I suppose I can." Annie managed to scowl; if she had any sense, she said indignantly to herself, she'd refuse right off now, while she had the chance. But no, no, she'd go on her traitor's errand and hunt round for that devil and his kin, and all she could hope for was the news that he was dead and buried in the mire at Prestonpans. If she came back with that intelligence, the journey and the risks of discovery by the Earl or Mr. Ogilvie would be well worth it.

"I'll collect some things," she said. "And I'll take Grandfather with me, if that's convenient to ye, milady."

"Take anyone you like." Katherine suddenly embraced her. "You're a dear, good girl, Annie, and I don't know what would become of me without you. If you go to Edinburgh for me, I shan't forget it, ever."

"Then put it out of your head for tonight," Annie said sharply. "One sign of anxiety and Mr. Ogilvie will suspect something. There'll be no trip to Edinburgh for me if he does, and if your father found out I were going on such an errand for ye, he'd have me hanged."

"He would," Katherine agreed. "But he won't know. I promise. No one shall suspect anything by me. And now I must go down. Thank you, Annie, and God bless you."

And that evening, as they sat at the long polished table in the Great Hall, she laughed and talked and displayed a fair imitation of her old sparkling self, until the Maclean was beaming and leaning across the table to her, and Henry watched her with a look of tenderness and joy, imagining that her gaiety, and the brightness in her eyes, was directed especially at him. And so it was. At him and at her father, and she acted so well that he came on her alone in the Green Salon after dinner, and hurried her into the garden where he made his request, very humbly, that he might kiss her. Unlike James, he was gentle; his fire was carefully controlled. There was no movement that might hurt her, no intimacy attempted which could offend her, and she stood with her arms at her sides while he embraced her and kissed her cold lips, and felt as if she were dead. When he stepped back, Henry looked down at her and shook his head, and she felt suddenly ashamed at having tried to cheat him.

"It was too soon," he said. "I'm sorry, my dearest."

"Please don't be sorry," she begged him. "I told you I didn't think that I could bear it yet. Tonight proved one thing to me, at least." She hesitated; in her soul she was bargaining, bargaining desperately with her own conscience and with God. I ask nothing for myself, the frantic cry went on, I ask only for him, that he is safe . . . and if You'll grant me that, I'll put all thought of him away, all lust and vengeance and

my poor misspent love, and marry this good man and be a
comfort to my father if only you will keep James safe. . . .

"What does it prove?" Henry asked her gently.

"It proves that all is not as lost as I imagined," she said
slowly. "Next time you touch me, Henry, I shall show you
what I mean. Now let's go in."

Chapter 5

THE STREETS of Edinburgh were so crowded that Annie and Angus had to push their way through. Above their heads the narrow houses leaned and almost met, shutting out the sky, and it was made darker still by the bright cloths and tapestries which were strung from window to window. The city was *en fête* for the Prince and his victorious army, and as Annie struggled after her grandfather she brushed against the soldiers of that army, Highlanders from every quarter of the kingdom, and it was one of these who nearly knocked her down. The Prince had given orders that the citizens were not to be annoyed; the penalties for molesting women or robbing or brawling were severe, and in spite of his charm, Charles knew how to enforce discipline. The Highlander stepped back with an apology. Seeing the sett of the Macdonalds in his plaid which she had come to know so well, Annie bit back her angry retort and managed to smile. Her grandfather was too far ahead to hear anything and the noise of carts rumbling and creaking down the cobbled streets was so loud that she had to shout to make herself heard.

"Can you help me?" she said. "I'm looking for James Macdonald of Dundrenan. Where will I find him?"

"At the house of a Mrs. Douglas in King Street. He's been sorely wounded. But the chief himself is at Holyrood Palace with the Prince if ye need him."

"I thank ye," Annie answered. "I'll go to King Street." She hurried past him and caught up with Angus.

"This is the devil of a place," the old man grumbled. "Pushing and shoving like a drove of cattle ... where's the place for her ladyship's silks? My feet are sore from these cobbles and I'm awful dry and weary!"

"At the end here," Annie snapped. "I told ye there was no need for ye to leave the lodgings, I could have found my way without ye!"

"Ye'll not go abroad in this place alone," the old man said. "God knows what harm might come to ye.... Ach, mind your way there, damn ye." He turned to shout at a carter whose horse was so close against them that it made him stumble. Angus had never stopped complaining throughout the journey. It was only his second trip outside his glen in all his seventy years and he considered the sprawling city a place of danger and perdition. The traffic and the noise upset him, and every stranger, including those who lodged in the respectable little house at the west end of the Mile, appeared as robbers or rogues with designs on Annie's virtue. When they reached the silk merchant's, he sat down on a stool with a groan and closed his eyes.

Annie announced herself as the maid of the Lady Katherine Fraser of Clandara, and the merchant himself came forward to serve her. Two apprentices brought out the bolts of silk and opened them on the counter.

"Her ladyship needs some white and silver cloth for a gown, and some blue taffeta, pale blue, not that dark colour. And some red velvets."

"This is a very fine specimen, beautifully embroidered and just come in from Lyons," the merchant said. He had supplied the lady of Clandara before and she was a good customer. "But of course if you think she'd be taken with it, I've a special weave which hasn't been shown to anyone yet. Magnificent, you see, but not cheap ... shall I have it brought out?"

"If it's the best, bring it," Annie said. "And don't think I don't know the price of good material. If ye're overcharging, I shall know it, man, and her ladyship won't buy."

The cloth which was brought out from the inner storeroom and unwound for her was so beautiful that even Annie's critical sense was satisfied.

"Pale yellow silk, and every thread of that embroidery is pure gold," the merchant said. "If ye don't take it now, there won't be a yard left by the week's end. Every lady in Edinburgh is ordering a new dress for the Prince's ball at the end of the month. Is your lady coming?"

"Her ladyship is not a Jacobite," Annie snapped. She fingered the material. Mrs. Douglas at King Street ... She glanced up into the man's expectant face and shrugged. "You're sure none of this has been sold to anyone else?"

"You can see for yourself, the bolt is uncut," he answered.

"Mr. Dugal," Annie said after a moment, "before ye tell me the price of this and I tell ye it's too much, can you satisfy my curiosity?"

The merchant smiled. "I can try. I know most of what goes on in Edinburgh. What do you want to know?"

"Do you know anything of a Mrs. Douglas who lives in King Street?"

Dugal hesitated, but he had a shrewd instinct which had done as much towards furthering his business as the excellence of his wares. That instinct told him that the sale of the fabulously expensive material depended on what he told the sharp-faced little servant.

"Mrs. Douglas is a good customer here," he said. "She's lived in Perth for the last year or so, but she's reopened her house in King Street now. She's a widow and a very rich one."

"I hear she's turned her house into a hospital for the wounded from Prestonpans," Annie remarked.

Dugal grinned. He leant over the counter towards her. "A hospital for one," he murmured. "There's the son of one of the Prince's chieftains staying there now—has been since the battle. I heard she followed him from Perth. He was near death when they brought him back. Her maid was here a few days ago, ordering for the ball I told ye about, and she said his life was despaired of for a week or more. He's comfortably set up there, I can tell you. Mrs. Douglas has spared nothing on him. 'Tis said she nursed him night and day herself."

"Thanks." Annie returned to the cloth once more. He was not dead, and the mysterious Mrs. Douglas was his mistress. Her lips tightened angrily; so much for his love for the Lady Katherine. Had he appeared before her at that moment, Annie would have cheerfully spat in his face.

"Annie!" Angus had woken up and he called over to her. "Are ye no' finished yet?"

"No," Annie snapped. "How much is this? And no robbery, mind you!"

"A guinea a yard," Dugal said. "And there's twenty yards there; enough for a fine ball gown."

"I'll take it. And fifteen yards of that white silk, and the same of the pale blue taffeta. The velvets can wait for another time. I've overspent with that yellow stuff, and I dare say my mistress will think I've been cheated. Deliver it to my lodgings this evening, and give me the bill for her ladyship."

She gave the merchant their address in the city and then, followed by Angus, went once more into the street. To the old man's annoyance she insisted on taking a circuitous route back to their lodgings, and the way took them down King Street where a passer-by pointed out a large stone-built house as the residence of Mrs. Douglas. Dugal was right when he said she was rich; Annie thought bitterly that it must be one of the finest houses in Edinburgh, with its large windows and carved oak door.

"What are ye staring at?" her grandfather grumbled. "Have ye never seen a house before? Come on, girl, for God's sake. . . ."

He was too tired to wonder why Annie did not answer back, or why she was unusually silent for the rest of the walk. But the next time she saw a Macdonald walking past them in the street she turned aside and spat into the road.

"I must say, you've taken very good care of him, Janet." Hugh Macdonald raised his glass to her and finished his wine. They were sitting in Janet's withdrawing room in the big house past which Annie had walked only a few minutes before. It was a pleasant room, with a high, plastered ceiling and handsome furniture. Janet was as elegantly dressed as usual, but to Hugh's intensely critical eye, red did not suit her, and it accentuated the lines of tiredness and the lack of colour in her face. She had nursed James without sleep or respite for a week, while his life hung by a hair and the fever from the infected wound rose to the point of crisis. By that week's end she looked an old woman, and though he was safe now and allowed out of bed, she had not quite recovered.

"I thought he was going to die," she said. "There was a time when the fever was highest that I was sure of it. And he wouldn't fight." She turned round and faced Hugh. "He lay there and gave in. I nearly went out of my mind watching him. He was delirious too, and he kept talking and muttering." She went over to the table and poured some wine for herself. Hugh saw that her hand was shaking.

"Do you know what changed it? Not my nursing. Oh no, my dear sir, never think that! He called her name when he was wandering, over and over like a lost man crying out, and do you know what I did?"

"No," Hugh said very quietly. "What did you do?"

"I took hold of his hand and said, 'I am here, James,' and immediately he sighed and held onto it, and from then he fought his fever and grew better." She swallowed the wine and leant back in her chair, her eyes closed, her face plain and drawn until she looked almost ugly.

"I didn't know you knew about it," Hugh said at last. "How did it feel to pretend to be her? I wonder you were able to. . . . But women have such unexpected depths."

"Women in love will do anything," she said bitterly. "And God knows how much I love him! Tell me something—did you know her? What was she like?"

"In all the years from our boyhood upwards," Hugh answered, "I thought I knew my brother. I thought I knew him until he met that woman. But you asked me what she was like. Very beautiful. Red hair, blue eyes . . . beauty, yes, beyond a man's imaginings, but as I tried to tell him once, all-cats are grey in the dark and all women the same in the end. . . . I remember he nearly knocked me down for saying it. I can see I've upset you by saying she was beautiful . . ."

"He told me," she said. "That's all I know. At least I know the colour of her hair and eyes. Go on, Hugh, you can't hurt me. Nothing hurts as much as ignorance now."

"She needed a damned good thrashing," he said at last, and his pale eyes were very narrow. "I thought that from the moment I first saw her. Too much of a mind and a will of her own. Spoilt and determined and falsehearted like all her breed." He leant forward towards her. "How much else do you know, Janet?"

"Nothing, except that they were going to be married."

"And so they were," he nodded. "Against our wishes and the wishes of her family. They defied everyone, both of them, and in the end both sides gave in like the fools they were. To make it short, Janet, her brother refused his help to the Prince and on a point of honour we had to kill him. At least I killed him, because James wouldn't. And they strangled his messenger and sent an impeachment to the courts charging us with murder. And she cast off James without even listening to his explanation. Just because of her brother!" He laughed suddenly, and it was the most unpleasant sound that Janet Douglas had ever heard.

"If I ever get my hands on her," he said softly, "I'll kill her. I owe that to my brother for all he's suffered."

"At least now I know what I have to fight," she said. "And believe me, I am going to fight her."

"I know you are." Hugh laughed again. "You're a determined female, aren't you? But you're what James needs, if he's not to end up dead or out of his mind. I had an uncle once who went mad. He was very like James. Mad with fighting and whisky, and he had to be shut up with two strong men to keep him quiet. Perhaps it's in the blood. Who knows? Who cares?" He yawned and stretched out to refill his glass.

"You care," she challenged him. "I don't pretend to understand you but I know you care for James."

He watched her for a moment over the rim of the glass and, as their eyes met, hers did not turn away. She stared him out until he began to smile his usual twisted, mocking smile.

"I do believe you're not afraid of me," he said.

"Then you're wrong," Janet answered. "Because I am. But that doesn't mean I won't look you in the eye. Besides, we're allies, you and I. We both love James."

"Love is a word I've never understood," Hugh said. "But I suppose that what affection I am capable of feeling is taken up by that fool of a brother of mine. I admired him so much when we were boys; he was always so damned brave and so bold and he cared not a damn for God or man . . . and now he lies back ready to die of some stinking bullet wound and only the name of that cursed woman brings him back to life. As I said, if I ever get the chance, I'll kill her. And now"—he rose and, going to Janet, took her hand—"my dear hostess, I must pay my respects to my brother upstairs and then be gone. I have an appointment for this evening. A charming, innocent, immensely wealthy child who is infatuated with me. If her dowry is big enough I will probably marry her."

"She has my sympathy," Janet said dryly.

"My dear Janet." He paused in the door. "Don't you think she has mine? Farewell. Take good care of my brother." And he laughed again and shut the door behind him.

Later that evening, a tray with two places on it was brought upstairs to the big bedroom where James had lain for over three weeks. He had come very close to death, so close that he could remember very little since his wound began to hemorrhage in the tent at Prestonpans; the journey back to Edinburgh in rough carts filled with wounded was a confusion of pain and fever and lapses into unconsciousness. He could remember the incredible luxury of Janet's bed and the coolness of the sheets, and hushed voices in the room, but the recollection was so blurred and the impressions of people and time dissolved so quickly into each other that he had given up trying to discover where he was and abandoned himself to a sickness which was as much in his soul as in the festering infected wound.

He had been aware of death and for the first time in his life he felt the sweet temptation that beckons the dying to surrender and have done with pain and struggle. And in the haze of fever and pain he had forgotten himself and cried out for the only solace his empty heart desired in those last moments. "Katherine! Katherine!" And he thought he saw her coming to him, and a hand took his and a voice said: "I am here . . ." and then, suddenly at peace and happy, convinced in his delirium that she was with him, he found the will to live. And when he woke, the fever was low and it was Janet he saw bending over him, her tired face wet with tears. That was the only time that he had ever seen her cry, and now she was herself again; calm and efficient and tactful. When he didn't want her, and he said so brutally, she left him without reproach, returning later with something he needed, always smiling and indulgent, as if his angry moods and sullen ingratitude were the whims of a sick child. And in spite of himself he was grateful because he knew that she had saved his life, and more grateful still because she never spoke of it or asked for thanks. And he had begun to sense that the hand which had transmitted hope to him and the voice which called him back to life were hers. But it was never mentioned, and for that too he thanked her secretly.

They dined together most evenings, and the doctor she engaged said he could go downstairs and later dress and walk about a little. By the end of the month he would be well enough to return to his duties with the Prince. Charles himself had been to see him once; it was a signal honour which caused much jealousy among the stronger clans who had also suffered dead and wounded, but it bound James to him as he had never been bound before. And it made Janet Douglas love him. Whatever those close to him said, accusing him of recklessness and pride and vanity, Charles did not share his family's failing of forgetting those who served them in adversity.

"I hope Hugh didn't tire you," she said. "I've brought some peaches; they've ripened beautifully this summer. Let me peel one for you."

"I've had enough," he said. "You've hardly eaten anything, and you look tired. I shan't be lying here much longer. I told that old fool if he didn't let me up, I'd get up and walk back to Holyrood myself!"

"Don't be so impatient." Janet cleared the tray away and rang for the maid who looked after James. "If you reopen that shoulder, you'll be lying here for weeks, and heaven knows how I should bear it!"

"Heaven knows how you bear it now," he said. "But I must remind you that I didn't ask to be brought here ... there must be other houses in Edinburgh besides yours. . . ."

"I know you're better, because you want to quarrel," she said calmly. "But you're not quite well enough to do it yet. In a week's time I'll bicker with you to your heart's content. But if you're going to be angry I'll go downstairs."

"Go where you please," he snarled, suddenly angry with her, but angrier still with himself. "No doubt you've found some lonely gentleman in the Prince's service who needs a companion for the night. Go down and go to hell!"

To his surprise she did not move. Her face went very white, and the bright blue eyes grew dark. He had never seen her angry before and it gave him a feeling of intense relief.

"If you ever say anything like that to me again," she said, "I'll have my servants drag you out of that bed and throw you into the street. And since you mention it, I do need a companion, so let's hope you pay me that much back as soon as possible."

He lay back on the pillow and laughed. "I'll pay for it now, rather than be one moment more in your debt! Come here, my ministering whore, and let me show you whether I'm recovered yet or not!" He caught her arm and when she pulled away from him he winced and swore. Immediately she stopped, leaving her arm in his grip, and at the sight of his face twisted with pain, she leant down and kissed him on the lips. His other arm came up and held her; she could see that his wound hurt him, but nothing would persuade him to release her or admit to his own weakness. His mouth came down upon hers and he kissed her fiercely, and she abandoned herself to it, hungry and trembling, until at last he let her go and fell back, white and sick with the effort.

She leant over him and smoothed the lank dark hair from his forehead. When he opened his eyes she smiled at him, and her face was soft and beautiful with tenderness.

"If you were sick to death you'd be worth twenty men in their full health," she whispered. "It's no good, James; there'll never be another man except yourself. I beg of you, don't taunt me with that any more. But even if you do, I shall forgive you. If you spat in my face I should still love you. I always will."

It was the first time that she had ever said it to him, and when he did not answer, she turned to go. But as she did so, he caught her hand and held it.

"Stay with me." The voice was so low she could hardly hear it. "Stay with me as you did that night." And turning his head away from her, James wept.

"Near to death," Katherine whispered. "I knew it, Annie. I told you I knew something had happened to him. . . ."

"That was a month ago," Annie said sharply. They were alone in Katherine's bedroom at Clandara, and nothing she had said about the mysterious Mrs. Douglas had affected her mistress like the repetition of the merchant's words. "He was brought back near to death. . . ."

"He's fully recovered," Annie said again. "I've told you so a dozen times, milady. I don't know why you're sitting there with your face as white as your gown, when there's nothing wrong with the villain!"

Katherine looked up at her; she was indeed pale, and her eyes were swimming with tears. "How do you know?" she demanded. "How do you know he's all right when you don't even know the nature of his wounds? He isn't dead, that's all! He may have lost an arm or a leg . . . he might even be blinded. Oh, merciful God, why didn't I go myself!" And she covered her face with her trembling hands and began to weep.

Annie looked at her in mixed exasperation and distress. The exasperation won. "Well, that's fine gratitude, I must say! There's a great fool I was, risking my very neck to go on your errand, and all ye say is ye wish ye'd gone yourself! And so do I wish it, milady, so do I!"

"Oh, don't be so foolish, Annie. Of course I'm grateful . . .

but don't you see that this is worse than before? Knowing him wounded, nearly dead, and not knowning how or whether he will have to fight again ... Annie!" She got up suddenly. "Annie, it's no use, I'm going to Edinburgh!"

"Mother of Jesus!" The oath escaped Annie before she could help herself. She stared at Katherine as if she were mad. "Go to Edinburgh! And for what, may I ask ... to find him? Oh, milady, I think ye're out of your head. . . ."

"Perhaps, perhaps I am." Katherine went to the wall mirror and wiped her face; it stared back at her, drawn and desperate, the face of the woman who had cursed James and sent him away with words of the most remorseless hate. She should have been glad; she should have been full of vengeful feelings, but instead her heart was aching with anxiety and there was nothing left with which to pretend to herself that she did not love him still.

She did not move from the mirror but spoke aloud in front of it, watching herself. "Oh, my God, what a fool I've been. That's all I want, just to see him and tell him, and then go away and forget him forever. . . ."

"Ye'll never do that," Annie said bitterly. "Look well at what you see there; look at the dark shadows and the lines from crying and worrying. . . . What are ye doing to your beauty, and all for the sake of a man who's hardly lost you than he's bedded down with someone else! Have ye no pride, milady ... how much did he love you that he could find this widow so quickly? Dugal said she followed him from Perth."

Katherine shrugged. "I don't care who he's found," she said. "I don't care about anything except knowing he's whole and strong again. And I'm going to find out." She turned and mocked the anxious woman who stood watching her. "You'd be happy to see me married to Mr. Ogilvie, wouldn't you, Annie? Kind, safe Mr. Ogilvie ... well, you never will unless I see James Macdonald once more."

"And your father," Annie muttered. "What of him ... what will he say to this?"

"He won't know," she answered. "Edinburgh is a large city. There are hundreds there seeking the Prince's audience.

When I go there I shall go with Mr. Ogilvie and Father can't object to that. In fact"—she began to touch her hair and straighten the neck of her white dress—"I know he'll welcome it. He's as fond of the match between Henry and myself as all the rest of you."

"Go if ye must," Annie said at last. "But if ye do find him, no good will come of it." She turned her back on Katherine and went into the clothes closet. The two women did not speak again while Katherine dressed for dinner. And that night it was she who suggested to Henry that they wait on in the Green Salon after her father had retired.

"My beloved, am I hurting you?"

"No, no, you're not hurting me at all. . . ."

Katherine drew his head down and shut her eyes and let him kiss her over and over again, and she linked her hands behind his neck and waited for the response which she knew would not come. His hands were firm and they trembled as they touched her, but the touch meant nothing. Her body was stiff and lifeless; she felt the discomfort of his urgent kisses and the strain of his embrace and endured them in horrible calm. There was nothing in her experience to prepare her for the travesty of love in which the object of it was a cold spectator. She pitied Henry so much in those moments when he murmured his longing for her that she could only nod and urge him on to kiss her because she could not bring herself to tell the final lie.

It seemed impossible that she had once held another man and returned every caress until her passions threatened to swamp her self-control completely. And more impossible still that she had only to think of him for those same sensations to return. At last she could bear it no longer. She drew away and asked Henry to compose himself and give her time to do the same.

His handsome face was flushed and happy.

"Oh, Katherine, if you only knew how I have longed to do that . . . for all these weeks it's been a torment to me!"

"It needn't be again," she said gently. "Dear Henry, I'm not worthy of you, not worthy in the least." And this she meant with all her heart. But she went on for the same reason as she had submitted to his love-making.

"I've kept my promise to you in the garden, haven't I? I told you all is not lost."

He turned to her, so painfully eager that he stammered like a boy. "Do you mean that you love me . . . Katherine?"

"Be patient," she said gently. "Please be patient. Remember what I've suffered. Don't ask me to love you yet."

"I know." He bent and kissed both her hands. "I'm selfish and thoughtless. Forgive me, my dear heart. I won't try to hurry you."

She got up and began to walk up and down. "It's this house," she said. "It's so full of memories of the past. Robert's death and my betrothal . . . everywhere I turn I see reminders. Henry, if only we could go away!"

He stared at her in surprise. "Away? But where, my darling? I can only offer to marry you immediately and take you back with me to Spey House . . ."

"No," she said quickly, "no, that's not what I want. Not yet," she amended. "Henry, I'd like to go to Edinburgh! Annie has told me it's full of people and there's so much excitement with the Prince there. You were going to see him anyway! Why not take me too, just for a visit? Father won't refuse, he'll be delighted. . . . Annie says there's a ball at Holyrood at the end of this month—we could go to it and present ourselves."

"Katherine, Katherine, wait a moment," he protested. "Why do you want to go to Holyrood? Your father won't allow it, you know that."

"Oh yes, he will, if you ask him." She came back and sat beside him, and gave him her hand. "Please take me; it's the one thing in the world I really want to do. Take me to Edinburgh. I'll have a new gown made and we'll go to Holyrood and see the Prince. After all, if you're going to fight for him, I ought to see him too. . . ." He was unable to resist her, and he believed that the gloomy atmosphere of Clandara was a powerful factor in her attitude towards him. Without reminders, in a city where life was full of excitement and expectancy, he would have a chance to awaken her love as well as her gratitude. He had been swept away by the power of his own passion, but a few moments of reflection afterwards had shown him that Katherine's submission was not the same as her response. She did not love him and he knew it. But she would, either before marriage or after it. He did not care which came first.

"We will go then," he said gently. "I'll ask your father."

She looked at him and on an impulse reached forward and kissed him. "Dear Henry. Thank you."

"No thanks are needed," he said quietly. "I only want to make you happy."

"They're going to Edinburgh tomorrow," Jean Macdonald said. "I heard that maid of hers talking to the steward about it. She's going with them."

The Countess was sewing by the window, making the most of the fading autumn light. When it grew dark she sat alone with Jean, sometimes talking but more often in silence, for her eyes hurt her and she was unable to embroider by candlelight without incurring violent headaches. The Earl had kept his promise to Katherine. He had not come to his wife's room again. The marks he had left on her face and body had disappeared. The bruises had faded but the mark on her mind was a permanent one. She no longer dreamed of him and woke shrieking until Jean ran in and calmed her, but she sat for hours without speaking, and often there was a vacant look in her pale eyes which frightened the young girl. Her mistress was a little turned; she was apt to sit there smiling at nothing, and when the maid asked her what was amusing her, she only shook her head and did not answer. But the smile was full of meaning; it flickered across her colourless lips as pictures flickered through her mind, pictures of death and torture, fire and disaster in which the Earl and his daughter struggled and shrieked in helpless agony.

She raised her head and stared at Jean, frowning a little. "Who's going to Edinburgh, did you say?"

"*She* is," Jean repeated. "And this Mr. Ogilvie who's been staying here. Tomorrow; I told you, milady."

"Ah, so you did. Mr. Ogilvie . . . I seem to remember him. He used to visit here. A very quiet and pleasant gentleman with as much spirit in him as a sheep. He was her suitor too, now I recall. . . . How James would laugh if he could see them. I expect she's going to marry him."

And the Countess' face grew dark and her lips twisted angrily. "James never had her," she went on under her breath as if she were speaking to herself. "He was a fool; I know he had the opportunity and she wouldn't have refused him. I remember seeing them come in from the Ladies' Walk after that ball, and her face was so full of concupiscence it made me sick. Quite sick. Henry Ogilvie won't satisfy her the way my cousin James would have done. He is so big and strong, Jean, so much a man. . . . When I was a girl I used to shut my eyes and dream of him and imagine . . . oh, you've no idea what I used to imagine," and she laughed.

The maid looked away in embarrassment, her cheeks scarlet. The Countess sometimes rambled on like this, her talk full of sly sexual allusions. And then she would suddenly go into her bedroom and shut the door and Jean would hear her weeping.

"I thought perhaps we might get a message to Sir Alexander," Jean mumbled.

"What message? Come and release us, leave the Prince and your commitments and come, rescue poor ugly Margaret and her little maid from the hands of Clandara. . . . Don't be so foolish. The Macdonalds would do nothing for us now. Now is not the time," she said, suddenly incisive and so clear in speech and manner that she seemed a different woman. "I shall know when to send for them, and then they'll come."

"But when she's gone, do ye think ye'll be safe here with him?" Jean whispered. "How do we know he won't get drunk one night when he's alone and bethink himself of you again . . ."

"He won't," the Countess said. "He must have promised her, his darling child. . . . Can't you hear them, Jeannie? 'Don't beat her to death, Father, it's unworthy of you.' 'As you wish, Katherine my child . . .' My God, when I think I owe her anything, I'd rather I was dead!"

"If I only knew how we could escape," the maid said. "Why won't ye let me ask her, milady? She helped us before, she might do it again. Let me send a message to the Macdonalds, they must be with the Prince. How do you know he won't let you go? It affords him no pleasure to keep you here now. Let me try!"

"No," the Countess said sharply. "I forbid you. You're a good girl, but you're a fool. He will never let either of us go. And one day he'll regret it, and so will she, that beautiful red-headed whore with her kind deeds and her eyes all wet with lust for James. Ogilvie indeed!" She laughed again. "But I suppose even a sheep is better than no ram at all. . . . I wonder how beautiful she'd look if she were left to wither away a little? Like me. . . . You're not withered, Jean. Come here! Come here, girl, don't be frightened!" She raised her hand and touched the round pink cheek of the girl standing awkwardly in front of her, her eyes looking at the floor.

"You're young and bonny still," The Countess said. "And here you are, shut up with a dead woman, losing your own youth and all its promise and not a word of complaint. But don't be troubled, Jean. It won't be forever. I'll get you out in time for some good lad to make you happy and give you what you ought to have. I'll not leave you here to grow like me. But you must be patient a little longer. Then we shall have our vengeance. I promised, don't you remember? And after that you will be free. Now, get me that book on the table over there. I want to read awhile; the light is gone for sewing now. Though who knows what use these samplers and covers will ever be to anyone? That's the one. Thank you, my child."

Jean gave her the book and lit the candles in the room, placing one by her mistress' elbow after she had drawn the curtains.

Tomorrow the Lady Katherine and her guest would leave for Edinburgh, and Jean, who had never left her glen until she came to Clandara with the Countess, envied them bitterly. It was easy enough for her mistress to sit in her chair and talk of patience and a revenge which was to come. But Jean was young, and her heart ached for the freedom of her own lands and the company of her own people. She was not troubled by the lack of love or the diminishing prospect of marriage and a croft where she might live and raise her children. And the more she listened to the sad and horrible dredgings of her mistress' mind translated into words, the less she wanted any part of such things. But she wanted her freedom, and she wanted freedom for the Countess while she still had enough sanity left to benefit by it. She busied herself preparing the Countess' supper table and wondered whether she dared defy her orders and approach the Earl's daughter before morning.

"Jean!"

"Yes, milady?" She turned round guiltily as if her mistress had divined what was going through her mind.

The Countess smiled at her. "You are not to go near her, do you understand? Not one word!"

"No, milady." Jean sighed and went back to her work.

"And don't sigh," the Countess called over to her. "I've told you. I shall know when to send for our people." She sat back and began to read her book and Jean finished the table and curtsied before going down to the kitchen to fetch the tray with supper for them both.

She saw Annie in the corridor and slipped quickly past her without a word. Early next morning, at the window, she and the Countess watched Katherine and Henry Ogilvie set off on horseback with their servants for the capital.

The palace of Holyrood was blazing with lights; there were torches flickering along the Mile as a long line of carriages drove up and the guests alighted and went in for the reception and ball the Prince was giving, and the entrance was crowded with people who watched the gentry and nobility and their splendidly dressed ladies. It was in unusual spectacle for the people of Edinburgh; the Palace had been empty for many long years, garrisoned by English troops and occupied by visiting dignitaries from London who did not think fit to entertain the native families in the palace of their ancient kings. Inside, the long dark halls and passages were full of people, all making their way towards the audience chamber and the state reception room, where the ball was being held, and the sound of music drifted out into the night and some of the spectators formed their own reels in the roads and began to dance.

Some of the proudest and most powerful men in Scotland were present there that night, and some of the loveliest women, but when Katherine came up the staircase on Henry Ogilvie's arm, every head turned to stare at her and the whispers followed her as she walked. Mr. Dugal's yellow silk had been made into a magnificent formal ball gown, its skirts held out by wide panniers on either side, the tight bodice cut low and ending in a point below her waist. The gold thread glittered in the lights as she moved, and in her left hand she carried a yellow silk fan with golden sticks. It had taken Annie three hours to dress her and arrange her hair high on her head, with three bright red curls falling over one shoulder, and she wore the pearl and diamond ornament which had once held her wedding veil. Excitement had made her pale, and the faint shade of rouge on each cheek emphasised the startling colour of her eyes.

As they reached the entrance to the audience chamber, Henry paused for a second and whispered to her. "You are the most beautiful woman here tonight; everybody has been staring at you and asking who you are! I'm almost afraid I shall lose you. . . ."

She smiled up at him nervously. "You won't, dear Henry."

"Not even to the Prince?" he murmured.

"Least of all to the Prince."

As they walked into the crowded room and took their places in the line to be received, she began searching among the scores of faces for the one she had come so far to see, but though there were many men as tall as James, and once she started and turned white under her rouge; when the man in a scarlet and green tartan coat turned towards her, she saw that though the build was similar it was not James. At the far end of the long room there was a crimson and gilt throne under a canopy; it was empty and all eyes were watching the door through which the Prince would enter. A woman on her left leant towards her and said: "Have you seen him before? We've travelled fifty miles to get here. I'm so excited I can hardly stand!"

"No," Katherine answered. "No, this will be my first sight of him too."

"They say he's the handsomest man in the world," the lady sighed. "Everyone tells me he could charm the birds from the trees if he wished. My niece has been here since September and nothing would induce her to come home once he returned from Prestonpans." She lowered her voice a little more. "They say he's fond of the ladies," she added. "There's fierce competition among them. My poor little niece is madly enamoured of him herself, but she hasn't a chance, poor child. Such a pity—think what an honour it would be!"

"Yes indeed." Katherine gave her a smile and half turned away. More guests were coming through the doors.

"It might be different with you," the woman continued. "Not many women here tonight can compare with you." She tapped Katherine gently with her fan. "I wish you luck," she whispered.

"Thank you." Katherine touched Henry and he turned to her immediately. "When will he come?" she asked.

"At any moment now. Here is a gentleman usher. He must be coming."

The gentleman in a dress of blue with gold facings raised his tall cane of office with its white and gold ribbon and struck the floor three times.

"My lords, ladies and gentlemen. Pray silence for His Royal Highness the Regent Prince Charles!"

The room was divided into two lines, making a pathway for the Prince to walk between them. The usher stepped aside and through the doorway a tall young man in a coat of silk tartan and white silk smallclothes advanced into the room with the Dukes of Perth and Atholl just behind him, followed by Lord George Murray, Cameron of Lochiel, and half a dozen officers. She was so busy scanning them that she hardly saw the Prince. But none of them was James.

Charles was walking slowly down the line, pausing to go from one to another of the guests; the women curtsied to the ground and the men bowed, and after he had spoken a word or two he nodded and passed on, preceded by the usher, who announced the names of those the Prince wished to meet. To Katherine's surprise he stopped before her, and when her name was called he held out his hand and smiled. She kissed it and curtsied very low.

"I have not seen you here before," Charles said. "You must be a kinswoman of Lord Lovat."

"Yes, I am, Your Highness. A distant kinswoman."

The bright brown eyes gleamed at her. His round small-featured face was not as handsome as she had expected; it was too young and smooth. "I bid you welcome," he said, and the faint foreign lisp was more pronounced. "It seems there is no end to the delights of Scotland and the beauty of her ladies is high among them. I hope you will not leave us too soon."

She curtsied again and he passed on. She was surprised that he did not stop and speak to Henry Ogilvie. When he took his place on the throne, the lines broke up and crowded round that end of the room, everyone hoping to be noticed and calling out to speak to him, and there were angry faces and jealous mutterings among those who had not been personally received.

"It's just as well we're not staying long in Edinburgh," Henry said. "You've already made a hundred enemies among the women here because he singled you out." On an impulse he lifted her hand and kissed it. "I'm very proud tonight," he said. "And the day you are my wife I shall be prouder still."

"He's very young," she said. "He doesn't look much like a Stuart."

"His mother was Polish," Henry answered. "Come, my dearest, shall we go to the ballroom now, or would you like some supper?"

"I'd like to go through the rooms and see the people," she said quickly. "We can sup later."

"As you wish. Follow me; the ballroom is through that doorway there."

She did not want to dance; when he asked her, she only

shook her head, and abandoning all caution, she began to turn and look among the dancing couples, watching for the face of James among the men, and when Henry spoke to her she answered briefly without really listening. He was not in the ballroom, and not among those who had been presented. But more were still arriving, and now the Prince himself had joined them and was dancing with Mrs. Murray of Broughton, the pretty young wife of his secretary, and one of the many ladies who were reputed to be his mistress. There was one chance, Katherine thought desperately, one place where she had not looked and where James might be. The young Duke of Perth came up to her and bowed.

"My compliments, Lady Katherine. It's a long time since we met but I can only say you are more beautiful, if that were possible." They had met once or twice in the past three years, and she had always liked him. He was a delicate man as a result of an accident in his youth, but he was gay and gallant and equally popular with men as well as women. He had a rare spirit of generosity that made him many friends.

"I'm glad to see you," she said. "And glad you recognised me after all this time. I hear you're joint commander of the Prince's army."

"I am." He grinned at her. "And a strange bedfellow I make with Lord George Murray, I can promise you! But if you'll forgive me, I've spent all day bickering round the council table and I'm dying for some entertainment. Mr. Ogilvie, sir, may I claim the lady for this reel?"

"With pleasure." Henry bowed and Perth took her hand and led her into a set.

"He looks sour as the devil," the Duke murmured to her. "Are you engaged to him? I thought there was some talk of a marriage for you, but I forget who the fortunate man was . . ."

"Not Henry," she said quickly. "But it's possible he may be. One day."

"Then he *is* fortunate." Perth smiled at her. "How is your brother Robert? I don't see him here."

The reel ended and she curtsied to him. She could see Henry waiting for her by the door leading to the audience chamber, but he was talking to an elderly couple. She turned quickly to the Duke. "Where is the supper room? I am dying of hunger."

"Through this door and down the passage. Let me escort you. If Mr. Ogilvie won't call me out!"

"No, thank you." Katherine smiled and put her finger to her lips. "I have an appointment with someone there. Just let me slip away."

"Then there are two fortunate fellows," Perth laughed and kissed her hand. "So be it; I am always unlucky!"

She edged her way through the crowd and passed quickly through the doorway and found herself in a long stone corridor. The supper room was at the end and she could see that it was crowded like the ballroom. Two men were walking towards her, one was talking to the other, his head half turned. Only when they were almost face to face did he look up and then she stopped, her fan falling to the floor, and found herself looking into the eyes of Hugh Macdonald.

"Do you like my dress, James?" Janet closed the door and came into the middle of the room. She looked extremely handsome in a gown of pale blue velvet, the bodice and sleeves edged with silver lace, and two rows of large pearls arranged in festoons round her neck.

James looked up at her and nodded. "You look very well. Blue suits you."

She saw to her surprise that he was not yet dressed, though she had sent one of her servants up to help him more than an hour ago. His tartan coat was still on the back of the chair and his peruke stood on its mahogany stand.

"We will be late," she said quietly. They had not quarrelled since that day when he asked her to stay with him. And she had never once referred to it, but her heart was full of hope, and she submitted to his moods and attempts to provoke her with inhuman patience. He was a proud man, and she had seen him in a moment of weakness and seen his tears; it was not likely that he would forgive her for it for a while, until he could forgive himself.

"Shall I help you, James?" she said gently.

He shifted irritably in the chair. His wound was healed

now and he had resumed his duties with the Prince. But the doctor warned him against overtaxing his strength. It was nearly the end of the month and the rumour was that the royal army would begin its march to the south very soon.

"I'm not in any mood for dancing and dandling after you in public," he said. "Why don't you go and leave me here?"

"Oh, James." She came towards him quickly, her disappointment showing on her face. "James, don't say that now. I've been so looking forward to it. . . . I ordered this dress specially and you told me we could go."

"You can go," he pointed out. "I've no objection. You have your dress and there's no reason why you can't go to Holyrood and show yourself off if you've a mind to. But you're not showing me off. I've changed my mind. I'm not going. And you can ring for that damned fool of a servant and tell him to put those clothes away and get me out my ordinary coat and breeches."

"Please." She stood before him, turning her blue feather fan over and over in her hands, struggling not to cry as if she were a small child suddenly denied a treat. "Please, James. I don't want to show you off. I only want you to come with me because I won't enjoy it if you don't."

"And I shan't enjoy it if I do!" He stood up and went to the door and opened it. "You'd better go or you'll be late. Hugh will take care of you; or David. They're both there." He shrugged and spoke less harshly. "Besides, if I see Lord George there tonight, I'll probably knock him down. I've had enough of listening to him blocking every plan that has an element of chance in it. How the hell does he expect to win, without taking a risk now and then? Oh, go on, woman, for God's sake. I'm tired and I'm no fit company for you tonight. Go to Holyrood and enjoy yourself."

"Wouldn't you rather I stayed with you?" she asked him. "I will, if you want me to; the ball means nothing to me without you."

"No." He came up to her, suddenly ashamed of himself, and angry because he was so ashamed. He owed her so much that he could never repay in the way she wanted. He could make love to her again, and he did, but that was not enough. He could not love her, and he could not pretend any longer that she did not love him. He lifted her face and looked at her. "I can't understand how such a clever woman could be such a fool," he said. "Go on to Holyrood, and see if there isn't a man among them there who's worthy of you. And that's not a jibe, I promise you. Anyone in the world would be better for you than me."

"I am the best judge of that." Janet managed to smile up at him, but he saw her eyes were full of tears. "Even when you're cruel to me, I'd sooner have it than another man's kindness. Very well, I'll go. I'll be back before morning ... perhaps I'll see you then?"

"Perhaps. You usually do."

He shut the door behind her and went back into the room; he knocked against the chair and angrily kicked it over. Now that she had gone—he could hear her carriage moving away outside the front door—he was restless and half regretful. There was nothing to do in the empty house; he had no stomach for books and no wish to sleep. He could go down to the drawing room and get drunk, but that prospect only bored him. He had not wanted to go to Holyrood with Janet, and make small talk to the men he saw every day surrounding the Prince, and answer the enquiries about his wound. He did not want to dance reels with Janet or with any of the other women who would be there, all of them with one eye on a place in the Prince's bed. How disappointed they would be to know that the Bonny Prince of their imaginings was much more interested in tactics and winning the war than he was in any woman. He had the pick, and he had taken none.

After a moment James pulled hard on the bell rope, and Janet's servant came running upstairs to answer it. The man knocked and came in, blinking nervously. He was terrified of his mistress' lover; once or twice James had boxed his ears for some omission, and cursed him as often as he spoke to him at all. He was a Lowland Scot, and quite unable to appreciate the regal manners of the Highland gentry to their servants. He would have despised James if shown the intimacy with which he treated Murdoch, and he hated him for the brutality which was the reverse side of that particular relationship. That was the one wish Janet had refused to grant him. She would not allow the Red Murdoch into the house to care for James. Not a girl in her service would be safe, and the men would have left her within the first day.

"My coat," James snarled at him. "And my hat. . . . I'm going out."

Ten minutes later was in the streets and walking as far away from the bright windows of the palace as he could. It was inevitable that he should eventually turn in the direction of the city's brothels, which he knew so well from his student days at the university. He had not been there for a long, long time. He had forgotten the charms displayed by an honest whore; he said that to himself and laughed aloud. In the clear air his head felt hot and heavy as if he had been drinking or the fever had returned. He had been three long weeks in that house, suffocated by its atmosphere, by the clean sheets and the excellent food, and the ministrations of her doctor and her servants and herself. God damn it, he had nearly died there. And when he was better he had taken her into his bed and exhausted himself in the effort to escape his own misery and wipe out the debt he owed her. Too long with an amateur whore, skillful and patient and cursed rich. . . . He saw a familiar doorway, half open to disclose a plump bedraggled girl sitting on a stool with her skirts tucked up above her knees, drinking ale out of a pot and giggling to someone he could not see. He felt in his pocket for his purse; there were two guineas in it. Enough to get drunk and have half a dozen of the miserable women in the street. He pushed the door back and went in.

"Don't tell me," Hugh Macdonald said, "that the Frasers of Clandara have changed their mind and joined their Prince."

The old smile was on his face again, but his eyes were like steel as they looked down into Katherine's; he had recovered his composure within seconds.

When Katherine answered, her voice trembled, and she thought suddenly that if it had been James himself she would have fainted at his feet. "Step aside, please. I have nothing to say to you."

Hugh went on smiling; he said softly to the startled man beside him, one of the principal tacksmen on the Dundrenan lands, "Leave us, Ian. I'll follow you later." Then he put out his hand and caught her arm. His fingers suddenly tightened on it until she winced. "I hope you're not going to escape so quickly," he said. "I never expected such a pleasure . . . Lady Katherine, after all this time. Am I hurting you?" He looked down at her hand. "Is this the one that struck my brother in the face? I ought to break it for you. What are you doing here?"

She faced him defiantly; after the first shock, her courage had returned. "I came to find James. I heard he was wounded. Hugh, for the love of God, tell me how he is!"

"Well!" He regarded her with the same smile, his head on one side in mock amazement. "Am I supposed to believe that you care what has happened to him? How touching! I suppose you hoped he was dead!"

"Would I be here if I did?" she demanded. "If you're not going to answer me, then let me go. If you don't, I'll scream loud enough to make you."

He did not answer her at once, and she could not see anything in the cold inscrutable face to tell her what his thoughts were. "We can't talk here," he said suddenly. "I've come to know this palace well; there's a little anteroom down that passageway at the end of some stairs. Come with me if you want to know how James is. . . ."

Something in his eyes warned her not to go with him; something she had seen long ago at Clandara on the night of the ball when she had surprised him watching her.

"Why can't you tell me here?" she said.

"Because my father and David will come out of the supper room at any moment and it as much as my life is worth to be seen talking to you. What are you afraid of—I always thought you had the spirit of a man. Or is this concern for James a lie?"

"Take me to the anteroom then." She rubbed her wrist; it was aching and there were red marks on it.

She followed him down the narrow passage and they suddenly seemed very far from the noise and the crowds, and at the head of a steep staircase she paused. He held out his hand to her and after a moment she put hers into it. "Such trust," he said gently. "Don't you know if I chose I could throw you down those stairs and you'd probably break your neck?"

Katherine looked at him and shrugged. She felt so exhausted and shaken that he had to catch her firmly and lift her down the first few steps. "Hugh, I have a strong feeling that you are going to kill me. I had it in the corridor and I have it now. But if you will only tell me about James first, you can do what you please. I have no wish to live without him."

He turned on the tiny landing and opened a small door set into the wall. The room was a disused guard room; one small window showed a square of black sky with a few stars shining. It was so dark that she could hardly see the outline of his face as she came close to her.

"Firstly, I killed your miserable brother. I ran him through the back because James had lost half a dozen opportunities of killing him. I wanted you to know this first."

"He told me; I didn't believe him." Her voice was a whisper.

"You should have done; James is no liar. Now I promised to tell you how he is . . . he's safe and well, my dear Katherine. He had a nasty wound, but it's healed up and he's back with the army. And he has a very satisfactory mistress, very rich, very handsome, and quite determined to marry him. Personally, I think she'll succeed; she's a woman of great character. And he's perfectly contented with her. He's quite forgotten you. Have I kept my word and told you all?"

"You have." She closed her eyes. She felt sick and faint and at the same time as if she were in the middle of a nightmare and that the tiny dark room and the man standing so close to her that she could feel his breath, were about to dissolve in the light of day in her own bedroom.

"You made him suffer," he whispered. "He was like a madman for a long time until I found this woman for him and she brought him back to sanity. He came back and .

begged you and you struck him, didn't you ... and cursed him? He told me so. He told me he knelt to you. . . ." Though she could not see him she knew there was no smile now upon his face. "You shouldn't have come here—it may be days before they find you. . . ."

When his hands came up and closed over her throat she gave a little cry and stumbled backwards. Her foot caught against a stool which had been upended in the corner and it fell with a clatter.

"Who's there? Who's on the stairs? ... Answer or we fire!" The shout came up to them and it was followed by a beam of light that swayed with the movement of a lantern.

She saw his face for a moment and it was twisted, the mouth pulled back over his teeth, the narrow eyes glinting as if he were a demon instead of a man. She pulled back from him and opened her mouth to scream. The cry was choked back by his hand which fastened over her mouth, and then, in a horrible travesty of James, he changed his grip and, seizing her in his arms, he kissed her. The touch of his mouth awoke her strength. She began to struggle fiercely, flighting the powerful arms that held her, seeking to wrench herself free from the gagging kiss. And then the beam of light became a glare that fell upon them, and suddenly he let her go, his face a mask again, the mocking smile beginning to turn the corners of his mouth, and he turned to the two members of the Prince's guard who had been patrolling the park lower passages.

"You damned fools," he said softly. "Can't you see you are disturbing this lady and myself?"

The men were Highlanders from the glen of the Macgregors. They stared suspiciously at this member of another clan, and then at the shadowy woman, half hidden in the little room.

"We heard a noise," one of the men explained. "You must remember, sir, there's a price on the Prince's head and assassins creeping over from the English border. We have orders to shoot anyone caught skulking in the palace. Ye can think yerself and the lady lucky we didna fire at ye first."

Katherine pushed past him before he could answer them; she saw one of the younger men staring at her with contempt.

"Where are the state apartments?" She was trembling so violently that she could hardly speak.

"Up the stairs, lady, and back down the passage at the top."

She did not look back at Hugh; she lifted her skirts and stumbled up the narrow stairs down which he had helped her and, finding herself in the same dim passage with the lights of the main palace corridor at the end, she began to run.

"Och, my God, my God!"

Annie knelt beside her, bandaging her wrist with cold cloths soaked in vinegar to take out the bruises. They were alone in Katherine's room at the inn where Henry had taken rooms for them, and they had sat there since dawn while he waited impatiently downstairs. She had said nothing to him of her encounter with Hugh; she had found him in the palace, searching anxiously for her, and whispered that she felt faint and overcome and begged to be taken home. He had not questioned her; he had ordered their carriage immediately and brought her back to Annie. And now Annie knew what had happened.

"If you tell Mr. Ogilvie I'll never forgive you," Katherine repeated. "If you dare to speak one word of this to anyone I'll dismiss you!"

"You'd let that scoundrel try to murder you and not take a revenge? Ye're mad, milady. If Mr. Ogilvie knew that he'd so much as touched ye—if he saw your wrist all marked like that—he'd call him out and kill him!"

"He'd call him out," Katherine said, "and *he'd* be killed! Do you think he could match swords with Hugh Macdonald? Annie, he's one of the best swordsmen in the Highlands . . . nothing would gladden him more than to butcher Henry as he butchered Robert!"

"When I think of it"—Annie's voice trembled—"when I think of that room and him with his hands round your neck . . . Mother of God, I feel like going out in search of him myself!"

"It doesn't matter," Katherine said wearily. Her head ached and her bruised wrist was throbbing painfully. "Nothing matters any more. I've found out what I wanted to know and that's an end of it. James is well now, and he's the lover of this Mrs. Douglas, just as you said, Annie. Handsome and rich . . . those were his words. And he's forgotten me."

"I told ye so," Annie said fiercely. "Ye didn't need to come here and risk your life to hear it from someone else. Forget the villain! Put all thought of those misbegotten Macdonalds out of your head!"

"I will," her mistress answered. "I will now, I promise you. Go down and tell Mr. Ogilvie I'm sleeping. Tell him it was the excitement and the heat that overcame me."

"Promise to sit where ye are then," Annie said. "I'll be back in a moment and get you into bed. My poor wee lamb," she added gently. "God's curse light upon them all!"

When she was alone Katherine leant back in her chair and closed her eyes. It still seemed as if the last few hours had been a nightmare; she could almost imagine herself in the little dark room and feel the pressure of those wonderful hands as they closed over her throat and her foot catching in the little stool whose noisy fall had saved her life. But more terrible still was the moment when he had taken her in his arms and kissed her, and she had felt some dreadful stirring of passion in him, cruel and animal and more terrifying than his attempt at murder. She began to shiver, and even the memory of James was suddenly tainted with the horror she had experienced with Hugh. They were brothers; the grinning, savage killer who had held her and defiled her was the same blood and bone as the man she had loved, the man to whom she would gladly have submitted. She touched the wet bandage on her wrist and shuddered. He had taken a mistress; even while she lied to those who loved her and made a fool of Henry by bringing him to the city full of false hopes in order to search for James, James was with another woman, a rich woman who had nursed him and driven all thought of her out of his mind. She felt suddenly sick with disgust for herself and shame for the deceit she had practised on the tender, honourable man who was even then waiting down below for news of her.

Slowly she got up out of the chair; the pink dawn light was spreading over the sky and through her window she could see the shafts of golden sunlight touching the rooftops of the city. When Annie returned, she found Katherine kneeling by her bed, her head resting on her clasped hands. Her prayer had been short, but she felt it to be the most sincere that she had ever spoken to her God, a God she had neglected in her bitterness and loss and her unlawful passions. She had prayed for forgiveness and for forgetfulness. And in return she had promised to marry Henry Ogilvie.

"I reassured him," Annie said. "I did as ye said and told him you were fast asleep and there was no cause to worry. You'd be fresh and well after a few hours' rest. He was terrible anxious, the poor man." She looked at Katherine and then glanced away. "He loves you very much, milady. I know ye'll be angry with me, but I must speak my mind. Ye could do far worse than settle for him."

"I know that." Katherine spoke very quietly. "I've done with Edinburgh and all that's in it. We'll go home tomorrow, Annie. I shall try and persuade Mr. Ogilvie to leave the Prince and come back to Clandara with us."

The little cavalcade of horses riding northwards out of Edinburgh paused on the crest of a steep ridge. Before them the countryside rose under the shadows of the mountains and fell into the plunging valleys beyond which Clandara lay; behind them, three hours' ride distant, the city of Edinburgh spread out under the sentinel castle, still flying the flag of England in defiance of the Prince who had not troubled to waste men and ammunition on reducing it.

Katherine was not tired, in spite of the arduous ride which was becoming slower and more exhausting as the track grew rougher; she had spoken very little to Henry Ogilvie, who kept at her side, and as if he sensed her wretched spirits, he let her ride on in silence. When she drew rein and turned in her saddle, he did the same and, behind them, Annie and Angus with two pack horses and their luggage paused and stretched.

"Why have you halted, Katherine?"

She did not answer him at once. It was impossible to describe the despair and pain which suddenly assailed her as she gazed backwards at the city. A moment of weakness had made her stop for a last look at the past, for she felt that all her life was being left behind in Edinburgh, and every memory of it was poisoned by grief and shame and a savage sense of waste. Love was behind her too, and trust and joy; why had she halted? ... For one mad moment she was tempted to turn and tell him why, and see his happiness and faith destroyed, and then perhaps she might escape the destiny which seemed to drive her to him when in her heart she did not want to go. The temptation came and went and she shrugged.

"I have never seen this view. Look, Henry, what is that enormous cloud of dust? Down there to the south!"

He twisted further still and followed her hand as she pointed, and down below them there was a haze which moved outwards from the city like a snake; the air was full of dust and from the heart of it the sun struck flashes. And then a faint sound came to them upon the wind, borne so fitfully upon the changing currents that it might have been the wind itself that cried in imitation of the pipes.

Ogilvie shielded his eyes with one hand; the column was long and moving at a steady pace; the flashing lights were bayonets, the distant sounds the music of the clans as they marched out to war behind their chiefs.

"That is the Prince's army," he said slowly. "They're moving southward towards England."

The moments passed and still they waited, all silently watching the army creeping forward on its journey to the English border.

"May God go with them!" Ogilvie said suddenly.

"Why do you say that?" Katherine asked him. "Do you regret not joining them already?"

She turned away, unwilling to watch or to think that down below the men she had seen at Holyrood, charming, lighthearted Perth, the strange young Prince with his bright brown eyes, and many hundreds more were marching against the power of England and might never more return.

"I have never said I wouldn't join," he said quietly.

"But you're coming back with me!" she exclaimed. "You would have been down there with them otherwise."

"I'm seeing you safely to your home," he corrected. "My poor Katherine, I know how much the thought of this war horrifies you—your heart is not in it, and there's small wonder. But as I sit here and watch *them,* I know my place is there among them. There goes the Prince of Scotland, and the Ogilvies of Spey shall go with him. Just as soon as I've returned you to Clandara. Come, my beloved. You wouldn't have it otherwise. Would you sooner have me hang back like that poltroon Charles Macleod, or fight against my own like the Campbells?"

"I don't want you to die," she said slowly. "And as I watched them go I felt that they would die. All of them, sooner or later. I had hoped you were not mad like the rest."

"And now that you find I am," he said gently, "you will have to forgive me. Come; it's a long ride from here on."

The streets were full of cheering people; women threw kisses and ran up to the Prince's stirrup, and he smiled and waved and promised them victory, while the war rants of the clans were played behind him, and the Highland army marched out of Edinburgh. His Life Guards, commanded by Lord Elcho, rode with the Prince at their head, followed by the mounted troops of the Lords Balmerino, Kilmarnock, and Pitsligo, and the seventy Hussars under Baggot. Seven thousand infantry, one thousand of whom were Atholl men under the command of Lord George Murray, seven hundred Camerons and the same number under the Duke of Perth, and all the Macdonalds, Stewarts, Robertsons, and Gordons followed their chiefs and their Prince on the road to England, and sang the war songs of their clans on that bright November day. His piper marched beside each chief, and just behind the piper marched his boy, apprenticed to him and his personal servant, many of whom had taken charge of the pipes at Prestonpans while the piper drew his broadsword and charged into battle with his clan. Sir Alexander Macdonald of Dundrenan rode with his two elder sons on either side, and the younger David just behind, and the Macdonald piper played the fierce traditional marching tune, the words and melody of which were as old as the soil on which Dundrenan House was built, three centuries before.

Sir Alexander glanced at his eldest son. James had recovered from his wound; the arm and shoulder were a little stiff, but that was no great trouble in a left arm which was protected by his buckler in a fight.

And a fight was what he needed most, his father insisted again and again in the intervals between their frequent quarrels and his angry discussions of them with Hugh. He had come to rely more and more upon his second son; normal contact was now so difficult with James that he found it impossible to avoid conflicts of opinion on subjects about which they normally agreed. It astonished the old man that his son should have found personal favour with the Prince; and yet when he listened to the bitter wrangles which took place among the Prince's council and sometimes joined in them himself, he had to admit that James and Charles shared the same reckless impulses in their estimate of the campaign.

Danger and uneven odds only spurred Charles and urged him to defy them; he fretted under the restraining influence of his older advisers like Lord George and Sir John Macdonald, who had come with him from France. He was full of hope, hope that all England would rise in his name when he came among them, hope that the armies of King George of England would run from him before the gates of London as they had run at Prestonpans, and whatever the older and wiser men on his council said, he much preferred the advice of men like James.

"Where's Mrs. Douglas?" Sir Alexander hissed at Hugh. "I suppose she is following again."

"No," Hugh answered. "I called on her two days ago and she said she had business to attend to; her house must be shut up and her servants dismissed. As far as I know she's going back to Perth."

"Thank God for that," Sir Alexander said. "No merchant's daughter is going to sit at Dundrenan."

"We could make use of her money," his son pointed out. "After this campaign we'll be a sight poorer."

"If we win, we'll have reward enough from the Prince," his father retorted. "And if we lose, my son, we'll either be dead on the field or dead on an English scaffold. But we won't loose, be sure of that. Victory is all about us today! Only wait till the English Jacobites have their first sight of the Prince!"

"Aye," Hugh said softly. "He says they'll rise in thousands and sweep him on to London."

James had come up closer beside them. "Who needs the English?" he demanded. "We'll carry the Prince to London without the help of any of them. . . . Do you need them, brother? By God, I'd rather trust to my own sword than to the sorry loyalty of that sorry race!"

"For once, you're right," Hugh said. "I don't think they'll rise. I think they'll lie low and wait and let us shed our blood. . . . I dare say they'll all raise a bonny cheer for us if we win, though."

"You're both fools," their father snapped. "If we weren't counting on support from the loyal English, do ye think we'd be mad enough to invade England? Of course they'll rise, they'll rise as soon as we cross the border!"

The brothers exchanged a look behind his back as he pressed forward.

A new roar of cheering greeted the Prince and the van of his army.

"James," Hugh said suddenly, "do you think we'll win?"

For a moment James did not answer. He rode at a steady walk, keeping his fresh and irritable horse under a short rein. The noise and the press of people were making the animal very nervous. "That's a damnable question to ask now," he said at last. "We must win; it's the end of us all if we don't. But personally, I'm relying on nothing but the men who are marching with us now."

"Father said victory was all around us," Hugh said. "I wish I could see it as he does. But I can't, brother, and I don't think you can either." He shrugged and took off his bonnet to a group of ladies waving from a window. "It's not important. We're not a family who've paid too much attention to survival. If there's a bonny battle and a lot of dead English, I shall be content. After all," the twisted grin flashed out at James, "I'm not the eldest son!"

By evening the cavalcade had left the city far behind and the dust had settled; the army was already on its way by the west coast route to the English border.

The house in King Street was shuttered and empty; the furniture was shrouded in dust sheets and the valuables packed away, and its mistress rode out of Edinburgh three days after the royal army had left, on her way to Perth. She was travelling part of the way in a hired carriage with her luggage following by pack horse; she had brought a great deal of household goods and clothes in order to equip the house in the city for the comfort of the man she had finally parted with after their most bitter quarrel.

Janet had hardly slept for the past three days; her head ached and the uneven jolting of the ill-sprung carriage made her wretchedly uncomfortable. And again and again on that long, exhausting journey she relived every word and incident of the quarrel which had ended their liaison. James had not been at home when she returned from Holyrood after the ball. She had sat up in her dress, tired and anxious, until the dawn came and in the early hours she heard his heavy step upon the stairs. When she went out to meet him she saw at once that he was drunk. He had stood leaning against the wall, staring at her through narrowed, red-rimmed eyes, swinging his bonnet to and fro in his right hand, and suddenly she heard him laugh. And then he told her where he had been, and he told her very slowly and in such detail that she flinched and shrank away. But flight was not permitted to her. He caught her wrist and held her, his face a few inches away, glaring at her as if he were mad, describing the caresses he had exchanged with the whores in Temple Street, comparing their diseased and dirty bodies with hers until quite suddenly she struck him. And then he let her go, one hand to his face, and when he spoke she could have believed that he was sober. "You cannot even strike me without reminding me of her." And she knew that it was not to any of the wretched strumpets he referred. It was then that her temper broke, and it broke as it had done only once before in her life when the miserable husband who had squandered her money and betrayed her with her own servant girls had come whining back and demanded her submission to him.

It was then she unleashed the weeks of pain and bitterness and blighted hopes upon the man who stood before her, the stink of the brothels clinging to his clothes; that was when she reminded him of the money she had spent for his comfort, the nursing, the scandal she had incurred, the ingratitude and boorishness, and now this unspeakable insult. Last of all she lashed him with her knowledge of his past. The name of Katherine Fraser fell upon him like a scrouge, and with it came her scorn for him and her admiration for the woman who had rejected him. He had not answered her; when she was finished she leaned back trembling and exhausted, waiting for a blow, linging for the release of violence because she already knew that she had destroyed her happiness he had deliberately made her do it. But he had not touched her. Instead he walked past her to his room and at the door he turned.

"There's nothing so vile-tongued as an unpaid whore. I see how true that old saying is now. I shall be out of your house within the hour."

And within an hour his belongings were removed by his clansmen and the door shut with a bang upon them. When his brother Hugh came to see her a day later to ask what had happened and say good-bye before the army left, she had recovered her calm, and matched his mocking curiosity with her usual composure. The interlude was over; she was returning to Perth, and she would be glad to give his regards to her sister-in-law Margaret. And then when he was gone she had been very busy packing up the house, very efficient and capable and quite unruffled, but she did not sleep and the cook asked her mistress plainly what was wrong with the food that she sent every meal back to the kitchen without eating anything.

And in the privacy of her hired carriage, jerking and swaying along the rough road back to Perth, Janet gave way to the unbearable pain of that dreadful parting and to her reckless self-reproaches, for now his drunken insults seemed no worse than many others she had suffered. He had often taunted her openly with her lack of morals, and until that night she had answered him coolly, turning the barbed words aside with cynicism, pretending that, whatever he said, he could not hurt her. But the hurt had been intense and the strain of hiding it tremendous; the rare flashes of tenderness, the moment when he held her hand and wept after his recovery, a hundred incidents in their profoundly satisfying physical relationship seemed to show in retrospect that he was softening, and she had hoped more strongly and strengthened her formidable will in the battle for his love. And then she had thrown everything away. Already when he left her house forever she was ready to crawl on her knees after him and beg him to return.

She leant back and closed her burning eyes. Within the next few weeks the real battles of the war would start and he might lie rotting on some English field or suffering in some English jail, and she would never know his fate or have the power to help him. And all for the sake of that woman whom she had never seen, but whose description Hugh had given her. She felt as if she knew that face so well in her imagination on that the real woman would be instantly recognisable. Beautiful, aristocratic, wilful, and proud . . . Even the blow Katherine Fraser struck in anger was superior to the one she had given him.

They had been travelling for three hours when the coachman felt a sharp tug upon the cord with which his passengers communicated with him. Slowing the tired horses, he leaned down from the box. The lady was halfway out of the window; her hood had fallen back, and the wind was whipping the black hair around her head. She looked wild and her face was wet with tears.

"Turn back!"

"What's that, lady? Speak up, I canna hear ye!"

"Turn back! Go back to Edinburgh at once."

He halted the coach completely and climbed down. "I'm tired for Perth," he said stubbornly.

"And I hired you," Janet said fiercely. "Turn back and do as you're told. If you can reach the city before dark I'll give you twice the fee."

The next morning Janet had converted some of her jewels into gold and hired the services of a groom and a maidservant. By noon she was riding hard out of Edinburgh in the direction of Carlisle across the English border. The Prince's army were expected to reach there in the first week in November.

"Katherine, I must talk to you. Come into the library." The Earl of Clandara closed the door behind them both; his daughter had been at home for less than a week, and Henry Ogilvie had announced his intention of leaving them and raising his clan for the Prince. The Earl had watched them closely since their return, and what he saw did little to satisfy his wish that Katherine should commit herself before Ogilvie left. She looked pale and strained, and made excuses not to be left alone with him; her father noticed all these signs of indecision and they angered him. As he looked down at her in the long room, its blazing fire and tallow candles lighting up the shadowed walls, he was frowning and irritable.

"You've been home for four days," he said abruptly, "and I wish to know what you've decided."

"Decided about what?" Katherine asked. "I don't understand you, Father."

"You understand perfectly well, my child. I gave Henry permission to take you to Edinburgh because you told him it might help you to make up your mind. Well, he's leaving us in a few days and I want to know if it has."

She faced him calmly; there was none of the friction or inequality which she used to feel when the man in question had been James. How old she had grown since then; the comparison almost made her smile. So old and so utterly without expectation of happiness. She did not want to quarrel with her father; he too looked worn and racked and the night before she had noticed how his hand shook at dinner.

"Let us sit down," she said gently. "There, Father, by the fire, and I will sit by you." She came and sat on a stool at his feet as she had not done since her childhood when she and Robert curled up by the winter fires and asked him to tell them stories.

He put out his hand and stroked her head. "I've become a disagreeable, petulant old man," he said suddenly. "Forgive me; I didn't mean to growl at you just now. Tell me the truth, child; do you not want to marry him?"

"I don't know," Katherine answered. "He's such a good man, so kind and gentle . . . I know you want it, Father."

"I do." The old man nodded, and turned her face up to him. For a moment they looked at each other and he said quietly: "Katherine, I am no longer young. Since Robert's death I have lost my taste for life; when I die, what will become of you, my only child, and this estate, without a man to protect you? And if there are no heirs it will pass to some distant kinsman who won't love Clandara and care for its people as you and I have done. If you marry Henry, I know that you and Clandara will be in good hands and that the sons you bear will inherit it. I don't want to die and leave you alone, my daughter; this is no world for a single woman of beauty and position and some little wealth. You should have a husband. If it is Henry, I shall be truly happy. But I won't force you against your will."

She turned and caught his hand in hers, and on an impulse she kissed it. It was strange how her love for James had sapped all her affections. Only her love for Robert had survived, and her feelings for her father had been cool to the point of hostility. As she made the gesture of tenderness and submission to him then, the lost filial love crept back a little, and with it a deep sorrow for the misfortune her ill-judged love had helped to bring upon him.

"If it will make you happy," she whispered, "then I will marry him. I owe you peace in your last years, my poor dear

Father, and I owe Clandara a son to inherit. You're right; it would be better for us all."

"Tell him tonight," the old Earl asked her. "The poor fellow is sorely disappointed at the way you've been avoiding him."

"I will," she said. "The sooner it is done, the better I shall feel about it."

"Thank God," he said. He bent down and kissed her on the forehead. "You will be happy; he will make you so, I know it."

"Perhaps." Katherine stood up and for a moment turned away from him. "I'll go and find him now before my courage leaves me."

The candles in the Green Salon threw their locked shadows on the wall, making the image of the man stooping with his arms about the woman into an enormous blur. Katherine's eyes were closed; her lips submitted, her body was unresisting. She felt terribly weak and tired, and only afraid that when he released her she would break down in tears. Nothing had changed; she could not feel the slightest stirring for the eager and impassioned man she had just agreed to marry. Whatever he did, she might have been dead in his arms. At last he let her go, and when she tried to hide her head against his shoulder, he made her look at him. His eyes were curiously detached and kind.

"You don't love me, do you, Katherine?"

"No." It was a wretched whisper, blurred by tears. "Oh, Henry, how can you forgive me!"

"Forgiveness isn't necessary," he said gently. "My beloved, I have known from the first that you felt nothing like that for me. You made no pretence. . . . It is still James Macdonald, isn't it? Don't be ashamed, my love, you can tell me."

"I don't know what it is," she murmured. "I thought it had died so many times but still it comes; he comes, like a ghost . . . but I don't love him—I can't! Henry, knowing this, do you still want me?"

"I have wanted you all my life," he answered. "I am not surprised that you don't care for me as I do for you. But if you marry me, my darling Katherine, I promise to spend my life making you happy and helping you forget. I ask nothing but your patience in return."

"I shall love you," she said at last. "I know I shall love you."

"I know it too." Henry smiled down at her and kissed her gently. "Will you marry me before I leave to join the Prince or must I wait and claim you when we come back victorious?"

"When you come back," she whispered, and despised herself for escaping once again. "It won't be long."

"A month or two at the most," he told her. "Within that time we shall have conquered England or else be fleeing back to Scotland. Will you marry me if I'm a fugitive?"

"I'd marry you whatever you were." For the first time she smiled and a little of her old spirit flashed at him. "If I know the canny Ogilvies, they're not often slow to find a way out, and you'll be safely back at Spey House with a ready explanation!"

"I must go back to Spey," he said. "I have to raise the clan and equip them and myself and see what money I can bring the Prince. I was talking to your father last night and he agrees that I can catch up with the army in England in about a month if I leave Clandara quickly. And now that we're betrothed"—he broke off to kiss her hand and then her cheek—"I can return and prepare with all speed. The sooner gone, the sooner I shall return to you. I know your father will be happy."

"You will be like the son he lost," she said. "He has always loved you. And he does know, Henry, because I told him before we spoke. He is overjoyed and already talking about grandchildren."

"Our second son shall take your name," he promised her. "There'll be a Fraser at Clandara in the direct line and we'll claim for the earldom for him from the Prince. Clandara will be safe and so will you."

They kissed again and then agreed that he should go alone to seek formal approval from the Earl. When he had gone, Katherine went out into the Great Hall, half in darkness except for two guttering pitch-pine torches, and walked slowly up the stone staircase to her own apartments. Annie was dozing in her chair by the door, a piece of sewing on her lap where it had fallen when she slept, but she woke at the sound of her mistress' step and with an apology hurried to help her undress.

"Ye're pale, milady," she scolded. "Why do ye sit up so late from your bed? You've never recovered your own bonny colour from the night ye went to Holyrood. Here, stand still and I'll untie the laces on your stays."

Katherine stepped out of her red velvet dress and Annie eased the tight whalebone corselet off. She stood by the mirror in her white shift and white stockings and looked at herself.

"I'm going to me married, Annie."

"God be praised! Mr. Ogilvie?"

"The same. I accepted him tonight and my father is delighted. Are you delighted, Annie? You've hinted at it often enough. Are you pleased now?"

"It's of small importance what a servant like myself thinks, and well you know it. Are you happy, my dear lady? Say you are, for that's all that matters!"

"Happiness is not a word I know any longer." Katherine pulled the shift over her head and Annie covered her with an embroidered nightgown, ruffled at neck and wrist and hem. It hung straight down to the ground, loose and fastened high. The glittering yellow gown she had worn at Holyrood revealed far more of her body than the robe in which unmarried ladies went to bed.

"I am not expecting love and all its fancies." Her voice was so bitter, it was hard and ugly. "I am marrying a good man who loves me because he will care for me and for Clandara and because my father wishes it. And I owe him a placid year or two before he dies. But don't ask me if I'm happy, Annie."

"Ye will be." She knelt down and put on Katherine's velvet slippers. "Time will teach ye wisdom, milady, and teach ye the joy of a good and kindly husband. If I'd ever found one I'd not be the crotchety old spinster that I am now." She looked up into the beautiful unhappy face, and her heart ached. As usual, whenever she was touched, her tone grew particularly sharp. "Now go to bed and put some colour in your cheeks. Ye can talk all ye want about the wedding to-morrow! And God help me, I suppose I've got to be dragged to live at Spey House with you! There's never a thought for me in it at all . . . Spey House!"

She tucked in the covers round her mistress and put one candle on the table by her bed, its little silver snuffer in the chamber stick. And then she suddenly lifted Katherine's hand and kissed it, her face flushing awkwardly. "God bless ye, mi-lady. And pay no mind to me. I'd sooner die than stay at Clandara or anywhere else without you."

When she had gone, Katherine lay until the candle flame burnt down and expired with a greedy hiss. A month or two at the most, Henry had said. If he were right, then she would be married by the spring, and he would be beside her in his family bed at Spey House, his head on the pillow near hers, his hands stretching out to take her, his body reaching its tri-umph within hers. And from it, she would conceive his chil-dren and watch them grow, and her days would be filled with the duties incumbent upon the mistress of a great house and an estate; there would be new friends and relatives by mar-riage whom she would have to cultivate and please. The old Mrs. Ogilvie of Spey, half remembered as a frail and homely little lady who was devoted to her only son . . . A whole new life, leagues away from Clandara and the lowering mountains that were reflected in Loch Ness, and the places where she had ridden out in secret to meet her lover. The hollow where she had felt the earth beneath them move and the day turn into night . . . There would be nothing of that in the bed at Spey House; she would not dissolve and flow away on the stream of Henry's passion. She would submit and endure, but that was all. Love would never come again. When Annie woke her in the morning she was unusually gentle, for it was obvious that Katherine had cried herself to sleep.

On November 17 the city of Carlisle within the English border surrendered to Prince Charles, and he entered the city itself on a white horse preceded by a hundred pipers and a jubilant army who had so far encountered only token resistance. All the omens were good; the people they had seen were not unfriendly; their reactions were those of curiosity and, living so close to the borders of Scotland, they were not as alien to the invader as the English people farther inland. Carlisle surrendered and its fears, like those of Edinburgh, were allayed by the excellent conduct and restraint of the Highland troops, whose only crime against the civic sense of what was proper was their uninhibited use of the streets for natural functions.

The Prince was in residence at the castle and those in his immediate council were there with him; the rest, including the Macdonalds of Dundrenan, were quartered in the houses of the local gentry and in the town itself. Janet Douglas had been living quietly in a rented house outside the city walls; she had seen the Prince's army lay siege to Carlisle and finally march into it triumphant, and two days later she drove in herself in search of James. She soon learnt that the Macdonalds of Dundrenan were guests in the house of a Catholic gentleman called Wykeham, and at seven o'clock on the evening of the nineteenth she was admitted to the room where Hugh and David and two of their tacksmen were drinking and playing cards.

"Good God!" Hugh sprang up in surprise, and the others rose more slowly after him, staring at the tall woman who was almost hidden in a long blue cloak and hood.

"Janet Douglas ..." he said. "Well, well, I might have known it. Come, sit down and let me present James Macdonald, the son of Angus, and Ian Macdonald of Dungall. Mrs Douglas, lately come from Edinburgh. My brother David you know only too well."

"Your servants, lady." The two tacksmen bowed. Both of them were distantly related to their chief, and both held a large acreage and high responsibilities at Dundrenan. A glance from Hugh was sufficient, and they excused themselves. He took Janet's cloak and called for a glass of wine for her. It was served by the Red Murdoch, who bowed low before her with no trace of recognition on his ugly, freckled face.

"I see James is here," she said. "That's one licence I wouldn't allow him, to have that savage in my house."

"Murdoch is no savage," David interposed sharply. He had not spoken before. "He's one of the best men with dirk and claymore at Dundrenan. And he's loyal to us all to the death!"

"Pay no attention to my brother," Hugh said lightly. "He and our more brutish tenants have much in common. He loves poor Murdoch; he once saw him cut a dead man's throat and it won his heart forever. It was the brother of James's betrothed, as a matter of interest."

"Don't please." Janet shuddered. "Hugh, where is he and how is he? I've travelled night and day to find him and I'm not going to sit here wasting words."

"Why didn't you tell me the truth at Edinburgh?" Hugh demanded.

"Because I was too proud. He'd hurt me beyond endurance; we had a bitter quarrel and I said things for which he will never forgive me."

"If you are so sure of that, why are you here?" he countered.

"Because I don't care!" she said. "I don't care what he says or does to me. I can't live without him. And if you laugh at me, Hugh, I'll throw your wine in your face."

"Come." He shook his head at her and his light eyes were gleaming. "Come, this is not the calculating Janet that I know. . . . You're not the kind of woman who throws wine and makes a scene. You are above all that, unlike the rest of us poor mortals. But content yourself, I'm not going to laugh at you, and if I do, I'll take good care to hide it. I'm glad you've come. He needs you."

"Is he here?"

"Upstairs." Hugh nodded. He put out his hand. "I shouldn't try to go to him. I must warn you, my dear lady, that he's not alone."

Her pale face did not alter; no colour came into it and her very fine eyes stared straight and coolly into those of Hugh. "What manner of woman is with him?"

"The lowest. He seeks nothing else. He found this drab in

some whorehouse last night and sent for her again this evening. He's drunk too!"

"And you and his father have done nothing to stop this?" she demanded.

He shrugged. "He's not the man to let us interfere. There's a madness in him, and he's fleeing from it. Father doesn't understand this; he thinks he'll sicken of debauch and come to his senses cured, but I do not. He's still fleeing that damned woman, that's the trouble." For a moment a frown showed in contrast to the eternal mocking grin. He had told no one of that meeting at Holyrood and of its failure. He would never tell anyone because in the few seconds when he held Katherine in his arms and kissed her to prevent her crying out he had wanted her himself. For that moment of weakness he hated her more than he had ever hated anyone.

To his surprise Janet put down her glass and got up. "I'm not afraid of a common whore," she said. "Take me to his room. I'll get rid of her. Wait, my purse is there on the table, if you please. No doubt I'll need it."

"As you wish." Hugh opened the door for her. "Up the stairs and the door immediately before you on the landing. I still think it would be better if you didn't go."

"Thank you for your solicitude, but I'm no swooning gentlewoman. My father was a merchant and my mother's people lived in a miserable croft and slept on the floor with their animals. Don't worry about me, Hugh. If I need help I'll call you."

She did not knock on the door; she opened it and pushed it wide and walked into the middle of the room. There were two candles burning by the side of the disordered bed; James lay upon it, half covered by one of the sheets, and by his side a young, bedraggled prostitute looked up from her ministrations in alarm. When she saw that the intruder was a woman, she began to shout and curse, and the drunken man on the bed opened his eyes and struggled up onto his elbow.

"Hold your tongue and get out or I'll call the watch for you!" Janet's voice cut through the obscenities. She advanced to the bed and picked up the girl's shabby petticoat. "Dress yourself and begone, or I'll have you whipped through the streets at the cart's tail! Dress, and be quick!"

There was something about her that made the strumpet pause. She climbed out of the bed and began to pull on her clothes. "He owes me for tonight," she said.

"How much?"

"A guinea," the girl spat at her. "And cheap at the price or the drunken dog. Look at my arms!"

"A crown," Janet said coldly, "and not one farthing more. That pays for a bruise or two. . . . What were you doing, trying to steal his money when he was asleep? You're a fool if you were. He's just the man to break your neck."

"What the hell are you doing here?"

Janet turned away and looked at James. He glared back at her, his eyes half closed and reddened, the shadow of a beard on his face. "Never mind that now. When we're alone we'll talk. Here's your crown, now go! And if I find you near this house again I'll have the skin flogged off your back!"

At the door the strumpet turned once more; she wasn't more than twenty and as the light from the landing candelabra fell upon her Janet saw with horror that her hair was red.

"Curse on yer both. I hope I've given 'im the pox!" And then she fled down the stairs.

Janet came to the bedside and looked down at him. He looked older and thinner, his face was wolfish now, the cheeks fallen in and the bloodshot eyes blazing with drink and confusion and rage at her.

"How are you, James?" she said gently. "How is your wound?" There was a livid scar upon his shoulder near the chest; she touched it gently with her finger. For a moment he did not answer her.

"Why have you followed me?" he said at last. "Why can't you let me go to the devil in peace?"

"Because I think you need me," she said quietly. "And judging by what I find here tonight, you certainly do. Sit up and let me make you comfortable. Pooh, this room stinks of that creature. I'm going to open the window."

She went to the door and called out. "Hugh, could someone bring James some clean linen and something to eat for us both?"

He sprang up the stairs and made her a sweeping bow. "As you command, dear lady. By God, I'll never underestimate you again. I dare say we shan't be seeing you again tonight?"

"It's unlikely," she said coolly, "unless he decided to throw me out when he is sober. But we shall see."

Within an hour he was changed and bathed and they were both dining from a tray sent up with Murdoch. There was a decanter of excellent whisky on it, and after they had finished, Janet joined him in drinking it as she had done the first night they met at her brother's house in Perth. She raised her glass to him.

"Your health, and our reunion."

"As you wish. My health and our reunion. Tell me something, have you not one jot of shame, to come breaking in here and turn a common whore out of my bed ..."

"You are always asking me if I am not ashamed," she answered, and she smiled. "And I always disappoint you. I'm not a bashful woman, James. Surely you know that by now. I told Hugh a strumpet doesn't frighten me. You forget I've had a husband. I've turned them out of the house before."

"A nice comparison." He raised his glass. "My thanks."

"You know very well I'm not comparing," she said. "My husband never once did anything that made me happy except die. I wouldn't have walked down the street in pursuit of him, much less from Edinburgh to England in the wake of an army and in the middle of a war. You should be flattered."

"I am. Didn't we quarrel, you and I? I've been drunk the last two nights and I get fuddled in my mind. I found that little slut and there she was in the whorehouse, dancing in her petticoats under the torchlight, and her hair was red ... red as the fire itself. I took her then and again tonight. I found her sneaking round my pockets and I shook her until her head almost fell off her dirty little neck." He leant back in his chair and scowled.

"They're dirty, these English. Their women are dirty, and low-tongued, and they say these are not really the English, these vermin in Carlisle are closer to the Scots! A dirty little thief, and poor at her trade ... Pass me the whisky, Janet. Don't fret yourself, I'm not drunk now and I shan't get drunk. I'm in attendance on the Prince tomorrow."

"If she was all those things, why did you choose her twice?" she asked him.

He glanced up at her and his black eyes were full of unhappy mockery, more at his own expense than hers. "For the colour of her hair," he said. "You knew that. You're a clever woman, Janet. Why did you ask?"

"Only because I wondered if you knew," she answered. "And now all I can offer you instead of her is a Scots whore, and a black-haired one at that!" She faced him boldly, and began to smile.

He felt suddenly as if she were as potent as whisky or opium; however he twisted in the effort to escape her, however cruelly he abused her kindness and scorned her generosity, she managed to survive and find him yet again, and always at a time when he was low and tempted to take advantage of her.

"I will never love you!" He said it as a challenge, calmly and deliberately, and it pleased him to see her face flush.

"I know that," she said. "There is no need to say it."

"There is need," he insisted. "You must know it and accept it. I can never love you, Janet, no matter what you do for me, simply because I love someone else, and nothing that has happened in the past or will happen in the future can change that. I admit this to you, because I must if I am going to let you stay tonight or any other night. But speak of it outside this room and I will kill you. Is that understood?"

"It is, James. I don't expect you to love me; I know that you can't and I am content to have what is left of you."

"So be it then." He rose and held out his hand to her. "Come to bed."

When he slept at last, she rose and snuffed the candles and closed the window, for the room was growing very cold. Whatever their quarrels or the circumstances of their meeting, the cravings of their strong and urgent natures found perfect satisfaction, made all the keener by the contrast of her sexual submission to her normal independence. The same fierce fusion, the same cataclysm had been reached, but it had left his heart untouched as always and hers ever deeper in its subjection to him. She was back with him again, but nothing had changed since the night they first met. She dressed and slipped quietly out of the house, returning to her own coach, where the coachman had taken refuge from the cold inside it and was fast asleep. In the early hours she reached her own house three miles outside the city and went to bed.

When the Scots army marched out of Carlisle en route for Manchester, Janet was among the crowd of wives and daughters and women of the streets who followed in the van of it.

Chapter 6

FROM CARLISLE the Prince's army marched by Penrith and Lancaster to Preston and walked unopposed into Manchester. No blood had been spilt and it seemed to the superstitious Scots that they were advancing through a sleeping enemy. People in the larger towns gave them a welcome, but it became more obvious with every mile of their advance that the expected rising of the English Jacobites was only a figment in the mind of their Prince and the more fanatical of his advisers.

Throughout that long march, only a few meagre hundreds joined them, and three hundred of these were raised in Manchester itself. Reports from Wales encouraged Charles, where a powerful landowner, Sir Watkyn Williams-Wynn, sent word that he was gathering an army and would soon be on his way to meet them. But against these hopes the pessimists balanced the number of desertions, which had depleted the Prince's original force to less than five thousand men. The clansmen were many hundreds of miles from home, and they were unsuited to a long campaign; they were weary and homesick and there had been no battles or the rewards of plunder to encourage them. Day by day they lagged behind and slipped away.

At Macclesfield, on the first of December, the Prince and his council received word that the main English army numbering ten thousand men was at Lichfield under the command of the Duke of Cumberland, the son of the King of England and a veteran of the Flanders war. It was a bitterly cold night, and Charles sat at the head of the table in his greatcoat; some of his commanders were wrapped in their thick plaids for warmth. Lord George Murray was now in undisputed command of the forces. He rose, bowed to the Prince, and opened the proceedings.

"Your Royal Highness, lords and gentlemen. It's already known that the enemy's main force is at Lichfield; their purpose there is clear. We are to be stopped and engaged before marching farther on London. This meeting has been called to decide whether to accept that challenge or avoid them and march southwards, leaving Cumberland at our rear."

He glanced towards Charles and cleared his throat. "In my opinion we should avoid a battle at all costs. Desertions have brought us down to half the strength of the enemy. Our men are in no condition to face the veterans of Fontenoy with a commander like Cumberland at their head; the country here is flat and unsuitable and we have no cavalry. Theirs is exactly seventeen miles away at Newcastle-under-Lyme! If we stand now and lose, the whole cause is lost."

"And if we avoid them, what then?" Lord Ogilvie asked.

"We continue to march on London," Lord George said. "But if we don't receive news of Williams-Wynn and the Welsh, or proper support from the English Jacobites, then before God, I doubt if we ought to go further!"

At the far end of the table the Macdonald of Dundrenan and his sons sprang to their feet. "If you're suggesting retreat, my lord, we beg the Prince to disregard you!" Others began to argue, some shouting the Macdonalds down, a few supporting them.

"Gentlemen!" Charles struck the table. "Enough of this! The English will rise when they're sure, and I know the Welsh are loyal to me ... I have no doubts!" He looked around him at the sullen faces, some of them a little ashamed. "All I ask of you is a little patience. A few desertions and you talk of throwing victory away and going back to Scotland. Where is your spirit, gentlemen? Where is the spirit that brought you to me when I came among you with only seven men?"

"We are far from home," Gordon of Glenbucket said slowly. "We are here here in the midst of the enemy, and they *are* the enemy, believe me, for none but those few poor fellows at Manchester have joined us and there's no sign of more. My men are losing heart; I see it every day. If they fought the English now I wouldn't answer for them."

For a moment there was silence; the Prince's face had flushed when he addressed them. Now he sat pale and angry, trying not to lose his temper. "Proceed, Lord George," he said.

"I will take a small force towards Congleton and Cumberland will follow me, thinking he is pursuing you, Highness. That will leave you free to take the main army on the road to London, and we will meet up at Derby once I have drawn the English off. At Derby we can think again."

That evening Lord George selected his regiments for the feint with Cumberland and to James's relief, the Macdonalds of Dundrenan were not included. They were to remain behind with the Prince. At dawn they began the long march towards the English capital, but the march ended at Derby, only twenty-six miles farther on.

Janet had taken lodgings in the town. She had been waiting nearly three hours for James's return from yet another council meeting; the supper prepared for him was ruined and she had given orders to the sullen English servants to provide some cold meats and a fowl, and then dismissed them. It was long past midnight, and as she sat before the fire she almost fell asleep. They had marched into the city and received a cautious welcome and a minor demonstration of sympathy, but the general apathy was turning into coldness, and there were rumours of unrest among the Highlanders. There had been no battle and Lord George had carried out a brilliant manoeuvre which drew the Duke of Cumberland and his army towards Wales, allowing the Prince to reach Derby unhindered, where Lord George had quickly joined him. Now the same question was on every tongue, from the poor bewildered clansmen to the highest ranks of the chiefs. What now? Advance further into the unknown, without support from the English people and with Cumberland's army at their backs, and yet another army waiting before London, or admit that they had failed and turn for home? The sound of the

than once on the long march the Prince refreshed himself from a small flask of brandy which he carried on his person; it was a habit which was to grow with the years. On the twentieth of December, the army forded the risen waters of the river Esk and once again stood upon the soil of Scotland.

When the council proposed the time-wasting pursuit of capturing Stirling, while the pursuing English army made straight for Edinburgh and took command of the city, the Prince was too disheartened to argue. Lord George's authority was all the higher because he had fought a brilliant rearguard action with the advance dragoons of the Duke of Cumberland's army and sent them flying back in defeat. He felt sufficiently confident by then to demand that the Prince submit the further conduct of the war to a committee, and in his letter he pointed out the disadvantages of the Prince's constant interference in the decisions of his commanders. It was the greatest humiliation which had so far been forced upon Charles and this time he did not submit.

He absolutely refused Lord George's advice, and the army set out from Stirling for Bannockburn where it was hoped they would engage the main English army under the command of General Hawley, whose nickname of "The Hangman" was well illustrated by the gibbets erected in the squares all over Edinburgh in expectation of the prisoners he hoped to take among the rebels. But they were occupied by unfortunates from the English army, executed as a punishment for General Hawley's defeat at Falkirk close to Bannockburn, where the English troops broke and ran from the Highland charge as they had done at Prestonpans. For a brief time the fitful light of victory shone on Charles once more, only to fade and be extinguished at the news of the Duke of Cumberland's arrival to conduct the war against him. Lord George and the chiefs were filled with prophetic gloom. Their council had brought Charles back to Scotland and it was then mercifully unknown to him that the messenger from Sir Watkyn Williams-Wynn had ridden into Derby just two days after he had left it, with the news that Wales was ready to rise for him. Now the same fainthearted voices cried out against following the victory at Falkirk by a battle with Cumberland at Bannockburn. They once again cried for retreat, and by then Charles and even Lochiel and his very few supporters were too dispirited to resist. On January 30 the army began its march back into the Highlands just five months since its triumphant advance upon England. Even at Falkirk it might not have been too late to drive the English out of Scotland and secure a respite for the rest of the spring and summer, when much might have been accomplished, including even aid from France. But Cumberland marched northwards unhindered, followed by his supply ships, while the forces of Charles dwindled from retreat and sickness in the bitter weather. Falkirk was to be their last victory.

The Countess of Clandara smiled up at her stepdaughter. It was a smile which made Katherine feel uncomfortable; whenever she saw the Countess that same smile greeted her, friendly and unvarying, and indefinably repellent. And yet on the rare occasions when Jean Macdonald slipped downstairs and begged Katherine to come up she could not refuse to see her. The Countess was never allowed out of her room; for her own safety she was advised to stay out of sight of the Earl, and her only source of news was Katherine. Jean heard little or nothing unless she eavesdropped in the kitchens, for none of the household servants spoke to her.

"It's kind of you to come," the Countess said. "I try not to trouble you more than I can help."

"It is no trouble," Katherine said quickly. She looked round the bleak room; it was badly lit and the fire in the big grate smoked. Outside the windows the wintry sky was growing very dark. "What can I do for you?" she said.

"Just talk to me a little and tell me what is happening in the outside world. Sit down, please. Do you know, I feel sometimes as if I were already in my grave in these two rooms. . . . What has happened to the Prince and his army?"

Katherine shook her head. "Nothing but failure," she said slowly. "They have come back to Inverness; half their number have deserted and the Prince is in despair. The English army are coming up through the countryside towards them, burning and hanging in every town and hamlet where they pass."

"How terrible," the older woman said. Her voice was very flat, almost uninterested. "But they won't harm you; the Frasers didn't join."

"Some of them did," Katherine answered. "Lord Lovat sent his son to the Prince; he's the head of our clan and for all I know we may be punished without any discrimination being made whether we joined or not!"

"I can't believe that," the Countess said. "Even in the '15 they didn't punish those clans who stayed aloof." Her smile diminished a little and then suddenly it disappeared. "Have you heard if the Macdonalds are still with him?"

Katherine turned away; she did not wish her stepmother to see the colour that rose in her face at the mention of that forbidden name. She looked down at the ring which Henry Ogilvie had given her and twisted it round and round upon her finger until the central sapphire was hidden in her palm. "I know nothing more than what I heard in Edinburgh," she said. "They are still with the Prince."

"They would be," Margaret Clandara said. Her eyes began to glitter. "I can't imagine Sir Alexander or James and his brothers deserting, can you? I imagine that when the final battle comes they'll be at the forefront of it. . . . James was such a great fighter. You have no idea how much he loved to fight; his spirit was too wild for this dull age. A few centuries ago he would have been a king. . . ."

"If you are going to speak of him"—Katherine stood up— "then I shall leave you. I'm surprised at your lack of tact, madam. I have never reminded you of my dead brother or of the betrayal I suffered at James Macdonald's hands. I never thought it would be necessary."

"Don't be angry," the Countess said quietly. "Now that you are betrothed to someone else, I thought your heart was mended. Forgive the indiscretion; I meant no harm."

"I know." Katherine did not sit down again. She had stayed long enough and there was something in the atmosphere which troubled her. She was glad to escape, and she said good night to her stepmother and left as quickly as she could. At the door, the Countess called her.

"When will Mr. Ogilvie be back? When will you be married, my dear Katherine?"

"God knows. He's gone off to offer his services to the Prince. He says he's in need of every man now, and as far as I know he'll be joining him at Inverness before the end of the month. As for the wedding—after the battle, I suppose."

"After the battle," the Countess repeated. "Of course. Good night, Katherine. I will remember your intentions."

"And to whom will ye address them, milady?" Jean came out of the inner room and closed the door. She knelt down and began poking the fire and feeding it with logs.

"To the devil, who else! Did you hear what she said, Jean? Ogilvie's gone to join the Prince's army. Ha-ha, I wonder what will happen when he comes face to face with the Macdonald? . . . She's wearing a ring too, and talking of a wedding after the battle. There'll be no wedding! James will kill him if the English don't! No one ever took a woman from James, even one he didn't want."

She began to rock backwards and forwards in her chair, staring at the fire. "They're at Inverness, Jean. They're at Inverness with the Prince!"

"What good is that to us?" Jean answered sourly. "They're at Inverness and we're shut up here."

"Not for long, Jean." The Countess turned to her and her sallow face was flushed; she looked excited, almost gay. "While I was asking her questions I was thinking. There's going to be a battle . . . win or lose, there'll be Macdonald's left alive at the end of it, and where will they go when it's over but home to Dundrenan. And how far from here will they pass on their way? A mere ten miles! Don't you see, you foolish girl, the time is coming when we'll send that message to them you've been blabbing about—and they'll come here in force and set us free."

"How?" Jean asked. She had witnessed these outbursts before, and seen the aftermath of tears and hysterical despair. "Wouldn't it be better to run away? Now that the fiend himself is often out for half the day and night seeing to his own affairs, why don't we fly, milady? The doors aren't locked on us; I could choose a good time and we'd be away without a soul seeing us."

"Away on foot, and most likely captured half frozen on the moor," the Countess retorted. "I wonder what my husband would do to us both then ... I'll wager that wretched daughter couldn't save us. You're a fool, Jean. I've no mind to crawl out of here like some beggar woman. There are too many marks still left on my back to let me walk away without revenge. We'll wait for our kin, you and I. And then we shall see what we shall see." And she laughed. "As for that noble stepdaughter of mine, I'll pay back her acts of charity to me by giving her to the Red Murdoch as a present! Do you remember him, my child? A great ugly man with hair and beard as red as her accursed hair, naked as a baboon under the plaid. . . . How I shall laugh, Jean. How I shall stand there and watch it and laugh." She looked up suddenly and saw the girl's expression as she watched her. "And I'm not mad," she said. "Unless it's mad with hatred. I just pass the time sitting here by thinking. And my thoughts amuse me, that's all. You know I'm going to send you to our people, don't you?"

"I shall be ready," the girl answered. "And the sooner the better. Now I'll bring up your supper, milady."

"As you please," the Countess said. She leaned back in her chair and smiled. "I'll make that devil watch," she said to herself. "I shan't let Alexander kill him, I'll make them keep him alive so he can watch her. . . ." There were nights even now when she awoke in terror, dreaming that Clandara was standing by her bed, that the hands which had never once caressed her were tearing her fiercely out onto the ground, and that the upraised fist would crash into her unprotected face. Once when he was drunk he had dragged her by the hair; as she screamed he kicked and belaboured her, and shouted, "For my son, for Robert," with every blow, until he lost his balance and fell back against the bed. He had stood there cursing at her as she tried to crawl away. Jean thought that she was crazy. Margaret knew it and it amused her. Mad ... a little perhaps. What punishmnt could she devise for the man who had starved and scorned her body and then maltreated it so that the marks would never heal?

She got up and began to walk about, opening and closing her fists; the sound of that restless pacing was the only sign of her existence in that house. The cause was ruined. She had understood Katherine well enough, but the news hardly affected her. Like a trapped animal, her mind pursued its vengeance, unable to consider anything beyond that one obsession. The ruin of her Prince and her family and many of their friends did not concern Margaret any more. It seemed unreal beside the pressing urgency of her plan for Clandara and all its occupants. When Jean came back with her supper, she found the Countess back in her chair by the fire, gazing into it and smiling. Neither of them spoke again.

"Why don't you marry him, Katherine?" The Earl stood warming himself before the blazing logs in the library fire. He looked down at his daughter, who was sitting in a highback chair, her hands listlessly in her lap, staring at nothing. "Well," he repeated, "what point is there in delaying? Henry is coming back before the end of the month just to see you. Why don't you send him a message that when he comes you'll marry him?"

"Why do you want me to hurry?" she asked him. "There's a battle to be fought, have you forgotten? Supposing he is killed . . ."

"All the more reason," her father said. "You may well be carrying the heir to the Ogilvies and to Clandara by then. Katherine, for the love of God, be sensible and show the poor fellow a little kindness. There is no time for delay now. Scotland is blazing round our ears; those dogs of English are destroying everything they can lay hands upon, and I tell you plainly that since that young madman has gone off to enlist with the Prince, his only hope is to be married to you, so I can plead for him later."

"You are so certain they'll be defeated," she said.

"As certain as that the night follows the day," her father answered. "There's not a chance for any of them. Damned fools! They're dealing with an experienced general in this

German Duke; he's fought in Europe and he knows the science of war, not like our gentlemen amateurs, bickering among themselves! The Stuarts are lost, and so are all who follow them. I said that before ever this war broke out. At least there'll be a few like ourselves who will survive the English vengeance. And I don't want my family to be wiped out, either by wars or the lack of heirs to follow me. Katherine, it is your duty to marry Henry while you can. As your father I ask it of you. See if you can give me a grandchild before I die. You owe me that at least."

She looked up at him and her pale face flushed. He had not reproached her for Robert's death since that terrible day at Ben Mohire. But his eyes were hard now; there was no sympathy in them for her excuses and hesitations. He wanted the wedding and he wanted a child to take the place of the son who had been murdered by her lover. He was right; she did owe it to him. And she owed something to Henry too, before he went out on his impossible quixotic venture into a war which was already lost.

"If you want me to do it, then I will," she said. "I'll write tonight to him."

"I'll have it sent to Inverness tomorrow," the old Earl said. He came over and bent down, kissing his daughter's cheek. "Thank you, my child. Now you're being sensible. All will be happy for you yet, you'll see."

She got up and returned his kiss, and curtsied to him as she said good night. When Annie came to undress her, she told her to wait. The night, though very cold, was fine and clear, and she went to the window and opened it, looking up at the dark sky which was full of glittering stars. Behind her Annie shook out her velvet dressing gown and laid the lawn nightgown on her bed.

"What is it, milady? Tell me, please."

"I'm going to marry Mr. Ogilvie at the month's end. My father has insisted upon it."

"Then you should be very happy," Annie said. "Why postpone it longer, when there's a chance he may be killed? . . . Ach, you ought to be smiling, milady. Come, leave that window before ye catch your death of cold!"

"I wonder where he is?" Katherine said suddenly. "I wonder if he's still with that woman?"

"God protect us!" Annie stared at her in horror. "Are ye talking of that murderer again, after what his brother tried to do to ye? Are you mad?"

"No, just curious." Katherine closed the window and turned round. "I wonder if he loves her?" she went on, almost as if she were speaking to herself. "I can't imagine it. He was never capable of love."

"I'm glad to hear you say that," the maid said fiercely. "How can you mention him and a man like Mr. Ogilvie in the same breath? I won't discuss him with ye ... it's wrong and it's a morbid sin against the one you're going to marry!"

"He's a good man," Katherine said slowly. "How strange, there couldn't be a greater contrast to James Macdonald in the whole of Scotland. Virtuous, gentle, honourable, kind ..." She laughed suddenly and beckoned Annie to begin unfastening her dress. "And yet I shall never love him, never. Now tell me I ought to be smiling and happy, you foolish creature!"

"I can't tell you anything," Annie muttered. "Except that I'm sure ye'll bless the day you married him in the end."

"No doubt," Katherine agreed. She stepped out of her dress and Annie removed the tight bone corselet. She stood in her shift and then suddenly pulled it off and waited naked for a moment, while her nightgown was opened up and drawn over her head. "When I'm too old to remember and my blood is too sluggish to run fast for any man, then I'll bless the day. But not before. Leave me now, Annie. I'll snuff my own candles."

"Good night then, milady." For a moment Annie hesitated, then suddenly she put her arms around her young mistress and hugged her awkwardly. "Be patient," she whispered. "They tell me love breeds love. I'm sure it will be so for both of you."

Katherine lay back and smiled at her as she went out and the door closed. Under the sheets she slowly touched her own body, coolly as if it belonged to a stranger. It would be as chilled and stiff under the hands of her husband as it was under her own; his touch had never roused her, his kisses and the circumspect caresses she had permitted him might just as well have been bestowed on someone else for all the effect they had upon her. And always afterwards the thought of James came creeping back into her mind like a serpent, slipping past the barriers she had erected, stinging her with memories when the blood sang in her head and the vision blurred and her fiercely independent spirit implored the absolute subjection of her body. It would never be like that with Henry. It would never be like that with anyone again.

Two weeks later she knelt before the altar of the family chapel at Clandara with Henry Ogilvie beside her and took her marriage vows.

"A healthy and long life of happiness to both of you! To you, Katherine, and to my new son, Henry!" The Earl raised his glass and the half dozen guests assembled in the Green Salon did the same. The toast was drunk and the glasses flung into the fireplace where they smashed to pieces. It was the custom to hallow the toast by making sure the glasses never held wine for another.

Two elderly cousins, their close neighbours Lord and Lady Glendar and their niece Fiona, and Mrs. Ogilvie of Spey were gathered round the bride and groom. Katherine stood close beside Henry; she wore a white dress, simply cut and frilled with rows of exquisite lace, and her family's jewelled headpiece glittered in her hair. She did not look pale because Annie had insisted upon roughing her, and the paint disguised the fact that there was not a vestige of colour in her face. Everyone agreed that she looked beautiful, and Henry's arm was round her waist, and he had her other hand in his, the hand on which his new ring shone.

His mother gazed at them both with moist and happy eyes. She had always liked Katherine, in spite of the fact that she was such a beauty and of imposing presence, and her son was so happy that she discounted all her fears. Dear Henry; her maternal smile of pride and tenderness shone on him like sunshine. He looked handsomer than she had ever seen him in his wedding suit of pale blue velvet and the kilt woven of fine silks. She went to the Earl and said gently, "What a splendid pair they make, my son and your daughter. This is a very happy day for me."

"No happier than it is for me," the Earl answered. "I've known Henry and loved him as if he were mine own. Now I have settled Katherine safely with him, I have no cares left in this world. Let me get you something more to drink, madam. Davie, bring the wine here for the Lady of Ogilvie."

It was a very small wedding, quite unlike the pomp with which the Frasers married off their children, but all their close neighbours were with the Prince at Inverness, and there was little enthusiasm for extravagance in the countryside. The doom of defeat and retribution hung over so many families that pride alone would not have permitted them to drink and celebrate in the house of one who had remained neutral.

Lord Glendar moved over to speak to Katherine. He was a small man, middle-aged and nondescript in appearance, but he was very rich and influential, with distant kinship through marriage to the treacherous Earl of Breadalbane and his Campbells. He had no sons and he had not joined the rising himself; that and his connection with the Campbells, who were as busily despoiling their own people as the soldiers of the King of England, ensured for him the safety of his family and the immunity of his fine mansion. He bowed to Henry and kissed Katherine's hand.

"My compliments to you both. You look exceedingly well, my dear, and I may say that this is a doubly happy occasion for me; firstly, I haven't seen your father since July, and secondly, I find you married to someone of whom everyone heartily approves."

He could remember that ball so well and seeing her sweep past him on the arm of James, her flushed and lovely face upturned towards him, his dark one bent down to hers. The old nobleman glanced across the room towards his niece; she was talking happily to Mrs. Ogilvie. Remembering the unwelcome suit of Hugh Macdonald, he frowned and moved away. The silly child had been quite besotted for a time. Luckily she was well under age and sufficiently frivolous to be quickly diverted by the other eligible young men who came to call on them. It had taken a bloodthirsty murder to break

Katherine from her engagement to the elder Macdonald. How very fortunate, he thought, as he made conversation with one of Clandara's old spinster cousins, how very fortunate that she was safely bestowed upon such an excellent, sensible husband as Ogilvie. Lord Glendar was convinced that the management of a large house and the regular births of children were the only possible means of happiness for any woman. His ideal was the serenely settled matron who gave to her husband the absolute obedience she herself exacted from her children and her servants. His own wife was a delicate, nervous woman who had lost four children in infancy and now devoted her time and energy to his orphaned niece. When Fiona was married, he did not know how his wife would occupy herself. . . .

At that moment Fiona Mackintosh of Glendar made her way to Katherine. She was very pretty, with a rosy complexion and soft fair hair; her hazel eyes shone up at Katherine and at Henry, and she exclaimed in admiration of the elegant dress and its abundant lace.

"I'll just go to my mother, sweetheart," Henry said. He squeezed her hand and moved away. And when he was gone the young girl glanced quickly after him in the direction of her uncle and aunt.

"Lady Katherine, I must speak to you. Can you come over to the window with me? . . . I mustn't be overheard."

"Of course. Come, I'll show you this picture in the corner, by the north window. No one will disturb us for a moment."

"Thank you."

They were apart from the rest now, apparently absorbed by the small landscape before which they were standing, and Katherine said quietly, "Tell me, what is the matter, Fiona?"

"I don't know how to start," the girl began. "To you, of all people. But there's no one else I dare ask. . . . Lady Katherine, do you know what has become of—Hugh Macdonald?"

To her surprise she saw the genuine colour rise in Katherine's face and when she spoke her voice was strained and shaking. "Why do you mention that name to me on this day? What is Hugh Macdonald to you?"

"I love him." The answer was very soft, almost a whisper.

The large bright eyes looked up at her; she reminded Katherine of a small trusting animal. "My uncle forbade me to see him again or think of him. The last time was in Edinburgh when we went to see the Prince. I saw him then and I expected we would be formally betrothed. But my uncle heard things and suddenly turned against us. He doesn't know I ever think of Hugh now, but with all these stories of the retreat and the battle that's coming . . ." She hesitated, and then hurried on. "I wanted to know if he was safe . . . I thought you might have news. . . ."

"I know nothing about him," Katherine said. She took the girl by the elbow and their backs were turned towards the room. "All I know is this; you are the most fortunate girl in Scotland to have been saved from him in time. You say you love him. . . . Let me tell you this: if he did not seduce you, it was only because he wanted to marry you for your money. It was he who killed my brother Robert, killed him from behind like some low footpad in the back streets of Inverness. Put him out of your head and your heart, and thank God for your escape. That's all I have to say to you."

"I understand," Fiona Mackintosh said. "And I'm sorry if I've caused you any pain by asking you. But I did know he was a bad man, you know," she added gently. "Everyone knew it. But that doesn't stop me loving him any more than it stopped you loving his brother. Excuse me, Lady Katherine, I see my aunt is coming over."

"Why now, what were you talking about, my love?" Henry had come back and he put his arm around her tenderly. "You look distressed."

She looked up at him and managed to smile. "We were talking about my trousseau," she said. "And I'm afraid the poor child was woefully disappointed when I told her how meagre it was. I had so little time after all!"

"You shall have all the fine things you wish," he said fondly. "As soon as this business is over and we can be together in peace, I shall personally supervise your choice. I have decided views on what you should wear, my darling one, and from now on you shall do nothing without consulting me." He laughed and kissed her, and she felt the pressure of his arm as it tightened on her and his lips hesitated against her cheek.

"How nice it is to see you two." Lady Glendar came up to them, followed by the Earl of Clandara. "So few young people show their feelings now; we went to the marriage of some cousins of mine a few months ago, and they stood like statues beside one another, not a word or a kiss between them . . . so discouraging, I think, for the future. . . ." She wandered off, and within the next half hour the others took their leave. By late afternoon only Katherine, her husband, and her father and mother-in-law were left. They dined quietly, and throughout the meal she maintained her calm and responded to the smiles and banter of the two old people, both of whom were mellowed by emotion and, in the Earl's case, by a prodigious amount of whisky. She had only to look up to see Henry watching her, his face suffused with tenderness and pride and the longing to be alone with her at last. She drank his health and her mother-in-law's, and deliberately did not dawdle because her pride would not allow it. And when the time came for them to say good night, she kissed her father and Mrs. Ogilvie and went upstairs on her husband's arm.

The Earl had given them the state rooms for their apartments; as a child Katherine used to wander into the big bedroom with its vaulted stone ceiling, and climb up onto the bed where three sovereigns of Scotland had once slept during their visits to Clandara. The rooms had been dark and musty with disuse; now they were aired and full of lights, with large fires blazing in the grates of the bedroom and the antechamber.

Her nightgown and robe were laid out ready, and Annie and one of the little castle maids were waiting for her, standing very straight and solemn, and when she came into the room they curtsied. Henry left her for his anteroom and dressing closet, small rooms which had been used by one King and two Princes in the past, and there his own Ogilvie servants attended to him.

Katherine did not speak to Annie. She smiled at her, the same stiff smile which had scarcely left her face throughout the day, and allowed her to brush out her hair and scent it, and help her into the huge crimson velvet bed which stood in the middle of the room upon a dais. When the red and gold hangings were drawn she lay alone and isolated. The bed was so big and the canopy above her was so high that she felt like a child again, exploring it as if it were a ship.

She lay and waited for Henry and thought of nothing. They were staying at Clandara for the next two weeks; there wasn't time for him to take her back to Spey and introduce her to his tacksmen. That would come later, when the rising was over. And if the worst befell, he was prepared to flee to France and negotiate a pardon from there with the English government. Henry was full of optimism; he had a solution for every problem, and she knew that the source of his optimism was his happiness with her. Nothing could darken his world now that she was securely fixed in it; her influence vas as brilliant and as immutable as the sun's place in the universe. The marriage might be her father's last insurance for his name and his estates, for her the payment of a debt she owed and a final surrender of her doomed and misdirected love, but for Henry it was life. He would go out to fight for his Prince and his country as if the possession of her was a talisman against death, the same talisman which would protect him from arrest and punishment and ruin. . . .

When he opened the curtains she sat up.

"If you had been asleep," he said gently, "I would not have woken you tonight."

"I know," Katherine answered him. "But I was waiting for you."

He was gentle, tender, and finally carried away by the force of his own passion; it swept him on and on, surmounting her wretched attempt at participation, ignoring that attempt's collapse and the painful, unresponsive surrender which her body made. The consummation came and after it he slept, one arm across her; a little later she removed it very gently so as not to wake him. She had expected to cry, but no tears came as a relief; she felt exhausted and wretched, and her unhappiness was passive as if it were already the pattern on which her life would develop. At last she slept. When morning came, he made love to her again, more slowly and with an expertise which only made the ordeal worse for her because it prolonged the act and she felt nothing. When it was over he took her in his arms and kissed her.

"Poor little Katherine," he said gently. "Thank you, my love, for all you've given me, and don't despair. Give me a little time."

She did not answer him because she couldn't, and wisely he did not press her. It would have been easier, she thought over and over again in the days of that wretched honeymoon, if only he had been less kind, less desperately in love with her. If she had been able to hate him or criticise him for one single moment's inconsideration, she might have hated herself a little less. But Henry was not to be faulted; she was alone with her own sense of betrayal, and pride forbade her the relief of making anyone her confidant. She snubbed Annie until her anxious hinting ceased, and to her father she presented a smooth face which told him nothing. If she were unhappy, then that unhappiness could not be shared. In his own way he loved her, and now that his son was dead, Katherine was all he had to live for, that and the grandchild he wanted so much. She could not burden him with a reproach, and once when he asked her if she was contented, she managed to kiss him and murmur that she was. He accepted her answer with relief and did not ask again.

The days passed, and the torture of lying in her husband's eager arms increased rather than slackened with repetition, because now that his own fierce desire was gratified, he had begun to woo her, trying with every caress and every lover's trick to force a response out of her body. And there were times in the last few nights before he left Clandara when she prayed that it would come, not for herself but to please him, and because without it she feared that she would never have a child. And all her feeble hopes were fastened on that child, so longed for by her father, and by Henry. She could devote herself to a son, and perhaps motherhood would reawaken the capacity for love and give some meaning to her empty life.

The night before Henry left, the crisis came, and unexpectedly it came from him. She lay naked at his side, her eyes closed, submitting to every intimacy he inflicted upon her, and suddenly she shuddered. He felt the movement of revulsion and immediately drew back. In the darkness he sat up and his voice was unsteady, like the voice of a stranger.

"Why did you marry me? Answer me, damn it, why did you marry me when I disgust you?"

"Don't say that, please," she whispered. "Please, Henry. You said it would take time . . ."

"Yes, a lifetime! You lie there, stiff and shivering, and think I do not know how you detest it all! But if it were he who did this to you, he who held you in his arms, ah, Katherine, that would be so different, wouldn't it? He is the cause of all this coldness in you . . . he's still in your heart, that murderer and scoundrel, and I know it. By God, if I ever come against him I'll kill him, and perhaps when you know he's dead you'll turn to me a little!"

"That isn't true," Katherine protested. "You have no right to say that to me. . . . I never pretended to love you; you took me knowing I did not!"

"I didn't know you still loved *him*," he answered. "And however much I loved you, I wouldn't have married you if you had told me that."

"What can I do?" she said. "What do you want from me? I've given all I can . . . there's nothing left."

"There's nothing left for either of us," Henry said, "as long as you're betraying me in your heart. I've been gentle and I've been patient. I thought that love would come, that I could reach you. . . . I was so sure. . . . God in heaven, what a fool I've been."

He dragged back the curtains and in the moonlight she saw him looking down at her. She pulled up the sheet to cover herself and he seized it and threw it back. "You are my wife," he said, "and I've a right to see you if I wish. You don't appreciate a gentle hand. So be it! Close your eyes and make believe you're lying with your brother's murderer, if that will make it easy for you."

She tried to fight him then, but she was overwhelmed and hurt, and suddenly his brutality and anger were a relief: she wept in his arms and when it was over he sprang out of the bed and left her.

When Annie came to dress her in the morning she saw the marks on Katherine's arms and her thin little face turned pale.

"Spare me," her mistress said. "No questions, no reproaches against him, Annie. I deserved it, and he was man enough to deal it out. At least I can respect him now."

She was still in her wrapper, her long hair hanging down her back, sitting before the toilet table while Annie laid out her riding clothes, for she was expected to ride part of the way with him, when Henry came into the room. He stood looking down at her and for a moment neither of them spoke.

Katherine turned to Annie. "Leave us, please. I'll ring when I want you."

"Very good, milady." She passed Henry without looking at him and at the door she turned. "If ye need me, I'll be nearby."

He was already dressed in trews and riding coat, his hair hidden under a short curled wig tied back with the white ribbon of the Stuarts. He looked drawn and there were sharp lines in his face which she had never seen before.

"Katherine," he said at last, "Katherine, I've come to ask you to forgive me."

She shook her head. "There's nothing to forgive. I am the one who needs forgiveness."

"I didn't want to hurt you," he said slowly, "I didn't mean to; if you didn't love me before, I know you must hate me now."

She got up and came to him and, putting out her hand, she took his. "I could never hate you, Henry. I've hurt you so much that if you hadn't turned on me I couldn't have borne it. . . ."

"You don't love me, do you?" he asked her. "Don't be afraid to tell me the truth, Katherine. What happened last night will never happen again, I give you my word. Whatever you say, I won't reproach you now."

"No," Katherine said. "No, I don't love you, Henry. I don't believe I ever will. There's nothing I can say to soften it; there's nothing I can do to right the terrible injury I've done you."

"You can forgive me for last night," he said unsteadily, "and say that in spite of all that's gone before, if I return you'll take me back and we can try again. I've said so often that love comes in the end, and like the fool I was, I expected it in a few days and nights. But now I know that I would rather have you on your own terms and keep hoping, than not have you at all. Can you grant me that one hope before I go?"

"I am your wife," she said gently. "If you want me, I shall be waiting here for you."

"Life isn't at an end for you, my love." He stepped close to her and took her in his arms. "We have so much, so many happy years of friendship, long before this shadow came to blot out all our happiness. We will regain it, given time."

"We may," she whispered. "Who knows? You're a very good man, Henry. . . . If only I had married you three years ago and never met that other one—how different everything would have been today!"

"The past is past," he said. "There's little profit out of thinking of what might have been—only of what still may be. And you know that I love you? Nothing has ever altered that and nothing ever will."

"I know," she said. "Take care, try and come back to me. We may make something of our lives together. I give you my word that next time I will try."

"That promise would drag me from the grave," he said. "Pray for me, Katherine. In victory or defeat, I will return to you. Kiss me now, before I go."

"I shan't ride with you," Katherine said. "We'll part here, alone."

He kissed her slowly, and she put her arms around his neck.

"One thing more," she whispered. "Don't look for James Macdonald. Don't tempt our fate. . . ."

He left her without answering, but at the door he turned and looked at her. "I told you last night, if I come against him in battle or out of it, I shall kill him. God bless you, my love. Farewell!"

On Tuesday morning, April 15, 1746, Prince Charles Edward was established in Culloden House, the evacuation home of his old enemy Duncan Forbes, Lord President of the Council of Scotland and supporter of the English King. It was a fine house in a beautiful setting, and the whole of the Highland army was drawn up in the country surrounding it. The world had come to Inverness two days before that the Duke of Cumberland and an army of ten thousand men had reached Nairn, followed by their supply ships along the eastern coast. The last battle was approaching, and the scattered troops were rallied; Cameron of Lochiel marched sixty miles from Achnacarry and the Duke of Perth brought back the Army of the Spey, an army too weak and ill equipped to challenge the enemy's crossing of the river Spey. By forced marches and incredible endurance, Charles's troops joined him at Inverness and then on to Culloden. And at Culloden, after a brave review of his army, it was decided to try again the tactics of surprise which had won him victory at Prestonpans.

The Macdonalds were there with their men; the old chief sat his horse with his three sons on either side, their piper playing before them, and only a third of their original levy drawn up behind. The rest had succumbed to cold and irregular rations or had slipped away during the long weeks of waiting. The Macdonalds had gone with Perth to the Spey, and marched back at the Prince's summons without food or rest for two whole days. The men were swaying on their feet with hunger and fatigue. Sir Alexander was gaunt and red-eyed and his edgy temper flared at his sons.

"While they sit deliberating in Culloden House, arguing and swilling brandy, when in the devil's name do we get either to fight or rest? Hugh, go down there and find out what's happening. Did they send for us to come all this way just to hold a review?"

"The English are at Nairn," James snapped. "That's all we know, and that's all we're likely to know till they come up on us!" He was so tired that he could hardly sit his horse. None of them had eaten more than a few crusts of bread and they had drunk only what they could buy or steal from the few miserable hamlets they passed through; their men had had less. "If we fight now, we haven't a chance," James said. "We need rest and our people need food. The same is true of the whole army. Tell them that, Hugh, when you go there."

"I will," Hugh called out to him; he kicked his tired horse until it broke into an uneven gallop down the grassy slope towards the Lord President's mansion. While they waited, the chief and James and David dismounted, and ordered their men to stretch out on the ground and snatch what rest they could. The hours passed, while the councils continued at the house, and when at last Hugh came back to them it was nearly dusk and turning very cold.

"We're to creep up on them and attack by surprise," he said. He was out of breath, and his thin face looked thinner still with fatigue. "Another Prestonpans, that's the plan. You should have seen the Prince! He threw his arms round Lord George's neck and wept with joy when that old misery agreed to take the initiative for once! Come on, Father! Rally the men, we're to march as soon as it is dark."

"March!" James stood up, wrapping his plaid around him. "Look around you, brother. If you can get another five miles out of these people of ours, it'll be a miracle."

"A miracle is what is needed," Sir Alexander said. He settled his bonnet on his shorn grey head, and cursed the cold, the lack of food and supplies and the whole war, which he was sure was lost even before they met with Cumberland. "Piper, play up! David, you're half asleep still, ye damned fool! Get to your horse. James, go round and make sure none of these laggards try to slip away. . . . We're marching to Nairn to take the Duke of Cumberland by the breeches! Away with you!"

"Why tonight?" James asked Hugh as they began to ride slowly out. "Why this sudden decision when half the army is tired out and empty-bellied?"

"Because today is the Duke's birthday," Hugh replied. "Our spies came in with the story this morning; he's issued a ration of brandy to the men and they're all making merry there without a thought of danger. I know we're tired, brother, and I'm as weary and hungry as the rest, but if we can catch them unawares tonight, catch them sleeping off their little celebration—we'll massacre them! And that's our only chance. I don't fancy meeting ten thousand of them, *and* artillery, on open ground when they're sober, I can tell you. Come on there, don't lag behind." He turned in his saddle and shouted at the straggling group of Macdonalds. "Keep up there, or I'll take my sword to you! Jesus, what wouldn't I give for a warm bed!"

At eight that evening the Prince's army gathered itself for the long night march to Nairn; Lord George was in the van with the Camerons, the Appin Stewarts, and his Atholl men, and behind him came Charles and the rest. The angry reproaches and exhortations of the Macdonalds to their unwilling men were repeated throughout the straggling clans that cold and misty night. Everywhere the Highlanders were falling behind, some sleeping where they lay, others complaining that they were being asked to fight on a drink of water and a dry biscuit, which was all the rations issued them that day. The carts carrying their food had not arrived from Inverness because the Prince's secretary, John Hay of Restalrigg, had omitted to assemble them. This inefficient and timorous man had replaced the energetic Murray of Broughton when the latter fell ill, and the wretched troops had him to thank for their empty bellies and sinking morale. The march was doomed from the beginning; a third of the army had drifted back from Culloden to Inverness in search of food and rest and when the dawn came up over the moor they had not reached Nairn and the drums of the English army were already beating the general call to arms. Within sight of the enemy, the Highland army halted, and at last the word was passed back along the line: "Retreat back to Culloden."

James turned his horse's head and pulled at his father's bridle. Sir Alexander had been dozing; he awoke with a start.

"James, what the devil are ye doing . . ."

"Turning back," came the answer. "We're in sight of Nairn and it's too light to go any farther. There won't be a Prestonpans this time. Tell the piper to play, Father. We've no need to hide ourselves from Cumberland now and the men will need the music to make them walk another step."

"God damn it," the old man said. "All these miles for nothing."

"If those swine of English advance on us today, they'll cut us to pieces," Hugh said slowly. He glanced quickly at his father and brothers as they rode back over the wet and treacherous moor towards Culloden.

"Others have left the field and made for home. Why don't we do the same while there's still time?"

The old chief's haggard face turned red. "Abandon the Prince?" he shouted. "Never! As long as there's breath left in my body, I'll stay on and fight with him. You can turn tail if ye wish, but don't let me find you at Dundrenan or I'll kill you with my own hands."

"I never thought you were a coward." James glared at him. "I've no great opinion of you, Hugh, but I never thought that! Run if you will, but I stay with the Prince."

"And I," David said. He turned away from his brother and spat.

Hugh shrugged, and to their surprise he laughed. "Calm yourselves," he mocked. "I've no mind to run away. I only thought for a moment that it might be sweet to live a little longer instead of dying in this dismal place. That's all."

"Better to die than live dishonoured," his father answered coldly. "You may be my son, Hugh, but there's something in you I don't recognise as being part of a Macdonald."

"It's only common sense," his son retorted, "and I haven't enough to make me leave you. I'll die with you then, if that's what you want. We'll all go back to Culloden and die for the Prince. I only hope he's grateful for it." And he began to whistle the same stirring tune the Macdonald piper played.

By six o'clock the clans were back where they had started, and the weary officers descended upon Culloden House at the Prince's invitation to breakfast off his own supplies. He did not share it with them, for he had ridden back to Inverness to bring food to the field for his men.

James and his father threw themselves down on a bench in

the main hall of the mansion, tired and wet and covered in mud from the long ride, while the Red Murdoch and Dugal, the chief's servant, brought them some oatmeal scones and cold meat, and jugs of the fine claret which had been discovered in the cellar. They ate and drank in silence and all around them the officers of the other clans were taking what rest they could once they had eaten. A few were arguing in angry tones, and there was a pause when the Prince came through, as dirty and fatigued as they were themselves. The steward of the house came up to him and bowed.

"There's a roast side of lamb and two fowls prepared in the dining room for you, Highness. I'll have them served as soon as you are ready."

"Distribute them," Charles said wearily. "I cannot eat while my men are starving."

He ran up the stairs followed by Colonel O'Sullivan, his quartermaster, and the Macdonald of Clanranald, Kinlochmoidart's brother. There were half a dozen officers who had come from Inverness with him, and among them James recognised Angus Ban, one of Macdonald of Keppoch's sons.

"We'd despaired of you," James shouted across to him. "Come and share what's left with us!"

"Greetings." Angus bowed to Sir Alexander and dropped down beside them. "We've marched day and night to get to Inverness in time only to find the army moved out here. Tell me the news; I've heard nothing but the wildest rumours and my father is like a lion; it's more than any of us dare to ask him anything."

"He smells defeat," Sir Alexander said, "and so do I. You'll have to bear with his temper, Angus; he's good reason for it."

"Is it true Cumberland is at Nairn?"

"No longer," James answered. "They were already assembling and taking down their tents as we turned back. We tried to creep up and take them by night, but it was useless. Our men and everyone else's were too hungry and too tired. We wasted what was left of our strength on a night march and then had to retreat. Cumberland is marching after us."

"Will the battle be today?" the young man asked. "I wish

my father wouldn't fight; he's over old for it now, and he's tired out. Even one day's rest would make a difference."

"So the English must think," James said. "And that's why they'll come at us today. What news from Inverness?"

"Little enough." Angus finished the last of the meat and swallowed some wine; he wiped his mouth on his sleeve. "A few more recruits for the Glengarrys, but not as many as were hoped. The Ogilvies of Spey have joined us; the Ogilvie himself came into Inverness with two hundred and fifty men, fresh and eager to do battle." He held out his cup and James refilled it.

"Take care with that," he warned. "It's a good French wine and stronger than the wretched stuff we're used to drinking. You'll need a clear head later on. Two hundred and fifty Ogilvies—we'll need every man of them."

"It's surprising they came," Angus said, "considering the Ogilvie is newly married. . . . They say she's a rare beauty." He looked up at James, and his freckled face wrinkled in a grimace. "Ach, of course you should know better than I—I'd quite forgotten. It's the daughter of Clandara that he married—Katherine Fraser."

Sir Alexander raised his head and glanced quickly at his son; he had been dozing again, half listening to the chattering boy. James was in profile to him; he could see nothing but the dark skin turning very pale and the muscles in the side of his jaw slowly hardening under the skin.

"Why," Angus Ban said, "what have I said? Why do you look like that?"

"He married Katherine Fraser. Isn't that what you said?"

"I did," Angus repeated. "A few weeks ago, it seems. That's why I said it's surprising he could tear himself away. I've never seen the lady but I remembered when I told you that you used to know her . . . wasn't there something about a match between you?"

"There was," James said very quietly. "A wedding was arranged. Your father came to our betrothal ball."

"That's over and done." The old chief spoke up suddenly and he glared first at the innocent Angus and then at his son. He knew that soft voice and the meaning of that blazing eye.

"Much good may it do the Ogilvie to marry *her!* James, where are you going?" His voice rose in alarm. James looked down at him; he was buckling on his sword and there was murder in his eyes.

Keppoch's son turned to Sir Alexander; he was flushed and stammering. "I beg your pardon, I had no idea I'd said anything of importance. I assure you," he said to James, "if I had thought ... I wasn't with my family at the time—I went to stay at Sleat for a visit and it must have been then ..."

"It must," James agreed. "Where is this Ogilvie of Spey? At Inverness, you said?"

"James!" His father sprang up. "James, I forbid you! You damned madman, he's her husband! Isn't that enough for you; doesn't that prove her worth, if proof were needed? Sit down, I command you!"

"He's on his way here," Angus Ban interrupted. "He should be here within the hour."

"My thanks." James bowed to him. He took his bonnet up and pulled it on. "I'll go and meet him. I want to offer my congratulations."

"James ..." Sir Alexander shouted after him, but his son was pushing through the crowd and the next moment he was gone.

"You blabbering fool," the old man snarled, turning on the innocent harbinger of bad news. "Do you know what you've done? My son has gone to kill him! Get out of my sight before I break this wine jug over your thick head. . . . By God, wait till I see your father!"

Angus jumped to his feet and, still mumbling his apologies, he fled. When Sir Alexander managed to get to the door and force his way out of the house there was no sign of James.

At five o'clock that morning the army of King George of England, led by the King's son, William, Duke of Cumberland, struck its tents and to the measured beat of drums began its march from Nairn towards Culloden. It numbered six thousand four hundred foot soldiers and two thousand four hundred horse, and the Duke himself rode with it, accompanied by his second in command, the infamous General

Hawley who had been ignominiously beaten at Falkirk, and the members of his staff. The birthday which the Duke had celebrated only the day before had been his twenty-fifth, and the rest of his staff were men as young as he was. Lord Cathcart, a veteran of Fontenoy who had lost an eye, was the same age as the Duke; Lord Bury, heir of the Earl of Albemarle, was only twenty-one, but he had been an ensign in the Coldstream Guards since his fourteenth birthday; and Colonel Joseph Yorke, scion of the ancient and mighty family of Hardwicke, was a seasoned twenty-two. To these young men, aristocrats of wealth and influence, the war was rather like a hunt in which the quarry were uncivilised foreigners who had dared to oppose the sacred authority of England and the King, by taking arms for a renegade Catholic Prince who should by rights have been handed over for immediate execution as soon as he landed on Scottish soil.

They were unmoved by the splendour of the country through which they had passed; the grandeur of the mountains, the majestic isolation of the sweeping moors, and the great blue lochs found no responsive chord in the hearts of officers or men. It was a savage land, unblessed by roads or tidy villages on the pretty English model. The people north of the Tweed were as alien to the men of Cumberland's army as the savage Indians in His Britannic Majesty's American colonies, and almost as far divided by their language, customs, and religion.

The fact that these despised people had dared to cross into England and march as far south as Derby was an added insult to the well-bred gentlemen whose families had fallen into such a vulgar panic at the threat of invasion. To Cumberland himself, the rebellion was an act of insolence against his father which he was determined to punish with Teutonic thoroughness. He was a fat young man with a rather porcine cast of feature and prominent black eyes, little imagination, personal courage and a horrible lack of human feeling which encouraged flogging and hanging as a normal means of keeping discipline among his troops. General Hawley was no better; his language was as foul as his temper, and the defeat inflicted upon him at Falkirk added personal hatred to his natural penchant for extreme brutality. These were the men who led King George's army, and their attitude to the war and those who fought against them faithfully reflected the feelings of His Majesty. From Aberdeen to Nairn, they had hanged and burned without mercy and often without troubling to make distinction between the innocent and the guilty. The rough and destitute men who comprised their army and suffered the rigours of campaigns abroad and army discipline for the pay of three shillings and sixpence a week proceeded on their way to Culloden behind the tapping drums with the hope of loot and the fear of the drill sergeant's lash to encourage them. En route the Duke stopped at Kilravock House and imposed himself and his officers upon the laird for a brief rest while the main force went on their way.

Only a few hours earlier, Prince Charles had stopped there and taken food and drink, a fact which the frightened owner did not try to conceal from his English guests. The Duke was in a good humour that morning, and with a battle ahead of him, he had neither the time nor the inclination to take vengeance. He accepted the laird's excuses with a smile of understanding, and Kilravock House and its inhabitants were spared. By noon he had joined the army of Culloden; within clear sight of them, the Highland forces of Prince Charles were drawn up upon the soft and hilly ground of Drummossie Moor.

The clansmen of Ogilvie were marching down the Inverness road and by nine that morning they sighted the mass of the army at Culloden. Henry rode forward towards the fine mansion standing in its park and woodlands, stopping to enquire of one of the many groups of officers where he might find the Prince.

"At the house, sir. But don't look for food for your people; we've none for ourselves and we're still awaiting the issue of what the Prince brought back from Inverness." As he rode by, Henry was surprised to see men lying fast asleep beneath the trees; everywhere he looked he saw signs of disorder and, what amazed him most of all, positive sullenness and apathy.

It was a cold day, and the clouds were gathering above in grey masses, threatening rain.

He dismounted outside the entrance to Culloden House, throwing the reins to one of his men, and ran up the steps to the main hall. He stopped a tall Highland officer who was leaning against the wall eating a piece of bread and meat; he was surprised to recognise the rich and elegant Lord Lewis Gordon, the younger son of the Duke of Gordon.

"Henry Ogilvie! Welcome and greetings. We heard you were on your way and thank God for it. How many men have you brought?"

"Two hundred and twenty at the last count," Henry answered. "What is the position, sir? Shall we do battle today?"

"Undoubtedly." Lord Lewis yawned. "They know well enough we've been up half the night trying to take them by surprise and they probably know that the army hasn't had more than a biscuit and a little water in its belly for the last twenty-four hours. The Prince himself went into Inverness to bring back the meal carts, but it's too late now. The whole thing is too late. Have you eaten?"

"Not since yesterday," Henry said. He was looking around him at the groups of weary men, eating like humblies with their bare hands and drinking wine out of the bottle. Some of the greatest names in the Highlands were being called back and forth, and those who answered to them were as tired and dirty as the clansmen he had seen sprawled out asleep on the bare ground outside. He turned to Lord Lewis.

"What has been happening here? I've never seen such chaos. You all look to me as if you've fought a battle, rather than are just about to!"

"That's exactly what we have done," the young man said. "We've fought for two long months, Mr. Ogilvie, against desertions, lack of funds, and the quarrelling of the Prince with Lord George Murray. No wonder Murray of Broughton fell ill, or said he did! Now there's such an utter fool in his place that he didn't make provision to feed the army, and the men are fainting for want of food. Fight a battle!" He laughed and, bending low, retrieved the bottle which he had placed between his feet. He raised it to Henry.

"I give you a toast, my dear sir. To the battle. Now excuse me; the Prince is upstairs if you've a mind to see him, but I'm going back to the kitchens. I have a notion this will be my last meal."

Henry turned to the stairs, but a gentleman in the livery of the Prince stepped across and held him back.

"If you're seeking the Prince, he's seeing no one now," he said. "He's with the general in chief and the Duke of Perth. Wait till he comes down."

"I've brought two hundred Ogilvies with me," Henry said. "How shall I dispose them?"

"The Prince will tell you."

"My thanks; in that case I shall take everyone's advise and get something to eat and drink."

"Through there," the gentleman said, pointing to an open door across the hall. "There's a sideboard laid out in there, and there's plenty of wine. The rogue who owns this house left an excellent cellar behind him."

The room was crowded; Henry had to push, constantly apologising and greeting men he knew, before he could reach the table. He was about to take a bottle of wine and fill his pocket with oatcakes, for the meat had all gone, when a voice said just behind him: "Ah, here come the laggard Ogilvies at last. And this, with his back to me and his hand round a bottle of another man's wine, must surely be their chief!"

Voices in the room were dying away; suddenly it was very quiet. He turned round and faced the man who had insulted him. And though they had never met, he knew at once that the tall, dark man, his black eyes glittering and his mouth drawn back in a sneering smile, was James Macdonald. He looked steadily into the swarthy face and read murder in the blazing eyes, and very calmly he looked from the face to the hand which was gripping the long thin dirk in his belt.

"I am the Ogilvie of Spey," Henry said. "Your name, sir?"

"James Macdonald of Dundrenan. I heard you had decided at last to throw in your lot with your Prince, and I hastened here to find you and tell you that the last rank in the battle is reserved for those who took so long to show their loyalty to their Prince."

"If you are trying to provoke me," Henry said, "why don't you do so clearly, so that all can hear you?"

"If you prefer it," James said very softly. There was not a sound to be heard in the room; a little circle had cleared round the two men as they stood facing one another.

"You are a coward," James said. "You had the temerity to marry a lady to whom I was once betrothed and that offends me. The marriage offends me; but you offend me most of all." He stepped forward and struck Henry a violent blow across the face. "Come outside and defend yourself," he sneered. "If you are not as afraid of me as you are of the English . . ."

Henry touched his face; a crimson weal was rising down the side of it, and blood oozed from a broken lip. The blow had been a savage one; custom demanded a light slap as a means of challenging an enemy. James had struck with all his strength.

"I shall kill you," Henry said. "I had that intention anyway when I set out. Not only to avenge the insults you've offered me, but to take justice for the death of my wife's brother and my old friend, whom you foully murdered from behind."

"Congratulations," James said softly. "I was afraid from all I'd heard of you that even a blow like mine wouldn't have brought your sword out of its scabbard. Follow me!" He threw his handkerchief at Henry and then turned and pushed his way out of the room. At the door he paused, looking back over the heads of the crowd to the man who followed him. He felt exhilarated, almost as if he were drunk. Lewis Gordon had told him where Ogilvie was, and he had forced his way in after him, determined to insult him past bearing and provoke the quarrel which would mean his death. James did not doubt his own skill, and the intensity of his jealous hatred gave him unnatural strength. Hate would sharpen his eye and quicken his thrust. She had taken a husband, had she, and a handsome one with a fine house and money and a good name. . . . As Ogilvie caught up with him, he bent and said under his breath: "Did you really imagine that I would let another man take my place with her? . . . Did you think I'd let her marry and forget me? If she takes a dozen husbands, by God, I'll kill them all, starting with you!"

"If you speak of my wife once more, you scoundrel," Henry said, "I'll stab you where you stand."

"Ah, has she enslaved you too?" James jeered. "Has she talked of love to you and melted in your arms, in that sweet way she has? ... Don't place too much reliance on it, sir. She'll have forgotten you after I've killed you as quickly as she's forgotten me. Come. Let's make an end."

"One moment!" The Duke of Perth stood before them. He was pale and unshaven, and his face was drawn with sleeplessness and worry. In spite of themselves, James and Henry stopped. "I hear you're about to fight a duel," the Duke said. "Is that correct?"

"It is," Henry answered. "I must ask you to step aside, Your Grace."

Perth glanced at his injured face and turned with a scowl upon James. "Your doing, I see," he snapped. "Now listen to me! The Prince is coming now, and the army will take its final position for battle within the hour. If either of you dares to persist in a private quarrel at this moment I'll send men after you to shoot you down! The English are two hours' march away from us, and we need every man. . . . Mr. Ogilvie, go and see to your clan if you please. Take them up to the moor and dispose them on the right behind Clan Chattan. You, sir"—he put out his hand as James tried to step forward—"stay where you are. Your father is searching for you."

"You have no right to stop us." James turned on him furiously; had his opponent been the Prince, he would have done the same. "This is a matter of honour. Just give me ten minutes"—he glared at Ogilvie—"and it will be over. Ogilvie, are you a man or the coward I called you, that you walk away with that mark upon your face!"

Henry looked at him; he was not a bitter man or one who harboured wrongs, but the pain of his parting from Katherine had been with him all the way from Spey, and the nightmare of their last night together had haunted him with shame and remorse ever since. And now the cause of it all stood within a few feet of him, the man whose arms had spoiled her for his, whose cruel and evil mouth had touched hers, whose hands had been at liberty to touch her before they drew a sword against her brother. . . . He had never really hated in his life before, but now his hatred came up into his heart and filled it full. There was a bitter taste of blood in his mouth.

"I'm going to kill you," he said slowly. "But I came here first to fight the Prince, and that's what I am going to do. After the battle we shall meet, Macdonald, and I beg of you, take care today. I don't want the English to deprive me of my purpose."

"Nor I," James snarled. "I'll wait for you, sir, sword in hand." He turned round to the men grouped near them and then to Perth himself. "I call you all to witness that the Ogilvie has promised satisfaction. If we both survive and he refuses to fight me, I claim the right to dagger him where he stands."

Perth turned his back on James. The meaning of the quarrel was becoming clear to him; Katherine Fraser . . . she had lately married the man James was challenging to the death. He had always disliked the savage son of the Macdonald chieftain. Now he could not trust himself to speak to him. He said to Henry: "Go on, sir. Nobody here doubts your courage. I order you in the name of the Prince. Go to your people and prepare them on the field. This business between you and the Macdonald can be settled later. That is, if either of you is left alive after today!"

Word had gone through the countryside that a great battle was about to be fought and since dawn the people had been coming from Inverness and the scattered crofts along the moor to the brae of Creagan Glas to watch the Prince and his army fight the English. It was bitterly cold and a sharp wind whipped the faces of the women and children and the gentry who stood upon the open ridge, the same wind with its burden of rain and sleet which was lashing into the faces of the royal army drawn up upon Drummossie Moor below them. A thousand yards away the thicker mass of scarlet which was King George's army moved towards them; the jingle and roll of their artillery train could be clearly heard, and with it the steady tapping of the drummers keeping the beat for the men.

It had seemed at one point that Cumberland might have to fight without his guns. The army had moved to the southwest, with the Moray Firth and the Nairn Valley on its flanks, and it marched upward over the soggy heather towards the plateau of the moor, its guns rumbling behind upon the Inverness road until the route took them the same treacherous, boggy path as the infantry. And a tattered Highlander had risen from the roadside and offered to guide Colonel Belford and his artillery an easy way up the steeply sloping ground. Within half an hour the guns were sinking and tilting in the ooze of the White Bog, and when the Colonel sent for the guide who had so skillfully misdirected them he had vanished. But if the Colonel was in despair, the Duke of Cumberland displayed his usual resource and energy and ordered the troops of Cholmondley's and the Royals to pull the guns onto firm ground. Their efforts and the despatch of horses from the rear rescued the artillery from the bog where the the unknown patriot had led them, and the Duke's army rolled forward to Drummossie Moor.

Upon the brae, there were many women and children of Clan Chattan come to watch their men in battle and to go down and care for them afterwards and bring them home if they were wounded or dead. Some merchants from Inverness had travelled out to the bleak moor and a minister or two. The Catholic priests were down below with the clans, armed with sword and buckler.

The wild skirling music of the pipers rose up through the driving rain and darkening cloud, carried for miles by the wind; the sound of it made the advancing redcoats glance sideways at each other, and the men of General Hawley's companies muttered uneasily under their breath. That same sound had presaged the terrible fighting at Falkirk when their nerve had broken and they fled the savage enemy. Thirty foot and thirty dragoons had swung from the Edinburgh gibbets after that defeat as a reminder to the rest not to run away again. Drums competed with the pipes, and slowly the English army moved, grouping and regrouping in companies as their commander disposed them for battle. Across the moor the Highland army waited, drawn up in a long uneven line on the spine of the ground. The Atholl men under Lord George Murray held the position to the right of the Prince, a position of honour which belonged by rights to all who bore the name Macdonald, given them by Robert the Bruce after Bannockburn as a sign of their courage in the battle, and now grudgingly renounced in favour of the unpopular general in chief.

The Camerons, the Stewarts of Appin, and the Mackintoshes, Farquharsons, Macphersons and MacBeans, all members of Clan Chattan, the Clan of the Cats, stood to the right and centre and the left line was held by men of the Clan Chisholm, the indomitable Clanranald, Keppoch, and the other setts of the great Clan Donald, in which the chief of Dundrenan and his three sons stood. Behind at the centre, Prince Charles himself waited on a grey gelding, surrounded by his bodyguard of Fitzjames Horse, now reduced to the strength of half a troop, and beside him the royal standard blew back in the wind.

From Creagan Glas, the spectators strained forward, huddled in little groups, the women drawing their plaids over their heads and hushing the crying children who dragged at their skirts. The few people of quality stood apart in scattered groups, and among them, wrapped in a cloak, her horse tethered to a bush on the hill below, Fiona Mackintosh stood to watch the battle in which Hugh Macdonald fought.

For the past three days she had listened to the talk of Cumberland and his army—its strength, the number and size of his guns, the perfect training and discipline of his troops—and through it all there ran her unspoken horror lest the man she loved should fall victim to his efficient, hateful machine of war. Her uncle had talked on, thanking God again and again that he had not committed himself to joining the doomed Prince and his cause, bewailing on the other hand the rashness of various cousins who had ignored his advice and gone to offer themselves and all they had to the

young man at Inverness. Lady Glendar said very little; it
seemed to Fiona that she was watching her a little anxiously,
and had she dared, she might have silenced her husband for
Fiona's sake. But Fiona had not given herself away. She was
awoken at dawn by the sound of the English army marching
from Nairn only a mile or two away, and she had dressed
herself and crept out of the house and taken one of her
uncle's fastest horses to ride to the royal army at Culloden.
But standing on the bleak brae, her courage faltered and the
tears came, running down her face as fast as she wiped them
away.

"Are you here alone?"

Fiona looked round and found a tall woman in a crimson
cloak and fur-lined hood standing beside her; she had seen
her among the group of people from Inverness, standing a
little apart from them.

"You are alone, aren't you?" she repeated. "This is no
place for a girl to be caught by the troops of either side when
the battle is over. We'd best stay together. Don't cry; tears
won't help them now."

"There are so many of the English," Fiona whispered.
"And our people are strung out so far. . . . Is your husband
down there madam?"

"No." The strange woman shook her head. "My lover is
fighting today. I'm Janet Douglas. What is your name?"

"Fiona Mackintosh of Glendar. I know who you're
watching for; it's James Macdonald of Dundrenan, isn't it?"

"How did you know?" Janet asked her.

The girl's white face had flushed. "Because I've heard
about you from Hugh, his brother. Listen! You can hear the
English drums. . . . If Hugh's wounded I shall get him back
to Dundrenan. I took my uncle's best horse . . . it'll carry us
both. And if he's dead," she said passionately, "I'll lie down
there and die beside him."

"He won't die," Janet said gently. "Hugh has a charmed
life. I only wish I felt the same of James." She looked quickly
at the small white face, pinched with tiredness and emotion,
and remembered the mocking voice of Hugh that day in Edinburgh when James was recovering from his wounds. "I

have an appointment for this evening. A charming, innocent, immensely wealthy child ..." Fiona Mackintosh. Of course. This was the pretty heiress whose uncle had rejected Hugh's proposal. She had always suspected that he felt more for his intended victim than he would ever have admitted, even to himself.

"Look!" Fiona said suddenly. "The redcoats are moving up—they're coming closer. ..."

Below them the final manoeuvre was taking place; when it was over only five hundred yards separated Cumberland's army from the Prince's forces. The two women turned instinctively and Janet put her arm around Fiona.

"Pray," she said fiercely. "Pray that we'll win. And pray for James and Hugh, wherever they are." For a moment her face contorted, and the arm around Fiona trembled. "If he dies," Janet said, "if he dies, I shall have nothing left to live for. ... And even so, he never loved me. I wonder where *she* is, that cursed woman. I don't see her standing here to watch and pray for anyone. ..."

"If you mean the Lady Katherine," Fiona said, "she's married. Her husband is the Ogilvie of Spey, and he's down there with the Prince. I was at their wedding. You've nothing to hate her for now, Mrs. Douglas. She belongs to someone else, and I believe she's miserable enough."

"What waste and folly," Janet said suddenly. "And what a fool I am to stand here shivering in this foul wind ... and yet I can't help myself, no more than you."

"You love him," Fiona said simply. "Just as I love Hugh. I knew he wanted me for my money, but I didn't mind. He could have had it all. ..."

As she spoke, there was a sharp crack in the silent air, and simultaneously puffs of pale smoke burst out along the front line of the English battalions and the first cannonade roared overhead and fell in a hail of shot among the men of Clan Chattan. The battle had begun.

Chapter 7

"HAVE YOU seen her ladyship?"

The steward at Clandara shook his head; he was hurrying across the Great Hall to the Earl's study with a bundle of papers under his arm when Annie stopped him. "I've not seen her since early this morning; she may be out riding, ask your grandfather."

"He's asleep in the kitchens," Annie said. "And I've looked all over the house for her."

"She's out for a walk then," the steward said. "I can't stand here wasting time with you, his lordship can't be kept waiting."

Annie muttered angrily and turned away. She had not seen her mistress since dawn; she had dressed her and brought up some breakfast and hot chocolate on a tray to her room, and after that Katherine had disappeared. Pulling her shawl over her head, Annie opened the heavy door into the outer courtyard and set out to look for her.

It was a cold day and the sky was dark and overcast; the sullen clouds flew before a biting wind. "Out for a walk," Annie grumbled to herself. "What a fool the woman is! She'll catch her death if she is, that's certain."

There was no sign of Katherine in the formal gardens at the back of the house, and with increasing anxiety Annie went to the stables to look for her. One of the Earl's grooms confirmed her fears. The Lady Katherine had taken her horse out very early and gone riding alone. She had not said where she was going, and refused his offer to accompany her. Seeing Annie's worried face, he added, "There's no harm

now, lassie, if she goes off without Angus. There's no Macdonald left within many miles to harm her."

That at least was true, but Annie ordered the groom to
have her grandfather's old mount made ready, and hurried
back to the castle to wake him. "Ye ought to be ashamed,"
she stormed at him, "sleeping away there while her ladyship
goes out alone and runs into God knows what dangers! Get
up and rub the sleep out of your eyes. . . . Your horse is
ready, go and look for her!"

"Aye," the old man said, stretching himself. "I dare say I
know where she'll be too."

"Oh, do ye?" Annie faced him angrily. "And how would
ye know something about her ladyship that I do not?"

"Because she's been going back to the same place ever
since Mr. Ogilvie left to join the Prince. She's over at Loch
Ness, where she and the Macdonald used to meet. I'll go and
bring her back if that'll ease ye." And he pushed past her,
whistling triumphantly. He did not often get the better of her.

The waters of Loch Ness were steel grey, its surface
rippled by the gusts of wind, and the bare trees, not yet in
full bud despite the month of April, bent and swayed by its
shores. In this lonely place under the shadow of the mountain
Katherine tethered her horse and walked up to the place on
the rising ground where she and James had lain in each
other's arms nearly two years ago. It was not her first visit, as
old Angus said; she had ridden out here many times in the
last few weeks since Henry had gone to call out his clansmen
and join the royal army.

This time she had not wanted even the old man as witness,
and drawing her tartan cloak around her, she sat down in the
hollow and leant back until the smell of the heather was so
strong and with it the memories of that other day when she
had lain back, pressed down by the weight of James's body,
that she covered her face and slowly wept with shame and
the most torturing regret. She had married Henry for nothing, given herself in haste to a man she did not love and
never could in the hope that the union might give a grandson
to Clandara. But now she knew that hope was vain. And she
knew too that whatever happened and in spite of her promise

she could never return to Henry as his wife. Above her the wild heron flew, and its cry echoed out over the Loch. In vain. The bird's call seemed to mock the bitter words that came from her own heart. In vain. Robert's death and the loss of James, poor Henry's unrequited love and failed marriage, her father's grief and the ruin of her own life. There was no child, no desire for the future, nothing left but bitter memories and the agony of her love which would not die.

She had not had the heart to tell her father or to disclose to Annie that she was not with child; and yet she saw the question in their eyes when they looked at her, and a letter had come from Henry's mother, full of affection and hope, asking for news of her and writing proudly of her son. The old lady was on her way north to take shelter with her Macleod cousins until the war was over. Spey House was too close to the gathering armies for a woman to remain alone. The letter spoke hopefully of the time when Katherine could join her and they could wait together for Henry's return. There was no sign of the fear she must be feeling for her only son. She was a brave woman, and Henry had inherited her quietness and her courage. But they would never meet again, for Katherine knew now she would not leave Clandara and go back to Henry if he survived the war. The short, unhappy marriage was already over. She had never belonged to anyone but James Macdonald.

"Milady! Milady, are you up there? Come down, it's Angus!"

She rose, brushing the heather from her dress, and began to walk down the hillside towards him.

"Annie sent me," the old man explained. "She's been awfu' anxious for ye, knowing ye were out alone. I'll bring your horse now, and we'd best start back."

"There was no need," Katherine said. "Nothing is left that can harm me now."

They rode slowly back down the Loch shore and turned their horses' heads for home. And two miles from Clandara they saw a little group of men stumbling through the heather, and as one fell and his companions tried to drag him upright, Katherine broke into a gallop and came up with them. Two

knelt beside the fallen man, and she saw that they were
young, and the plaid of the man they were supporting was
soaked in blood. Their torn and dirty tartans were of the
Chisholm sett, and they crouched back when she came up to
them, the youngest of them grasping a naked dirk.

"Who are ye? Stand away, woman, or by God, I'll cut
your heart out!" The wild, bearded face that glared at her
was gaunt with hunger, and the bare chest was covered in
dried mud and scored with half-healed cuts. Katherine
shouted to Angus and the old man slipped from his horse and
ran to join her.

"I'm the daughter of the Lord of Clandara," she said. "Put
up your dirk, we mean you no harm, we only want to help
you. Who are you and what has befallen him?" She pointed
to the groaning man upon the ground. He had come to the
end of his strength and lay back on the ground, his head supported by the third man, and blood oozing from a blackened
hole in his ribs.

"We're Chisholms," the bearded clansman said. "Sons of
Dugal, who you see here. The battle is lost, and the Prince is
fleeing for his life. We're trying to get home before the English find us."

"The battle . . ." Katherine tore off her white scarf and began to wipe the fallen man's wound; he moaned and winced
and every movement brought more dark blood until the scarf
was sodden with it. "The battle is lost?"

"Aye, and lost is the cause with it. We've been fleeing for
two days with those dogs behind us, hunting the clans down
and murdering them where they find them. Get to your
home, lady, and bolt fast the door before they come. . . .
We'll make our way as best we can!"

"He's dying," Katherine said gently. "He'll go no farther.
You can put him on my servant's horse and come with us.
We'll shelter you. Angus, come and help them!"

"God's grief," the old man muttered, "God's pity . . . easily
now, I'll hold the horse still. . . . Can ye sit, man, if I support
ye?"

"Take me home," the dying man whispered, his grey head
propped against Angus, while his son's hands lifted him and

eased him onto the horse's back. "Take me home and bury me. I've done . . . Aah, Jesu receive me! Jesu . . ."

"He's dead," one of the Chisholms said. "Lay him across the beast."

"Come back with me," Katherine said. "We'll feed you and find some clothes for you and send you on your way with horses. Come now, don't waste time! Where were the last English soldiers you saw?"

"Outside of Inverness, lady. We carried our father to a croft we found beyond Drummossie Moor and hid him there for the night. But the soldiers were searching everywhere, and they were shooting every man they saw, wounded or no. We set out again at dawn and struggled here on foot, sleeping in the heather. . . . They must have found the poor woman who sheltered us, for we saw the smoke and flames of burning crofts all round that place. We've eaten nothing since the crusts she gave us." He stopped, panting for breath, and for a moment he swayed. Angus came up and tried to help him, but the clansman shook him off.

"Mount up beside your father," Katherine said. "And your brother can ride behind me. Angus, there's not room for all of us, and we daren't waste time walking you back with us. Make your way on foot and I'll send men out to bring you back."

She mounted and the younger Chisholm, his face grey with shock and weariness, climbed up behind her. He had not spoken a word, but she felt his body trembling as he put his arms around her waist.

"Follow me," she called. "We'll be in Clandara in an hour or less, and you'll be safe!"

She kicked her horse into a gallop and they sped down the rough moorland towards the distant castle, Katherine turning to make sure the second horse with the dead man and his son were following, and at last she shouted back to him and pointed at the grey stone turrets on the side of the hill.

"Walk your horse, we're almost there and the path is very steep. Hold on now," she said to the silent, trembling man behind her. "In a few moments you'll be safe inside."

"You fool!" The Earl stood facing her, his face pale with

rage and fear. "Do you know what you've done? The English have won and you've brought fugitives from the field into our own house! Do you know what this will mean if they're discovered? I've questioned them and no quarter's being given. . . . Every house is being searched for rebels. Neutrality won't save us if it's known that we took them in!"

"What should I have done," she asked him bitterly, "passed by and left them on the moor to die or be caught and murdered? No, Father, I'd rather they came and sacked Clandara than have such treason to my people on my conscience. I'm not afraid of what I've done. Thank God, I've no cause to be ashamed like you!"

"Chisholms," he raged at her, "blood cousins of the Clan Macdonald! Did you know that when you brought them here? Oh, God give me patience with you. What is to be done with them?"

"They're being fed and given clothes," she answered coldly. "And horses will take them back to their own glen. We will bury their father here, out on the moor. A night's rest, that's all they ask of you, and you'd refuse it! Where is your heart, Father, what has become of you? . . . You didn't want to fight, so well enough, but have you joined the English, your country's enemies?"

He turned on her angrily. "What influence will I have on Henry's behalf if it's discovered that I gave them even a cup of water? You accuse me of betraying my own, in your high-handed way—but have you thought of that? What of your husband—I see no sign of fear for him, no thought, no loyalty . . ."

"He may be dead," she said at last. "And if he's not, he wouldn't want his life from you at such a price. No more would Robert listen to you, if he were alive today. Turn them out if you must, Father, but I'll ride home with them myself and see them safe!"

"My son died because of you," the Earl said slowly. "If it weren't that I hope for a child from you, I'd thrust you out and shut my doors on you forever for what you've said and done today."

She looked at him then, and he was silenced by the hatred he saw on her face.

"There is no child," she said. "And never will be one. I tried to pay my debt to you for Robert, but there's no coin in the world which will suffice. I cannot give you back your son or myself my brother. And I have lost the man I loved forever. My grief must be enough for you, Father. It's all I have to give you now." And she turned her back on him and went out of the room.

The next moment the Earl came to the open door and shouted for his steward. "Donal, where are those men my daughter brought into the house?"

"Below, my lord, having their wounds dressed by the women. . . . Her ladyship said . . ."

"Pay no mind to what she said," the Earl snapped. "Have the dead man buried at once and see that the grave is well hidden. And turn the Chisholms out by nightfall! I want no trace of them here and if anyone speaks of their presence at Clandara, I'll have their throats cut! Is that understood?"

The steward bowed. "It shall be done, my lord."

"And tomorrow you're to ride into Inverness and see if you can find out what has become of Mr. Ogilvie. From now on, the castle gates are closed to all rebels, whatever their clan. And send word out that any tacksman or humbly of mine who shelters them shall suffer death!"

In her rooms above, the Countess waited impatiently, walking up and down, stopping to listen by the door. Lately she had spent more and more of the long hours in bed, sewing and talking to herself; now she was dressed, her greying hair hidden under a linen cap, and her hands pulled at her skirts and twisted in and out of each other as she waited. At last the door opened and she sprang forward eagerly.

"Jean! Who are they, what news?"

"The Prince has been lost," the girl said, and her voice faltered. "His army fled the field. Ach, I've just been down talking to the bearded one she brought back with her . . . the other's out of his wits. He lies there trembling and mouthing." Jean suddenly put her two strong hands to her face and began to cry. It was the first time Margaret Clandara had seen her weep for years. She came and shook her, her pale face thin and sharp, her eyes glittering.

"Stop that!" she commanded. "Stop that at once, you idiot girl! I want to know who they are and where they're going. What else did the man tell you?... Come on, speak up!"

"They fought at Drummossie Moor," Jean mumbled. "At the end of it the place was four deep in Highland dead and wounded. And afterwards the English gave no quarter.... They're Chisholms, milady. And *he* is turning them out! They're being sent away tonight, without even a horse to carry them...."

"He would," the Countess said. "And better they go than stay here to be handed to the English. They're our blood cousins, do you realise that? Stop crying," she said angrily. "Don't you realise what this means? Did you ask them about our kin at Dundrenan? Did they see them, did they fight nearby? Oh, you stupid ox, must I box your ears for you to make you answer me?"

"They were in the same line," Jean said; she wiped her eyes with the backs of her hands like a child. "The one below said they made the charge together. Our people fell like leaves."

"But some escaped," the Countess urged her. "Some *must* have escaped!"

"I asked him that," the girl said. "It was difficult, milady, I didn't like to harry them with questions. They're so distressed and the poor silent one, lying there shivering from head to foot!"

"What did he say?" the Countess said. She was calmer now and her voice wheedled. "Come now, Jean, think of my anxiety ... did he see any of my cousins leave the field alive?"

"The chief, he thinks," Jean answered, "but he could not be sure."

Margaret smiled and, taking the girl by the arm, she brought her to the fire and gently put her in a chair. "Calm yourself now," she said. "You're a good girl, Jean. I didn't mean to be impatient with you. It's an ill wind, my child, that blows nobody any good. Sit quietly now and listen well. You say they go tonight?"

"As soon as it is dark," Jean muttered. "Even the Fraser servants were ashamed to hear it. They had their father with them but he died as they tried to lift him onto old Angus' horse. He's been buried out on the moor where none will find his grave."

"You must go down again," the Countess said. "You must go down and promise to steal a mount for them, and in exchange they'll do a favour for me. They will do it, won't they, if you get a horse for them?"

"What do you want?" the girl asked her.

The Countess gave a little laugh. "I want them to find Sir Alexander or any of his sons and give them a note which I shall write. It shouldn't be difficult; the Chisholms' glen is not more than a few miles from Dundrenan. It won't be much to ask in exchange for a mount on which to get there, will it?"

"No," Jean said. "No, if I can do that for them, they'll be grateful. I trust the bearded one. He'll keep his word. But how am I to get a horse for them?"

The Countess tapped her cheek. "You're a good girl, but you're not as clever as you might be. . . . She will get one for them if you go and plead with her. She brought them here, didn't she? Her soft heart must be bleeding for the poor rebels, her own Ogilvie among them! She'll get the horse, and they'll do me the favour. Get up now, child, and go see if you can find her. Don't wipe your cheeks, a few tears will look all the better. I'm going to write my little note."

Embarrassed by having sat down in the presence of her mistress, Jean got up and curtsied. She wasn't really thinking of the note or of whatever plan was forming in the Countess' mind. The words of the hunted man were ringing through her aching head, and the fate of her own humble kin was still unknown. Macdonalds had charged along that shattered line, broken by withering fire from the English guns, falling as they ran, while those behind leapt over them and raced towards the waiting enemy.

"The Prince is a fugitive too," she said. "God knows what will become of him. . . ."

"God knows," the Countess said patiently. "But he'll find

friends to aid him. Don't fret for the Prince, Jean; he'll get away to France. Go on now. Find Lady Katherine as I told you."

Across five hundred yards of moor the air was black with the smoke of the English cannon. It roared and rumbled and belched out its volleys of heavy balls, which crashed into the massed ranks of the Highland army, killing and maiming men four deep. Clan Chattan and the Camerons of Lochiel were scythed down by the continuous fire; the music of the pipes cried on through the appalling din, and the shouts of the Highland officers "Close Up," "Close," told how the cannon were thinning their ranks. Fire swept the Appin Stewarts and the Atholl men, and bowled down the lines of Frasers, and still the time passed and the men of the Prince's army stood their ground, falling and dying even as they shouted in protest, begging for the command to charge their enemy and escape the murderous bombardment.

For fully fifteen minutes the clans waited, until at length Lochiel himself, standing at the head of his men with the cannon balls roaring past him and the screams of his dead and wounded drowning the rant of his piper, sent a message to the commander of the right flank, Lord George Murray, that unless he was given leave to charge he could not, and would not, hold his men.

Behind the second line of his army, Prince Charles sat on horseback watching the confusion of smoke and listening to the horrible sounds of the bombardment, and the sight seemed to immobilise him. A ball fell so close that his horse dropped under him, and the body of his groom was cut in half by a direct hit.

"Permission to charge, Highness! Lord George says he can't hold the line any longer. . . ."

At last the responsibility for which he had craved so long belonged to Charles alone; Lord George, his hated opponent, was begging for the order, and he alone could give it. And at that fatal moment he wavered, for he knew that he should have given it himself ten minutes ago. His voice hoarse and shaking, he shouted above the uproar to his aide, Lachlan Machlachlan.

"Give the command for a general advance against the enemy!"

Lachlan rode off, waving his bonnet and cheering, but before he had reached the front line to deliver his message a ball smashed him from his horse and dropped him dead upon the heather. And so the clans waited while hundreds died without even seeing the faces of their enemy. It was the men of Clan Chattan, the Mackintoshes and their kin, who broke away, led by their officers. With a great yell of their ancient war cries, the Mackintoshes shouting, "Loch Moy! Loch Moy!" as they ran, the clan began their charge through the smoke towards their enemy. That was when the English artillery received the order to change round shot for grape.

The rain and sleet had stopped some time ago; its work of soaking and freezing them was over. Now death came sweeping down upon the running hordes of men, as thick as the sleet itself, a deadly hail of lead, nails and iron, and the men began to fall and those behind leapt over them, and still they fell. And on the right of them, the men of Atholl and the Camerons and Appin Stewarts were charging, and the withering fire swept through them. Cameron of Lochiel, the fighting chief, fell as he ran, both ankles broken, and as he lay he shouted to his people to run on and leave him. What was left of the right flank of the Highland army was but twenty yards or so from the first line of Cumberland's infantry when the first discharge of musketry was fired into the charging Highlanders. The first ranks fired, reloading while the second and third ranks loosed their roll of musketry. Those of Clan Chattan and the Camerons and Atholl men who slashed and stabbed their way among the English front-line troops fought on right through to the second-line regiments of Howard's and Bligh's and there they fell, some with as many as twelve dead men to their credit. The Colonel of the Clan of the Cats, MacGillivray of Dunmaglas, crawled through them mortally wounded, fell forward into a little stream, and drowned.

And among the fighting groups, the old Machlachlan chief,

whose son had died with the Prince's message undelivered, died on the bayonets of his enemies, and with him perished nearly all his people. In the centre and right of the moor the dead covered the heather four deep.

On the left the long line of the great Clan Macdonald, its pipes playing, each chief running ahead with his bodyguard of two picked men, his sons in command of the companies behind him, began to move up the sloping ground that fronted them and onwards towards the English regiments of Poultney and the Lowland Scots regiment known as the Royals.

"Claymores!" The command was shouted up and down from officer to officer, and with a fierce yell the men of Keppoch, Clanranald, Glengarry, and Dundrenan raised their swords and surged forward to charge at last. Sir Alexander Macdonald was ahead of James and Hugh, he stumbled over the rough ground, his eyes watering with the smoke that drifted thickly over the battlefield, and all around him the deadly grape shot sang, and cries arose from the clansmen who ran with him, as men threw up their arms and fell, or doubled up and rolled in agony upon the ground. He paused only for a moment, and that was to see if his sons were following, and through the noise he heard James's voice raised in a savage yell; on the left of him, Hugh was ahead; he glimpsed the tall figure of his second son as it passed into the wreathing smoke and then it disappeared.

"Charge on," the old man shouted. "Follow me!"

Out of the mist a charge of grape shot tore into the man beside him; with a terrible scream he dropped his sword and fell forward on his shattered face and died. And then James came to his father, yelling at their men to pause, and he flung the old chief to the ground.

"You dog," Sir Alexander bellowed at him; he struggled to rise and began striking at his son. "You dog, would you have me hide like a woman? ... Get up, God damn you, and go on like a man!"

"Let them come to us," James shouted back. "Stop the charge and let the men fire their pistols. That may bring them forward. God's life, we can't even see them in this smoke and we're being cut to pieces! Do as I say!"

"Fire your pistols," Sir Alexander shouted. "Take shelter and fire; we're going to draw them out from behind their cannon. The cowards," he raged, "the dirty skulking cowards! Come out and fight with us, you scum of England!" He raised himself up and shouted at the hidden enemy. "Come out, you dogs, and kiss the Macdonald's steel!"

"Where's Hugh?" James asked him as he crawled away.

"Gone to the front and doubtless broken through," his father snarled.

The pistols of the Macdonalds cracked out through the thundering artillery, and the sound of their shouts and jeers reached the English officers of the line and caused them much amusement. A breeze was coming up and it was blowing away the powder smoke; it revealed the Macdonalds a hundred yards distant from the English, and even as the officers watched, their guns swept the ragged Highland line with grape shot and the dreaded musketry began. From his horse on a rise behind the Royals, the Duke of Cumberland adjusted his short telescopic glass and brought the left flank of Prince Charles's army into focus. The advance had strung them out unevenly; to the right of them the Chattan men and the Stewarts and Cameronians were throwing themselves on death and already a little trickle of them were turning back and running towards their own second line. But the line on the left, where the different setts of the Macdonald tartans glowed in the grey light, was standing still, firing its few forelocks and pistols spasmodically at the unmoving British line.

"Good God," the Duke remarked, handing the glass to Lord Mark Kerr, "look at that; our men are shooting them like rabbits!"

"They're going back," the dragoon commander said.

Cumberland took the glass again. "Only to reform. See, they're charging again. Good God," he repeated, "have you ever seen the like? . . . I must say, they make excellent targets!" and he laughed.

Down on the bloody moor, James rallied his desperate men once more. Their old-fashioned firearms and pistols were flung away upon the ground; the ruse had failed and twice already they had advanced, jeering and yelling, through the murderous fire, only to be beaten back and then re-form and try again. And a third of all who bore the name Macdonald were already dead or wounded on the field.

"Once more," James yelled. "Claymores, my people! Follow the chief!"

His father lived by some miracle, though shot had torn the skirts of his coat and whipped the bonnet from his head. As he ran forward once again, his broadsword flashing in his hand, he roared with hatred and contempt. James leapt after him; he had flung off the plaid that protected his left arm; he carried only his buckler and his broadsword and the dirk grasped in his left hand. His face was streaked with sweat and dirt and blood ran down the side of it from a scalp wound. All around him was death; his feet stumbled over bodies as he ran, he trod on them because he had to, and then he added the wild fierce yell of his own voice to the terrible clamour around him, through which the grape shot whined and whistled and the methodical English musket volleys cracked like whips. And then, within twenty yards of that line of redcoats and the sticklike legs gaitered in white, the muskets levelled pouring fire, the men of Dundrenan faltered as the survivors of Cameron and Mackintoshes met them running back.

Through the red haze of blood and smoke James paused and saw his people waver, some of them turning, running, only to fall with their backs towards the enemy. Madness possessed him then, the madness of despair and hate. He stood with his arms wide, cursing at his clansmen, and the sound of his voice was drowned by the thud of hooves as the troopers of Kingston's Cavalry rode down upon the remnants of Macdonald regiments from the left.

Sir Alexander and the Red Murdoch found him, standing alone upon the field, cursing the English soldiers who had ceased their fire for fear of hitting their own horse, while individuals among them took careful aim at the mad Highlander. Balls ploughed into the ground beside him and sang past him; his father seized one arm and Murdoch grabbed him from behind, and the strength of both dragged him backwards and pulled him into a stumbling run. Men were fleeing round them, and the dreaded cavalry were wheeling among the scattered groups too tired or hurt to run away, and their sabres flashed among them. Somewhere on the moor the old Macdonald of Keppoch was being carried off, dying from a ball in the chest and a smashed arm, supported by weeping Angus Ban, his son, and members of his clan. As the Macdonalds of Dundrenan turned to fight Kingston's troopers, Keppoch died of his wounds in a miserable hut beyond the moor, and his son crept out to flee to his own home afar off by Loch Lochy.

Trooper Edwards of Kingston's was a young man from the Midlands; at twenty-four he had seen service in Flanders and considered himself as seasoned a cavalryman as any in the troop. He had been riding down the fleeing Highlanders and sabring them without so much as a blow being aimed at him when he set his horse at the tall kilted soldier, his officer's coat in rags and a red-bearded savage, naked but for his kilt, helping him on with the aid of another older officer. Edwards thought that the big one was injured and, with a shout to his friend Trooper James to accompany him, he wheeled his horse round and galloped across the heather in pursuit.

He never brought his bloodied sabre down upon their heads because the tall one sprang and caught him by the jacket, tearing him from the saddle. He fell with a frightful yell and it was the last sound he made because James drove his dirk into his throat. Trooper James was not a coward; he saw what had befallen his old friend Edwards and he charged down upon them. His sabre came down upon the upturned shield of the Red Murdoch, its blade slid off the brass edge and sliced deep into Murdoch's bare arm. As it did so, Sir Alexander sprang from the heather where he had been waiting and fired his pistol into Trooper James's unsuspecting face.

"Two horses," James gasped. "Mount up, Father. . . . Murdoch, come with me!"

"I'll not be coming," Murdoch muttered. "My arm is all but off, Lord." He sank to the ground and the heather was red where he knelt. "Take the horses and may God go with ye!"

"Murdoch!" James knelt beside him and eased him gently down, folding his own coat under his head. One look assured him that Murdoch would go no farther. The arm was almost severed and the sabre stroke had cut an artery.

"Leave me now," Murdoch mumbled. "We've shared the same breast for milk, and I've courage enough to die like the milk brother of my chief's son. Farewell, Lord, and you, my brother. God go with the House of Dundrenan. . . ."

"Hurry," Sir Alexander shouted. "He'll be dead in a few minutes! Mount and for God's sake let's ride off. Some of our people are ahead . . . I'm going to look for Hugh and David."

They found David, unwounded and surrounded by a dozen trembling, exhausted clansmen in a deep dip in the moor, so deep that it was almost a ditch and served to hide them from the pursuing cavalry. Hugh was not there nor among the scattered Macdonalds, numbering fifty in all, who were all that could be rallied at the end of the day. It was Janet Douglas who found Hugh.

Henry Ogilvie died at the hands of a Campbell; they met in the desperate melee which followed the retreat of the Highland right flank after the massacre by cannon and the musketry and the brief and terrible hand-to-hand fighting by the Camerons and men of Chattan against the infantrymen of the first British line. He had fought blindly, killing with the broadsword and the dirk, and sustained wounds in the legs and right arm which he was too confused and fighting mad to notice. When the retreat began, Henry fell back with what was left, and as he paused to help an injured Ogilvie to his feet and drag him out of range, the hidden company of Ballimore's Campbells leapt a stone wall to the left of them and rushed among them to do battle. And Henry fell under the sword of one of these. He died immediately; the confusion of the battle and the Campbell war cry "Cruachan! Cruachan!" ringing out above the crack of musketry and the fierce clashing of sword and axe against buckler were the last things he heard. The scene of the battle and the face of the man who leapt in front of him, his broadsword flashing downwards, were the last things Henry saw. There was a great pain and a cry and then nothing. He lay where he had fallen, surrounded by the dead of his clan, for two days and nights and was buried in one of the communal trenches which served the Highland army as a grave.

From Creagan Glas, the watchers saw the Prince's army break and flee. Janet and Fiona Mackintosh stood holding fast to one another, and as the lines below them thinned and scattered and the belching cannon roared, Fiona hid her face and wept like the other women and many of the men who watched with them.

Janet's eyes were dry; the agony in her heart was too intense to express itself in tears; instead she stared down over the smoking moor, blackened with bodies and moving groups of men, and did not move or speak.

Only when the cannon were silent and the distant yelling of the clans had stopped did they hear the drums of the Duke of Cumberland's army beating the advance along the line and see the redcoats moving forward in correct formation, marching over the dead and wounded until they stood upon the ground held that morning by the Highland army. Only then did Janet turn the trembling girl inside her arm towards the moor below.

"It's over," she said. "Come down now, and we'll take our horses and see what has become of James and Hugh."

"I couldn't watch," Fiona whispered. "When I saw them falling and the men turning back, I couldn't bear to watch. . . ."

"Where did you leave your mount?" Janet asked. The crowds upon the brae were dispersing now, muttering among themselves. Some of the women of Chattan were wailing, their plaids pulled over their heads.

"Hurry back to Inverness, ladies," an elderly man advised them, shepherding his wife and daughter with him. His name was Farquharson, and two of his sons were fighting on the moor that day. He never knew the fate of either. "Don't waste time here; I've seen some of the English cavalry riding out after our soldiers. It's not safe to stay so near the battle now. Come, Annie and Margaret, make haste!"

"My sons," his wife moaned. "Where are my sons? . . ."

"There are the horses." Fiona pointed to the horses tethered below the brae among some bushes. "The bay gelding over there . . ."

Janet had begun to run, pulling the girl after her. Everywhere people were slipping and stumbling down to the hollow, and some were seizing horses and riding off with them.

"Come on," Janet shouted, "they're stealing the mounts! Come on, for God's sake, or we'll be left stranded on foot here!" She grabbed the reins of the gelding and led it to where her own mount was tethered. "Here, get up," she said. "Hurry, I can't hold both!"

"Where are we going?" Fiona said. "How can I find Hugh . . ."

Janet looked up into the white and drawn little face, the mouth quivering like a child's; she reached up and squeezed the girl's cold hand. "We'll go together," she said. "Hold him now, I'm going to mount."

"Give me a place." A man came to her stirrup and caught the strap. "I've walked for miles . . . I'll never get back in time."

"We're going to the moor," Janet said. "Not Inverness. Let go my stirrup!"

She pulled her horse round and, followed by Fiona Mackintosh, began to ride out of the shelter of the brae and down towards the river Nairn. They crossed by a stone bridge and, moving at a steady canter, began to round the edge of the moor behind the former English position. And that was where they met the first of the refugees from the battle. Suddenly men came at them out of the heather; men in rags without weapons, running and stumbling, panting like animals, men staggering from wounds and falling, only to rise and try to walk a few yards farther. And seeing the horses, they waved and shouted, some crying piteously for help. Fiona was the first to stop. She reined in and jumped down, going to the aid of a wounded man who had fallen only a few feet away from her. And immediately others surrounded them, and her horse was caught by half a dozen hands so that it reared and plunged with fright. Janet would not have stopped. Janet knew that their only chance was to ignore the men on foot, to ride over them and the wounded and to stop for nothing. But now she had no choice. She came back to the place where Fiona knelt, watching helplessly as the desperate Highlanders fought over who should have her horse, and the wounded man in her arms groaned and twitched in pain.

"Why did you do it? Why did you stop? . . . Oh, God, don't you know they'll never let us mount again . . . stop that, you damned thief! Leave my horse alone!" She sprang up from Fiona and ran the few feet to wrestle with a big, wild, bearded man who was struggling to climb on her mount's back.

"Hold back! Mackintoshes hold back!" The man in Fiona's arms managed to shout the order, and sullenly it was obeyed.

"What are you ladies doing?" the wounded man asked them; his face was grey with pain and he gasped as he spoke. "Don't you know the English dragoons are riding down everyone they find . . . man, woman, or child? They're killing them all. . . . For God's sake go back before some of their horse come up. I'm done, girl, can't yet see that and let me be?"

Fiona bent over him, the tears running down her face. "I am a Mackintosh of Glendar, niece of Glendar himself. I will not leave you."

Janet came up to her. "Do as he says!" She knelt beside the dying Mackintosh. "Were you near the Macdonalds of Dundrenan? We're looking for the chief and his sons."

He shook his head. "They took the left line today. I heard some of the men of Clanranald saying it was unlucky. Not as unlucky as the right where we stood. Lady, take Miss Mackintosh out of this place. My people won't take the horse from her when they know who she is. Mount up behind her and begone while there's still time. I'm their tacksman, but if I die while ye're still here I cannot answer for them them. . . ."

"I'm going to find the Macdonalds of Dundrenan," Janet said. "I'm not leaving the moor until I do. But I'll do it better alone and on foot. Here!" She turned to the big man who had tried to take her horse; he stood sullenly and stupidly by its head, one hand holding the reins, watching his officer on the ground.

"You can have the mount," Janet said, "if you take Miss Mackintosh back to Glendar. The Lord Glendar will care for you there and help you back to your own glen. As for the gelding, let two men take it, and make what speed they can. Come, Fiona, leave him now and get on my horse!"

Fiona stared up at her and shook her head. "I will not leave him," she repeated. "I shall stay with him until the end and then I am going to go with you and find Hugh. I heard what you said: I'm coming with you."

"Ah no," Janet said gently. "No, you're not. I was mad to bring you this far. You're not staying here to be raped and cut to pieces by the English." She turned to the man half lying in the girl's lap. "These men will obey you. Give the order!"

He raised his head and, gathering his ebbing strength, he called out to the big Highlander. "Take her! Ride for Glendar! As for the other horse, two wounded men may have it."

The bearded man came up and between them he and Janet dragged the struggling, shrieking girl to her feet and Janet held her while he mounted.

"I'll find Hugh," she promised. "Be sensible now, you've done your best. I can hide and wait until they've gone. . . . It's easier for one. Hold still, or I'll have them tie you to the horse!"

"I said I would die with him," Fiona wept. "I want to die. . . . I want to stay here and die with my own people and with Hugh." She was choking and hysterical, and when the clansman reached down and lifted her up in front of him, she sobbed and let herself be taken.

"God go with you," Janet called out, and the next moment the horse was galloping away, back towards the river and the bridge.

Janet knelt in the heather, and the dying man whispered to her: "They've taken the other horse. You're on foot now and alone. Take this, lady. Ye may need it."

She took the pistol from him and hid it in the belt of her dress under the red cloak. "On the left of the line," she said. "Nearer to Culloden House than here."

"Look in the little bothies," he whispered to her. "Many wounded took shelter there.... But if you hear horsemen, hide yourself. All ours fled with the Prince ... there's none left now but the dragoons."

As she began running onwards through the heather, Janet heard a new sound, a sound so strange and full of unfamiliar pitch that she stopped for a moment to listen. After a moment she went on while the dreadful noise grew louder. It was the crying of hundreds of wounded men, and now she found herself passing little groups of dead and injured as she walked, and in the distance, near the centre of the battlefield, she heard the crack of shots and frightful cries. She crawled forward through the grass, and only a hundred yards away she saw three English soldiers shooting and bayoneting the fallen enemy. For a moment Janet's tremendous self-control gave way; she hid her face in the short heather and fought the impulse to spring to her feet and scream and scream. The moment came and she conquered it; she lay very still until the noise of English shouts abated, and when at last she raised her head and looked above the ridge, the soldiers were gone and no one lying near was moving now or crying out.

All through that long afternoon she picked her way through the human debris of that battle in which a thousand of the Prince's men had lost their lives. The Camerons and men of Chattan, the men of Atholl and the clansmen of the Duke of Perth lay all around her, and she ignored them, turning away from those who were yet alive and undiscovered by the English. Not till she saw the Macdonald setts lying in the reddened ground did she begin to search among the dead. Many times she threw herself down and hid as the English cavalry patrolled the battlefield, searching for fugitives or for the living among the heaps of dead, and when either were found, they were killed without mercy.

It was growing late when Janet found the first little bothy about half a mile from the rise on which Prince Charles had watched the battle. It was a crude hut without windows, thatched in peat, mud-walled and -floored, and when she staggered to the opening she saw movement in the darkness and heard the sound of someone groaning.

"Are there Macdonalds here?" she called out.

A voice answered her from the stuffy gloom within. "Aye, three of us, men of Clanranald. And others too whom we don't know. For the love of Christ, bring us some water. . . ."

Stooping, Janet went inside, and very slowly she scanned the desperate faces turned towards her; now that her eyes were used to it, she could see well enough to recognise that none of the unconscious ones was James.

"Water!" Hands caught at her skirts, and now they were as red as her cloak.

"Macdonalds of Dundrenan . . . are any here?"

"There's one in the corner there; we brought him with us. But he's dead now. 'Twas the son of the chief. . . ."

He lay on his side, his head leaning back against the wall, and both his legs were broken and torn by a direct discharge of grape shot. She knelt beside him, trembling, and turned the cold face towards her. The dead man was Hugh Macdonald. As she knelt there and very slowly took her hand away and let his head turn back to the wall again, the party of Cobham's Dragoons found the bothy. They fired their pistols into it first and killed two of the injured men; then they came one by one through the low doorway, and the setting sun shone for a moment on their sabres. That was when Janet found the Mackintosh's pistol.

One of them was coming nearer, stepping over two bodies, while his comrades cut down the Clanranalds. She had never fired in her life before, but she brought the pistol up with both hands and pointed it at the dark stooping figure with the curving cavalry sword half raised in his right hand, and taking aim at him, she fired. The sound of the shot cracked through the tiny place, and the air was acrid with powder. She got up and stood before the body of James's brother and a second later the dragoon lurched forward and fell.

In the shouts and cries that rose from the wretched hovel that afternoon, one of the younger members of the troop, who had remained on his horse, swore that he heard a woman's voice cry out above them all: "God save Prince Charles!" He never knew whether his imagination, already overburdened with the horrors he had witnessed and in which he had unwillingly participated, played him a trick, or whether indeed a woman was among those killed in the bothy. He never knew because he was too sick and nervous to ask his fellows when they came out; but one of them was wounded, and while the wound was being dressed the rest set fire to the thatch and burnt down the place and the dead who were left in it.

Chapter 8

FROM THE red stone house in Inverness belonging to the Dowager Lady Mackintosh the Duke of Cumberland issued orders for the apprehension of all rebels who had fled the field and for the disposal of all who were still lying wounded out on the moor. The Duke was in a good humour, but his general mood was severe. Inverness and the surrounding country reminded him constantly of the untidy state into which Scotland and its people had fallen, and he directed the operations for restoring it to order with the zeal of a butcher in a slaughterhouse. For two days and nights the Highland wounded lay on Drummossie Moor, stripped of their clothing by the beggars who crept down upon them searching for loot, their own womenfolk and kin kept back by the bayonets of the English sentries who mounted guard upon the place. Their cries for help made people living on their farms in the vicinity cover their ears and draw the blankets over their heads at night.

There were many who found some of these pitiable creatures crawling at their doors, begging for water and food, and those who took them in were soon to learn the meaning of the victor's wrath. On Friday, detachments of the British army marched out to the moor and began searching the farms and bothies around it. Every man found breathing among the heaps of dead upon the field was shot or bayoneted and the houses which had sheltered any able to escape were burned to the ground with the fugitives, and those who had befriended them, bolted inside.

From their hiding place three miles distant, all that was left of the Macdonalds of Dundrenan watched the spirals of smoke rising into the pale spring sky. Sir Alexander had gathered his people together in a wood near Castle Hill; there they had taken an accounting, tended the wounded, and buried some who had since died. There were little more than fifty left, and James had sent for every man among them to come before the chief and say if he had seen Hugh Macdonald after that first wild charge. And that was how they heard of the wounds which felled him long before he reached the English infantry. One clansman had seen him fall, and another, running for his life, had seen him carried from the field by men of another branch of the Clan Macdonald. This man stood before his chief and told what he had seen.

"How grievous were his hurts?" Sir Alexander demanded.

The man glanced down and muttered, unwilling to look into the fierce face. It was not always wise to bring bad news to the Macdonalds of Dundrenan.

"Answer," James said. "How grievous? Could he have lived?"

"His legs were smashed," the answer came, "and there was blood all over him. I think he would soon be dead, Lord."

"Who took him?" James asked again.

"Men of Clanranald, I think," the man answered. "In the confusion I could not be sure. But I saw the Lord Hugh's face as they carried him and I knew him. I am not mistaken about that."

"No," Sir Alexander said slowly. "You are not mistaken. What is your name?"

"Ian, son of Dugal." The clansman glanced up at him quickly.

"So, Ian Macdonald, you saw your chief's son being taken off in need of help and you ran on and left him to the charity of the Clanranalds?"

The man turned very pale; he stared into the faces of his chief and his two sons and saw that sentence was pronounced upon him. He fell on his knees. "Lord, there was nothing I could do . . . he was past help and all about me were flying from the English grape shot!"

"Do you not know," Sir Alexander demanded, "that your duty is to the chief and his blood first and to yourself the last of all? You've broken the clan law, Ian, son of Dugal. To him who leaves my son to die and saves himself, life shall not be granted." The old man's yellow eyes blazed at him. He turned to the men standing around him and pointed to the wretched clansman. "Take him and hang him!"

As the man was seized and dragged off, Sir Alexander covered his face and his people crept away, leaving the chief alone to grieve with his two sons.

"He's dead," James said at last. "At least we know he's not lying out there suffering. Don't grieve for him, Father. Hugh never feared death."

"Aye." Sir Alexander raised his head. "Hugh was afraid of nothing. No son of mine would be taken prisoner, Hugh least of all."

"They're not taking prisoners," James said. He stared out across the ground at the edge of the wood and pointed to the fingers of smoke. "Those are crofts being burned. . . . Father, you'll have to rouse yourself. Hugh may be dead, but so are three quarters of our people with him. Where do we go now? Search parties will be coming this way soon—are we to wait here and fight?"

David, sullen sombre David, came over to where his father sat, his head sunk between his shoulders, and kneeling down, he put his arm around him. "Father's done with fighting," he said slowly. "Stay behind with some men if you wish, James, but I'm taking him home to Dundrenan."

"You come with us, James," the old man said. "I've no mind to lose another son or one more man for a cause that is lost. We'll gather our people and go home."

"Dundrenan can be defended," James said. "It's not the first time we've faced a siege. Let them come to Dundrenan for us—by God, they'll find a welcome waiting for them when they do!"

"I told you," Sir Alexander said. "I've done with fighting! When we are home we'll set about making what peace we can. Come now, David, give me your arm to lean on. James, send the word out that all must prepare themselves to leave the wood as soon as it's dark. We'll be better keeping to the open country and leaving the roads alone. That's the way the English will be marching."

As night came, the little company of men began their silent journey out of the sheltering wood, led by their chief on the horse taken from the dead English dragoon, with James riding the second mount beside him and David walking at his father's bridle. During the night they stopped at a small burn and drank, and ate the few fish they caught in it raw, for they dared not risk a fire. By dawn they were well to the west of Inverness, turning towards Dundrenan, and James disposed his people in a pease field where they were ordered to lie silent and out of sight on pain of being left behind. Hunger tormented them, and many were so weakened by superficial wounds and lack of food that they dropped down and waited mutely for death to overtake them. Only the fierce will of their chief's eldest son, and their terror of his anger, made the rest of the Macdonalds struggle onward. James was everywhere among them, cursing and exhorting, often driving his men to obedience with blows. They hated him and they muttered, but his orders were obeyed. And that was how he brought the little company within sight of their home at Dundrenan, and it was in the early dawn, as they prepared to march the last mile, that the two men of Clan Chisholm found them with their cousin Margaret's message and the news that a detachment of English cavalry had ridden over from Inverness the previous day and were in occupation of Dundrenan House.

The elder Chisholm took a sealed paper from his ragged plaid and handed it to the chief of the Macdonalds.

"We've searched far for ye, Lord," he said. "Night and day we've watched and waited for ye so that our promise might be kept to the lady of your name who saved our lives."

"What lady?" James demanded. "Where have you come from, and why is there no word or sign from him?" He pointed to the younger man, who stood silent, his eyes passing vacantly from one to the other.

"He has not spoken since the battle," the Chisholm answered. "We brought our father away from the moor and that was when the daughter of Fraser of Clandara found us and brought us to her house for shelter. My brother here has lost his mind. I have to keep him with me."

James came close to him. "The Lady of Clandara gave you shelter?" he asked. "Speak up, man. The lord's daughter, you say?"

"The same." The Chisholm nodded. "But 'twas not she who gave this letter for ye, nor who smuggled horses to us when her father turned us out. 'Twas the other, the Macdonald lady, who is kept close prisoner there. She saved our lives when the Fraser would have delivered us to the troops of the English. We gave our word to find ye and deliver what she wrote. The bond is honoured now."

"We thank you," Sir Alexander said. He put the letter in his coat. "What are the English doing at Dundrenan?"

"Searching for ye," the Chisholm answered, "and looting the house. Some of the women escaped but others are still kept within for the soldiers. We've heard cries, but the few men left there are dead or made prisoner and there's naught that my brother and I could do alone, save wait for ye and warn ye."

"How many are there?" James snapped.

"Fifty or more, with horses, fully armed."

He turned to his father and David. "Fifty! Are we to stand here while they rape our women and steal our goods? Is this your 'peace,' Father?"

"Lord," the Chisholm said, "may a poor humbly speak?"

"Wait, James," Sir Alexander held up his hand and nodded to the clansman. "Speak on."

"If you go against them, you will all be killed or taken. I see many of ye here, but tired and sick and hungry as we were when we fled the battle. Nothing can save your women or bring back your servants they have killed, and the same is being done to every house whose chief fought for the Prince and to every farm and croft belonging to the clans. Take your people, Lord, and go into hiding until the fury is over. Our home is gone; we found the Campbells driving off our few cattle while the croft burnt to the ground. We hid and watched it being done, for it's better to have life and wait for vengeance than throw all away. I shall take my brother into the mountains and wait for quieter times."

"Wise words," the old man said. "Wiser than yours, my son." He turned to James. "We stay here until a decision can be made. If we attack Dundrenan, it must be in the dark. Meantime, let our people stay low. Let us see what is in Cousin Margaret's letter. . . ."

Captain James Booth of Lord Mark Kerr's dragoons glanced quickly at his reflection in the mirror on the wall at his left and, satisfied that he presented all that could be required of a well-favoured English officer, made yet another attempt to be friendly with the Lady Katherine Ogilvie.

Two weeks earlier, he and his company had come to the gates of Clandara demanding admittance. They were making an inspection of all the big houses in the area to the south of Loch Ness, while their comrades of Cholmondley's dealt with the gentry, and their tenants, to the west.

There was a list at the Duke's headquarters in Inverness of those clans who were in rebellion, and Captain Booth had received orders to billet himself on the Earl of Clandara and make discreet enquiries whether his loyalty to King George was genuine. It was more than likely that many of the cunning Scots had abstained from the battle from self-interest rather than from a sense of duty to their rightful King. Any one of these found harbouring the rebels was to be counted equally guilty and placed under arrest. But the Captain could find no fault with the Earl. He had been welcomed politely to the castle and offered its hospitality for as long as he wished. None of the Earl's tenants had taken up arms, and the thorough search instituted the same day discovered no fugitives hiding in the castle. The Captain and two young ensigns were given comfortable rooms and invited to share the Earl's table and consider themselves his guests. In return, the officers behaved with tact, and their men billeted themselves and their horses in the outbuildings and so far no incidents had occurred.

But if the Earl was friendly, his daughter Katherine remained hostile and silent. Her attitude was a disappointment to the Captain; he considered her to be one of the most beautiful women he had ever seen in his life and he was only too anxious to be amiable. He found the Scots an irritating mixture of barbaric feudalism and outrageous pride. Many of the hovels he had burnt were so crude that they were fit only for animals and the wretched people in them who fled before the sabres of his troopers were little better than savages. He could not understand them when they cried for mercy in their uncouth language and he would not have spared them if he could. He was a little irritated to find that the great mediaeval castle was in many ways more luxurious than his own modest manor in Suffolk, and that the Earl was a man of such wide culture that he was often at a disadvantage with him. He did not like or trust the imperious old man, and he was becoming very angry with the Lady Katherine, who wore deep black and did not scruple to tell him as soon as they were introduced that she was the widow of a man who had fought for the Prince at Culloden. Once or twice, after a particular rebuff, the Captain found himself wishing that the Frasers of Clandara were not so well within the law. In his own eyes, the Captain considered himself a model guest; he was courteous and appreciative and avoided all mention of their purpose in the neighbourhood. He had done nothing that could give offence and the only man in his troop who had been caught stealing from the castle servants' quarters had been summarily hanged as an example.

And still the Lady Katherine avoided him and when he tried to speak to her she stared at him with such contempt and dislike that he stammered and blushed like a boy. It made him very angry, and because of it he ordered a second search, even invading the rooms where the Earl's wife was confined, in the hope of discovering some compromising secret. His encounter with the eccentric Countess and her maid had yielded nothing. He was forced to accept the Earl's curt explanation that she was a little crazed, and he abandoned his search in some discomfort.

He advanced farther into the Green Salon, and the woman sitting sewing by the window looked up at him. "I hope I'm not disturbing you, madam."

Katherine put down her sewing and began to fold it up. "I was just leaving, Captain. Please make use of my room if you wish."

"My room." He grew red at the tone and the implication that he was intruding.

She was gratified to see the round young face flush with embarrassment. He pulled at the tight white stock above his blue-faced scarlet coat and stood still. He had such an ordinary face, with undistinguished features and curiously sharp brown eyes, and she hated him as if all her hatred for his King and his victorious army were concentrated on that one pompous young officer who would have smirked and strutted at the slightest encouragement from her. She wondered what the women of his country would do if the Highlanders of Prince Charles were in occupation of their country and invaded their homes and had the insufferable impudence to expect them to be friendly. She knew her father hated him too, but he concealed it, and forced his people to do the same. One hostile incident would be enough to signify their sympathy with the rebellion and bring the punitive squads out from Inverness to burn and ravage their lands as they were doing to the Chisholms and the Mackintoshes and the Macdonalds in the area.

Every day Booth and his men went out to hunt for fugitives; Katherine noticed with horror that they never returned with prisoners, and one night at dinner she saw the Captain take out a fine gold watch which she knew he had not possessed before.

I *am* disturbing you, I see," he said stiffly. "I must protest, madam, that whenever I come into a room you always make a point of leaving it!"

Katherine stood up. "You are here at my father's invitation, sir. Not at mine. I find it extraordinary that you expect Henry Ogilvie's window to treat your presence here as if it were a pleasant social call."

"I am sorry about your husband," he said stiffly. "But if he had not taken arms against his King he would be with you now."

"King George was not his King!" Katherine retorted.

"What do you want from me, sir—must I call on God to save Prince Charles? I will, if it will give you the excuse you need to arrest me."

"If I wanted to arrest you"—the Captain stepped up to her, barring the way to the door—"if that was what I wanted, I could have done it long ago! Don't make any mistake, madam, I can do what I please and order what I please here. But we're not punishing anyone except the guilty, and it seems your family are not guilty. As for your feelings, I can hardly punish a woman for the treason of her husband. All I want," he said angrily, "is that you should stop treating me and my two officers as if we were cutthroats!"

"When I think of my husband and so many that I loved—" But it was not Henry who was in her mind then as she stood confronting the enemy; it was not his memory that brought the tears to her eyes and made her so far lower herself as to weep in front of the Captain. It was James who haunted her. James dead on that dreadful field, James lying for two days and nights among the wounded until the execution squads of Cumberland marched out and killed him where he lay. Suddenly she began to cry, and her tears touched the heart of the young man standing in front of her; he had seen many women weeping in the last few weeks, some of them as wellborn and as proud as the beautiful widow of the traitor Ogilvie of Spey. But he had seen their suffering quite unmoved. He was a soldier and accustomed to unpleasant duties, some of which, like the summary execution of the savage Highlanders, gave him a sense of satisfaction. He was quite unprepared for the effect that Katherine's tears had upon his feelings. He took a step nearer her.

"Please," he said, "please don't cry. If there's anything I can do ... If there's a chance that your husband might be alive ..."

"There's no chance at all," Katherine answered. "My father has made enquiries everywhere among the prisoners in Inverness; my husband was last seen fighting the Campbells. We have presumed him dead." She wiped her eyes and composed herself, and as she did so and saw the young man watching her, she suddenly decided to disguise her loathing and make use of him. With an effort she smiled. "I'm sorry I was so rude to you, Captain Booth. You have been very kind. Please excuse me, I was overcome . . ."

His response was so immediate that, had she been less bitter, Katherine would have felt ashamed. He went red again to the edge of his tight curled wig and offered her his arm. "Come and sit down," he said. "Can I ring for anyone for you? Do you want your maid?"

"No, thank you." She shook her head. "There's nothing anyone in this house can do to help me. Captain Booth, have you ever lost someone you loved?"

"My mother," he said slowly. "I was very fond of her."

Katherine leant towards him. "Then you can imagine what it is like not to know whether that person is dead or not?"

The Captain stared at her. "But you said it was certain that your husband . . ."

"I'm not talking about my husband," she said. She decided to gamble everything on his vanity. "I feel I shouldn't burden you," she said. "But I cannot help myself. Can I trust you?"

The sharp brown eyes gazed into hers and then he looked away. "You know you can, madam. Are you in trouble?"

"No," Katherine said gently. "And I wouldn't take advantage of your chivalry to ask you to help me if I were. I am asking for something that only you can do for me—if you will. But it's not against your honour, Captain. All I want is news of one of the rebels . . . whether he's a prisoner, or dead. . . ."

"Why can't your father make enquiries for you?" He was still in doubt about her; his natural suspicion and dislike of the Scots fought with his increasing interest in the woman and the hope that gratitude might induce her to make some return to him. He was not even sure of what kind.

"You don't know Scotland, do you, or you wouldn't ask that question. I had a suitor once, long ago; my father disapproved and married me to someone else. I dare not even mention his name. Captain, can you find out for me what has become of James Macdonald of Dundrenan? That's all I ask."

"I wish I knew," he said curtly. "For he and his father and

a number of their men are on my list of fugitives. We've been out searching for them the last three days. The Cholmondleys went to Dundrenan to wait for them, but the Macdonalds didn't go back there, and if they do now, they'll find it burnt to the ground. So far he has escaped; there are quite a number of dead British soldiers scattered round this countryside to prove it."

She turned on him then in triumph; she didn't care what he thought of her then, nor was she afraid. Nothing mattered but that James was still alive. "Oh, thank God," she said. "Thank God and thank you too, Captain, for giving me the best news of my life."

"You surprise me," he said stiffly. "I thought you were mourning your husband. If I were you I shouldn't rejoice too soon. We're searching the woods round Loch Ness this very afternoon; there's a rumour that the Macdonalds have been seen in that area. Have no doubts, your lover will be caught and executed. We'll find him and punish him if we have to search the Highlands from coast to coast!"

Katherine moved away abruptly, leaving him standing, glaring after her, but at the door she turned. "You will never capture James Macdonald," she said quietly. "You poor, tame Englishman—if you ever do catch up with him, I pity you!"

As she shut the door he heard he laughing. The Captain left Clandara early that afternoon. He had sat through the midday meal with the Earl and Katherine and hardly spoken. His two junior officers were stiff and glum, and the Captain behaved with pointed rudeness by leaving in the middle of the last course and ordering his ensigns to saddle up and be ready to set out. He turned curtly to the Earl.

"Your pardon, Lord Clandara, but we have a special area to search today. I hope you will excuse us!"

"It seems I have no choice."

Katherine saw her father's pale and angry face and, leaning across, she whispered to him to be careful.

"Take your leave then," he said. "We will excuse you."

When they had gone, he snapped his fingers angrily and

the two menservants drew back their chairs, and he took Katherine's arm and went down the Great Hall to the library.

"Ill-mannered dogs," he said. "They should sit with the servants! I've half a mind to tell that puppy to behave himself or take his men elsewhere!"

"He's angry with me," Katherine said. "I snubbed him this morning. He'll recover his temper."

"Has he been troubling you?" The Earl turned to her quickly. "Tell me, my child, has he offended you in any way? By God, if he has . . ."

"No, Father. You know how awkward-mannered the English are. He's just a harmless oaf, that's all. And even if he weren't, there's nothing you can do without losing your neutrality. I only hope you think it's worth it."

He looked up at her as she stood before him, dutiful and polite and faintly hostile. "You have never forgiven me for turning out those Chisholms, have you?" he said.

Katherine shook her head. "No, Father, and I never shall. Is there anything else you want now? Your books, or Dugal to come to you?"

"There is nothing I want," he said slowly. "You may go." She curtsied and went out, closing the door gently, and he heard the sound of her steps as she crossed the Great Hall. He was beginning to hate her and she was all he had left in the world.

Angus had saddled her horse, protesting all the time that the countryside was no place for anyone to ride into these days when troops of cavalry were roaming the moors and some of the fugitive clans were robbing their own people of food and clothing. Katherine did not argue. She had changed her dress and she waited in the stables while Angus saddled her mare; when he began taking down saddle and bridle for himself, she stopped him.

"I'm going alone."

"That you're not!" The old man's mouth fell open and then snapped shut again. He shook his grey head and repeated it. "That you're not, milady. If ye insist on going out, then I go with ye. Otherwise I go now and tell his lordship!"

"Angus." Katherine spoke very quietly. "You are my servant and your obedience is to me. Those soldiers have gone after the Macdonald of Dundrenan and his men. I'm going out to see if I can find them first and warn them. And you are not coming with me. If you dare to tell my father I shall let him know you accompanied me on those secret meetings at Loch Ness, and I wouldn't give much for your skin after that. Bring my mare out, and tell them to open the gates!"

She rode out into the open country, guiding her horse down the steep hillside away from the castle, and when the ground flattened she broke into a canter. Five miles to the west by the head of the Loch there was a wood where she and James had often ridden; it was thick and riddled with small paths. Men might hide there undetected for days, snaring what game they could and creeping to the Loch at night for water. She would look there first. As she rode she thought of what that wretched Englishman had said. "The Cholmondleys went to Dundrenan to wait for them, but the Macdonalds didn't go back there, and if they do now, they'll find it burnt to the ground. . . ." James's home was destroyed, his lands forfeit, and he and his father and his men were fugitives. But he was still alive. Joy and thankfulness filled her heart, and for the first time in many weary months Katherine knew what it meant to be happy again. Nothing mattered to her at that moment; her marriage with its tragic disappointment to the kind, deserving Henry, and then his death . . . all he futility and pain which had oppressed her ever since the poor fleeing Chisholms took their brief refuge in Dundrenan, all vanished now, because the greatest grief of all was gone. James still lived, and even if it cost her own life she would find him and warn him that the dragoons were in the district looking for him. That was why she had not taken Angus. For if she didn't find the Macdonalds, they would certainly find her. Whatever happened, she didn't want poor faithful Angus to be killed.

At the edge of the wood she dismounted and, leading the mare, began to walk through the trees. The little wood was very quiet, the sun gleamed through it, patterning the mossy ground, and twigs broke under her horse's feet. After a few moments she stopped. There was not a sound, and yet her mare heard or sensed something, for it whinnied. Far to the right, another horse whinnied in reply. Katherine turned the mare's head and began to lead her in the direction of that sound. Someone was in the wood, and that someone had a horse. If it wasn't James and his people, it must be some other fugitive.

Katherine had seldom been afraid in her life. Now as she went deeper into the shadowy wood it seemed darker and colder and the patches of sunlight grew less. Some of those who fled the battlefield had turned robber, and lay in wait for travellers, killing them and stripping them of clothes and money. Not all those who fought at Culloden were English on one side and Scots on the other. Supposing that the wood hid a party of marauding Campbells ... Rape and death might be at the end of that path where she was walking. For a moment she panicked and stopped, and then suddenly the wood was full of terrible sounds. There was a wild yell and just ahead of her a man came crashing through the trees, a big bearded man, naked except for the kilt, and behind him others followed, but these were men in the scarlet and blue of the English cavalry, and one of them ahead paused to take aim and fired at the running Highlander. She heard her own voice shrieking, and the mare took fright and plunged, almost knocking her down.

"James, James!" she began to scream. "James, the English are upon you. . . ."

"Someone stop that woman's mouth!" an English voice shouted behind her, and the next moment she was thrown to the ground, and the weight of a man's body dropped on hers. The trooper wasted no time. He pulled her head up by the hair and drove his fist into her chin.

When she regained consciousness Captain Booth was bending over her.

"I might have guessed you'd try to warn him," he said. "How very foolish of you . . . didn't you think we'd be looking in a place like this?"

She moved her head away; there was the taste of blood in her mouth and her arms ached, for they had tied her wrists behind her back. She tried to struggle upright, and he watched her contemptuously.

"I saw someone running," she whispered. "I thought for a moment . . ."

"One miserable rebel, that was all," the Captain answered. "You've betrayed yourself for nothing, madam. Your Macdonalds are not here."

"That's all I care about," she said. "Will you be good enough to untie me, sir? When my father sees me and hears what you have done, he'll accuse you to the Duke of Cumberland himself."

"Much good that will do him," the Captain jeered. For the first time since he had met her he felt superior. The dishevelled woman lying on the ground, her beautiful face streaked with dirt and blood and her arms bound awkwardly behind her, was suddenly at a level with all the rest of her countrypeople, outlawed and hunted down like dogs.

"The Duke is not merciful to traitors," he went on. "And you have proved yourself no less. Warning a rebel is as bad as harbouring one. You are under arrest, madam, and you'll go with an escort to Inverness tomorrow morning. Like all your people, you made one serious mistake. You underestimated us."

"I didn't," Katherine said slowly. "I knew you for an illbred cur the moment you walked into my sight. And you'll never capture James Macdonald!"

"Sergeant Brewster! Is that business done yet?"

"Aye, sir. We found nothing on him."

"Very good then. Untie the Lady Katherine and detail two men to take her back to Clandara Castle. She's to be confined to her rooms and a sentry posted outside her door. No one is to see her until I return with the troop. Quick now!"

The trooper pulled her to her feet; her head ached and her jaw throbbed; she stumbled and almost fell. He called another man to hold her upright while he cut her wrists free.

"Can you ride unaided, ma'am?" he asked her. His tone was respectful, for this was the daughter of their host and a great lady. He was not so gentle with the women of the poorer classes who had fallen into his hands in the last few days. "If you feel faint, you can ride in front with one of my men."

"I'm perfectly able to ride," she answered. "I'd rather *walk* back than share a horse with one of your soldiers."

"As you please." Sergeant Brewster took her arm, and though she tried to wrench it free, he held it a little more firmly, privately thinking what a pity it was that the Captain had to be there when they came upon her in the wood. He was bored with stripping and hanging their miserable, half-starved men. A woman like this one would have been a change. They could have buried her afterwards and no one need have known.

"This way, if you please." He led her down the path and there she saw the troopers' horses tethered in a clearing, her own mare among them. They must have been waiting there while the men searched through the wood and flushed out the poor man she had seen running for his life. Two men led their horses and hers forwards and the sergeant escorted her farther out through the trees until they came to the edge of the wood. There she mounted and her escort, two stiff and wooden-faced young conscripts from the Suffolk estates of Captain Booth, closed in on either side of her.

"Back to Clandara," the Sergeant barked at them. "Under close confinement in her rooms and a sentry posted outside till the Captain gets back. Ride close now. And don't try to escape them, ma'am," he added. "They'll ride you down in a minute; they're both good lads."

At the edge of the wood, the sun blazed down upon her as she rode back to the castle, and something made her turn and glance back. At the very edge where the wood ended she saw the naked body of the bearded man swinging from a tree.

Annie had been crying for an hour; her thin little face was pinched and blotched with weeping. When they brought Katherine back, she gave a wild cry like an animal in defense of its young and flew at the impassive soldiers with her fists. One of them had pushed her hard back into the room, and then the door was shut and the sentry took up his post outside it. She gathered Katherine in her arms, and a moment later the Earl came and they could hear him shouting at the sentry, until the man said loudly: "Stand away there, or I'll use the bayonet. I've my orders. None goes in there until the Captain comes."

"Don't try him, Father," Katherine called out. "He'll do what he says. I'm all right, I'm not hurt!"

"She is too!" Annie called out. "Her sweet face if all marked ..."

"Be quiet!" Katherine ordered. "Do you want that English brute to kill my father? Father, don't listen to her. I'm not hurt, I tell you. I went out riding and I came upon them hunting a poor man down in the woods by the north shore of the Loch. Now go away, I beg of you. The Captain will be back soon and then you can see me."

"I'll have every man in the castle up here in five minutes and I'll personally cut your throat, you swine," she heard him shouting at the sentry.

Thrusting Annie aside, Katherine came up to the door. "I went to warn the Macdonalds of Dundrenan," she said loudly. "That's why I was arrested. Will you still come up and free me now?"

He did not answer at once, and behind her she heard Annie gasp. A moment later they heard the sound of his steps as he turned and walked away down the long stone corridor.

"Ach, my God," Annie whispered, "what have ye done?"

"He won't be back now," Katherine said. "Annie, help me, my head's swimming."

She gave herself up to Annie then, and while she was busy bathing her mistress' face and hands and gently brushing her hair, and helping her into a dressing robe, Annie remained calm.

"You're out of your mind," she said over and over again. "Risking your life to go looking for him ... have ye forgotten that murderous brother and the danger ye put yourself into at the palace? ... What would they have done if you had found them? Did ye think of that?"

"I didn't care," Katherine said. She felt strangely lightheaded, almost exultant. "They won't capture James. I know they won't!"

"Ach, how foolish, how foolish," Annie went on. "How will we put this right now, with that great oaf of an officer? . . . Your father will have to explain it. . . ."

"It's beyond anything Father can say to him," Katherine told her. "Poor Annie, I've got to tell you. This isn't just an escapade, and these people are not chivalrous gentlemen playing at war. . . . Look at my face if you don't believe me. I went there to warn a proscribed traitor, and that Captain told me I would be sent to Inverness tomorrow and charged with treason. I want to ask you if you'll come with me. I don't know what manner of place they'll put me in before I'm given trial."

That was when Annie began to cry.

"You must understand," the Captain said, "that I find this personally very unpleasant. But I must carry out my duty, Lord Clandara, and Lady Katherine's action has given me no choice."

The Captain and Katherine's father were facing each other calmly, and in the young man's opinion he was conducting the interview with authority and tact. He felt very pleased with himself and very confident that the arrogant old man was about to humble himself and beg. Whatever he did, nothing would secure his daughter's release. She had laughed at him and called him a poor, tame Englishman. In the stinking prison at Inverness she would have time to regret that remark.

"My daughter is under arrest in my house," the Earl said. His light eyes glittered at the Captain. "I would like to hear your explanation of this circumstance. Then we will discuss the merits or demerits of her action and what I propose to do about it."

Some of the Captain's composure deserted him at the tone in which the Earl delivered his remarks. He felt almost as if he were on trial. "This morning your daughter asked me to do her a favour," he snapped. "She asked me to find out if a certain James Macdonald of Dundrenan House was alive or dead. I was able to tell her that unfortunately he is very much alive, and that I was engaged upon a search for him. I can assure you, my lord, she made no secret of her attachment to him, and to the infamous cause for which he fought."

"Young man," the Earl said curtly, "there is no need to use long words with me. Be plain. My daughter asked after this traitor, and you told her he was still alive."

"I did," the Captain said stiffly. "And acting on that, your daughter rode out this afternoon to look for him and his people and warn him. I rather expected that she might. She came into a wood up by the shore of the lake there—"

"You mean the Loch," the old man interrupted. "We have no *lakes* here. . . ."

"Don't try me too far, sir," the Captain barked at him. "One more insult and I shall leave you to make your own deductions."

"That would be most unwise." The Earl regarded him with a curious little smile. "I have friends, sir, in very high places. No stain of disloyalty shows on me. Beware how you conduct this business. Go on, my daughter came into this wood . . ."

"We were searching for rebels, and one of them had been hiding there. He ran out and your daughter must have mistaken him, for she began shrieking. I heard her myself. 'James, James, the English are upon you!' Most regrettably we had to silence her by force. I have many witnesses among my men, Lord Clandara. She herself did not attempt to deny it."

"No," the Earl said at last. "No, I can well believe that. It seems the case is proved then." His face was quite composed. It was impossible for the Captain to guess his thoughts. "I had an only son," he said at last. "He died; I had a son-in-law; he too is dead. It seems that only James Macdonald of Dundrenan lives. When my daughter told me why she had been brought back a prisoner, I thought afterwards it might have been a lie to make me go away and leave your sentry unmolested. Now that I know it's the truth the matter's altered. Captain Booth, what she has done to betray allegiance to the King of England does not concern me. If it were only that, not one of you would leave Clandara alive. I tell you this so that you may not think it possible to call the child of a chief to your justice. It is my justice which counts at Clandara. But because of my daughter's betrayal of her own blood and my authority, I shall let you take her to Inverness tomorrow. I do not even want to know what becomes of her. If you will excuse me now, I should like to be alone."

The ruins of a great house stood open to the sky; its walls were blackened by fire and the upper floors were charred and crumbling. Shreds of silk hung down from one wall, and they were all that remained of the Grey Salon, prepared so carefully by James Macdonald for his bride. The Macdonalds of Dundrenan had taken refuge in the ruins of Kincarrig, and no one had thought to search the relic of an old clan feud. They lived in the cellars and in the outhouses, and little bands of them went out by day, with James or David in command, to search for English troops and catch them unawares when they were looting the poor crofts. Those they caught were killed quickly, but when there was time to spare they took prisoners and questioned them about the movements of their regiments. Few refused the Macdonalds information, and afterwards their burnt and mutilated bodies were left hanging near the mountain roads as a warning to those who came in search of them.

Food was scarce; the Macdonalds trapped and fished, and cooked over a fire in one of the cellars at Kincarrig which was well below ground and no light could be seen. Most who had fled from Culloden had left their arms behind, but the muskets and bayonets of their victims were distributed among them and they had taken many horses. The Macdonalds wore English coats over their kilts, the facings and insignia ripped away. Their numbers had diminished. Some had left their chief at Dundrenan and gone back to protect their own homes if they could. There were taken by the soldiers in due course and shot; afterwards their few sheep or cattle were driven off, the crude farming implements chopped up, and their families, often stripped of their clothes, were left in the empty crofts to starve. Whole families fled westwards to the mountains and the sea, hoping to escape the punitive detachments in the bleak, wild country, and many of them perished from cold and hunger on the way.

Slowly and methodically the victorious British army advanced through the Highlands, burning and killing and gathering the people's means of livelihood, so that the scattered farms were empty of animals and tools and there was nothing left for those who stayed behind. Old men who remembered the rebellion of thirty years ago had never seen anything to equal the slaughter and destruction inflicted on the people by the Duke of Cumberland. For the Macdonalds of Dundrenan, the centuries turned back; they lived as their wild ancestors had done, pillaging and killing, and the old chief sat in the ruins of Kincarrig wrapped in his plaid, and his men brought him the heads of English soldiers and stray Campbell militiamen as a tribute.

Hate had taken possession of him. Hidden among the low hillocks outside Dundrenan, he had watched his great stronghold burn to the ground, and heard the wagons rattling down the rough tracks as the English carried off his silver and possessions. When they had gone he led his men into the smoking ruins, and there they found the corpses of his servants, and one young girl, her ravaged body arranged with horrible obscenity upon the open ground. While his sons stood beside him the old man suddenly raised his arms and called on God to bear witness to his oath that not one man, woman, or child of English blood, or any Highlander who submitted to them, should go unpunished as long as he had strength to hunt them down. Then he took his sons and his people back into the open country; it was James who suggested they make their headquarters at Kincarrig.

Word reached them through some fugitive Grants that the Prince had escaped and was on his way to Moidart with the crippled Cameron of Lochiel and a few followers, to await a French ship which would take them to France. It was decided by Sir Alexander that, as heir to the chieftainship, James should leave them and go after the Prince. Kincarrig would not conceal them forever, and if he were captured with his father and David, the Macdonalds of Dundrenan would be leaderless and the clan would disappear.

James's fierce arguments had been overruled. Nothing mattered now but the continuance of the clan, and the Prince would need every loyal subject to support him in exile and work on for the cause. James would have to escape with him to France and continue the fight from there.

It was late afternoon when David returned with half a dozen men and came to report to his father. The old man sat upon a stone and one of the young boys who carried the pipes stood by him, attending to his needs and singing to him as his own ancestors had done to the wild Macdonald chieftains centuries ago.

"What did ye find?" Sir Alexander demanded. David untied a little bag and laid it at his father's feet. A few silver coins, some buttons, and a woman's metal locket on a chain were in it.

"These, and three troopers," Daivd said. "There's a detachment of cavalry five miles from here and these three soldiers were out alone, resting round a burn by the Black River Bridge. We have their arms and horses outside. They had bread with them and one of them carried some brandy. I've got it for you."

"Poor taking," James said. He had come out from the ruined stables. He looked gaunt and wild and his dark face was bearded; an English bayonet was hanging at his belt beside his dirk. "Did any of them speak?"

"One did," David said. "We kept him alive for a little time and by the end he cried so hard for his life that I gave it him, and we buried him alive." He laughed. "There is a detachment of cavalry at Clandara; he was able to tell us that."

Sir Alexander leaned forward. "Guests, no doubt," he said softly. "Guests of him who sent the Chisholms out to die?"

"Received there in all honour," Daivd said. He did not look at James. "Clandara is their headquarters while they search the area."

The old man leant back and kicked the coins and trinkets aside. "Give these to those who went with you today. And you, boy, go and bring the brandy. We will have a conference, my sons."

He was watching James as they sat down and he took the

first drink from the bottle. None of them had tasted anything but water since the morning of the battle. The old man's eyes did no flicker or leave his eldest son's face; they had fought together and lived through hardships and dangers, buried their dead and killed their enemies and walked through the smoking ashes of their home together, but he was not satisfied with his son. There was a doubt, and it came to him sometimes at night, when he lay in his plaid on the ground and thought of his second son whom he had never loved as much as his first. And he had come to the conclusion that his preference was mistaken.

Hugh, mocking, merciless Hugh, was now dearer to him in memory than the son who had given such terrible proof of his weakness in the past. Hugh would not have loved the daughter of their enemy. Hugh would not have changed colour when the two Chisholms mentioned her name, and even then when David spoke of Clandara, the old man had seen James start. His son was not true, he thought. There was still a weakness in him. And now weakness of any kind was a crime, a treason to all that remained of the clan. The chief took out the stained and creased letter which he had kept in his doublet, and opened it out.

"Listen, my sons," he said. "Listen again to what our cousin Margaret says. 'On the night of the first full moon the north postern gate will be left open for you. Come while the house sleeps and you shall easily overcome them. I have lived and suffered only in order to take my revenge upon them, and I charge you with it, my cousins and kinsmen. Every month at the full moon, I shall leave the north gate unlocked until you come.' What does this say to you, my sons?"

"It says that Margaret wrote this when the castle was not garrisoned by English troops," James said. He met the look of his father and his brother David without betraying anything. But even though a cold wind blew, the sweat was shining on his forehead.

"And since when have you been afraid of a few sleeping English?" the chief demanded.

"I am afraid of nothing!" James said. "And by God I've proved it often enough!"

"It's not your courage I question." His father spoke softly and his yellow eyes were cunning. "I know well enough that there's not a man living of whom you are afraid. So why do you make the troopers your excuse? Isn't this better and better, that the English should be there, sleeping and all unaware when we come upon them? We have men, and horses now, and arms for everyone. "Why"—he turned to David—"we will slaughter everyone in the castle in their beds! And isn't that what troubles *you!*" He rounded suddenly on James. "Come now, David and I are not deceived—it's the woman, isn't it? That's why you talk about the soldiers . . ."

"That is a lie!" James shouted. "There's no woman who means anything to me!"

"I'm glad to hear it," Sir Alexander said. "Consider, my son. We hide here like vagabonds in all that the Frasers left of your home—that splendid home you prepared for her so carefully. We have lost everything, lands, houses, everything. We are hunted like dogs and even this place will be thought of in the end. While our enemy, the traitor who would not join his Prince, sits on his estates only a few miles distant, closing his doors to fugitives and entertaining Cumberland's troops. What do you suppose they speak of, when they're at dinner there? The raids they've made, the crofts they've burnt, and the women they've ravished while their husbands look on at bayonet point? It must be entertaining stuff! I wonder how the Lady Katherine likes it."

"How do you know she's there?" James countered.

His father laughed. "Oh, she'll be there, protected by her traitor father, pretending to mourn for the honest man who married her and whom you would have killed. Whatever he was, no English troops would have made their headquarters there if he were still alive! So no woman means anything to you—and yet you would have killed him, you were so jealous!"

James looked at him. "All that is in the past. It was a moment's hate and madness. I repeat, no woman means anything to me."

"If you are going to join the Prince as titular chief and go to France, then you will have to earn that privilege," Sir

Alexander said. "And if you can't, then I shall give your right to David here. You owe me this, James. You owe it to me to prove that you're no longer guilty of that love."

"I am no longer guilty of it," James said slowly. "I'm as eager to attack Clandara as you are."

"I want more proof than that," the old man said. "I took an oath in the ashes of Dundrenan that no one who harboured our enemies should be spared. I shall keep that oath and I lay it on you also. Not one man, woman, or child shall be left alive in Clandara. And you, James, will redeem your honour by putting her to death yourself."

"This is what you ask of me?" James's dark eyes burned into the yellow ones.

"No," his father answered shortly. "It is what I *command*. And now go and summon our people. Tonight is the full moon, and tonight we attack Clandara!"

James rose and bowed to him. As he walked away, David turned questioningly to his father.

"Will he obey you?"

"He will," Sir Alexander answered. "His pride will make him. And when it's done and Clandara is in ashes, then I shall die happy. If he'd refused, I think I would have had him killed. Come, drink from the bottle, David, and then pass it to me. It's growing cold and we've a long way to ride."

"If Margaret fails, and the gate is not open ..." David said.

"It will be open," his father answered. "I know it. We will get in."

Annie had gone down to get her mistress some food, in spite of Katherine's protests that she wanted nothing, and in the long dim corridor leading to the kitchens she came upon the Countess Margaret's maid. For the first time for many months, Jean did not back against the wall to let her pass.

"My mistress wants to know what has befallen," she said. "Is it true there are soldiers guarding Lady Katherine?"

"It is," Annie almost spat at her. Her swollen eyes filled up with tears again. "And you can tell your mistress this—milady is being taken away to prison tomorrow and all on account of your cursed family! She was out trying to warn that devil James Macdonald when they caught her. Now get out of my way before I box the head off your shoulders!"

Jean turned and slipped past her and ran back upstairs to the Countess' rooms. She shut the door quickly and her mistress came out from her bedroom. To Jean's surprise she had rouged her face; the effect was grotesque, and even more so was the yellow velvet gown trimmed with lace which the little maid had not seen her wear for years.

"She's under arrest, milady," she said. "I met her maid in the passage below and she told me it was on account of the Lord James. She was caught by them, trying to warn him. . . . They're taking her to Inverness tomorrow!"

"I don't believe it," the Countess said. "I don't believe they'd dare. . . . Taking her to Inverness, did you say? To prison?"

"Yes," Jean muttered. "I've heard them talking in the kitchens about how they keep our people at Inverness. They're terrible places. . . ."

"I expect they are," the Countess said. "She wouldn't look so beautiful after a while spent in Inverness. . . . It's a pity she won't be going."

"Not going? But why not?"

"Because by tomorrow she and everyone in here except you and I will probably be dead!" the Countess said softly. "I said in that letter to my cousins that on the night of the full moon I'd find a way to let them in if they came here. We know they're still alive and somewhere near. The Chisholms must have found them. And tonight *is* the full moon. Why are you looking at me like that, girl? Close your mouth, it's hanging open like an idiot's!"

"Tonight, milady . . ." Jean stammered, staring at her. For the first time in all the years she had served her, she felt as if the Countess were positively evil.

"Yes, yes, yes!" Margaret said angrily. "Tonight is the full moon! And when the house is sleeping, you're going to creep out and unbar the north postern gate. You know the one, set back in the wall. . . . It's easy, it's only a short piece of iron;

a strong girl like you can lift it out of the socket and a hundred men can slip through there without being seen."

"But if there's a sentry," Jean protested.

"Sentry!" her mistress snapped at her. "What sentry, you fool? Why should they post sentries here? Who do they expect to attack them?" She came close to the girl and caught her by the arms. "I'd go myself, you miserable little slut, but I haven't the strength to lift it. No one will question you, even if you are seen. I'd be detained at once by one of these damned servants if I tried to even leave my rooms. You're going to do it, do you hear!"

"Yes, milady. I'm not afraid. I'll open it." Jean moved away a few steps, rubbing her arms. The Countess' hands had left red marks upon them.

"Think of it, Jean," she exulted. "Think of all the years we've spent in this place, insulted, despised ... think of the nights *he* used to come here drunk and tear my clothes off my back and beat me like a dog on account of his son! Did you think I'd forgotten? Did you think I'd weaken and let it go unpunished? There won't be one of them alive by morning.... *He* and his daughter and his English officers! I saw you looking at me just now, child. I've rouged myself and changed my dress."

She looked down and pulled at the low bodice of her old dress, exposing her thin, sallow breasts. "I want my cousin James to see me looking well," she said, half to herself. "He must have forgotten me by now. When he comes, I want to surprise him."

Something stirred in Jean; much as she hated all the Frasers, and especially the Earl, she felt a momentary compunction for the woman who had risked her safety for the sake of James Macdonald. For the first time she used her name respectfully when speaking of her to the Countess. "But will our people kill the Lady Katherine?" she said. "When they know what she tried to do ..."

The venom and rage on her mistress' face made her step back. "Will they kill her? By the living God they will, if the clansmen haven't torn her to pieces first! Now go down and get me something to eat and see what more you can find out. I'm hungry. And I'm excited too."

She went back into her bedroom and Jean could hear her singing softly. Through the half-open door she saw the Countess standing by her mirror, examining herself slowly, and again she tugged at the neck of the dress. Quickly, the girl turned away and went down to the kitchens. There was something horrible about that glimpse of the plain, greying woman, preening herself in a dress she had never been young enough or beautiful enough to wear. Jean shuddered and put the thought of it out of her mind.

The Earl dined alone that night in the library, leaving Captain Booth and his two junior officers to eat in the Great Hall. He was sitting by the fire, as comfortable as his devoted servant Dugal could make him, with a cushion behind his head, his books and whisky by his elbow and the candles placed for him so that he could read if he wished. There was a knock on the door, and Angus came in, bonnet in hand, and when the Earl beckoned him near, he fell on his knee.

"What is it?" Clandara said sharply. "Why do you disturb me at this hour?"

"Is it true they're taking her ladyship away tomorrow?" the old man mumbled. He looked up into the stony face above him and his eyes filled with tears. She was going away, that was all Annie could tell him and all that anyone knew. There had been no word or sign from her father and the old man could bear the suspense no longer.

"It is perfectly true," the Earl said. He had been drinking whisky since the Captain left him, and it had produced no effect on him at all. He felt completely empty and sober.

"In God's name, then," Angus quavered, "what are we to do, Lord? Have ye no orders for us, so as we can stop them? The servants sent me to ye, and I'm afraid there'll be fighting with these dogs of soldiers before the night's over!"

The Earl sat upright. "Tell the servants this. My daughter goes to Inverness tomorrow for the crime of trying to aid Lord Robert's murderer. She went to warn the Macdonalds of Dundrenan. For this I have disowned and abandoned her and I command my people to do the same. After tonight her name will not be spoken in this house. Anyone who provokes the English troops will be hanged. Make that clear. Now go."

He watched the old man shuffle away, and turned back to his whisky. It had done much to relieve him after Robert's death, but now the hollowness could not be filled. "Too many deaths," he said aloud to himself. Robert and Henry, and now Katherine too, for the woman who betrayed her brother's memory and her dead husband's name was not his daughter but a stranger whom he was never going to see or think about again.

He was alone, and all he loved were dead. There were no grandchildren to inherit the great castle and carry on his ancient name. Some distant cousin would be found to take it all when he was dead, and for their sake and to keep his clan together, he must find the will to live the trouble out and see the Highlands at peace again. After that, the sooner he was free of life, the better. After a time he remembered something; the thought came to him slowly and he digested it over another glass of whisky, remembering too how he had always thought the same thought at about that time. His wife was still in the castle; strange that he should have forgotten her. Of course she was still there. The Captain had come upon her in one of his searches, and he had explained her presence as a prisoner with the excuse that she was mad, and the Captain had obviously agreed with him. Margaret Macdonald. The others would be caught and killed in time, and there would be no case for Robert's murder brought against them now. They were proscribed by law. There was nothing he could do about Margaret as long as the troops were at Clandara, but when they'd gone, there would be no one there to interfere. . . . That promise made to Katherine was no longer valid. He sat on until the decanter was finished and at last Dugal and one of the menservants came in and carried him up to his bed.

"He'll do naught," Angus said. "He said she went to help the Macdonalds of Dundrenan and he's disowned her. Her name is forbidden in the house!"

"Ach, let him tell me that!" Annie blazed. "Did ye not

know why she went, Angus, and why weren't ye with her, now that I think of it?" In her grief and terror she turned furiously upon her grandfather.

"I knew it," he retorted. "She told me so, and it was no surprise to me. Nor is it to anyone who knows her. She's loved that scoundrel from the first moment and only her father wouldn't admit it! Anyway, she wouldn't *let* me go with her. What are we to do, Annie? There's no help from him at all...."

"Then we'll do without it," Annie said fiercely. "She's upstairs there with the ruffian standing by the door, and her own father hasn't even been to see her.... Angus, go among the men. See how many ye can call on and we'll try and rescue her tomorrow."

"We can lay in wait for them on the Inverness road." The old man's eyes gleamed. "They won't send more than two or three men to escort one woman prisoner ..."

"Two," interrupted Annie. "I'm going with her and no one's going to stop me."

"Two women then." Angus nodded. "Ye're a good girl, Annie. Don't fret now. No matter what the Lord says, we'll think of something. All my life," he said, shaking his grey head, "I've obeyed the Lord in everything. But I'm not going to obey him this time. Give her ladyship my greeting and tell her not to fret herself. We'll find a way."

Chapter 9

As soon as it grew dark the Macdonalds began their long march to Clandara. They came out of the ruins of Kincarrig like shadows, those unmounted moving beside the chief and James and David and the tacksmen who had horses. They had taken off the jingling bridles and stripped the saddles of insignia or ornament; the horses were as silent in their movement as the men, and no bright metal gleamed in the light of the big moon which rose above the mountains. It was a glorious night, still and cool, and the beauty of the wild country in the moonlight was such that even the poor ignorant humblies' hearts were filled with pride and sorrow for the plight of Scotland, ravaged by the invader and humiliated by defeat. Somewhere among the mountains their Prince was a fugitive like them, and in spite of the price his enemies had put upon him, none had been found or ever would be, base enough to give him up.

A few were with him and others still were waiting to join him far off in the Western Isles where a ship might take them to France.

In the foul prisons at Inverness, the men who had fought for him lay starving and dying of wounds, and the gibbets in the city were hung with rotting corpses.

The holds of the English ships anchored in the Tay were filled with prisoners awaiting transport to London where they would be tried, and the sufferings of those battened down among the ballast stones and bilge water was even greater than the miseries of the men in confinement ashore.

The land was full of miserable fugitives, many of them innocent civilians whose crime was the name of a clan who had fought at Culloden, and little children perished in the hills while Cumberland's troops burnt and looted their homes in the glens. Under the bright moon, the men of Dundrenan rode out to pay back many wrongs. Death and rapine and destruction had fallen on their families and they were outcasts with no hope of pardon and no place to lay their heads. They had been told where they were going, and all that afternoon they had been sharpening their weapons and priming the few pistols they possessed, and the lust for vengeance dulled their hunger and their weariness. At the head of them, James rode a big black horse which he had taken from the trooper at Drummossie Moor. He had been organising the men and inspecting their weapons, and he had not spoken again to his father except to come and tell him they were ready to start out.

Broadsword, dirk, and the curved English bayonet hung at his side, and a pistol was in his belt. His mind had accepted what he was going to do; now it seemed inevitable that he should kill the woman he loved, because the love itself was an inexpiable crime and she as guilty as her father of treason to her country and her people. And somewhere in his soul his fierce jealousy rejoiced; another man had married her and known her, and for that he could never forgive her. He would have killed Henry Ogilvie because of what he had enjoyed. Now he would make sure that there would be no other men. He wondered savagely what manner of men the English officers were, those honoured guests of Lord Clandara, and whether one of these were not being made more welcome still. . . . She had married Ogilvie; that surely was proof enough of her unchastity, and hadn't he held her trembling in his arms and felt the eagerness of her response until he had to tear himself away? Even believing him her brother's murderer, her hungry lips had welcomed him in the garden at Clandara. Janet, half forgotten now, as he imagined living safely in her house in Perth, had taught him a great deal about the depth and power of female sexuality, but unlike Katherine, she at least had loved him, with a strength and unselfishness that never wavered. Unlike the false passion of the woman he had loved with all his heart. His father was right.

The ruins of the great house which he had dreamed of living in with her were all that were left of his hopes and his incredible folly, and while he lived like a bandit in his own lands, she entertained his enemies and smiled at them across the table in Clandara. That thought more than anything made him mad; as mad with jealousy as when he faced her husband at Culloden House and challenged him to fight. He wanted her death; he wanted to punish her for her venality and himself for his weakness. He would obey his father. . . .

They dismounted at the Black River Bridge and led the horses over at a walk. David pointed silently to a large mound of freshly dug earth by the side of the track. James remembered the English soldier who had been buried there alive, and turning aside, he spat upon the grave.

"We should go faster," he said. "Tell my father we should ride on and let the rest catch up on foot!"

"You tell him," David answered. "You know the way to that place better than any of us!"

The old chief had not dismounted; he looked down at his eldest son and smiled. It was not a pleasant smile, for he saw the look on James's face, and it was full of pain and hatred.

"I'm glad to see you eager," he said. "It shows your heart is in the business. When it's done and you're a man again, you'll bless me. Tell our people to increase their pace. We'll need time to dispose ourselves while one of us tests the gate. I want to catch them sleeping sweetly."

One of the tacksmen came up to James and held his horse as he remounted. "I was thinking of Murdoch, your milk brother. How he would have relished this!"

James turned on him with an oath. "Get back behind! There's to be no talking!"

Sir Alexander crouched low on his mount's back; his plaid was wrapped tightly round him and his bonnet pulled down; the eagle feather of the chief was broken and it drooped. He watched the little scene and shook his head.

"I'll be behind you, my son, when the moment comes. . . .

For, by God, I don't trust you. . . . David, go on in front. The ground's clear ahead and we'll make speed."

By three o'clock in the morning they reached the north shore of Loch Ness, and as they rounded it, on foot now and without a word passing between them, they saw the crenellated turrets of Clandara Castle outlined in the bright moonlight on the side of the hill.

Captain Booth was not a sentimental man; when he did marry, and there was a well-connected and modestly endowed young woman in his home county whom he had already decided to honour, he would treat his wife with the right mixture of firmness and fairness and proper affection which would ensure that he was master in the relationship at all times. He had a natural distrust of extravagant emotions; the word "love" was one he used as a verb rather than a noun. He could truthfully say that he had loved a number of women in his twenty-three years, beginning in the accepted fashion with a little servant in the house when he was fifteen and she an experienced village slut of thirteen. He had done no more than kiss the hand of the respectable young lady he intended to propose to when he returned to England, and he was quite prepared to supplement her inadequacies as a lover by taking a discreet mistress later on. His world was very orderly and its patterns were straight and rigidly adhered to; there was no provision in any of them for a woman who risked her freedom for a man to whom she was not even married, or for a father who coldly abandoned his own daughter to imprisonment and did not even wish to be told of her fate.

The Captain sat down to dinner in a pensive and uncomfortable mood, and he left it feeling positively confused and rather angry. He felt he had a right to be vindictive. His efforts to treat the inhabitants of Clandara as equals whose loyalty entitled them to consideration had brought him nothing in the way of gratitude and a situation in which he found himself punishing a woman who had insulted him, only to end by feeling embarrassed and guilty about her. Her taunt still stung him; so too did the bitter insult spat at him in the woods when she lay at his feet, and even her bonds didn't quell her insufferable pride.

It would have been so much easier if her father hadn't broken every rule of gentlemanly conduct by callously consigning her to the Captain's custody. "I do not even wish to know what becomes of her." The Captain was deeply shocked. He had been armed against protests, threats, pleas for mercy—even bribes; he had already experienced them all in his dealings with these extraordinary, uncivilised people. But the relentless attitude of the Earl towards his only child, however she had sinned against their tribal customs, was something which the young Englishman could not understand. It had the one effect which he had believed impossible. It made him sorry for his prisoner, and it stirred some curiosity in him about this love of which she spoke and which had so much power over a mere woman. He could not imagine the future Mrs. Booth doing what Katherine Ogilvie had done. After the port was served and his ensigns had irritated him by their cheerful discussion of the extraordinary day's events, the Captain sent a message that he was coming up to see the Lady Katherine.

"Plead with him," Annie entreated, "beg him! What does it matter, milady, so long as he doesn't take ye to Inverness?"

Katherine shook her head. "I never thought I'd hear such advice from you," she said gently. "What would you have me do, Annie, go on my knees to him? How do you know," she added, "that his price may not be higher than just pleading . . . have you thought of that?"

Annie turned pink; the struggle between her sense of outrage and her shrewd countrywoman's assessment of the proper values showed so plainly on her face that Katherine nearly laughed. She felt so tender and grateful to the plain little woman, her poor face blotched with crying and her sharp brain working furiously in an attempt to save her mistress. Finally Annie made up her mind.

"If ye'll forgive me," she said, "I think even that would be worth it if it would keep you from their prison. Ye're no virgin now, milady, and honour is all very well, but how do ye know what your situation might be later on? Do what the ruffian asks, and we'll find some way to make up for it later. . . ."

"By cutting his throat, I suppose," Katherine said. "No, dear Annie. I shall neither beg him nor take him into my bed. He can do what he pleases with me."

"Don't ye understand?" Annie wailed. "Your father has given you up—you haven't a friend to help you now except us poor servants in the castle, and there's little enough we can do to save ye until ye're out of here and on the road to Inverness! Why is this scoundrel coming up here, but he's some plan in mind to let you go?"

"I don't know why he's coming and I do not care," Katherine said. "And you are not to egg the men on to do something foolish tomorrow." She took one of Annie's rough hands in hers. "Don't *you* understand, I'm finished with pretending now? What I did today is what I should have done— I tried to help the man I love. And I do love him, Annie. I've never *stopped* loving him. Robert's death, all our grief and disappointment, even what his brother tried to do to me— nothing has killed my love and nothing ever will. I've known another man and God rest him wherever he is. If he came back tomorrow by some miracle, I couldn't even let him touch me. As long as James Macdonald lives, that's all I want. As for my father—we have given each other up. I have no one left now but you and my few friends in the castle, and I don't mind. Let that English pig come up, and don't you dare to say one word to plead for me, or I will never forgive you. Do you understand that?"

"Ach, very well," Annie sighed. "I'll tell him he can come up now. At least let's see what he says. . . ."

The last time he had seen her, only a few hours before, she had been struggling in the grasp of Sergeant Brewster, whose evil mind he had read as clearly as if the soldier had shouted its content aloud, with her riding dress crumpled and dirty, her hair hanging down her back, and her lovely face disfigured with dirt and blood from the soldier's blow. Now she faced him calmly in her own room, as beautiful and self-composed as ever, with nothing but a bruise near her mouth as evidence of the rough treatment she had received.

"What do you want, Captain Booth?" Katherine said. "I was about to go to bed."

He was in the superior position and it gave him the confidence to ignore the snub. "I came for two reasons, Lady Katherine. Firstly, to make sure that you are ready to leave in the morning, and secondly, to say how sorry I am that this situation had come about."

"I am quite ready," she said. "I have a small box packed. I presume I can take that?" He nodded. "And I should like to take my maid with me—provided that she is free to leave Inverness at any time. If you can't promise that, then I shall go alone." She glanced quickly at Annie, who she knew was about to protest, and made a sign for her to leave the room.

"I can't really promise you anything," the Captain said. "When you arrive at the capital you will be under the Duke's authority. I had expected that your father . . ." He hesitated awkwardly. "I had taken it for granted that he would be going with you and see the Duke's aide, Lord Bury. . . . I had thought at least he would have come up to see you himself. . . ." He looked at her almost appealingly. "Please believe me, Lady Katherine, I had no idea that you would be completely abandoned in this way. I really cannot understand it!"

"I told you, you don't know the Highlands," she said quietly. "In my father's eyes I have placed myself beyond forgiveness. The Macdonalds of Dundrenan killed my brother because he wouldn't join the Prince. Now do you understand why he had disowned me?"

"No!" Booth exclaimed angrily. "No, I don't! No Englishman would treat his daughter like this and leave her to a foreign army's mercy, knowing she might be tried for her life! Lady Katherine." He came close to her. "All this is outside my experience. I don't understand your customs and I hope to God I never shall. All I want to say to you is this: if there was any way I could reverse this thing, I would. But it's beyond my power. If I let you go unpunished for what you did today, I'd be courtmartialled, and believe me, in his present mood the Duke would have me shot. I daren't do it; my ensigns know, the troopers know—it's just not possible!"

"I understand that," Katherine said gently. She felt almost sorry for him. "I don't blame you, Captain. You are only doing your duty as I tried to do mine. I have no regrets; if I could give my life to save James Macdonald, I would do it gladly.

"He's very lucky," the Captain muttered. "By God, he is."

"Will you excuse me now?" she asked him. "I'm very tired."

"I'll go," the Captain said. "And once again, I'm very sorry. Please believe that."

"I do," Katherine answered. She felt very weary.

At the door he turned again. "I'll ride in with you tomorrow and see what I can do myself," he said, and then he went out and shut the door. She heard him snapping angrily at the sentry to relieve his feelings and then his footsteps died away along the passage and all was quiet again.

She did not call Annie immediately. For a few moments she sat on alone in the room among the things she had known all her life and which she would never see again. If the English released her eventually, her home would be barred to her forever. The best she could hope for was to take shelter with Mrs. Ogilvie if Spey House was still left standing.

Fate and their families had divided her and James and left them both as outcasts; he would never know what had become of her.

"Milady." Annie came in and knelt beside her. "Come to bed now, my poor lamb, and rest."

"It was no good, Annie," she said. "He had no dishonourable intentions. He only wanted to say that he was sorry. He's coming with us tomorrow to see what he can do."

"I know," Annie said. "I was listening at the door. Never mind, never mind. We're not at Inverness yet. When I've put ye safe to bed, I'll go and see my grandfather. He's waiting below."

She lit the candles in Katherine's bedroom and turned back the sheets of her bed and helped her into it. She leaned over her anxiously. "Will ye sleep now? Is there anything ye want?"

"Nothing," Katherine said gently. "Good night, Annie, and God bless you."

It was long past midnight and one by one the lights in the castle had gone out. The Earl was in his bed, deep in a drunken dreamless sleep, and Katherine slept at last, while Annie dozed uneasily outside her bedroom and the English trooper nodded at his post outside her door. Everything was very still with the living stillness of a great house full of people, and in the servants' quarters old Angus and half a dozen men were lying on their hidden weapons. They planned to leave the castle very early and lie in wait for Katherine and the escort on the Inverness road. Not one of them possessed a pistol; it would be swords and dirks against the sabres and firearms of the English cavalry, but not one of them drew back or counted the cost to themselves. In her rooms above the Great Hall, the Countess Margaret waited with her maid. Jean wore a long dark cloak and hood; now that the moment had come, she held her candle in a steady hand and all the fatalism of her Highland blood gave her a sense of purpose which was stronger than fear.

The Countess looked at the watch which she wore on her belt. "It's nearly half past one. Go and look out in the corridor and see if you can hear anyone stirring!"

Jean opened the door cautiously and stepped outside. She went a little way down the long dark corridor and listened. There was not a sound and no glimmer of light anywhere. "All are sleeping, milady," she said.

The Countess came out after her, holding the candle, shielding the flame with one hand. "Take this and go down now," she whispered. "Remember, if you're seen by any of the English, make some excuse about a lover. They'll believe you. The same excuse will serve you if one of the castle servants sees you; pretend to go to the stables where the troopers are. . . . Do you understand?"

Jean nodded. "I know what to say," she answered. "Rely on me, milady. I'll get to the gate somehow."

"Take out the bar," the Countess said. "Be careful, child, make no sound, for if you're seen, it will be the end of our plans and the end of us too. Lay it down quietly by the side of the wall and then come back as fast as you can.... Now go on, Jean, and make no mistakes."

"If they don't come," Jean murmured, "and that gate is found open ..."

"If they don't come before dawn," Margaret said, "then we'll know they won't be here tonight and you must slip down and put the bar in place again. It's easy, girl, there's nothing to fear!"

In the flickering light the maid looked up at her. "For nearly seven years I've lived in this place among these cursed people," she muttered. "There's no fear in my heart, only thankfulness to God that we will soon be free, and not without a proper vengeance!"

"Vengeance," Margaret said, "is all I care about. I want to see him die and I want to see his face as our men make free with his daughter. I want to walk among the ashes of Clandara.... After that, I've little care for what becomes of me." She smiled, a ghastly drawn smile, and gave the girl a little push. "Go! I'll watch by the window for you."

Down the long stone corridor Jean went, protecting the candle flame from draughts, her felt-soled shoes making no sound; down past the door where members of the Earl's household slept and on down the sweeping staircase and through the Great Hall. One of the Earl's hunting dogs was lying by the grate and, as she passed, it raised its head and, recognising her, lay down again. It was easy to open one of the doors into the courtyard from the servants' quarters. They were not even bolted at night, and she left the candle on a ledge half hidden in the wall.

The night outside was as bright as day, and the enormous silver moon hung overhead in a sky which glittered with stars. A very light wind blew, chill but not strong, and it bent the tops of the bushes as she turned through the courtyard and into the garden at the back of the castle. This was where the Macdonald of Dundrenan and Katherine Fraser used to walk, holding each other's hands, their heads close together and their pace the gentle gait of lovers to whom time was of no consequence. Jean used to watch them, full of disapproval, hating to see the son of her chief consorting with a woman from the Fraser clan, jeering at the wedding and listening to the jealous outbursts of her mistress. Her heart was hard with hatred for her enemies; there was no pity in it now for the woman who had proved her love for the Macdonald and was so soon to see him face to face. Jean had overcome her scruples. She did not intend to stand and gloat like the Countess.

She went through the garden and up to the high wall; a little to the left she found the north postern gate. When that was opened her part was played. The honour of her mistress and her own duty were satisfied; she did not wish to see what happened afterwards. Because they were Frasers, the way in which her people chose to kill them did not interest her. As for the English—she glanced behind her towards the dark mass of the stables where the Captain's troopers snored among the hay—it was more than likely that the Macdonalds would bolt them in and then set the stables on fire. From what she had heard of their treatment of the Highland families in the district, it would be no more than they deserved.

She lifted the iron bar with both hands, straining a little, and then gently eased it upwards and out of its sockets. It was heavy, but not in any way beyond her strength. She propped it against the wall, well out of reach of the gate so that, when it opened, the bar would not be knocked over. She tested the gate handle and it opened easily. She had a quick glimpse out over the well-lit countryside, with the distant Loch shimmering at the foot of the hill, and then shut the gate again. If the Countess' message had reached them in time, somewhere out there her people were creeping on the castle; the idea made her shiver suddenly. If they were out there, every Fraser and every Englishman at Clandara would be dead before dawn. Jean had only a brief knowledge of the Bible and she could not read or write; the saying she knew best was that dark promise of the Old Testament, "An eye for an eye and a tooth for a tooth."

The Frasers would pay very dearly for strangling the Macdonald's messenger and burning Kincarrig in their ven-

geance for Lord Robert's death. They would pay for not joining their Prince, and for every beating inflicted on the Countess by her husband. With a sense of justice and excitement,
Jean went back to the castle to report to her mistress that she
had done as she was told. There was nothing for them to do
then but wait.

James had ordered his men to tether their horses among
the trees on the Loch shore. Each man tied his mount and
then wrapped his plaid tight round his chest, and with dirks
and daggers in their hands, they began the ascent up the hill
towards the castle. They moved like shadows in the bright
moonlight, taking what cover they could among the scrub
bushes and the uneven places on the ground. But there were
no sentries on the castle walls and no lights in the turrets or
the outer wall. Half crouching, half running, James brought
them to the base of the thick stone wall, the same wall
beneath which their ancestors had beaten themselves in vain
two hundred years before while the Red Fraser defied them
from within and starved his hapless prisoners to death. But
this time there would be no siege; James waved his arm and
the chief and his brother came up close behind him.

"Where is this gate?" Sir Alexander said.

"Twenty yards farther on," James answered. "Wait here,
Father, and keep the men with you while I go forwards and
see if it is open. . . ."

The old man gripped his arm. "No," he said. "Let David
go. You wait with me. We will go in together, James."

They waited, lying flat and close against the wall, while
David crept round the base and disappeared. James did not
look at his father. He felt nothing; his emptiness was so intense that he moved by instinct. He might have been leading
an attack on any house where the English troops were quartered. Not until he was inside and the sword in his hand leapt
at the first strange face he saw would he allow himself to
think that he was at Clandara and that Katherine was asleep
behind those walls. David came back, slipping fast along the
ground.

"It's open. Margaret kept her word."

Sir Alexander looked behind him at the waiting file of men. He raised his arm and they began to run quickly forward. They went through the gate so swiftly that in less than five minutes every man was inside the wall. The chief looked round him; weapons shining in the moonlight, the Macdonalds clustered round him like a pack of wolves. He smiled a fierce smile at his eldest son.

"Lead us, James. You know the way in. And David and you, Douglas, have your daggers ready. Cut the throat of the first man or woman you see, but be silent about it. They shall have no warning until we're right among them.... Ready? Follow me!"

James led them the way he knew the best, up through the garden and into the walled terraces where he had often walked with Katherine, past the small summerhouse where he had waited for her so long ago, with his wild plea for forgiveness for the crime Hugh had committed. Memory returned to him; the dumb and empty sense of hatred vanished and his pain and jealousy swept over him like fire. Here, where he passed with his kinsmen padding like animals behind him, here he had held her and gone on his knees to beg her pardon. The powerful muscles in his belly knotted at the thought of that tense and frightened body yielding suddenly in his arms, of the fierce withdrawal and the stinging blow she gave him.

"Why are you hesitating?" An angry whisper reached him and he turned to see his father's eyes upon him, full of cruelty and suspicion.

"There is the door leading into the Green Salon," James answered. "From there we will be in the heart of the house. I'll open it now."

It was latched but not locked, and they stepped quietly inside.

"Beyond this door is the passage leading to the Great Hall," James explained. "Behind the screen there are the kitchen quarters. Let twenty men go down there and put everyone to the sword. Another ten go out of the Great Hall by the main door and across to the stables. Like as not that's where the English troopers are. Bolt the doors fast."

"Gather what wood and straw you can find and set them on fire," Sir Alexnnder added. "Cut down any of the dogs who break out through the flames. David, that will be your task. You take ten men and give our English friends a little roasting. The rest of us will go with you, James, and give our attention to the Frasers in the castle. Where are their sleeping apartments?" he demanded.

"Upstairs," James answered. "On the floor above this; that's all I know."

"Ach, we'll find them," the old man muttered. "We'll find where they're lying, and their friends the English officers. And such an awakening we'll give them! Come on!"

Captain Booth was dreaming. It was a confused dream in which he was pursuing a fleeing rebel, and the figure grew and diminished as the chase went on, sometimes so large and close that it was within reach of his sword, which then became too heavy to lift, or else so small that it became a running dot which he could not catch up with; just when the quarry came close again, it suddenly turned and looked at him, and as he raised his sword once more, the face he saw was that of Katherine Fraser, her red hair streaming in the wind, her mouth wide open in a terrible scream. It was the scream which woke him, and it came from below where some of the women servants had escaped into the Great Hall and were being caught and murdered by the Macdonalds. The screaming rose and fell, and as he sprang out of his bed, still dazed with sleep, groping for his pistol, the door of his room burst open and a man with a blazing resin torch rushed through it, his bearded face and matted hair illumined in the red light. Captain Booth never had time to fire his pistol at that face because another figure leapt at him and plunged a foot of steel into his middle. He gave a choked shout, half of warning, half of pain, and then he was stabbed again and again until his white nightshirt was soaked in blood, and the clansman with the torch shouted that he was dead, and the men ran out in search of other prey.

Farther down the corridor his two ensigns managed to make a fight for it. They fired their pistols into the doorway

and one of the Macdonalds dropped with a yell; the rest
jumped over his body and fell upon the two young Englishmen, who defended themselves as bravely as they could
against half a dozen attackers. They were lucky, like the Captain, for they died very quickly and were spared the agonies
of Sergeant Brewster and his troopers, who were roasting to
death in the locked inferno in the courtyard, while David and
his men stood guard outside, shooting at the twisted faces
which appeared at odd moments at the windows and firing
regularly into the blazing doorways to drive back the desperate men who tried to escape through the roaring flames.

Angus died in the quarters below, one hand under his
straw mattress searching for his dirk; he had no time to find
it. A blow from a broadsword killed him instantly. Somewhere in the castle a clock struck four; the chimes were lost
in the tremendous uproar which told of the arrival of James
and his father with their men among the private quarters of
the castle. They did not catch the Earl unawares; he had
awoken at the first sound, and hundreds of years of ancestral
experience told him exactly what had happened. Unlike Captain Booth, he was ready when they found his room, and he
went for them, sword in hand, and behind him his steward
appeared from an inner room, also armed, and a bitter fight
developed. Out into the corridor Clandara forced his two as-
sailants, and since they were ordinary clansmen and unskilled
at indoor fighting, he killed one of them and wounded the
other. There were blazing torches everywhere; some of the
wall hangings had been set alight, and through the smoke and
glare he saw the plaid and sett of the Macdonalds as they
swarmed through the rooms, some engaged in hand-to-hand
fighting with members of his household, others pursuing unarmed servants. And then the short thick figure of Sir
Alexander Macdonald came towards him down the corridor,
his dirty plaid wound round his arm, the dirk in his left hand
gleaming and the sword ready in his right.

They shouted together, the two mortal enemies, with their
agelong hatred burning their souls, and they met like tigers.

At the foot of the stairs at the end of the passage, the
Countess of Clandara stood in her yellow gown, with a

branch candlestick held high in one hand watching the slaughter and calling out directions to the Macdonalds.

"Through that door on the right there—the piper's boys sleep there!"

The three boys in their teens fled yelling from the Macdonalds, and the Countess held her candles higher and laughed aloud. It was she who cost the Earl his life. He was fighting Sir Alexander like a madman; they circled each other, lunging and parrying, and already there was a wound in the Macdonald's left arm where his enemy's point had ripped through the plaid in a stroke aimed at his heart. No one interfered in that combat between the two chiefs, and it might soon have ended with the death of Sir Alexander, except that Margaret Clandara came down the steps to watch. It was the movement of her yellow dress, seen in a flash as the Earl made a parrying movement, that distracted him for that vital second and took his attention off his enemy. And that was when Sir Alexander ran him through the chest. The last thing the Earl of Clandara saw before he died was the smiling and triumphant face of his wife bending over him. Very deliberately she spat on him. The old man stood watching her, leaning on his sword. His chest was heaving and the plaid round his arm was turning dark and wet from his wound.

"I wanted him to see her die," she said slowly. "I wanted him to watch while our men took their pleasure with her, and then you could have killed him." She looked down at the dead man and frowned. One hand touched the shoulder of her gown. There was a scar there, made by his riding whip, which all Jean's skill had failed to heal. "It was too quick," she said.

Sir Alexander glared at her; she looked strange and mad in the flickering light, standing unmoved as his men ran past her, shouting and laughing. Some of them were looting the rooms and the bodies. He looked round for his son James, and saw him coming down the corridor towards him, his reddened sword in his hand, half a dozen clansmen close behind him.

"Be content," the old man said to his cousin. "We've no time for rape and torture. It will be light in two hours, and this place will be a grave. I'll burn it as those swine burnt Dundrenan. James!"

He came up to his father quickly. He looked wild and his eyes were black and blazing; he did not even seem to recognise the Countess though she stood only a yard away, the skirt of her dress in a pool of the Earl's blood. Sir Alexander nodded downwards.

"He's dead," he said. "But he pierced me first and I'm losing blood. You'll have to gather the men and see to the firing of this place. Have ye done what I commanded yet? Have ye found her?"

In the light of the torches and the blazing hangings on the wall behind them, James stared at him and shook his head. The hand holding his sword tightened until it trembled. Suddenly his father raised his voice and shouted.

"No man is to touch Katherine Fraser! She belongs to my son! Where is she? Where is she hiding?"

"She is in her room up those stairs," the Countess said. She watched James and smiled. "It's the first room you come to, with a fine carved door. There's only her maid with her and one soldier left on guard. Up there, James. I'll show you."

His father's voice bellowed at him. "Go with her and do what has to be done. Take two men with ye, as witnesses. Ian and Angus—go with my son!"

It was Annie who woke Katherine, her face as white as chalk in the dim light of one shaking candle. "For God's sake, get up! There's murder broken out below. . . ."

Katherine stared at her, so exhausted that she was dazed with sleep; the yelling and echo of running feet seemed to her as if she were in a nightmare and the terrified Annie was a figment in her dream. "What is it . . . what's happened?"

"I don't know," Annie cried. "I heard terrible noises and there's a fire outside; the light of it woke me at the same time as the noise. That sentry's come inside and shut the door behind him; he's shaking like a rabbit. Someone's got into the castle!"

It came to Katherine the next moment who their attackers were—she heard a distant savage yell and recognised the war cry of the Macdonalds of Dundrenan. Annie heard it too, and shuddered.

"Jesus have mercy on us! It's them, and they're inside! Come out of your bed, milady, before they break in here!"

Katherine pulled on her dressing robe and fastened it automatically, hardly aware that her hands trembled. Taking Annie's hand, she ran out of her room into the outer chamber, and there she saw the trooper Captain Booth had placed to guard her. He was standing before the door, his pistol in his hand. He looked back at the two women and began to swear at them. He thought the Frasers were attacking the troops within the castle and for a moment his pistol pointed at Katherine and his finger tightened on the trigger. He was a young man and Scotland was his first experience of war. He had hated the Highlanders he fought and hunted down and he glared at his prisoner and her maid with murder in his frightened eyes.

"You two bitches'll be the first to die," he shouted. "When they come through that door, I'll put a ball through you!"

"Save your fire for them," Katherine spat at him. "Those are the Macdonalds of Dundrenan below. They'll kill us all!"

The soldier pushed his pistol into his belt. He had been out searching for the Macdonalds of Dundrenan for the past week, and he had seen enough English bodies hanging from the trees and pegged out upon the ground in the contortions in which they had been put to death to know what must be happening in the castle. Katherine ran to the window and looked out. Below, the whole courtyard was as light as day and the fire which swept the stables leapt and roared in the dark sky, showering the Macdonald who stood guard upon it with thousands of bright sparks. They could hear the cries of the men who were burning to death above the noise of the fire and the jeers and laughter of their tormentors.

"My brother's in there," the trooper said. His face convulsed; he looked as if he were about to murder both the women, and then they all heard the sound of steps running along the passage.

"Barricade the door," Annie screamed. "Quick, ye damned

fool, stop standing there doing nothing. Help us move the chest!"

They began pushing the heavy piece of furniture across the floor towards the door. The door itself was only closed; Captain Booth had removed the key and a small inner bolt to prevent his prisoner from locking out the sentry. There was nothing left them to keep the Macdonalds out.

Annie turned to Katherine. "Get to the inner room and hide there," she begged. "For the love of God, don't be found in here with him and me! Get under the bed or in the closet!"

"No," Katherine said. "I'm staying with you, Annie. They shan't find me cringing in a corner for my life...." James was coming; she knew it, and with it she felt the certainty of death. She would not hide from it or from him.

The chest now stood against the door, and the hurrying feet were so close that they could tell exactly when they started to slow down and in the next moment they would stop.

Annie turned to the soldier. "It's her they're after," she cried out. "If they see her they'll slaughter us both without mercy.... Make her go into the inner room, for God's sake!"

He was too afraid to doubt her; their attackers were outside and a heavy blow fell on the door. He could hear their voices, men's voices cursing, and one of them shouted fiercely: "Open, Frasers, open and deliver her to us!" That decided him. He rushed on Katherine and lifted her half off the ground, dragging her to the bedroom.

"Stop struggling, you bitch," he hissed. "Stop it or, by Jesus, I'll break your bloody neck!" He threw her into the room and shut the door. "Give quarter," he yelled. "We surrender to you. Give quarter!"

Annie shrank back against the wall as the chest began to slide back under the pressure behind the door. She watched it in terror, and the door behind it widened, and then she saw the Macdonald himself standing there in the opening, with two men behind him. On the far side of the passage, she could see the Countess of Clandara. She heard the soldier's cry of "Quarter" yet again, and James Macdonald pointed to him with his claymore. The two clansmen threw themselves upon him and he went down with a frightful yell. In less than thirty seconds they had cut his throat.

Annie sprang forward as she saw the wild, black-bearded figure in his torn and bloody plaid, the sword uplifted in his hand, turning towards the door behind which Katherine was hidden.

"Don't harm her," she shrieked. "God damn ye, ye black swine, it's for love of you she was arrested! She went to the Loch wood to try and warn ye!"

The black eyes blazed down at her; she didn't think that he had heard a word; he looked like the devil himself. She flew for the door and stood in front of it. James knocked her to the ground; in the haze of madness which possessed him, he did not notice that she was only stunned. The two men who had killed the sentry were behind him, and he roared at them to keep back. "I'll settle this alone," he shouted. "You heard my father—she belongs to me!"

When he opened the door, the room looked red; the redness was the light of the fire outside, and as he saw her standing against the wall in her long robe, he thought for a moment that she was bathed in blood. There would be no witnesses to this, no gaping clansmen should see him kill the woman he had once loved. . . . He kicked the door shut behind him and advanced on her, his claymore raised for a single stroke.

And then he hesitated. For a whole year they had not seen each other; now they were face to face. He had not forgotten how beautiful she was; that lovely face had mocked him from Janet's pillow and glided before his eyes when he was drunk in the arms of whores. He had not forgotten anything about her, except that the living woman who waited for her death with such dignity was a thousand times more potent than the phantom of his maddened jealous dreams.

Katherine looked up at him and her voice trembled. "James, be quick—that's all I beg you."

He cried out and she shut her eyes. The next moment she was in his arms, and his wild kisses covered her face and hair.

"My love ... my darling, forgive me, forgive me! I was mad, possessed. I couldn't have touched you. . . ."

She clung to him, her whole body trembling, fighting the sense of faintness which overcame her. "James, James ... I never stopped loving you. Believe that. Nothing else matters now."

"Don't faint, my love," he whispered. "Bear up. You're safe with me." Annie's words came back to him, and he lifted her face and looked at her. "You were arrested ... the girl said it was for trying to warn me?"

"They caught me in the woods by the Loch," she murmured. "I wanted to tell you they were hunting for you. If you hadn't come, they were taking me to Inverness tomorrow . . ."

He didn't speak because he couldn't trust himself. He held her tight against him, and for a moment hid his face against her hair. He felt as if his heart would burst. "Katherine, I'll get you away safe from here. Will you trust me?"

"I will," she said. "But how will we ever escape? Your own people will cut you down if they see you helping me. . . ."

"My father ordered me to murder you," he said. "But believe me, I'll fight our way out if I have to. . . . Come, hold tight to my arm!"

She stumbled over Annie's body at the door, and it needed all James's strength to drag her away. "I can't leave her," she wept, "I can't, I can't. . . . Oh, James, you didn't . . . ?"

"I only used my fist," he said. "She's not dead. . . . She'll likely escape Come on, my darling, there's not a moment to lose!"

He hurried her past the sentry's body and out into the corridor, and found himself face to face with his cousin the Countess. In the first second Margaret's instinct recognised that this was no vengeful captor bringing out his victim. He held her tightly to him for protection, and the sword he carried was for anyone who might try to get in his way and take her from him. She took a step towards them, her face contorted into a horrible travesty by hatred.

"You filthy traitor! You're trying to escape with her! You

traitor!" Her voice rose to a piercing scream. "Macdonalds! Macdonalds aye!"

"Come on!" James shouted, and together he and Katherine began to run, the Countess' shrieks for help ringing out behind them. At the end of the corridor they heard voices, the voices of his clansmen coming in answer to her call, and for a second James hesitated. Ahead of them he saw a half-open door. There was no escape from the passage and the men were coming up the stairs. He pulled Katherine into the room and shut the door. When he heard her cry out he turned quickly and gathered her into his arms, shielding her from the three bodies which lay on the floor only a few feet away from where they stood.

The Macdonalds had looted their victims, and she had just had time to see the upturned face of her father's valet before James hid her from the sight. Clinging to him, her heart racing with shock and terror, Katherine heard the pursuing Macdonalds running past the door, yelling to the Countess. Without James she would have stayed where she was, helpless to move until they came back and found her. But already he had opened the door and was pulling her after him. One look showed that the passage was empty. They ran to the head of the stairs and James thrust her behind him. The scene below was indescribable; furniture was smashed; the tapestries in the Great Hall had been torn off the walls and some of them were blazing. And everywhere there were the bodies of Frasers, men and women and even children, sprawled in heaps, and their murderers were bending over them, ripping the clothes away in search of a watch or a gold chain or a purse with a few pennies in it. Smoke hung over everything like a cloud, and there was an acrid smell of burning. The frightful screaming had ceased; there was no one left alive now, but a few wretches who had fled upstairs to the turrets, and Sir Alexander himself was hunting these.

Katherine came forward and glanced down. She turned so white that James gripped her round the waist. "Oh, my God . . ."

"We've got to go down there," he whispered urgently. "There's no other way. Brace yourself, and if anyone stops

us, get behind me. Ready, now, my darling heart. Hold tight
to me. We're nearly out!"

They went down the stairs at a run, so quickly that they
were past the men looting their victims, and one or two who
had found the Earl's wine cellar paused as they came up
from below with bottles in their arms, and the Macdonald
himself rushed past them with a woman by the hand. They
looked up and stared and then suddenly one of them opened
his mouth and yelled. " 'Tis the Fraser! 'Tis the woman herself escaping!" It was Dugal Macdonald, whose son Ian had
been hanged for deserting Hugh on the battlefield; he was
half drunk and mad with killing. He saw Katherine, whom he
had seen once in his life before when she greeted him at Kincarrig. He and his sons were humblies on the estate there,
and even in the gloom and smoke he recognised the flaming
hair and the lovely face which turned towards him for a moment. He dropped the bottles and they shattered round him,
the red wine splashing over the floor. He made a clumsy run
at her, and one hand caught the edge of her robe; he made a
sound like an animal, and the fierce snarl was lost in Katherine's scream.

James spun round on him like a tiger and took aim at the
hand holding Katherine's dress. With one stroke he severed it
from Dugal's arm, and the man fell howling in the wine
puddles. With a rush, James reached the doorway and, half
carrying Katherine, he raced down the steps into the courtyard. The confusion there made it easier for them to slip
back against the walls and towards the gardens. The blazing
stables were collapsing. James could hear his brother David's
voice raised above the crackle and roar of the fire, ordering
his men to keep away. Smoke and heat scorched them and,
bent almost double, they escaped into the castle garden and
began to run towards the north postern gate. It was open, and
unguarded. He felt her dragging on his arm, and he stopped
and lifted her. He did not know whether she had fainted.
Stooping, he carried her through the gateway and out onto
the side of the hill. Halfway down he stopped, sinking to his
knees in the heather, and laid her gently on the ground. His
own strength was taxed to the limit; he needed a moment to

get his breath before the long and rough descent by foot to the Loch shore and the horses the Macdonalds had left tethered there.

"James ..." She opened her eyes and immediately he bent over her.

"I'm here, my love, don't fear. We're on the hillside. Only a moment more and we'll seek our horses."

She put her arms around his neck and he heard her weeping. "Oh, James, James ..."

"Don't greet," he whispered, using the old Scots word his nurse had used to him, and he rocked her against his breast as if she were a child. "Don't fret, my darling ... you're safe now."

"I know," she said. "We're both safe and we're together. I mustn't be a weakling now. Hold me, James. Give me your courage." She put her hands to his face and held it; reaching up, she kissed him. They felt, both of them, as if the earth on which they lay had moved. "If we were caught now," she whispered, "I'd die happy."

"We're not going to die," he answered her. "We're going to get to the horses before they rouse themselves and come out looking for us!"

One man alone was guarding the horses hidden by the shore of the Loch; he started at the sound of feet running over the heather, his dirk drawn and ready. He was one of the few old men left among them and he had known James since he was a boy; not one of his kin was alive now; all had perished at Drummossie Moor or fallen into the hands of the English dragoons. The eldest and best loved of his four sons was the Red Murdoch, and his wife had given the infant James her milk. He put his weapon back as he recognised the son of his chief, and his eyes grew suddenly narrow as he saw the woman by his side, her hair flowing down her back, dressed only in a long white robe. He stared, and he knew her and for a moment he thought he was imagining what he saw.

"I want two horses, Andrew Ian," James said. "My own and the next swiftest to carry the lady."

The old man did not see James's hand creep to his dirk; he

only knew that this was the man who had held his dying son on the field of battle, the mighty one, the future chieftain. His heart was sad and sickened with death. He knew the woman and he knew what it meant when James asked him for horses.

"Ye'll find your mount there—by the bushy tree—I'll go bring one for the lady."

In the shadows of the trees they turned again to each other.

"Katherine," James said, "I don't know what will become of us. My people will be hunting us now as well as the English. I know where the Prince is hiding; I was going to make my way to him later. Our only chance is to join with him and escape to France. There's a French ship coming to take him off. It means many dangers and a lifetime of exile if we succeed in reaching him. Darling heart, will you come with me?"

Katherine took his hand and pressed it to her lips. "I belong with you, James. Where else would I go . . . whether to France or to eternity? It matters nothing so long as I'm with you."

Andrew Ian held the horse for her and stood a little back in the shadows as James mounted. He came forward and took off his bonnet.

"I've not seen ye," he said. "When they come, I'll be asleep."

Behind him the sky was growing light, but it was not the soft streaks of dawn which they saw, but the fierce red light of a great fire and the heart of it was high above them on the hill. For a moment Katherine waited, looking back at the end of Clandara.

It was the old man who touched her horse's flank. As they rode off, he waved and called out to them. "God go with ye!"

But already they were too far away to hear.

About the Author

Evelyn Anthony lives in one of England's venerable country houses, Horham Hall. She is married and the mother of six children. Two of her major historical novels (*Anne Boleyn* and *Victoria and Albert*) were published to widespread critical acclaim and are available in Signet editions. Her novels with contemporary settings—among them *The Poellenberg Inheritance, Stranger at the Gates,* and *Mission to Malaspiga* (also available in Signet editions)—have established her as a major writer of suspense.

⊘

Big Bestsellers from SIGNET

HANDY FILES AND CASES FOR STORING
MAGAZINES, CASSETTES, & 8-TRACK CARTRIDGES

CASSETTE STORAGE CASES

Decorative cases, custom-made of heavy bookbinder's board, bound in Kid-Grain Leatherette, a gold-embossed design. Individual storage slots slightly tilted back to prevent handling spillage. Choice of: Black, brown, green.

#JC-30—30 unit size (13½x5½x6½") $11.95 ea.
3 for $33.00

#JC-60—60 unit size (13½x5½x12⅝") $16.95 ea.
3 for $48.00

MAGAZINE VOLUME FILES

Keep your favorite magazines in mint condition. Heavy bookbinder's board is covered with scuff-resistant Kivar. Specify the title of the magazine and we'll send the right size case. If the title is well-known it will appear on the spine in gold letters. For society journals, a brass-rimmed window is attached and gold foil included—you type the title.

#J-MV—Magazine Volume Files $4.95 ea.
3 for $14.00
6 for $24.00

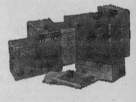

8-TRACK CARTRIDGE STORAGE CASE

This attractive unit measures 13¾ inches high, 6½ inches deep, 4½ inches wide, has individual storage slots for 12 cartridges and is of the same sturdy construction and decorative appearance as the Cassette Case.

#J-8T12—4½" wide (holds 12 cartridges)
$8.50 ea.
3 for $23.50

#J-8T24—8½" wide (holds 24 cartridges)
$10.95 ea.
3 for $28.00

#J-8T36—12¾" wide (holds 36 cartridges)
$14.25 ea.
3 for $37.00

Please send:

ITEM NO	COLOR (IF CHOICE)	DESCRIPTION	QUANTITY	UNIT PRICE	TOTAL COST

Postage and handling charges (up to $10 add $1.50) ($10.01 to $20 add $2.50) ($20.01 to $40 add $3.50)
(over $40 postage FREE)
I enclose ☐ check ☐ money order in amount of $ _____ Total _____

The New American Library, Inc. Name_____
P.O. Box 999
Bergenfield, New Jersey 07621 Address_____

City_____ State_____ Zip_____
Offer valid only in the United States of America. (Allow 5 weeks for delivery.)